THE KEEPERS

by Ken Trethewey

Jazz-Fusion Books

First published 1994

This second edition published February 2012 by:

Jazz-Fusion Books, Gravesend Cottage, Torpoint, Cornwall PL11 2LX, UK

ISBN 978-0-9570092-3-3

CONTENTS

Part One

Part Two

1	Henry Hall	2 Dec 1755
2	Henry Hall (epilogue)	19 Dec 1755
3	John Smeaton –1	15 April 1756
4	John Smeaton –2	1756-1759
5	Lizzie Knott	11 May 1759
6	Will Knott	11 May 1759
7	John Jennings	12 May 1759
8	Samuel Graves	14 May 1759
9	Josias Jessop	16 August 1759
10	Neptune	16 August 1759
11	Jacob Evans	May-October 1759
12	Tar	October 1759
13	Zachariah Mudge	October 1759
14	Sir Edward Hawke	24 November 1759
15	Regis du Plessix	25 November 1759
16	Tom Eliot	25 November 1759
17	Elizabeth Knott	December 1759
18	Geoffrey Marsh	December 1759
19	Jane Heal	February 1760
20	Isabelle du Plessix	February 1760
21	Jules Paulin	February 1760
22	Guy Rodier	February 1760
23	La Marquise d'Arranda de Darrax	February 1760
24	Pierre Gallond	9 March 1763
25	Jean-Paul Cartier	9 March 1763
26	John Hatherley -2	9-10 March 1763
27	Samuel Graves -2	10 March 1763
28	Finale	March 1763

Front Cover:
The Smeaton Eddystone lighthouse; photo ca. 1878 (anon).

Eddystone lighthouse paintings by Ken Trethewey.

PART ONE

1 GEORGE PRIDDY

Rock lighthouses are lonely places.

Amid hundreds of square miles of forbidding ocean, a lonely man stood watch in an impertinent structure. The tiny wooden tower was the only irregularity in so much sea, except for the red rocks on which it had been built. The man was the keeper of the Eddystone lighthouse and guardian of the lives of countless seamen, for should his feeble light fail to pierce the treacherous night, ships would surely stumble on the irresistible mass. It was here that the lead had been set for the rest of the world to follow. The unique rock lighthouse was in the hands of its two keepers without whom its construction would have been pointless. A new breed of man had been moulded, prepared to sacrifice a life in the company of fellow men and women and to substitute one of cramped monastic solitude. The Eddystone lighthouse was one of the world's loneliest places and no-one could be more acutely aware of it than Henry Hall.

Henry was a short, stocky old sea-salt whose face, which might have been hewn out of pink granite, was almost hidden by a tangled mass of greying, wiry hair. During his forty-two years on God's Earth Henry Hall had experienced almost everything that life was likely to offer with but one exception. Marriage had never come his way and he had not made any effort to seek it, for Henry was quite content to suffer his own company. His career as a seaman had taken him to every part of the globe, to pinnacles of success in battle and to the depths of despair in fever-ridden floating slums, but his iron constitution had never failed him. Apart from a dose of malaria when he was thirty-two and serving in a frigate off the west coast of Africa, Henry had been blessed with almost perfect health. Having reached in his sea-time the exalted and much feared position of bosun's mate, Henry had always tried to use his authority fairly, but responsibility for the discipline of a mixed bag of human life such as was to be found in a ship of His Majesty's Navy was always difficult. Henry shouldered his burden well, sought no-one's favours and received respect from everyone through dint of effort and self-determination. Then, by chance, the course of Henry Hall's life had taken a completely new direction.

Two men were required to keep and maintain a light on the murderous Eddystone reef that Henry Hall knew only too well. For generations, seafarers had tried to keep a healthy distance between the reef and their ships. Even so, there had been scores of wrecks and countless deaths, mostly in bad weather conditions or at night when it was so difficult to be precise about position at sea. Then one day a man was found who was prepared to take on the unenviable task of constructing some sort of warning light. London businessman Henry Winstanley built the world's first lighthouse on an isolated reef at sea.

Finding men to take on the challenge of living in such a remote and dangerous location was not easy, however. Whilst there were a good number of volunteers, the majority were of unproven reliability and character. It was necessary to recruit men who could be depended upon to keep the light burning during the hours of darkness, but perhaps even more importantly, men who could endure long periods of isolation and mental stress with no ill-effect. No matter how reliable the keeper, he would be useless if his mind became unbalanced. Henry Hall, a seaman between engagements and with a proven naval record, was considered to be a most suitable candidate. His physical stamina was second to none, he was clean, self-disciplined and totally convinced of the importance of the job he was being asked to do. He was also unmarried and quite happy to be confined to a small space in the middle of the sea with only one other human being for company.

So, after five years of keeping Winstanley's lighthouse, Henry Hall had become quite used to the life. There was the occasional company of George, his colleague, but he was on his own for most of the time as they kept watch and slept alternately. Henry had quite come to terms with his solitude and although there were periods of shore leave, he was always glad to return to his very own private retreat amid the waves. Here he was playing a vital part in the safety of his old shipmates. Here he was fulfilled.

Over the years he had made several good friends from amongst the numerous men who had shared his duties, for George was but the newest in a succession of colleagues. Many of those who had gone before him had found the loneliness too much to bear. George was different from the rest. Henry found George rather eccentric; they got on well together for most of the time, but George was inclined to become very moody. As a result, Henry had found their relationship becoming progressively more strained. Recently, George had been spending a lot of time out on the balcony and was unhappy for most of the time. For the past four weeks it seemed the George had done nothing but grumble about Henry who had almost reached the end of his tether. Nothing he could do seemed to please George.

Henry rose from his seat in the kitchen where he had been warming his torso and climbed the ladders through the bedroom into the lantern room. It was time to make a routine inspection of the candles as they cast their feeble lifesaving rays into the stifling darkness.

George was out on the balcony again. He was always out on the balcony.

Henry looked up at the cupola where the candles stood in a wrought iron ring suspended from the roof of the lantern. He could see that one of the candles was burnt away and should be changed. It might possibly last the night which was now nearly over, but there was no point in performing his duties shoddily. Henry was conscientious. Spare candles were kept in a cupboard in the bedroom below. As he put his foot on the ladder to make his descent, he shouted, "'E still out there, George? Fer God's sake, ain't ye 'ad enough yet?"

No answer.

Henry shrugged his shoulders and returned to the bedroom to collect a brand new candle. He fluffed up the wick between his thumb and forefinger.

"Tis all thy fault, 'Enry… ye done it."

A thin, sad voice seemed to come from the direction of the lantern room. George was obviously in a bad mood again. Henry lost his temper. Turning quickly to the ladder and gripping its sides bellowed upwards, "No, 't wasn't. 'E 'ad to go out on that damn balcony, didn' 'e?"

He released his grip and, holding the new candle at the bottom end, smashed it on a rung in a fit of rage so that the candle broke into five pieces held together by the wick. Instantly it fell limp like a drunken Romeo. Henry, the big, strong bosun's mate with the iron constitution, was crying. He blinked to try to see through the tears and threw the useless candle aside so as to wipe away the tears with his shirtsleeve.

" 'T id'n fair," he mumbled to himself and slumped into a heap on the floor. "'E always blames I. 'T were 'e as 'ad to go out there. If 'e 'adn' gone out there 't wouldn't a 'appen."

Everything had been well at the Eddystone lighthouse until that thunderstorm. The winter weather, which had arrived early in October, had been worse than usual. He and George had not seen a soul for about seven weeks except on a distant ship, but they were quite comfortable. They had plenty of food and were warm. Henry never complained about bad weather for he had seen many storms during his early years and had almost overcome his fear of the sea - if that were ever possible. Even here, trapped in the wooden tower, which sometimes shook as if it would disintegrate in minutes, he was not afraid. That storm, however, had been worse than most and the lightning had been the most spectacular he had ever seen. George, the fool, had insisted upon watching it from the balcony. He had a passion for watching lightning.

As he sat on the floor Henry pulled his knees up to his chin and hugged them tightly. He stared into the dim glow that seeped down from the lantern room above, his depression complete. Suddenly, there it was again. The fireball which had been pursuing him ever since that storm, burst out from the darkness, spinning towards him, spitting flame, twisting and turning, its heat scorching his face. He shut his eyes tightly and burst out crying again. He could still see the brilliant ball of flame, even through his eyelids. Then, suddenly, it was gone, over his head with an ear splitting whooooosh! Silence reigned in the lighthouse, except for Henry's blubbing. He dared not open his eyes and kept his face buried in his own embrace. For ten minutes, he sat totally still. Just as he was beginning to recover his composure, he heard George again.

"Told 'e 't were thy fault, didn' I?"

George was still sulking. He obviously was not going to be civil to Henry tonight. Henry had cried enough and was now past caring. He struggled hard to be rational. George could be civil sometimes. He had been quite civil when Henry had taken him his supper on the balcony. Henry could not understand why George was so upset with him now. He thought that George had forgiven him. No-one could have been lonelier than Henry Hall at this moment. George was no companion when he was in this sort of mood. It was not fair of him to go on blaming Henry like this. Henry had not wanted to go out on the balcony to watch the lightning. It was George - he had insisted. George had been a good mate until then. Now he seemed to think that everything was Henry's fault. Always blaming him, he was. Henry pulled himself together, jerked out his shirt tail and hooted mucus from his nose into it. He remembered the candle that needed to be changed and rose to get another. Yes, George was a good mate really. He had a good sense of humour, which Henry had appreciated. You need to have a good laugh sometimes. You could go mad in a place like this if you didn't have a good laugh.

Henry selected a new candle from the box, instinctively wiped it in his sleeve just in case there was any dirt on it, and climbed the ladder once again. The old candle had burnt out, to Henry's dismay, for he was always particular to keep the correct number alight. Despite the fact that it made only a slight difference to the light being given out by the lighthouse, Henry was always upset if he was careless in the execution of his duty. He reached up to the candleholder in order to clean out the excess wax and insert a new candle. It meant stretching up to his full height and reaching another eighteen inches above his head.

"Why don't 'e come in from out there, George? 'E must be freezin' cold."

George had gone out on the balcony again. He seemed to spend all of his time out there. Ever since the thunderstorm. He even preferred his meals out there. Henry had decided that George was loopy. Seeing that lightning had done something to his brain. All he ever wanted to do was wait around on the balcony until he saw more lightning. Anyone could tell him that he might have to wait months. There was no reasoning with him.

"'E goin' to sit out there all night?" Henry was beginning to get annoyed with George again.

"'E made us like this... 'T is all thy fault..."

Henry looked down from the candleholder as he stood on tiptoe. George was complaining again. Henry blew his top. "Who were it wanted to go out there in the first place? Not I, George, not I," he bellowed at the top of his voice. "I 's sick of 'e moanin' at I."

George shut up.

Henry, on tiptoe again, replaced the candle and lit the virgin wick with a long taper that he kept in a special box just beside the door to the balcony. Checking that the flame was burning steadily, he relaxed, blew out the taper and looked towards the balcony door. He guessed that George was sat in his usual place with his back to the tower staring into the night for another glimpse of the lightning. Henry put his hands on his hips and drew a deep breath. What was he going to do with George? If the fellow really had lost his mind, Henry would have to bear the burden of his watches until the next relief. That could be a long time away. He already had to do all the work, which, at present, he did not mind, but he didn't know how long he could keep it up. George was obviously not going to do his share at all. What else could Henry do? They were due for relief a week ago, but the weather had been so bad since that storm that there had been no opportunity of getting them off the rock. The small relief boat had to make a journey of about fourteen miles, and, in the sort of seas presently outside the tower, it was impossible. Henry was sure George must be sick. Why else would a man want to sit around all day looking for lightning? This man must be wanky. Come to think of it, he was a bit off his food too. Henry had taken all his meals up to him, but he had not eaten much of it. The seagulls seemed to have had a party with George's suppers. Yes, George must be a bit mental. A real head-case. It was a pity because George could have been a good mate.

He must be asleep now. He had gone quiet again. Perhaps he would be in a better mood when he had had a sleep.

Henry looked out of the lantern and realised that dawn was just minutes away. Whilst he had been so taken up arguing with George, he'd not even noticed the waxing of the morning sun in the southeast as it hoisted itself up from below the horizon. Soon he would be able to put out the candles. The portents were good for a clear morning to follow the fairly calm night. Perhaps the relief boat might come today?

Henry looked to where the rapidly reddening sky was trying to brighten up a very thunderous-looking cloud. Surely there would be no storm today? Not like the last one.

Then, from below the horizon there arose the most gigantic ball of fire. Henry was terrified. He wanted to cry out but couldn't. He just kept staring at the burning mass of hell-fire. It rose high up into the thundercloud and for a timeless second hung there like a demon, awful and omnipotent. Then it exploded in an instant with a colossal release of energy. From it came an infernal sphere, falling from the heavens like a burning boulder plummeting towards the sea and accelerating to enormous speed as it did so. Then, instead of crashing into the sea, it curved upwards into a horizontal trajectory directed straight at the lighthouse. Henry was mortified, but as if attracted by some strange new force, he pushed open the balcony door so that he could step outside for a better view. He was so keen to get out onto the balcony that he almost fell over George who was sat with his back to the tower. In the background, Henry could hear a noise like continuous thunder, a perpetual rumble, which began to reach a crescendo as the fiery globule hurtled towards him at immense speed.

Soon Henry had to shout at the top of his voice to be heard above the roar of the fire. It was the apocalypse. "There it be, George... that's what 'e bin waitin' fer. Are 'e 'appy now? Lucifer 'eself be 'ere to fetch us."

George said nothing.

As the fireball reached the base of the tower, it slowed right down almost to a standstill, as if it had reached its destination. It was so bright and hot that Henry had to shield his eyes and face to avoid pain. The noise was so loud that it seemed to be drilling needles into his eardrums. His rib cage vibrated in resonance with the tremendous bass volume from the object. Very slowly, the fireball rose in the air, its flames scorching the sides of the tower. Henry shrunk back against the side of the tower, trying to escape the singeing heat. His eyes were tightly closed now, but his vision was filled with brilliant light. And from the very depths of the fire he saw the face... that terrible, awesome face...

9

"All thy fault," screamed George.

"Shut up, damn 'e," yelled Henry in abject terror. "'e's 'ere, 'e's come fer us..."

The inferno rose higher and higher in the air. Henry sensed from the changes in sound and heat that it was now hovering above the tower. Suddenly there was the most gigantic explosion. It was as if all the heavens were showering down upon the lighthouse at once. The flash blinded Henry, and the force threw him through the open door of the lantern room. He hit his head on the floor and lost consciousness...

"Henry, where are you?"

Henry realised that someone was shouting his name. He opened his eyes and found himself flat on his back staring up at the roof of the lantern. He was cold. George must have left the balcony door open again. He was always doing that.

"Henry!"

"That 'e, George?" Henry got up onto all fours and discovered that he had a splitting headache. A face appeared on the ladder through the floor of the lantern room. It was not George, but Thomas Blomer, Henry's relief keeper.

"Ah, there you are, Henry. We were wondering where you were. Sorry we couldn't get here no quicker. The weather's bin a bit bad, in it?"

Henry wondered how long he had been asleep. "What time is it?" he asked his relief.

"About two, I think," replied the man who had come to take over the responsibilities, the loneliness.

"Dinner time. I must take George 'is dinner." Henry ignored Thomas and pushed past rudely. He had to go to the galley to prepare some food for George. "George gets annoyed wi' I if I's late wi' 'is dinner," he mumbled as he disappeared down the ladder to the kitchen below.

"Where is George, anyway?" shouted Thomas.

"Out on the balcony, I 'spect. Always out there 'e be. 'E likes watchin' lightnin'."

Thomas was a little confused. There had been no sign of George at all, which was most strange. He noticed that a cold easterly wind had caught up and was whipping into the lantern room from outside, bringing with it a most peculiar smell. He took the three necessary paces to the open, swinging door that led onto the balcony where George must be. The foul smell got worse.

Thomas's first sight of George was a pair of dark legs sticking out through the balcony rails. Strangely, they had been secured with rope to the rails. Then as Thomas stepped outside he met George face to face. Thomas found himself staring at an unrecognisable, bald, featureless head. It looked badly sunburnt and was beginning to decay. Then he realised that the hideous, faceless skull that had once been George was not sunburnt. It had been partly incinerated, fried alive. Clothes and skin alike were but charred remains, a hideous Negroid corpse, its teeth clenched in the agony of combustion. The stench was overwhelming - one of putrefying flesh, accelerated in its natural decay by the intense heating to which it had been subjected.

10

Thomas fell against the balcony rail to be sick. "How could a human being look like this?" he thought, as he emptied the contents of his stomach in a series of painful spasms. Having done so he tried to compose his thoughts. George must have died weeks ago. How could Henry have survived for so long, living in such close proximity to this... this monster?

Thomas stepped inside the lantern room once more and sat down on the cold floor to gather himself together. He realised that he was shaking with shock. Slowly the situation became clear. Thomas knew Henry well. He knew how Henry liked everything kept shipshape and orderly. Henry would have liked George to be buried properly - in a coffin. He would not have simply pushed George over the side. Besides, he might have been accused of murdering George if his colleague had vanished without trace. Henry had no choice but to keep the corpse out on the balcony.

Poor old Henry.

Then Henry appeared from below and, still ignoring Thomas, strode over to the balcony. Without going outside, he put his head around the corner. "George, yer dinner's ready. Are 'e comin' in to eat un or not? 'E idn' goin' to see no more lightnin' today so 'e'd best come in out the cold..."

2 HENRY WINSTANLEY

Henry Winstanley sat at a small bureau in the State Room of the Eddystone lighthouse and made notes in his diary.

26th November, 1703.

"Since my arrival yesterday the weather has progressively worsened. It would seem that this has so far been a thoroughly bad winter with a far greater number and degree of inclement seas than one might normally expect to pertain in the West Country at this time of year. Upon my arrival I set about a detailed examination of the structure in order to determine what damage, if any, had been caused since my last visit on 8th. August inst. It was reported to me from the outset by the keepers that severe vibrations of the tower were being felt from time to time and that they were very concerned about their safety. Notwithstanding these vibrations, which I myself have experienced, I am convinced that no serious weakening of the structure has occurred and that no major modifications will be necessary. Minor repairs of storm damage are inevitable in a structure such as this and of these there were but seven in number, all to outside fittings."

Winstanley was a natural diarist. His writing, punctuated by frequent dipping of the quill into the ornate silver inkpot, was technically neat and exhibited an efficient translation of imaginative thinking into detailed, thorough and often philosophical prose.

"Nevertheless I am concerned that the keepers may not be able to tolerate such disturbing vibrations without becoming much afraid as to their safety. The two keepers presently on duty are new to their posts, having been engaged at short notice, and consequently have yet to convince themselves of the soundness of my lighthouse. The tragic events of November 12th inst. have, no doubt, also weighed heavily upon their consciences, as indeed they have on mine. Having now discussed the matter at great length with all concerned I am determined to increase the number of keepers in my lighthouse to three at the next available opportunity. In so doing, any accident that might occur to one of them will leave the other two in control of the situation. They will then be able to continue their watches, albeit more frequently, and at the same time retain their sanity, by virtue of their mutual company, until such time as a relief can be effected. I understand that Mr Hall is responding well to medical treatment. The poor fellow saw his colleague struck by lightning during a particularly malevolent storm. One observer ashore reported seeing a most unusual lightning effect in the form of a ball of fire that travelled at great speed above the surface of the sea. I can only conclude that it was this extremely rare atmospheric phenomenon, which Mr Hall described so vividly as his nightmare, and which caused the particularly hideous death of Mr Priddy. Mr Hall was unwilling to dispose of the body into the sea for fear of being charged with murder. He courageously resolved to attach the body to the balcony until the relief boat arrived. Unfortunately it was a considerable length of time before this could be effected, and in the course of living alone with a corpse, the balance of Mr Hall's mind was disturbed. It is indeed fortunate that Mr Hall, who was the first keeper whom I employed and is well known to me, has the constitution of an ox and is sure to make a complete recovery. Any lesser individual would incontrovertibly be committed for life following such an experience. Nonetheless I find myself accepting some of the blame for had I employed three keepers from the first this terrible thing might have been partly avoided. As yet I have been unable to find a third keeper at such short notice. The two who now keep the light are naturally most apprehensive at present both about the vibrations and the recent tragedy. Despite all my assurances about the strength of the tower and the unlikelihood of such an event occurring again so soon after the first, they remain unimpressed. Only time will alleviate their misgivings."

Henry Winstanley had recently celebrated his fifty-ninth birthday and during his lifetime had managed to acquire a dazzling array of abilities and interests, most of which he somehow converted into profitable occupations. His home at Littlebury in Essex had been constructed more in the fashion of a fun fair than a house. It was filled with tricks and unusual effects to amuse the many visitors who paid a shilling each to pass through the turnstile that Winstanley had placed at the front gate. As a draughtsman he made a great deal of money producing engravings of the Stately homes of England, whilst a pack of ornate playing cards, which he designed, achieved considerable popularity and nation-wide distribution.

Perhaps the most famous of his creations other than the Eddystone lighthouse was a spectacular and novel entertainment centre, which he opened near Hyde Park and which was called *Winstanley's Waterworkes*. For more than thirty years people

Figure 1: Henry Winstanley's First Eddystone lighthouse (1698-99).

from all over England paid anything up to half a crown to view a dazzling display of fountains and other aquatic effects. Some of the creations achieved a combination of fire and water in wholly original concepts and the fame of the *Waterworkes* spread throughout the country.

The wealth he acquired over the years of success as a showman was invested in many areas, one of which was the purchase of five ships. To lose one of them on the notorious Eddystone Rocks in August 1695 was a severe enough blow to the jovial, sincere and talented Winstanley, but when news came that a second had met an identical fate, he hurried to Plymouth to investigate. There he uncovered a problem which had beset mariners and merchants alike for centuries past, but which he himself had only just begun to appreciate. In a typical surge of optimism and inventiveness he immediately resolved to eradicate the problem by the construction of a lighthouse, the like of which had never been seen before. Its design would be such as to compare with the Seven Wonders of the World, and would be an everlasting memorial to the outstanding genius of its creator. To his credit, he delivered what he promised and the Citizens of Plymouth were most grateful for it. An evil trap, lurking silently amid the busy seaway of the English Channel had finally been beaten.

Momentarily pausing for thought, Winstanley became aware of the decreasing level of light in the luxurious apartment he had so extravagantly included in his design. He placed his quill in the correct place on the inkstand and, rising from his padded chair, walked the short distance to one of the two sash windows. From this west-facing position some forty feet above the menacing waves he could see just how much farther the weather had deteriorated since he had last looked. The panes of glass were opaque as torrents of wind-swept rain beat against them. The skies, which could barely be discerned, were nevertheless conspicuous by their ominous hue. The naked Atlantic rollers sweeping in from the west towards Winstanley's position were expending their incalculable energy mostly upon the exposed rocks, for it was low tide. But the tide was beginning to rise once more, as also was the height of the swell, and Winstanley knew that before long the waves would be literally knocking at his front door.

Even as he watched, the opposing rhythms of swell and breakers would now and then become coincident, and for a few tense seconds be magnified into a gigantic mass of snarling power to beat the base of the tower with its awesome might. A shudder sufficient to jingle the crystal sherry glasses in the walnut drinks cabinet was gone again in a moment, but, along with its predecessors, had instilled a terrible uneasiness in the hearts of those present. Winstanley knew that the real test of his lighthouse was only just beginning. During the course of the three months that he had spent on his designs, he had, of course, made every contingency for the weather. Winstanley was prepared. He braced himself and opened the window sufficiently to allow him to pull across two heavy oak shutters. These, when barred and bolted in position, kept out everything, including the light. He re-closed the window, drew the Flemish velvet curtains and repeated the exercise with the other window. Having done so he set light to the candelabra and took up a towel to remove the rain and sea spray from his face and hair. Then, returning to his desk he noticed that his quill had been blown by the gust of wind onto the silk bed cover to leave a small but unsightly ink stain which he doubted could be washed out. Winstanley cursed and once more sitting dejectedly at his bureau, he returned the quill to its proper place.

He watched the flames from the candles flickering wildly as the gales infiltrated even this citadel. He set his mouth into an expression of determination. He could not surely have failed? His lighthouse was the greatest engineering feat since the mighty pyramids. It could never fall victim to the sea. He recalled a memorable

Figure 2: Henry Winstanley's second Eddystone Lighthouse (1699-1703).

conversation he once had with a particularly sceptical acquaintance, who was convinced that the lighthouse would not withstand another winter. At the time Winstanley had proclaimed that he wished to be present in his tower during the greatest storm ever. His friend had been impressed by Winstanley's courage (but little else) and the two men had progressed to a very lively and rumbustious argument about the merits and pitfalls of the design.

No-one could dispute the efforts which had been made to ensure a sound, safe construction, nor the enthusiasm with which Winstanley had set about the arduous and difficult job of building a lighthouse in the most exposed position in the world.

In July 1696, the first task in the construction of the tower had been to bore twelve holes in the chosen bedrock. Not a problem, one might think, for the cream of the available labour in Devon and Cornwall. Yet this very task had proved to be the most difficult of all because, after a tiring sea journey from Plymouth of anything up to eight hours, there were rarely more than a few hours of useful work which could be completed at any one time. Then there was the rock itself, so hard that the unremitting granite quickly blunted the sharpest tools, and the keenest wills. A mere twelve holes took nearly four months to carve with the sweat and pain of the workmen. Once the holes had been created however, it was a relatively simple job to fill each hole with molten lead and then insert a huge iron stanchion. Having finished this stage of the enterprise, the workers retreated from the reef for the remainder of the year to prepare for the next season of work. Because of the weather conditions work could not recommence until the following May.

In the summer of 1697, construction pressed ahead. The men became adept at transferring large pre-cut stones from tiny bobbing boats onto the reef. There they were cemented in such a way as to make them fast both to the reef and the stanchions. In this manner it was intended to create a solid regular base of stone upon which to build the lighthouse.

It was whilst this work was proceeding that a remarkable incident occurred. England had embarked upon another war with her continental neighbour and it was not uncommon for marauding French men-of-war to cause havoc on the South coast of England. Winstanley, fearful of being attacked, had asked for and obtained the protection of the Royal Navy and, on the days when work was being carried out on the rock, a frigate had been detailed off to act as guard-ship. During the first week of July HMS *Terrible* failed to arrive. Winstanley was not unduly concerned at first for, in truth, the working parties had not been troubled. But, sure enough, on the one occasion that they were unguarded, their luck ran out. Whilst all were engrossed in their work there was a dull thud followed rapidly by a high pitched whistle and a huge splash as a shot plunged into the calm water not fifty feet from where the men worked. Immediately they saw a French sloop bearing down on them. Stupidly, but instinctively, the workmen scuttled for cover, though there was none to be had on such an exposed position. There was no escape. Soon they were looking down the musket barrels of a dozen French marines. Winstanley was quickly singled out as the one in charge, for, although initially he played dumb, his very appearance made it abundantly clear that he was not a workman. Fortunately Winstanley had a good working knowledge of French, which allowed him to escape the violent arrest which would have otherwise followed, Nonetheless, he was removed by ship's boat back on board the enemy sloop. There he was chained and taken as a prisoner to France where his fate would have certainly been sealed if it were not for the chance remark of one of the King's minions. Louis XIV, a man of considerable intellect, seized upon the remark and enquired further. When details of the incident were made known to him he ordered the instant release of Winstanley and for him to be brought to court. The Englishman was surprised enough to be released, but his surprise turned to astonishment when he found himself ushered into the presence of the king of a nation with which England was at war.

Louis apologised sincerely for the trouble he had caused and said that he hoped the incident had not unduly delayed work on the lighthouse, for, although he might be at war with England, he was not at war with humanity. Winstanley was relieved and delighted, especially when given the opportunity to explain the principles of his design to the king. After an audience of about an hour he departed for England in ambassadorial style with numerous compensatory gifts. A minor miracle had occurred.

Despite losing two working weeks in the height of the fine weather season, Winstanley's men worked harder than ever to make good the deficit. Thus, by the end of the second season they had completed the solid cylindrical base. A round pillar of granite some twelve feet high and fourteen feet across had been secured to the Eddystone reef.

During the third season of 1698 work on the living quarters progressed quickly. Having once established even the most basic of accommodation a permanent team was victualled on the reef, thus allowing work to be done continuously, rather than on the odd occasion when the weather permitted Hence, by the end of the year Winstanley had finished his towers and, to the delight of the nation, lit his candles for the first time on the fourteenth of November. Then, like all true gentlemen, he retreated and allowed his two keepers to guard the light throughout the winter.

Henry Hall had been one of those two keepers, and by the time Winstanley returned in the spring of 1699 it was obvious, both from the reports of the keepers and the damage sustained by the structure, that the tower would have to be both strengthened and enlarged. Henry Hall reported that on many occasions the lantern had been completely doused by the waves and that the tower had shuddered so violently that they thought their end was nigh. Winstanley made a close inspection of the tower and decided to redesign it.

The whole of the summer of 1699 was spent in a major rebuild, The size and mass of the solid base was increased so that the new diameter was twenty-four feet, and the upper half of the tower was encased in stone and increased considerably in height.

Inside the tower the accommodation was spacious. A visitor entering at rock level would first climb a staircase to elevate him above the level of the solid base. Here there was a storeroom that held stock craned into the lighthouse by means of lifting gear mounted on the gallery. From here, the stairs led up past two sumptuous rooms which Winstanley used, but which could accommodate any visiting dignitary. First there was an ornate bedroom with fireplace and closets, next the Stateroom with its exquisite carvings and artwork. Above these rooms the staircase came out through a hatch onto the open lower gallery. This was the main observation platform but was also the site of the lifting gear. Also present was a fresh water tank for collecting rain from the upper levels.

A wooden staircase led from here up to the keepers' accommodation. First came the kitchen, complete with dressers, table, cupboard and the essential range. Then there was the bedroom with fittings for use as a dining room. Here also was kept a large stock of candles for the light. Finally came the lantern itself, a splendid room with six-feet high glass panels all around. In the centre suspended from the lantern roof was a magnificent chandelier capable of taking sixty candles. These, when lit, provided the feeble light which was to save scores of lives. Surrounding the lantern room was an upper gallery to which poor George Priddy had been lashed.

Apart from the rooms themselves, all fittings had been given considerable thought by Winstanley. The six large ornamental candlesticks, which he so oddly mounted on the outside of the lantern room above the gallery, could also be used as ladder supports when the glass was being cleaned. All manner of cranes and other lifting devices had been included to cater for every eventuality. The final touch was an engine to cast down stones upon would-be aggressors.

By the end of 1699, the new improved tower was finished and its keepers keen to exhibit its reassuring light throughout another winter. This time, surely, success had been achieved. The keepers continued to complain about the shaking of the tower in heavy seas, but Winstanley convinced them that this was inevitable and that he had taken account of it in his new design. Furthermore he could find no evidence of any weakening of the tower. Thus it was that the new Eddystone lighthouse became famous throughout the civilised world as the guardian angel of seamen, a marvel of the new engineering that was to revolutionise society. For three more years it cast its protective beams into the night. Henry Hall and a succession of assistant keepers kept the light burning through countless storms until the fateful day that George Priddy decided to watch lightning from the gallery...

There was a mighty thud and a shudder that seemed as if the whole tower might disintegrate. Simultaneously, above the sound of the howling wind, Winstanley heard the effects of breaking glass and men's despair. He aroused himself from his reminiscences and quickly moved to the door of the Stateroom. As he opened it a small stream of water washed over his feet. That stream was but a fraction of what was pouring down the staircase. Soon after it, splashing down the stairs two at a time came Josh Geadley, one of the two new keepers. He was soaking wet and distraught.

"Mister Winstanley, we've just bin hit by the greatest wave... It just poured in over the railings of the gallery where I was standing... I was washed clean off me feet. I've never seen aught like it!"

"Steady, Mister Geadley, there's nothing to fear. This has happened many times before. Indeed, I included the gallery in my design so that waves could wash through the lighthouse rather than against it. Rest assured, this lighthouse can withstand far worse than that." He smiled reassuringly at the worried keeper, though deep in his heart he was worried too. Although the tower had indeed suffered waves that swept in over the balcony, some sixty feet above the sea, he was not sure just how much worse the seas could become. Nevertheless, his outwardly confident, calming manner succeeded in settling his nervous employee, temporarily at least. The effect did not last long, for, just as Winstanley was closing the door of the State room to follow Geadley back up to the lantern room, another enormous wave swept into the tower from sixty feet up, causing cascades of seawater to pour through the hatch which Geadley had left open. As it toppled down the staircase, Winstanley had to hold fast to the handrail in order not to be swept down with it. When the downpour had subsided, Winstanley, soaking wet from the waist down, squelched upwards as fast as he could onto the open gallery.

As he emerged onto the platform, he found the weather to be far worse than he could have imagined. The sea spray alone was drenching, whilst the force of the wind made all movements extremely difficult and conversation impossible. He could no longer see the sea at all and periodically a wave came rushing up the side of the tower to expend the last of its energy through the balustrade. Having briefly looked out and been astonished by what he saw, Winstanley, with great difficulty, managed to reach and climb the stairs to the keepers' apartments.

The kitchen was almost totally dark. With the shutters drawn tightly across the windows, the only light was from a couple of candles burning animatedly atop empty bottles. As Winstanley paused, allowing his eyes to adjust to the light a breathless Geadley arrived. Then Winstanley noticed Geadley's partner. Harry Joggett the second new keeper was lounging in his favourite chair, the stove on one side, the table on the other. In his hand was a glass of gin and on the table a half-empty bottle. His tragic face was as white as the foam outside the tower and, as Winstanley watched, he drained his glass and stared limply into nothingness. From the smell of his breath and the volume remaining in the bottle Winstanley knew that Joggett had drunk far too much gin. Joggett had proved to be rather easily frightened since he had taken on the job of keeping the Eddystone light. Now the poor man, terrified by the storm, was seeking refuge in the anaesthetizing effect of alcohol. To some extent he must have succeeded for Winstanley observed that he was quite calm.

"Mister Joggett is in a bad way I fear," he remarked to Geadley.

"Yes, sir. I 'ardly knows how to stick it meself. I never thought the weather could get as bad as this. Just afore I come down, that big wave broke a pane in the bedroom. We didn't 'ave the shutters closed. I never thought as the waves could reach that high," Geadley's voice reflected the concern he was obviously feeling.

Winstanley too was shocked. "I must admit that we have never had panes broken in the bedroom before. That room is nearly eighty feet above sea level. My calculations did not predict waves of such a height."

"So much for your bloody sums," snapped Geadley angrily. "And what 'appens when the waves get so bloody high that they goes right over the top? Answer me that one, will you, mister bloody clever."

Winstanley bit his lip, but did not answer such a hypothetical question. For the first time he had admitted openly that he might have miscalculated in his estimation of the ferocity of the sea. He had been totally confident; now there was doubt. If the sea could reach such a height then the power of the waves could also reach far greater proportions, but how much greater?

His question was soon answered, for as he sat looking into the glazed stupor of Joggett there was an enormous thump which shook the tower from its ornate weather vane to its foundations. Simultaneously came the piercing sound of glass breaking into thousands of pieces. Winstanley began to rush up towards the lantern, but as he did so he was met by water pouring through every possible exit from the upper levels. The bedroom was saturated enough, but in the lantern he found a gloomy windswept scene of devastation. All but one of the panes that surrounded the chandelier had been pulverised whilst the leaded beading which supported them had been buckled and bent. Everywhere there was jagged glass; everywhere there was seawater dripping from the upper to the lower levels. Even the candles and the chandelier had been drenched. Never had Winstanley imagined this; perhaps one or two broken panes in the lower levels, but never destruction on such a scale.

The wind blasted its icy chill into the lantern room and a wet and cold Winstanley was forced to retire to the rooms below. There would be no light on the Eddystone tonight. In the temporary safety of the kitchen once more, Winstanley flopped dejectedly into the single vacant chair. The situation was not difficult to assess for there was absolutely nothing that could be done. They could only sit out the storm and hope - nay pray - that the tower would survive. There would be no rescue; no rescue ship could survive in the cauldron that existed outside the tower. There was no escape from the rock. They must remain calm and wait for the morning. Perhaps the storm would have blown itself out by then.

Winstanley became aware of a strange sensation. For a moment his balance seemed to desert him. Then he looked at the small amount of gin remaining in Joggett's glass. The liquid was swaying from side to side. Suddenly he realised that the tower was in motion. He had been either too occupied or too upset to notice it before. The tower was bending in the gale like a tree. Then Winstanley knew the meaning of fear. He knew the reason why Joggett was drunk. He knew the reason why so many men had petitioned him about the shaking of the tower. Winstanley feared for his life, for just like the finest oak tree could be uprooted in a gale, so even his lighthouse could be swept away in the wake of such incalculable forces. He had done his best to ensure that the tower was strong enough to withstand such might, but suddenly he knew just how powerful the elements really were. Nothing could resist such energy.

Winstanley fought with his fear, trying to appear calm for Geadley's sake, but a feeling of nausea crept into the pit of his stomach. Joggett was by now insensible, his head lolling limply downwards. Winstanley picked up the half empty bottle of Plymouth gin, put it to his lips and took a large swig. Josh Geadley, who had been sat on the floor resting his head in his hands, looked up and asked in a voice of unashamed desperation, "Is there no hope?"

"Of course there is hope," Winstanley lied. "This is the strongest possible design; it can take all of the force." He winced at the taste of the gin, but took another shot. An even greater thump occurred, followed by even more water, which rained down upon them and extinguished the lights. It was now dark outside, as well as in. Water fell onto the stove which began to spit and hiss. Geadley strived and eventually succeeded to light a candle. Winstanley shivered. He took another swig of gin in a vain attempt to acquire some form of extra consolation, but as he did so Geadley lost his temper. He strode across to where Winstanley had abandoned himself to his fate, and, snatching the bottle form the surprised man, smashed it on the stove.

"That's no bloody help," he said looking Winstanley straight in the eyes." Here we are in this God-forsaken death trap with all Hell outside the window, Joggett's pissed out of his brains and you're goin' the same way. Call yourself an engineer? If you wasn't 'ere right now I'd call you a bloody murderer but I don't think even you want to commit suicide. You'd best think of a way of saving our lives, and be bloody quick about it, or, so help me, I'll pitch you off that balcony"

Winstanley was so taken aback by his own feelings of failure and the onslaught from the worried keeper that he did not notice the frequency with which the waves were beginning to pound the upper half of the tower. Neither did he notice the degree to which the lighthouse was swaying or the onset of a particularly ominous creaking noise within its timbers. The motion of the tower was enough to disturb the equilibrium of Joggett's senseless drunken body, which slumped from the chair into a heap on the floor. It was a cue for Winstanley at last to find the courage he had been seeking. He picked himself up and grasped Geadley by the arm.

"Below... let's get below... the lower the better," he said, pulling Geadley towards the ladder.

"Too bloody right," moaned Geadley, "Don't take no engineer to work that out, dammit." Geadley checked himself. What are we goin' to do about 'im?" He indicated the prostrate wretch on the floor.

"Leave him here," said Winstanley callously. Then he set his foot on the ladder down from the kitchen. His reply was all Geadley needed to make up his mind.

"Not bloody likely. He's comin' too." Suddenly filled with remorse, Winstanley changed his mind and helped Geadley drag Joggett to the ladder. There he was bundled and pushed with the assistance of gravity in a downward direction. When they got to the lower gallery the boards were awash. No-one could have guessed that they were sixty feet above the ocean. Winstanley noticed alarming gaps between the planking. The lighthouse was swaying so much that all the joints were being forced apart.

Joggett was dragged to the next flight only with the greatest difficulty as more water surged over them. The floor was slippery and the spray blinded them. Once over the hatch they all fell into the hole that led down to the lower levels and a temporary respite from the appalling weather. Geadley, being the last man through, shut the hatch after him. It was by now just a token gesture for the water seemed to be pouring through every joint in the lighthouse. All the timbers were in motion as they tried in vain to absorb the stresses being placed upon them. As they did so, the creaking and groaning was clearly audible above the now tremendous roar of the wind and the sea. The three men retreated to the lowest possible level - that of the storeroom - where there seemed to be less motion of the tower. Such was the damage to the timbers, however, that cracks were appearing everywhere. The gales were screaming through every available crevice and a heavy spray of salt water permeated the atmosphere.

In their last refuge the two conscious men found blankets amid the stores and wrapped themselves up as best they could in the darkness. No candle could be lit in this water-borne hovel. Neither man could see the terror on the face of the other. The noise was deafening, but soon, above everything, there came the most almighty splitting sound as the carefully crafted woodwork of the upper tower was finally wrenched from the body of the lighthouse. With a calamitous crash, tons of timber, masonry and gilded panels tumbled down, only to be absorbed by the elements, which attacked the remains of the lighthouse with renewed vigour. From within their cell the prisoners of death cried out vainly to their Saviour.

"O Almighty Lord God, have mercy upon us thy servants..." The pitiful words too were absorbed. No mercy was forthcoming. For Winstanley, Geadley and Joggett it was a further half an hour of life in the presence of death, a further thirty minutes of the agony of expectation, a further eighteen hundred tortuous, fearful seconds before the mutilated lighthouse finally succumbed to the unrivalled power of the ocean.

The miraculous and unending cycle of life and death caused a strange twist of fate. During the death of Henry Winstanley another life was created which was to have a close connection with the Eddystone reef. In a small cottage at the edge of Bodmin moor Eliza Hatherley was giving birth. Her own pains of childbirth were overwhelmed by the noise outside of the Great Storm of 1703, but nothing could surpass her joy upon hearing the first cry of her son, John.

3 WILLIAM KNOTT

It was 1730 and times were hard. Well, William Knott thought so as he left Reach Farm to walk back to the tiny, tarred cottage where he lived on the beach at St. Margaret's Bay. It was dark, cold and stormy, as it seemed to have been for most of the winter, but soon the winter weather would surely abate and spring would arrive to allow work to begin again on the land.

Agriculture was not easy in this most southeasterly corner of Kent. The soil was poor and the land, high up on the chalk downs, was exposed to the biting winds that had swept across a thousand miles of continent. From spring until harvest the villagers worked on the local tenant farms to provide themselves with a meagre wage and a little free food. During the winter farm work was hard to find and the people were forced to resort to other means of survival. The proximity of St. Margaret's to the sea enabled them to supplement their income through fishing, but much more important to a large number of people was the income derived from smuggling.

Despite the fact that it was a crime in the eyes of the authorities, the people themselves had always considered it to be a rightful way of gaining small luxuries. Complementary to the contraband that came ashore through cross-Channel trafficking were the enormous quantities of goods salvaged from the numerous wrecks along the coastline. Indeed, it could be said that a good wreck might keep a family through the winter, one way or another. The beach where William lived had certainly seen its fair share of shipwrecks and, whilst William had always helped himself to anything that might come in useful, he had never become involved in smuggling.

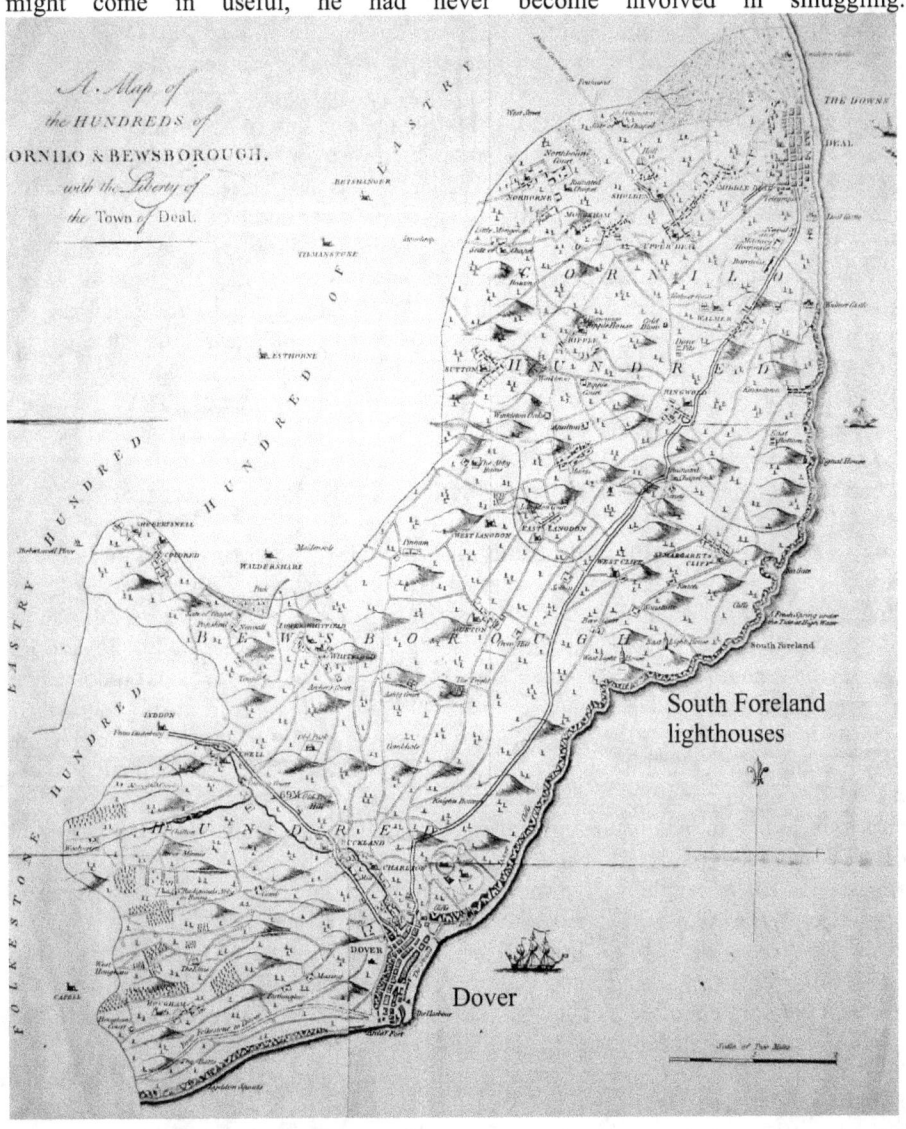

Figure 3: An old map of Southeast Kent, Dover and South Foreland.

23

The prolonged spells of bad weather had made life that much harder. The villagers were besieging all the local farmers with pleas for work and it was on this very business that William had been to Reach farm in the hope of securing employment with Edgar Pilcher. His mission had not been successful, although Pilcher had not refused him entirely. Such was the fluidity of labour that William had been encouraged to try again in a few weeks time when the weather had improved. So it was in a somewhat depressed mood that he was stepping out along the coastal track back towards the Bay, his coat pulled in tightly, his head bowed towards the weather.

The parish of St. Margaret of Antioch consisted of few more than a hundred and twenty souls living in two clusters. The larger was centred on the Norman church and several inns, some four miles from the port of Dover and half a mile from where the chalk downs come to an abrupt end three hundred feet above the sea. Originally a Saxon settlement, it had been set back out of sight of the marauding Danish pirates who were frequent visitors in those times. After dates ran into four figures, the Norman barons stabilised English rural life considerably, and then, in the latter end of the twelfth century, the church had been built. Despite the position of the village high up on the Downs there was comfortable access to the sea by way of a steep track into St. Margaret's Bay where the second small cluster of buildings had grown up next to the shingle beach. It was here that William lived with his family in a small cottage, tarred to maintain a waterproof integrity during the kinds of storms that had beset the area all winter.

William spotted a conveniently placed, well-rounded stone and kicked it as far as he could down the road. It bounced a couple of times and disappeared into the long grass in an adjacent field. He felt better temporarily. At twenty years of age he was dissatisfied with the way his life was going. He had been working on the land for eight years, had received no education, and whilst he enjoyed the outdoor life, working hours were long and the rewards were small. The prospect of scratching a living for a wife and family was low and if he was going to make anything of his life now was the time to do it. Living on the beach, it was not possible to completely avoid the trafficking in contraband which was continually taking place. Whilst he did his best to maintain an independent position, William had inevitably become involved in one or two close calls with the preventive officers whose job it was to catch smugglers. To be caught very often meant a fine or jail, and either would lead to hardship for ones family. The risk was a constant worry and he would be glad of the chance to live an honest life. In the *Green Man* over a glass of smuggled rum he'd conversed with many a sailor and had come to the conclusion that life in the Royal Navy would not be too hard. Fame and fortune could sometimes be won overnight and the accompanying adventures gave their participants many a conversation topic later in life. But William's conscience wrestled with his ambitions. How could he leave his family to go to sea? He lived with his parents who needed all the support they could get. Even William's meagre earnings provided them with enough to prevent them all starving. His father was twenty-five years older and much less able to obtain the sort of work a man half his age could do. Consequently, he concentrated mostly on fishing,

24

and shared a boat with John Parker and Finnis Bowers. The Knott family managed as well as most, but no better. To William, the only escape from his present life-style was to join the navy and he had made up his mind to do just that.

Squeezing his sturdy frame deep into the warmth of his coat to escape the cold he looked up at the sky. It was going to be a rough night. The strong north-easterly wind was blowing up a storm. Quickening his pace, William decided on a plan of action. He would wait until the worst of the winter was over and then leave home to join the fleet. His mother and father would have plenty of time to provide for themselves next winter. And, who knows, by then he might have made his fortune? No, even the ambition of a twenty-year-old had to assume realistic proportions. He had to admit that this was probably overoptimistic, but what could be worse than a life of spasmodic employment, the risk of jail and wondering where the living for the next winter was coming from?

He thought of the men at sea at that moment and wondered how he would feel on board a ship in the face of such a gale. "Any Captain worth his salt would not be at sea on a night like this," he thought, and kicked another stone.

He heard the sound of hooves. Not one horse but two. They were approaching fast from behind. The track was narrow and William had to stand well clear as two heavily cloaked riders galloped past him, hardly acknowledging his presence. William had no difficulty in telling who they were. It was John Tucker and John Bridges, the two preventive officers. For some years now it had been their unenviable task to combat the enormous amount of smuggling that was going on. They always seemed to be in a hurry and William could only guess their errand. He didn't know of anyone who might be involved in smuggling tonight but there was such a lot of activity that he couldn't possibly know about all of it. Whatever it was, he was glad not to be part of it. They looked as if they meant business. Surely, even smugglers had more sense than to be out on a night like this? Shipping would stand no chance, least of all the small boats used by those men. His mind went back to the Navy. It would be a hard life in the company of bitter, pressed men and criminals: the number of volunteers was few. And then there would be the long periods of separation from his loved ones. Elizabeth would understand.

Yes, his dear Elizabeth. She would be hardest of all to leave behind; but it was for her he was really going. What sort of life could he offer her in his present position? At sixteen, she was younger than he and, in her father's opinion, not ready for marriage. They would be forced to leave wedding plans for some years during which time William could be establishing a career at sea. Then, after a few years, he would be able to rent a cottage and start a family with her. As things were now, how could they possibly make a living? Others in his position chose to take the risk: look how their lives turned out! Many were hungry; infant mortality was high. Elizabeth deserved better than that. He knew she would wait for him if he went to sea. When he'd mentioned the idea to her that last Sunday afternoon, she'd not been delighted about the prospect of losing him for months, perhaps even years at a time, but at least she was mature enough to realise, even at her tender age, that their hopes of marriage within the next few years were slim. Yes, Elizabeth would understand.

William caught sight of a brilliant red flash up on the hill to his right and was momentarily taken aback. Collecting his thoughts he realised it was coming from the upper lighthouse. The keeper was obviously stoking the fire well tonight in view of the impending storm - not that there should be much shipping out in such weather. Nevertheless, if the light saved only one life its existence would be justified.

From there it was only a quarter of an hour's walk to William's home and a warming tot of rum. He was quite looking forward to lying in his warm bed and listening to the howling gale outside; he always got a great feeling of security from that.

He was pleased that he had finally made a decision about his future. His step was lighter and it did not seem quite so cold somehow. While the weather cursed, he would dream of the exotic worlds of the Orient and the Indies from the comfort of his bed... until tomorrow.

4 WILLIAM JENNINGS - 1

William Jennings knew it would not take place that night. The weather was far too bad. He'd known for the past three hours. but had been forced to come to Fan Bay in case those stupid Frenchmen attempted it. He consoled himself with the thought that any self-respecting customs man would be in his bed on a filthy night like this. He looked over to his left and saw the lights from the two South Foreland lighthouses. At any moment Jack Heal, the keeper of the lower lighthouse, would give a signal to the Frenchmen by obscuring his light so that only one of the two lighthouses could be seen at sea. Jennings was very doubtful that the French would come at all. The sea was running very high and visibility in the pouring rain was dreadful. Jennings and his men were already soaked to the skin and he would be very glad to go home. Despite the rain, he could feel spray in his face from the huge breakers over a hundred feet below. Looking out into the void he strained his eyes to see a vessel, although he knew there was none. Even Frenchmen would not risk it tonight.

Suddenly something changed. The light from the lower lighthouse had been screened. Heal had done his stuff - this time. The operation was greatly assisted by the use of the lighthouse for signalling and it had all been Matson's idea. But obviously it needed the co-operation of the keeper. At first Heal had wanted nothing to do with the scheme, but with the aid of bribery Jennings had obtained Heal's compliance. Heal was still not happy about his role in the affair. He was a man of conscience and took the responsibilities of his job seriously. So it had been necessary for Jennings to engage in a bit of 'friendly persuasion' to ensure Heal's assistance with his plans.

Eb Faller and Jake Dike were good at persuading people to do things. Cockneys both, they had learnt what it was like to be without and had had to fight for everything they owned. They were the linkmen in the operation. When 'goods' had to be transported to London they organised it; when labour problems arose they dealt with them. Jennings was left in an overseeing capacity, which he liked, except when the weather was as bad as this. But he was still answerable to Matson.

He looked around and could not see Faller or Dike but he knew they were there. Their job tonight was to be lookouts. Tucker and Bridges were getting too good at their jobs and were beginning to make life difficult for Jennings and his associates. Luckily, he had built up a good network of informers and often knew what Tucker and Bridges were planning. Jennings had received no warnings that his opponents would be in the area tonight and felt sure his men would not be disturbed. What a pity the night was almost certain to be fruitless.

Two o'clock. If it came at all it would be now. He would wait another half-hour and then get back to his bed. The weather, like the law, was an occupational hazard. At the time the runs were planned there was no way of knowing whether they would actually take place and the excess of bad weather this winter had caused too many cancelled landings.

He looked across at John Jale and Finnis Bowers who were waiting with him on the cliff top. Both looked thoroughly miserable and anxious to go home. It surely was a desperate trade they were all involved in! The trouble was that it was profitable. There was good money to be made in London: Ben Matson would bear witness to that. Matson was the mastermind behind the operations here in the Kentish countryside. A poor local boy made good, he'd worked hard all his life and earned not only a great deal of money but also the respect of all the local people.

Fortunately he'd had the benefit of many years when the authorities did little to combat smuggling. Matson had made full use of this opportunity to establish a countywide network of outlets for his merchandise and had only latterly made his most profitable contacts in London. This had led to the arrival of Faller and Dike and the organisation suddenly began to take on a more sinister aspect.

Wanstone farm, situated but a few hundred yards from where Jennings now waited, had been financed almost entirely from Matson's ill-earned profits and he'd always taken care to acquire the trappings of respectability, whilst maintaining his position at the hub of the undercover setup. He'd always remained one step ahead of the preventive officers, and few people knew of the scale of his associations with a major contraband gang. Jennings couldn't understand why Matson allowed landings to take place so close to Wanstone farm - it seemed to be inviting suspicion, but Matson was always too smart for the customs men. 'Goods' were never kept at the farm. Everything was removed from the locality almost immediately it was brought ashore, and Matson himself was never present at the scene of the crime. Not surprisingly it was almost impossible to pin a charge on him, No, it was he, Jennings, and all these other men who took the chances, did all of the donkey work. Bringing stuff up the cliffs was no joke: the path was steep and dangerous. Still, he could not complain for Matson paid him well.

John Tucker was in a hurry. He and Bridges were always in a hurry. He'd been a Preventive Riding Officer for some years. It paid him sixty pounds per annum as well as giving him a horse. The job had been created in 1690 when the authorities decided an attempt should be made to cut down the amount of smuggled merchandise escaping the various duties they were trying to impose. From the start they'd been fighting a losing battle and it was the likes of Tucker who'd had to soldier on against overwhelming odds. The worst part was that you could never convince the people that what they were doing was wrong. Perhaps it was against the law, but as far as they were concerned they were morally entitled to obtain their little luxuries as cheaply as possible. They'd little enough as it was without furnishing the taxman with more. Consequently, smuggling was a major occupation and there was little that he and Bridges, working alone against virtually the whole population, could do about it. They needed informers and that was why tonight was so important. They'd at last found a source of information, which, if it proved to be correct, would lead to an important capture. Eagerly - and carelessly - they rode towards Fan Bay.

Shots rang out; horses whinnied. Jennings realised that something unexpected was happening in the direction of the lighthouses. Instinctively, he got up and began to run frantically along the cliffs in the direction of Dover. Jale and Bowers ran too, but they chose to disappear down the cliff path towards the beach below which was being continuously pounded by the heavy seas. Jennings did not know what had happened but he was going to get away; nothing else mattered. He guessed that the lookouts had ambushed Tucker and Bridges, but Faller and Dike were capable of looking after themselves and he'd not considered going to their aid. Jale and Bowers would be all right on the beach. They couldn't get any wetter and they'd escape back along the shore to the Bay where they both lived. He could hear nothing but the weather. Whatever had occurred, it had been brief. His lungs were bursting but still he ran. You could take no chances in this business. Soon he would be able to cut across to the Deal road and thence back home. He was safe.

On the cliff path, Finnis Bowers was sliding more than running. The rain had turned it into a slippery and dangerous route and it was extremely difficult to see the path in the darkness. Though he had made the descent many times before, Bowers was terrified of making a false step and falling over the edge. Jale was behind him, panting furiously, and although they could hear no sign of pursuit, still they kept on going. Lower down, the spray was drenching. Fortunately, the tide was low. When they reached the beach they set off back towards St. Margaret's Bay keeping close to the foot of the cliff. Their progress was slow because of the difficulty of finding a way over the rocks in the darkness. Bowers hit his shin on a rock and cursed. He decided to go more steadily, realising that he could easily break a leg on such terrain.

Though he could not be sure, Bowers guessed that Tucker and Bridges had turned up uninvited and met their reception party. Faller and Dike were good at that sort of thing. Bowers was afraid of them (they all were) and he always kept well away from them whenever he could. They could be violent at times and it was best not to upset them. Jennings was a fool ever to have brought them down from London. They should have stayed in the East End where they belonged. Things had been much better before they came. There'd always been a spirit of comradeship amongst their group

28

before, but he could never look upon Faller and Dike in the same way. Still, he was glad they were on his side - he'd hate to have them against him.

Bowers and Jale said nothing to each other as they struggled on into the night. They knew what they had to do and that was to escape.

Faller and Dike were professionals: professional thugs, that is, the sort of men who find life dull without an occasional brawl. They knew their business. Customs men were their business. From the moment that they had heard the clump of four pairs of hooves heading towards them, Faller and Dike knew that the customs men were coming. It was too dark of course to see them, but who else could it be? Jake Dike clasped a six-foot staff tightly in his large hands and stood in the track that led along the cliff to where Jennings and the others were waiting. Faller remained hidden behind a small bush close by.

"Who goes there?" bellowed Dike in his best military voice. The horses loomed up at him out of the darkness. With remarkably swift reactions Dike leapt to one side and swung the staff at the dark, cloaked shape on the nearest horse. Either by chance or from the experience gained from years of skulduggery, Dike's instinctive aim was good. Tucker was knocked unconscious from his saddle by the single blow on the head. Bridges had slightly more time to react and attempted to defend himself by drawing a pistol from beneath his cloak. A figure came at him from out of the dark and he fired at it. To shoot from a moving horse using a pistol thrust from beneath a sodden and heavy cape required a good deal more luck than Bridges could muster. His wild shot missed Faller entirely. His horse took exception to the sudden noise and commotion in the darkness; it whinnied and shied. Bridges was forced to drop his pistol to maintain his place in the saddle, but his horse was in no mood to retain him any longer. He fell awkwardly into a clump of longish grass and felt his shoulder twist out of joint. Agony gripped his left side but still he staggered to his feet, only to be pounced on by Faller who clubbed him senseless with just two bloody strokes. It was all over very quickly.

Faller, hardly even out of breath, knelt for a moment over the lifeless body slumped in the grass. With the limited vision that the smothering darkness allowed him, he watched as the rain began to wash blood from Bridges' forehead into his hair. A fleeting second of remorse entered his animal senses, but was dismissed in an instant when Dike came to see if his friend was all right. The two men smiled grimly at each other and began to walk back along the cliffs to St. Margaret's.

5 JAMES HILL

Captain James Hill stood on the quarterdeck of his merchant ship *Prosperity* and knew deep down that he would not make it back to Dover. His first command was going to end in failure. The weather had been slowly worsening since the ship had left Falmouth in a lazy swell yesterday morning with her valuable cargo of copper ore bound for London. Only recently the value of the copper and other minerals beneath the Cornish landscape had been realised and mining was expanding at a colossal rate, bringing a new degree of importance to that county. As yet, facilities for dealing with the ore in Cornwall were few and a lot of the ores were being shipped out of Falmouth untreated.

Hill, too, had struck it rich, although not in mining. A Falmouth man, he had been working with the local shipping company, George Penrice and Son, for over ten years, most of which had been spent plying the Atlantic routes. The owners had right away considered him to be a man of potential and rapid advancement had come his way. Then, when the copper boom started, the company suddenly found a requirement for more captains and Hill had been one of the first appointments, confirming the company's high regard for him. He had certainly been lucky, taking command at the relatively young age of thirty-one and he was anxious to prove to Mr Penrice that his faith in him was well-founded. He had not been so lucky with crew however. The great demand for seamen in Falmouth at that time had forced the company to take on a larger number of inexperienced men than they might have wished and Hill had been forced to rely heavily on the few experienced crew he had on board. His second-in-command was an old first mate by the name of Clayson, whilst the helm was in the safe hands of John Hatherley, whom Hill had sailed with before. Despite the inexperienced crew, *Prosperity* had made excellent progress until now.

Passing Dover, Hill had been sure they would make a safe, if lumpy, passage and he'd steered a course well away from the Goodwin Sands, but there'd been a sudden deterioration in the weather, which, in Hill's limited experience of this particular route, he'd not witnessed before. The wind had veered to the northeast and lashed the sea into a most dangerous condition. With every second, the waves had seemed to grow until they smashed into the bows of the *Prosperity*, burying the forecastle in cascades of icy brine. Hill tried to turn back, but the withdrawal manoeuvre had only made matters worse. The severe rolling action when he brought her about caused the load to shift and now *Prosperity* was struggling back to Dover with a severe starboard list.

"Fifteen degrees to starboard."

With the gale at his back forcing him painfully into the guardrails, Hill bawled the order.

"Aye aye, sir," came the reply, and the wheel was adjusted accordingly to bring the ship closer to the land and to safety. Hill had made a mistake. Why had he not run for shelter in Dover when he first had the chance? Why had he tried to complete his journey and turned back only when it was too late? The answers were painfully obvious. On his first command he'd been so keen to do it right: to stay within the time schedule his owners were asking and to prove to them that they'd made the right decision in giving him command. Now his only hope was to try to make Deal, or perhaps St. Margaret's Bay. He strained his eyes towards the point where he felt sure the South Foreland beacon would be burning, but there was no sign except for a tantalising glimmer, which he knew to be the optimism of his imagination. There was no chance of seeing the light in these conditions and he knew it.

"Steady as she goes, Hatherley," he screamed at the stout Cornishman behind the helm.

"Aye aye, sir."

"Begging your pardon, sir." A third voice was heard through the din. It was Clayson, an old salt with many years more experience than Hill but who, for some reason, had never been able to convince his employers of his ability. It had been rumoured that many years before he had killed a shipmate after an argument, but Clayson had always hotly denied it and no-one knew of any evidence to substantiate it. However, mud sticks and it had inevitably held him back unfairly. Hill was always aware that Clayson was probably more qualified to captain the vessel than he was, but Clayson had never shown any ill-feeling and Hill respected him for it. He'd been given command and was keen to prove himself - or perhaps he had been too keen.

"She's taking in water badly now, sir. If we don't get that cargo back in place soon..."

"Get every man that can be spared below decks and start shifting that cargo," interrupted Hill, realising the position fully and not wishing it spelt out so vividly.

The orders were given and for a few seconds men scuttled about on deck, finally disappearing below to begin their impossible task. How could a dozen men make an impact on many tons of ore in the time being spared them? But it was their only hope. Running before the wind as she was, *Prosperity* was slightly less exposed to the brunt of the waves, but so ferocious was the sea that the decks were suffering torrent after torrent of frothing water. Hatherley struggled. Holding her on course was exceedingly difficult and he sweated voluminously beneath his well-tarred waterproof clothing. The list seemed to be getting worse and more of the starboard side was beneath the sea. Why had he left the comfort of his home in Calstock to come here? He wondered how long the storm sails would last. Already the immense stresses of the gale were causing a weakening of the lashings.

And then it happened.

Prosperity rode the crest of a gigantic wave and seemed to stand on end, bow downwards. The whole of the forward end of the ship was suddenly submerged by an enormous wall of water which ripped aft towards the quarterdeck, carrying with it most of the foremast. As it hit the deck the mast was smashed to pieces, most of which were instantly swept overboard In turn, this destruction had caused severe entanglement in the after rigging, and, just as Hill had picked himself up after diving for cover from falling woodwork, a second wall of water seethed over the bows.

"That's it," yelled Hill to Clayson. "Abandon ship!"

He had tried to avoid saying it. He'd prayed he would not have to say it, and when he did the words stuck in his throat. He yelled them again.

"Abandon ship! Abandon ship!"

The men below had just received their final orders and begun to emerge from their rabbit-holes as the next waterwall beat into the ship. Many of them were immediately plucked from their floating refuge and stuffed into the bowels of the storm, never to be seen again.

The more fortunate Hatherley had immediately set about releasing one of the boats when the ultimate order came, and, together with two other crewmen, had managed to divorce himself from the doomed ship just in time to see the remaining superstructure scythed to fragments. The luckless captain's last thoughts were to check for men below as a large section of the mainmast smashed down on his skull.

6 JOHN HATHERLEY -1

William Knott awoke with a start. He'd been sleeping badly due to the noise of the weather and it had taken him so long to get to sleep that he was annoyed at being awakened. Then he realised that someone was hammering at the door.

"William, Joseph, there's been a wreck... wake up..."

William leapt out of bed and quickly pulled on some clothes. His father, Joseph, and his brothers Henry and Thomas were soon gathered at the front door in the light of the caller's lantern. Henry Darby, another local fisherman, had raised the alarm.

"Come on," said Henry," there are some men washed up on the beach. They're pretty far gone, so it seems. I'll go and get more help."

Darby ran off to the other cottages as the Knotts headed towards the sea. The weather was appalling. The wind and rain beat straight into their faces as they struggled across the pebbles of the beach, their feet sinking up to their ankles in soft stones. Progress down the steep shingle beach seemed painfully slow and they all felt as though they were working a treadmill. Strangely, even against the din of the elements they could barely make out distant shouting as Henry mobilised assistance. They arrived at the water's edge soaked to the skin from rain and spray. William scanned the beach to the right and left. Nothing could be seen. They decided to split up. William and his father headed up towards the cliffs, while the other two brothers went in the opposite direction. Progress was slow in the darkness and William wished that they had not been in so much of a hurry for they had come without a lantern.

Suddenly, a few yards ahead, William was able just to make out dark shapes on the beach. Feeling rather like puppets with strings on their arms and legs, they plunged animatedly towards the survivors, if they could still be described as such.

A man was sprawled on the shingle, motionless. Nearby, a small ship's boat was high and dry, deserted by the ebbing tide. It contained two more wretched seamen. William and Joseph briefly examined the three bodies and found them to be as cold as winter waves. The one on the beach, a well-built young man in his early twenties, seemed to stir faintly as Joseph turned him over.

"This one's alive," said Joseph. "Let's get him back to the cottage. I don't have much hope for the others."

Breakers tumbled up the beach behind them, but with great difficulty the two Samaritans carried the survivor up the steep, slippery pebble bank. As they did so Stephen Peake, John Parker and Henry Darby came half running, half sliding towards them. The light from two lanterns bathed the rain-soaked scene and William squinted to avoid the sudden glare. Suddenly, from out of the night Finnis Bowers and John Jale also came staggering and offering assistance. William thought they looked unusually tired and wet for two people who had just got out of bed.

"We'll take this one to our house," shouted William's father. "I don't give much for the others' chances."

"We'll do what we can," replied John Jale, the Knotts' next-door neighbour.

"The doctor's on his way. I'll send him around to you when he arrives," shouted Henry, and, with the others, ran off down the beach leaving the two men to struggle with their cumbersome load. William's arms were tired and he knew his father's would be also but every second counted if they were to save a life. Exposure was a killer and if they didn't get him to the warmth of the cottage soon their efforts would be in vain. His calves ached so much from walking on an unsteady footing for so long that he thought he was going to collapse. His father's face showed too the agony he was feeling.

"Let's keep going," William encouraged, "It's not far to go now. Can you last out?"

"Just about, son. Reckon I'll need the doctor as well when he comes," he joked. William smiled grimly.

Mary, William's mother, was quick to open the door in response to his kick on the wood and told the two exhausted men to lay their load on the mat in front of the hastily rekindled fire.

"Get those wet clothes off him and get him into your bed, William," she ordered, her matronly instincts taking full command. As best they could they stripped him and struggled to get a clean, dry nightshirt over his large frame. Then with a final effort the frozen heap was deposited in William's still warm sleeping quarters. Extra blankets were purloined from the other beds and a hot drink found to try to revive the newcomer. Indeed, by the time these acts were completed the patient was beginning to stir.

"What's your name, son?" enquired Joseph.

"John Hatherley, sir," came the reply with great effort.

"Drink this down lad and rest easy: the doctor will be along shortly. You're going to be all right."

"Thank you very much, sir."

William detected a hint of real sincerity in the response and knew the survivor was grateful to be alive. He was certainly a lucky man. He thought of the other poor beggars on the beach, their limbs blue with cold. It was certainly a risk every sailor took when he went to sea, and now that he had seen so vividly the results of a shipwreck he began to have doubts about joining the navy. Certainly Elizabeth would be much less inclined to let him go when she heard about this episode. It was more than likely that the man lying in his bed was the only survivor from the ship's complement of perhaps a hundred - who knows? When William thought about the weather outside and the size of the waves pounding up the beach he wondered how anyone could have survived a shipwreck tonight. Yes, Hatherley was indeed a lucky man.

William realised that he, too, was soaked to the skin and shivering from the cold despite the warmth of the room. He found himself some dry clothes and put them on. By the time he had done this, Dr Dale had arrived looking worried and wet. William's two brothers, who'd had less luck in their area of search, followed the doctor into the cottage. They too had found a body on the beach, but the poor devil was already dead.

"How is he?" was the doctor's immediate enquiry.

"Surprisingly well under the circumstances, I should say," replied Joseph. "What of the other two?"

"Two?" said the doctor, surprised. "They've found five more so far and there'll be more."

"But how are they?" repeated William.

"All gone," said the doctor sadly. "Four were dead on the beach and the other lasted only a few minutes after we got him to Henry Darby's cottage. He lived long enough for us to discover that he was French. No, they'd been exposed to the cold and wet more than most men can stand. This fellow of yours is exceedingly lucky to have survived. Is he French as well?"

"No, he isn't," replied William, trying to understand why there should be English and French sailors on the same ship.

After the doctor had completed his examination, he diagnosed a case of simple exposure - not that there was anything simple about a case as serious as Hatherley's. In any case, the only remedy was plenty of rest, warmth and good nursing, which William's mother promised faithfully to provide. Hatherley was sleeping peacefully and when the doctor had left, Mary remained on watch, whilst Joseph and his sons retired to a restless sleep for what little remained of the night.

In the course of time, Hatherley made good progress and after a couple of days was sat up in bed and ready to talk to anyone who would come to his bedside to listen. The whole village was buzzing with the news, not only of the shipwreck, but of the attack on the preventive men on the cliffs. Whilst Tucker and Bridges were not the most popular men in the locality, the violence of the assault on them had been most out of character for local people to do it. Speculation was rife about the identity of the men who would do such a thing. Hatherley, however, had attracted the most interest and everyone had suddenly become concerned for the welfare of a stranger, apparently uniquely able to ward off the perils of one of the worst storms of the winter. Wreckage and more bodies had been washed up along the Kentish coastline and everyone carried the shipwreck around on their lips, the more so since there appeared to have been but one survivor. Hatherley found himself to be quite famous and the Knott's cottage at times was besieged with people clamouring to see him. He knew none of them, but they all appeared to know him well, and he soon found himself being addressed as the 'Lucky Cornishman.'

Elizabeth, William's beloved, had more than contributed to Hatherley's rapid recovery, and Mary had been delighted with the help she'd given her. Apart from that, it had given Elizabeth good reason to be in the company of William and she was naturally pleased with Hatherley's arrival on the scene, albeit under such dramatic circumstances. The 'Lucky Cornishman' himself could not contain his gratitude towards the Knotts for having saved his life. He thanked them continually and apologised that he would never be able to repay them.

It was early evening when yet another visitor arrived at the door with a much more serious air and announced himself to be one William Cooper, Senior Preventive Officer in the area. Treating the Knotts with unreasonable disdain he marched into the room where Hatherley was still in bed and began to launch a fusillade of accusations at the surprised patient.

"My name is William Cooper," he pronounced, "and it is my job in this area to investigate all illegal trafficking in goods from abroad. I have reason to believe that two nights ago in the region of Fan Bay you were involved in a highly illegal operation. This was to land alcoholic beverages and other dutiable goods, as yet unspecified, without paying His Majesty's customs duty. I shall hear what you have to say, but, if you fail to convince me of your true business, I shall arrest you on a charge of attempted smuggling and assault on His Majesty's customs officers. What have you to say?"

Hatherley was aghast. He had not suspected this and was quite speechless.

"Very well then. Silence is a true indication of guilt in my book. Get your clothes on."

"Just a minute," interrupted William, "this man is entirely innocent of this charge."

"How do you know?" Cooper swung around to face William with a savage look.

"Well, I... er."

" 't is true," said Hatherley. " 't were naught to do wi' me. I were a 'and on the merchant ship *Prosperity*. The Cap'n were James 'ill an' me bosses was George Penrice and sons of Falmouth. Us set sail from there early Thursday with a cargo of copper ore. Us run into a storm as us passed Dover. A real hoolie 't were. As the Cap'n tried to bring 'er about to run back to Dover, the load shifted. 'Er sunk not long after that. I got off wi' two other 'ands in a ship's boat and us managed to come ashore just below the light on the South Foreland. Trouble is, I were the only one as survived so I don't 'ave no witnesses."

Cooper was surprised. He hadn't expected such a lucid reply to his accusation. He struggled to find a response.

"Well then, er... how do you explain the casks of rum and whiskey which have been coming ashore today, to say nothing of dead Frenchmen and my officers with broken heads!"

"He doesn't have to explain it," defended William. "All you've got to do is check with the shipping agents in Dover."

35

That was the last straw. Defeated, Cooper accepted that his attacking tactic had been a dismal flop and reconnoitred his retreat.

"All right then, for the moment I'll leave it while I check out this story of yours," he said severely and trying desperately to save face, "but two of my officers have been seriously assaulted on the cliffs and there is no doubt in my mind that smugglers were at work judging by the wreckage being washed ashore. Make no mistake," he said, edging towards the door "if you're involved I'll see you pay dearly."

So saying, he turned and almost ran out of the door, his tail tucked firmly between his legs.

William and John looked at each other and grinned. The sudden relief from the tension of the past few moments made Cooper's antics seem quite comical and, reassured by the knowledge that the innocent had nothing to fear, they both relaxed.

"We certainly showed him the door, didn't we?" said William. "I must confess, he caught me off guard at one point and I'm glad you found your voice."

"From what 'e says I reckons they was out smuggling in all that weather," said John in amazement.

"It is certainly beginning to look like it. I wasn't aware of it, but I don't know about much of what goes on these days. I would say they tried a landing and came to grief. It's just an unfortunate coincidence that you came ashore at the same time. Come to think of it, I was a bit puzzled, when we were bringing you home last night, I saw John Jale and Finnis Bowers coming from the direction of the cliffs. They don't live in that direction at all and it's a funny time of night to be up anyway. I wouldn't be at all surprised if they were waiting for the Frenchies when things went wrong. It wouldn't be the first time the other side have tried a run in rough weather, but they must have been really crazy last night. We haven't had weather like that for years. If truth were known, they were getting desperate with so many runs being cancelled recently. Anyway, as far as Cooper is concerned, he'll get all the proof he needs in Dover to eliminate you from his enquiries, although he's bound to come back to ask more questions. I'll bet he's a good deal more polite next time. You can't really blame him for jumping to conclusions, though. I think anyone else would have done, the same."

"Ye got your alibi anyhow - savin' me like 'e did. My shipwreck 'll give thee something after all."

"I suppose it will, but if that's so then Jale and Bowers will get one too. I expect that's why they were so eager to help in the rescue. What are your plans from now on, John? Are you going to carry on working for the same company?"

William had wanted to ask John about life at sea, but after recent events he was beginning to have doubts again. It was certainly a dangerous occupation, but it had occupied his mind so much of late that he had to talk about it with someone.

"No, I'm finished with the sea now. I'm not quite sure what I'll do."

The definitive way in which he pronounced his retirement from the sea had suddenly sunk in and John realised that he had no other occupation to fall back on other than mining, which he hated. He would surely be out of his mind to go back to sea after this experience. On the other hand, it could also be said that lightning never strikes twice and the chances of him finding himself in a similar situation were fairly remote. Realising the seriousness of his position, Hatherley fell deep in thought. William, of course, had been secretly hoping that John would allay his fears of going to sea, but that seemed rather unlikely now. He explained the problem that had occupied him and John proved a sympathetic listener to William's woes.

"Well, I were in the same boat a couple of years back," explained John. "I were a miner back home in Cornwall. There's a real boom in mining down there at present - 'specially in copper. That's what us was carryin' on *Prosperity*. Ah, but 't is a 'ard life, minin'… all the day in a pitch-black 'ole with just a candle to give light on thy work. There's water pouring in everywhere and thee very often get soaked to the skin. When thee get to the top again after breakin' thy back all day 't is dark again, so thee never gets to see the sunshine, 'cept p'raps in the summer. That's 'ow I come to go to sea. I thought it'd be a challenge, and a 'ealthy one too, with all that fresh air to breathe instead of dust. Fer two years I've sailed up and down the Channel on merchantmen, goin' nowhere 't is true, but I quite liked 't. Then come that storm. 'T was the last time for me. I thought I'd seen everythin' 'til then. The Almighty threw everythin' at us. 'T were no way *Prosperity* could have survived the pounding 'er got that night, and Cap'n Hill knew it. But 'e also knew e'd made a mistake. 'T were in 'is eyes. 'E should 'ave sheltered in Dover but 'e didn'. Just why 'e didn' only 'e can tell, God rest 'is soul. No, Will the sea's not for me. I'm no hero, despite what the folks 'round 'ere think. Don't know what I'll do, but 't won't be that. Actually, I rather fancies bein' a lighthouse keeper meself. They say 't is a good job with everythin' provided - and that's half the battle these days, isn't it? What's the lighthouse 'ere like?"

William was silent for a time. A lighthouse keeper! Funnily enough, it had not occurred to him before, although just why he was not sure. It certainly was a good job, and responsible too. Just think of all those lives at sea dependent on seeing the light for safe navigation. Even if he didn't go to sea, he'd still retain a close connection with it.

"William, d'ya 'ear me?"

William suddenly felt guilty for ignoring John.

"Yes, John, I'm sorry. I was thinking what a good idea it was. I wouldn't mind doing that at all. That way, I could be with Elizabeth all the time and have a living wage and a house too."

Instantly, William was imagining himself in charge up at the South Foreland.

"But what about the lighthouse?" John asked again.

John was obviously interested in the South Foreland lighthouse and William was momentarily jealous in case John should steal the job from him, even though it was John's idea.

"Oh yes, it's a good station. There's an upper and a lower light. The keeper in the lower light is called Heal and seems to do the job well. He… what's wrong, John?" William noticed a look of puzzlement suddenly cross the Cornish face.

"There was only one light burnin' as us come to the shore, I swear. Why were that d'ya reckon?"

37

"That's funny, I'm not sure. As I say, Heal is usually reliable. Of course, it might have been the top light that was out, but the keeper there, Saul Goldsack, is a good man too. I wouldn't have thought that either of them would have gone to sleep and let their fires go out. They're supposed to keep them burning all night and usually do, to the best of my knowledge. The local people think quite well of both of them, although the fishermen in these parts don't like to admit that they find the lighthouse useful. They always like to let on that they know the area like the backs of their hands, but I'm sure it helps them find their way back home. Of course, when it was first put up most people hated it because they lost a good deal of the spoils they would have had from the wrecks during the winter. Now they've mostly got used to having it and they don't really mind. Yes, there was a terrific amount of ill-feeling at first, so father says. You see, for many of them what they got from the wrecks was the difference between living fairly well and going hungry in the winter."

" 't is still a bit like that down 'ome," said John. "There be a lot of talk about lighthouses in Cornwall because there be always so many wrecks. I'm sure as I wants to be a keeper on the Eddystone, though."

"Isn't that at Portsmouth? We've heard stories about it. It's a famous one that."

William's lack of education was manifest - not that John minded - he didn't know much about Kent.

"No, 't is about ten miles south of Plymouth Sound. Plymouth is in Devon, just over the border with Cornwall. Down that way, everyone talks about the Eddystone, it be the wonder of the age."

"Tell me about it, you've got me interested now!"

"Well, Winstanley built a lighthouse on the Eddystone because 'e 'ad several ships wrecked on the rocks. 'E were s'posed to 'ave been a bit queer in the 'ead and this lighthouse 'ad all sorts of funny things built on 't - really fancy t' were. Well, if thee ever been out to the Eddystone as I 'ave 'e'd never believe naught could be built there, let alone last a winter. Durin' it's first winter 't were damaged bad by the sea. Winstanley 'ad to virtually rebuild it to make it safer. 'E swore blind as the new lighthouse would never be so much as damaged and 'e used to tell everyone 'as 'e'd like to be in 't during the greatest storm there ever was. Would 'e believe it - 'e 'ad 'is way. 'T were in 1703 – the day I was born, so me mum told me, as us 'ad the Great Storm - your own good folks 'll remember it. 'T were the worst for years and years, and washed the lighthouse away completely with Winstanley and 'e's keepers in it."

"No survivors?" asked William, incredulously.

"None! And if 'e'd been out with I last Friday night 'e'd know why. I'm blowed if I can see how any structure on a rock in the middle of the sea can stand what us took."

"But isn't there another lighthouse there now?"

"Oh, aye. This merchant, Rudyerd, put up another tower a few years after Winstanley died. I think 't were 1708 when 't were in use again. Plymouth folk think 't is only a matter of time before it goes the same way as Winstanley's did, but 't 's done

38

all right so far. I wouldn't like to be a keeper there mind. They don't allow no women out there so 't is a job for bachelors and brave ones at that. No, I'll stick to lighthouses on land. There's a good one down the Lizard."

"Where's that?"

" 't is right down west of Cornwall, the most southerly point in England. I'd like to be a keeper there."

"I suppose you'd like the job here?" asked William, still conscious of the possibility that John was going to rob him of the chance of taking over at South Foreland, but he had reckoned without the strong ties of one's home country.

"Not really. Oh, 't wouldn't be bad, but not 'ere. Me 'ome 's in Cornwall and always will be. 'T is where I belong and I must get back there soon. I can't stay yer with thee kind folks much longer, now that I'm better. Thee been so good to I - I owe you me life."

"Nonsense," protested William, "any of the villagers would have done the same."

"Nevertheless, 't were thee and thy family as saved I and 't is thee I shall owe for the rest of me life."

It would indeed be time soon for John to move on and William knew that the family must let him. In the very short time in which they had known each other, the Knotts had all grown to like Hatherley a great deal and they would miss him and the breath of fresh air that he had brought to their lives. Already they had learnt about a part of the world and a way of life with which they had no contact before, and probably never would again. A man who, until so recently, had been a complete stranger, was now almost a member of the family, and had had a profound effect on their lives.

"Where will you go?" queried William.

"I'll go back 'ome to live with me own folk fer now. If I can't get a job as a keeper I might learn a new trade, I'm young enough. 'T is not easy getting took on as an apprentice, but I'll try, even if I 'as to go to Plymouth."

"How will you get back to Plymouth?"

"I'll go to the company's agent in Dover - they must 'ave one there. They owes I some pay. That should get I 'ome all right. How far be 't to Dover from 'ere?"

"Oh, about an hour's walk," replied William. "When will you go?"

"On Friday, if thee will 'ave I 'til then."

And go he did, but not quite in the way that he had planned. On Thursday, Hatherley and the Knotts returned to the cottage from the mid-morning funeral service for those who had died in the storm. Just after they had got back Mary found another visitor on the doorstep asking to see the survivor of the wreck. It was immediately apparent that this visitor was someone special from his style of dress and the fine brown mare that he had tied up outside the cottage. His voice showed none of the local inflections and instinctively Mary found herself trying to speak in her best Sunday accent in response to his questions, as if her education had been considerable, which it had not. The lucky Cornishman was ill at ease as he shook hands with the stranger,

39

remembering the row he'd had with Cooper, but to his surprise the gentleman announced himself to be a Mr Stephen Latham, Dover agent to the company which owned the *Prosperity*. Latham made himself entirely at home and his manner generally was totally sympathetic to John's plight. After all, Hatherley had been the innocent victim of an unfortunate chain of events. Having initially asked after John's health, and expressed pleasure with the positive answer, Mr Latham was most anxious to ascertain the details of the disaster in order to send a report to the owners. Hatherley told him as much as he knew, although even he could only guess as to why Captain Hill had erred - a matter about which there could be no doubt. Nevertheless, Mr Latham seemed pleased with his account, but expressed some disquiet about John's observations regarding the South Foreland light - or rather the lack of part of it. However he thanked John for his help and produced a small pouch in which there were five guineas. These he duly handed over to an incredulous John.

"Whilst there has not yet been time for communication with the owners, I am sure they would like you to accept this as part compensation for the misfortunes which have befallen you. I would be obliged if you would continue to serve on our vessels as a leading hand at twice your previous rate of pay. What do you say?"

" 'e be most kind, sir. I must say as 'ow I be quite taken aback b' thy kindness. To be honest, sir, I were reckonin' on a job ashore. That storm were too bad for me. I thought about bein' a lightkeeper. Even so, thy offer be exceedin' generous and I finds it 'ard to say no to 't."

"A lighthouse keeper, eh? I have some dealings with them myself, you know, or rather, I should say, with Samuel Weaver in Deal. He looks after the local lights and arranges for men to be taken on as required. We quite often do business together. I could recommend you to him if you like, but of course, I would prefer it if you would accept my offer."

"Thank you all the same, sir, but I don't wish to make me 'ome in this strange county so far from Cornwall."

"Then I take it you will accept my offer?"

"I will, sir," said John with only a hint of hesitation. The tragic events of a few nights past had now slipped into relative insignificance compared to the generous contract now on offer. William and Joseph Knott smiled at each other, remembering the degree of certainty with which Hatherley had declared an end of his marriage to the mariner's life. They knew he'd little choice and were pleased for him.

"In that case, take this letter to the address of the London agent which is printed there and he will find you a ship forthwith. It has been a pleasure to meet you Hatherley. I wish you every good fortune in the future."

After a few words of farewell to Joseph and the Knotts, Stephen Latham left the cottage with John somewhat dazed and not entirely sure what had happened to him. It was only after the sound of hooves had ceased and words of congratulations from his hosts that he began to appreciate his luck.

Next day he pressed two of his five guineas into Joseph Knott's hand, much against the latter's will, and said farewell to the family that had saved his life.

" 't will never pay for the kindness thee shown me," said John "but 't will certainly 'elp and thee must take it. I will always remember thee and I'll be back to see thee all one day."

Mary found tears blurring her vision as the door closed behind the Lucky Cornishman.

7 JACK HEAL

In the lower of the two South Foreland lighthouses, Jack Heal was stoking the fire that was to provide a warning light to any vessels at sea that night. It was one of those cold, still, moonlit nights when the elements seem to be resting from the exertions of previous days. Heal was grateful for the lull in the weather which had been so bad all winter. It was a lovely night - the sort of night when he realised how much he liked his job. The air was cold, but fresh and invigorating. Here in the lantern room next to the fire however, he was very uncomfortable. It could get too hot at times, but then he could go down below for a while. He looked out at the higher light and saw it burning brightly. Saul Goldsack, its keeper, always did his job well.

Jack's wife, Jane, and young daughter were safely in bed in the cottage below and the only noise was a gentle crackling from the fire which had temporarily died down a little as the latest batch of coal caught up. This was always a problem with coal fires - it was very difficult to maintain a constant light intensity. The owners of the lighthouses at the South Foreland, the Greenwich Hospital Trustees, had experimented to try to optimise conditions but had not really been successful. They were always getting complaints from shipping that one or both of the lights were not visible. These complaints filtered down to the keepers by way of the agent in Deal, Samuel Weaver, but it was not really the fault of the keepers and his reprimands never had much force behind them. At one time the lights had been merely an open fire atop each tower, but eventually it had been decided that the lights could be improved by enclosing them behind glass. It certainly made conditions better for the keepers, providing a shelter from the weather. It didn't however seem to reduce the number of complaints. Of course, Jack knew the reason for many of the complaints. He cursed the day he had submitted to the threats of those men, but when one's family is threatened sense of duty often goes by the board. He'd been in involuntary participation with the Jennings gang for the past six months - all winter in fact. He had been glad of the extra money and a few small luxuries that Jennings had given him, but he had a good job and he was very afraid of losing it. If his employers ever found out, he would be out of work immediately.

He remembered the night back in August when they had called on him and his family to propose their scheme. The thought of deliberately falsifying the lights from the Foreland seemed a dirty trick, but Jennings had pointed out that they weren't wrecking and he had to admit that that was true. The ships would still have the upper light to warn them, but they might get a bit confused about their position. All that was required was to screen his light on the seaward side for the space of an hour on the occasional night. Saul Goldsack in the upper lighthouse would see the light burning normally and suspect nothing. Jack had agreed to do it but only after some very nasty threats against his family had been made by those filthy, Cockney scum. How he hated those men. At least Jennings was a local man, but to live in fear of people who were not even inhabitants of Kent seemed far worse.

Seeing that the fire was well stoked and could be safely left for a while, he descended to the ground level coal store to get further supplies of coal up to the lantern level. The coal store was at the back of the tower on the landward side and in the bright moonlight he could see quite plainly without the aid of a lantern. It was considerably colder at ground level, away from the warmth of the fire and he shivered as he tackled the door fastening.

Suddenly the world fell about him, his head spun and a searing pain surged through his skull. The earth came up to meet him and before he had time to spread his hands to break his fall, he had smashed his front teeth and broken his nose in the impact with the ground. His vision flashed red... he struggled with sensibility. Could this be happening to him? He tried to roll over and found himself not only assisted in this process, but immediately crushed by a heavy object on his chest. The 'heavy object' was in fact Jake Dike, who then commenced to rain blow after blow into the hapless keeper's cheeks. Heal could only just retain consciousness as the numbing pain in his face seemed to penetrate every corner of his body, submerging all other senses like a drowning seaman. He became aware of voices but found vision very difficult as the blood trickled between his eyelids. Not only voices but muffled screams... his family... they were hurting his family. He summoned all his strength to cause his attacker to roll off, but in vain. The blows stopped; the pain did not. Spluttering and coughing blood that was flowing freely from his nose and facial wounds he rolled his head to the side to try to breathe. He caught sight of his terrified wife and daughter being dragged by the hair from their cottage in their nightclothes.

"Shut your noise," screamed Faller at the two petrified females in his grasp. "You don't inform on Eb Faller and get away with it.

"I didn't, it wasn't me... I swear... it wasn't me." Jack Heal found speech as well as vision difficult. His mouth was full of blood and loose teeth but he did his best - he had to. "You've got the wrong man. Please leave my wife and child alone."

"Oh we'll leave them alone all right," said Dike, still astride his helpless victim. "Get on with it Eb."

Faller was already locking the little girl in the coal store and having quickly done that began to rip the flimsy clothing from Jane Heal's attractive body. Jane began to scream uncontrollably but soon found herself, as well as her husband, pinned on the cold damp ground beneath the overwhelming strength and weight of her vicious and sadistic attacker. There was, of course, nothing her poor husband could do to prevent what followed, the terrible event being repeated by Dike after the two men had changed places. Tears now moistened the blood, which was beginning to congeal on Heal's battered face. Was there no way to appease these monsters?

"Please, please leave us alone... we'll do anything you say." His wife's pleas were unheeded.

Finishing his evil business with Jane Heal Dike set his eyes inches from hers and looked through them with all the malevolence he could find.

"Unfortunately for you, my cocker, we have not yet finished. If you so much as breathe a word of this to a living soul your dear little daughter will receive the treatment that you have just received, followed by the treatment that your stupid husband is about to receive."

"No. Please... No more..."

Dike went on unperturbed.

"Your husband is now going to pay the ultimate price for snoutin' on 'is mates. We can do without people like 'im. We should never 'ave gone along with Jennings' idea. Heal was a dead man right from the start and now his time's up."

"No, no, please don't do it," screamed Heal, desperate for mercy. "I'm innocent I tell you. I'll help you all I can, you have my word on it... just please let me go."

Jane was on her knees pleading with Faller and Dike to let them go, but it was no good. It was a matter of yards to the cliff edge where the chilling breeze flowed in from the void. Heal struggled once more with his captor but could in no way match his adversary for strength. With no hesitation, the mighty Faller lifted the screaming lighthouse keeper into the air.

"Dear God, please help me... what have I done... help me... please... please... oh, no, no..."

Tears streamed from his face as Faller launched him into nothingness. He felt the rush of cold air against his face, as the breeze became a howling gale. His face was sore, oh so sore. He spread his arms into the wind and flew...

8 SAMUEL WEAVER

It might have been one of those remarkable coincidences, those strange quirks of fate, which occur at the most unexpected moments, or it, might have been the work of the Almighty acting in His own strange way. William Knott was convinced that it was the latter. A matter of days after John Hatherley had occasioned a major event in the lives of the Knott family, another event occurred which surprised everyone in the locality. Jack Heal died.

Jack Heal had for the past ten years been steadfastly keeping one of the lights burning on the heights of the South Foreland, the closest point of approach to the troublesome French nation. Ever since Julius Caesar had come, seen and conquered, countless vessels of peace and of war had used the narrow stretch of water and made it one of the world's busiest seaways. The lunatic Roman emperor, Caligula, had seen fit in the early ADs to build a tower, probably containing a beacon, on each side of the Channel, but these had long since fallen into disuse. It was because of an increasing number of shipwrecks on the Goodwin Sands that shipmasters in 1634 called for the erection of a lighthouse on the South Foreland. Trinity House, who at that time were newcomers to the idea of lighthouses and were really little more than a seamen's charity, rejected the idea out of hand, claiming, amongst other things, that the light would be more likely to guide England's enemies to her shores. The urgency of the matter must have been recognised by the Privy Council at least, for in the same year it gave authority to Sir John Meldrum to construct the lighthouses at South Foreland.

In these pioneering days, it was necessary to obtain a patent from the King - a process that essentially amounted to asking his permission - before a lighthouse could be built. Once obtained, the patent allowed the lighthouse owner, in return for a nominal rent to the Crown, to exact a toll from every vessel passing the light. The rate of charge depended upon the tonnage of the cargo carried. This enabled the speculator to recoup his capital expenditure remarkably quickly and thence to make a healthy profit.

It was of course soon realised that it was very little use lighting an area of danger if the mariner did not know exactly which dangerous area it was. One light could be very easily confused with another just along the coast and the ensuing navigational error could prove to be as fatal as if the light had not been there. So it became necessary to make one lighthouse distinguishable from another, wherever possible. Apart from the two lights that Sir John Meldrum built at South Foreland, another was constructed on the North Foreland. To the west lay the single light of Dungeness. Thus all three stations could be unambiguous to the navigator who was at least aware of his approximate position.

The two lighthouses on the white cliffs of Dover were at first merely huts constructed of timber and plaster. On top of these was an open platform where a coal fire was kept burning in a cast iron grate. In return for the relatively small outlay and a £20 per annum rental, Sir John was entitled to charge a halfpenny per ton of cargo carried past the light. Soon he was making no less than £1,900 per annum and Trinity House, smarting with the knowledge that it might have been they who were making the profits, sourly complained to the King about profiteering.

Sir John employed an agent in Deal whose job was to manage the North and South Foreland lights, and to whom the light dues were finally paid after collection in Dover and other ports by the respective harbourmaster. The original lease granted to Sir John was for fifty years from 1640 onwards, but during this time it was taken over by Robert Osbolston. When that ran out in 1690, he obtained a renewal for a further thirty years. Osbolston was far more conscientious in his stewardship of the lights than Meldrum had been, and did his best to ensure that his keepers always performed their duty to the full. Around about 1690, the keepers experienced some difficulty with the Press gangs and came close to being conscripted on several occasions. They wrote to their employer to seek his help but Osbolston merely pointed out that if they attended to their duties at the lighthouse instead of going fishing during the day, they would have no cause to fear the Press gangs. He was genuinely worried by the matter, however, and wondered how it was possible for the men to keep good lights throughout the night if they had spent the previous day out in a fishing boat. The men were consequently forbidden to engage in any activity other than the one for which they were paid and accommodated. Osbolston even wrote to the parish priest and asked him to peep out sometimes as he went to bed and if he saw that the lights were dim, to reproach the men on his behalf.

In 1719, as the lease was about to run out once more, the ownership of the North and South Forelands lighthouses passed into the hands of the Trustees of the Greenwich Hospital who, to save coal, almost immediately enclosed the open fires behind glass. This move was not without its difficulties for the keepers found it necessary to use bellows in order to create sufficient draught for a good fire. Disillusioned with the change, the keeper at the South Foreland lower lighthouse had given notice and so it was that Jack Heal, a young man of twenty-two, had become a lighthouse keeper.

But ten years later, Jack Heal died.

William had known Jack fairly well, as those living in small communities must, but the keeper and his family had kept themselves to themselves. They seemed to like the solitary existence at the lighthouse and rarely entertained any of the villagers. Even Saul Goldsack up at the upper lighthouse openly admitted to the locals that he didn't socialise with the Heal family. Saul was a bachelor who would have been glad of a bit of company, but his relationship with Jack was purely of a business nature. Despite this, there was no animosity between the two men.

The circumstances of the death had been most unfortunate. In a most distressed condition, his wife awakened Saul early in the morning and told him that her husband was missing. The villagers were quick to organise a search party and it was not long before the terribly injured body of what had once been Jack Heal was discovered at the foot of the cliffs. His wife said that there had been an unusually unpleasant marital quarrel that night and it was generally concluded that the poor man's mind must have been disturbed sufficiently for him to commit suicide. His wife and young daughter were naturally heartbroken, Jane the more so since she seemed to think she had been responsible for her husband's death. If only she had swallowed her pride and made up with him before going to bed instead of putting it off until morning, he might still have been alive, she had told her friends. Soon after the body had been found she moved out of the lighthouse to find sanctuary with her parents at East Langdon.

William was greatly saddened by the whole affair, but felt that Jack's death was a divine act to give him the job he'd always wanted. After all, he'd probably not even have considered it if it had not been for the idea seeded in his mind by Hatherley. Even the Cornishman's arrival had been miraculous. No, the whole thing could not be a coincidence.

Saul Goldsack, on whom fell the lot of maintaining not one but two lighthouses, soon made sure that the Deal agent knew about the recent events. Samuel Weaver, whose job it was to manage the affairs of the three lighthouses at the North and South Forelands, was not slow to react either. His job too depended upon the regular and efficient exhibition of lights for shipping and he knew how difficult it would be for Saul Goldsack to keep both lights going, even for just a couple of days. So it was not long before he was on the carriage to St. Margaret's in search of a new keeper. He already had a good idea who he would ask to do the job. The story of the rescue had earned the Knott family quite a reputation and in Weaver's mind William was the only real contender for the job. The job was a rigorous one, involving long, unsocial hours and a good deal of hard work. The lighthouse consumed about a hundredweight of coal every night, all of which had to be carried by hand to the platform. This demanded a young, strong worker with a sense of public interest and reliability to keep the light burning well, even under unfavourable circumstances. William's reputation had illustrated all of these characteristics and Weaver had had no doubt in selecting him as the prime candidate. Could he persuade William to accept it?

William was cleaning and sharpening tools in the shed behind the family cottage when his father entered with a stranger.

"William, this is Mr Weaver, the agent in Deal for the Greenwich Hospital Trustees. You know that he is manager of the lighthouses up on the Foreland. Well, he is wondering if you would consider taking up the post as lighthouse keeper, now that Jack Heal is gone."

"Well, what do you say, William," asked Weaver impatiently. Strangely enough, William said nothing at first. He had no doubts about his inclination to take on the job, but it was simply that he could not believe his luck. Ever since he and Hatherley had talked into the night, he had thought of little else, and since Jack died, he had been obsessed with the idea. Still he said nothing. Samuel Weaver took it as a sign of disinterest and thinking he was going have some difficulty recruiting his man immediately started onto an offensive tactic.

"I can offer you secure employment, admittedly with difficult hours, but no more than you are used to I'm sure. You'll be provided with accommodation, free fuel and five shillings weekly, a perfectly adequate wage considering the extras. If you accept, I would like you to begin tonight and to that end I shall take you along to see Saul Goldsack, who I'm sure you know already. He will show you around the buildings and generally help you overcome the initial difficulties. The essential requirement is reliability, by which I mean the need to ensure that the light burns at all costs, whatever the difficulties, whatever the weather. If I did not feel that you were totally suited for the job, I'd not have come here today. The courage you showed in rescuing that unfortunate seaman recently tells me you will not be diverted from your duty as an honest citizen. What do you say? Will you take the job?"

By this time, William had had ample time to realise that this was indeed, happening to him. He suddenly became aware that the two men were silent and awaiting his reply with looks of puzzled anticipation. His moment had come, he must decide... quickly before Mr Weaver changed his mind...

"I accept," he said briefly.

"Excellent, then we will go up to the lighthouse right away." Mr Weaver was obviously keen to get his new recruit installed in his new job and little more than thirty minutes later the two men were standing outside the door of South Foreland upper lighthouse, home and place of work of Saul Goldsack. Saul was at the door within seconds of their knock and politely invited them both inside, away from the fresh easterly breeze, which had brought with it a lazy drizzle from the North Sea.

"Ah, William, so 't is you I'll be working with is it? I must say I'm delighted to 'ave you up 'ere on the Foreland, but tis unfortunate it 'ad to be under such circumstances." They all nodded. "Poor ole' Jack - such a dreadful thing t'appen."

"Yes, indeed," said Weaver. "He was a good keeper but I'm sure that William will not let us down. Now Saul, I am anxious to get back to Deal as soon as possible to conclude some business, which I had to leave in a hurry. Will you please give William all the help he needs to get the light operational tonight?"

Figure 4: An old drawing of the Upper South Foreland Lighthouse (anon).

"Of course, Mr Weaver; just leave 'im wi' me. I'll sort 'im out."

"In that case, I'll be on my way. Goodbye William and good luck. I shall come up again in two or three weeks with your wages and to see how you are coping. Until then, here is an advance of ten shillings, which should keep you going. Goodbye, gentlemen."

After he had gone, the two keepers began a tour of the lighthouse.

"I don't s'pose you've ever bin inside 'ere before, 'ave you?" asked Saul.

"No," replied William, "I've only ever seen the lighthouses from the road, although in fact it is not hard to imagine the inside."

"That's probably true. Well, this is my livin' room; 't is small, but comfortable. Only the two rooms - the bedroom's through 'ere. 'T is just about big enough for a fam'ly; I think your house is a little bigger than this."

William looked around the small wooden house. The walls inside had been roughly plastered and formed an effective seal against the elements. The whole living room was centred on the fireplace where all the cooking was done and which occupied a large part of one wall. The furniture was just the minimum, which might be expected for bachelor existence. There was a table and chair, a cupboard, and next to the fire the only item of comfort - a cosy looking rocking chair. In the wall opposite to the fireplace a curtained doorway led off to the bedroom, which was half the size of the living space and contained nothing but a small single bed and chest of drawers. Consequently, the tour of the quarters was soon over.

"Let's 'ave a look at the important bit then," said Saul. For this they had to go outside into the drizzle. The coal store was situated at the side of the house, its locked door to landward, and close to it was the stairway which led up at the back of the house to the lantern on the roof, one floor above the ground.

"The coal is delivered once a week by Peter, my younger brother, who brings over a cartload of half a ton for each of us. We don't 'ave to worry 'bout payin' 'im - Mr Weaver sees to all that. Obviously we burn the coal at different rates dependin' 'pon season and weather, but if we need more coal, we only 'ave to send Peter a message an' 'e'll bring more over right away. I'd say on average we get through about one an' 'alf 'underdweight a night, an' you 'ave to carry it all up to the lantern in a bucket."

The two men went up the flight of stairs to the lantern. William found himself on an octagonal wooden platform. All around him were thick glass sash windows that could be raised or lowered for cleaning, whilst in the wooden roof there was a wide flue to provide an exit for the smoke. There was no window on the side facing the land, for no light was required in that direction. Instead, there was the small entrance through which they'd come, the doorway set in a timber wall for added support.

"This is where it all 'appens," said Saul quite proudly. "As you can see, it all centres on this grate made of cast iron. You simply light your fire in the top of it and once a day clean out the ashes from underneath. 'T is a good idea to do this regular, as a build-up of ash reduces the draught an' you don't get such a good fire. 'T is 'arder to light too. You 'ave to use the bellows a good deal. Ever since they put in the windows, the draught 'as bin much less. As you can see from that pile of coal over there, you can bring up enough to keep you goin' for the whole night, pretty well. I'd say you' 'ave to stoke up at 'ourly intervals, or thereabouts. If you put too much on it more or less blots out the light so tis a good idea to keep it stoked pretty regular wi' just enough coal to keep the light up to a reasonable level. So you won't get much sleep my friend. When you get used to the life you can get quite good at takin' cat-naps and be sure you won't oversleep and let the light go out, but 'til you've bin 'ere for a while I wouldn't risk it. You'll not wake up when once you go to sleep and that won't please the sailors, or Mr

Weaver for that matter. I usually get my sleep in the mornin's. From daylight 'til early afternoon is enough for me. Well then, I reckon 't is all pretty straightforward. 'Ave you anythin' to ask me? I think I've told you more or less all there is to know."

"What about kindling wood?"

"Ah, yes, I'm afraid you 'ave to get your own. There's usually plenty of wood around, especially down on the beach. Funny really, isn't it, that we use kindlin' wood that comes from the wrecks we are tryin' to prevent? Yes, funny that. Anyway, the coal store is fairly dry an' you can stow it all in there. With practice, its surprisin' 'ow little wood it actually takes to light a fire. Don't forget to get it started well before dusk - that'll give you plenty of time to get the fire up to scratch before dark. Let's go over to your own place now and make sure everythin' is ready for tonight."

The lower lighthouse on the South Foreland was about three hundred yards away from the upper one and quite close to the edge of the cliff. It was almost identical to its relation up the hill, but William agreed with Saul that the living accommodation was marginally bigger. It was slightly better furnished too, and here the woman's touch was evident, in contrast to the bare, bachelor barracks of Saul Goldsack. Saul gave him the key to the fuel store and they checked the inside to find a good supply of coal and kindling wood. In the lantern, Saul had been busy and had made sure that there was enough fuel for the first night and that the fire was all ready to light that evening.

"You can't have been getting much sleep lately if you've had to look after both of these brutes," said William, his voice tinged with admiration, for, with so much work, Saul had kept the lighthouse in good shape.

"Not really, but then I knew 't wouldn't be long before another fella arrived. Now I've more or less got it all ready for you. All you've got to do is put a light to the fire tonight and stoke it regular. So I'll leave you to it, William. Come up any time if you 'ave trouble."

William thanked Saul sincerely for all his help and made it clear that, unlike Jack Heal, he, William Knott, was quite happy to receive visitors at any time. Saul was obviously very relieved to hear it although he didn't say so. He had found a new friend.

9 BEN MATSON

Ben Matson thumped his fist on the oak table and proved that wood was harder than flesh. His hand hurt but he was too angry to care much.

"Sometimes those men go too far, Jennings. Why didn't you stop them?"

William Jennings had been summoned to Wanstone farm to account for the actions of men over whom he had little control.

"Because I didn't know what they were going to," replied Jennings, indignant at being blamed for something in which he had played no part.

"How did they find out about Heal?"

"I told them," grudged Jennings, "but it didn't make any difference - they'd guessed anyway that it was Heal who tipped off Tucker and Bridges. They asked me point blank if it was him and I said that it was, but they said nothing to me about what they were going to do. The first I knew about it was when Heal's body was found. I never dreamed they would do anything so drastic as to kill him. After all, Tucker and Bridges didn't catch us - Faller and Dike saw to that - so they really had nothing to fear. All we had to do was go and put the wind up Heal and his family. Tucker and Bridges had no evidence and we were all in the clear. There was no problem at all. Then they had to go and do this. It's just as well that they scared Heal's wife so much that she won't talk, though I dread to think what they threatened her with to make her keep quiet. And now Heal's dead; we're right back where we started. We won't be able to use the lighthouse again unless we can persuade either Goldsack or the new keeper to co-operate."

"I've told you before, Jennings, that if you can't buy a bachelor then you'll never force him into co-operating. A married man can be blackmailed by threatening his family and I'm sure that's how they cracked Jane Heal. They threatened her daughter with the same treatment that Jack got. No mother or father is going to risk the life of a loved one so they always do what you want. It's much more difficult to get results by threatening a bachelor because he resists: he's got nothing to lose. In fact he will probably enjoy the chance to have a go at you. People don't worry about their own lives so much. Nevertheless, you must try to bribe the new keeper. Offer him a reasonable sum… discreetly. If it's turned down we'll have to think again. If he is married then we may have to use the same methods as we did for Heal, but if he's single like Goldsack then we may have some trouble."

By this time, Matson's anger had died down a little, if only from the physical to the verbal.

"And tell those idiots Faller and Dike that if I have any more trouble from them they're out. They take orders from you and there's to be no rough stuff unless you tell them. There's no need for it and it won't happen again, will it?"

"No, Mr Matson, I'll make sure they behave in future."

"See to it that you do. Now, tell me…" He got no further. The door was flung open and one of Matson's staff appeared.

"Mr Matson… the Preventive Officers… they're coming up to the farmhouse… they'll be here any moment now…"

He had hardly got out the words 'Preventive Officers' when Jennings had leapt to his feet and disappeared out of the door.

"All right, don't worry about a thing, Tom, we've nothing to hide. Just show them in here, I'll speak to them."

"Right you are, Mr Matson."

Tom left the room, closing the door behind him, whilst Matson strode over to the window. Just as his gaze fell on the scene of the courtyard, three riders entered the muddy enclosure, dismounted, and immediately approached the entrance to the farmhouse. Matson quickly removed himself from view and sat down at his large desk to make it look as -if he was busy with his accounts. Tucker and Bridges, bearing signs of having been recently injured and, led by William Cooper, wasted no time in entering the farmhouse. Even before Tom had chance to invite them to talk to Matson, the two junior officers rushed to the upper floor and noisily began to search for a secret cache of contraband. Cooper did, however, accept Tom's offer and entered the room where Matson had by now dropped his paperwork and approached the door to find out the cause of the rumpus upstairs.

"What's all this about, Cooper," he demanded.

Since you obviously have not guessed, I am carrying out a search of these premises for imported goods of an illicit nature. My officers are presently engaged in such a search on the upper floor and we shall not be leaving here until the farm has been thoroughly searched."

Cooper was always formal. That was the way he liked to do it. If he could use a word of two syllables instead of one he always did, even when he talked to his wife. He maintained that you must always let people know you mean business. If you weakened for a moment the criminals would take advantage of you.

"Oh come, come now, is all this really necessary?" soothed Matson, deciding that, although he was mad with Cooper, he ought nevertheless to humour him.

"What makes you think that I have anything to do with smuggling?"

"I have reason to believe that this farm has been used in smuggling operations and I intend to discover where the contraband is concealed." He wasn't going to admit that he was working on pure guesswork.

"What evidence do you have and on whose authority are you conducting this search? I have always kept my affairs perfectly legal and to the best of my knowledge this farm has never been used in the way you suggest. Neither am I aware that any of my friends or employees are engaged in smuggling. Anyone who tells you different is a liar. Now answer my questions. Whose authority do you have for this and on what have you based your evidence?"

Cooper refused to be drawn into admitting he had no other reason for the search than his theories, or that the only authority he had was his own. He substituted Matson's questions with his own in an effort to ease himself out of the tricky situation.

"Why is William Jennings here now?"

"Jennings? Is he here now? I didn't know that. I don't really know the fellow myself but I believe he comes here to court one of my wenches. I must have a word with him if he is here now, my wenches should be working."

"He was observed entering this farm about half an hour ago and he certainly didn't pass us as we came here."

"Tom?" shouted Matson, "Are you still there?"

"Yes, Mr Matson." Tom came in looking worried. "Those Gentlemen upstairs are making a bit of a mess. Wouldn't it be better if…

"Never mind that for the moment. Go and find Bess in the buttery and send her to me. And if William Jennings is there send him here too."

As Tom went out there was the sound of footsteps on the stairs. Then Tucker and Bridges came into the room and began searching it, Bridges somewhat hampered by the injury which had been caused to his arm that night on the cliffs.

"Oh, really, this is ridiculous. Do you always treat your men like this? Mr Bridges should be taking it easy with an injury like that."

Matson was beginning to lose his temper again, but Cooper ignored his remarks. He was dealing with a clever man and he knew it. He hadn't expected Matson's excuse for Jennings presence at the farm and was now worried that he would have to leave Wanstone having achieved nothing but the ignominy of his failure. The two searchers completed their task in the room and left to continue elsewhere. They had done their best to leave things more or less as they had found them, but they hadn't come for a social call and were not going to waste time tidying up and generally playing housekeeper. All walls, floors and even ceilings had been well prodded and tapped by Tucker in the knowledge that secret hidey-holes give themselves away eventually.

As every minute passed Cooper became more and more convinced that the raid was going to be a dismal failure. He had been relying on finding some evidence at Wanstone farm but had he known Ben Matson better he would have realised that Matson was much too smart to be caught with smuggled goods in his possession. Even the link, which he thought he had established between Jennings and Matson, was about to be badly broken. Without a find of contraband, Jennings was the key to his success or failure. Cooper was sure that Jennings had been involved in the smuggling operation, but the failure of Tucker and Bridges to catch anyone red-handed had left him once more without proof. One of his sources of information had died in dubious circumstances He suspected that Heal had been killed, but there was a complete lack of evidence - and Cooper was essentially totally impotent in the face of the serious offences being committed. So far he had no idea where the contraband was stored or how it was disposed of and the present search was a distinct act of stabbing in the dark in the hope of stumbling on something. It would have been good work to catch Jennings with Matson.

Bess came into the room after gently knocking twice.

"You wanted to see me, Mr Matson."

"Yes, Bess, Would you tell us exactly what is the nature of your relationship with William Jennings?"

"Me and 'im been courting now for almost a year, if that's what you mean."

"And when did you last see him - be truthful now, or it will be the worse for you."

Bess fidgeted with her apron and, looking at the wooden floor, spoke with some trepidation.

"He has just gone, Mr Matson. He come in the buttery about half an hour ago, but when the preventive men come he left quick out the back way and across the fields in case he got me into trouble with you." She looked at her employer earnestly. "He didn't keep me from my work, sir, honest he didn't."

"All right, Bess, you've been honest and I won't punish you this time, but don't let it happen again. I am paying you to work and not to skylark around for half the day with your fancy man. Now go back to your work."

Bess curtsied politely, thanked her employer and left.

"Does that satisfy you, Cooper?" demanded Matson.

Cooper knew that he was going to make a bigger fool of himself if he stayed any longer. Matson's air of total confidence had already indicated to Cooper that he would find nothing at the farm, however hard he and his men looked. He didn't waste any more time.

He turned and stormed out of the room, summoning his minions to his side with a bellow most unbecoming of a man of his station. The three men mounted their horses, Tucker helping his bandaged comrade into the saddle, and galloped out of the courtyard only slightly slower than they had entered it. Matson, on the other hand, was triumphant. He strode quickly across the yard to the buttery where Bess and Tom were deep in conversation about the events of the afternoon.

"Well done, Bess, that was exactly what was expected of you. Take the rest of the afternoon off. And don't speak a word to anyone about this, Tom. I am trusting both of you to say nothing of any of this."

And neither did they. Bess and Tom did as their master bade them. Bess would do anything to help her beloved Bill Jennings, but she was still unaware of the real reason that had brought her lover to Wanstone Farm.

10 STEPHEN PEAKE

It was always difficult to find room enough to stand, let alone sit, in the *Green Man* on a Saturday night. Stephen Peake, the innkeeper, was naturally pleased with the way his business was flourishing. It seemed that despite hard times, people were always ready to consume ale. A good drink was probably the only luxury the men in the village could afford. Uncustomed spirits too formed a good proportion of Peake's trade, although a number of elementary precautions had to be taken before he dared risk selling it. Nevertheless, it was difficult for the Riding Officers to prove the origins of the liquor, once landed, and business continued with relative impunity.

It was certainly busy on the Saturday night when Jack Knott and his brother Henry slipped in for some glasses of ale. Pushing their way through the throng of smoking, chattering, arguing and, most definitely, drinking customers, they exchanged many a friendly greeting. The public house was, after all, the main social centre of the village, and it was here that much of the true life of the village was conducted. Local politics and scandals were debated, small business transactions carried out, even the occasional marriage was arranged, but people came to the *Green Man* mostly to meet their friends and enjoy themselves away from the hard-working lives which they led by day.

Despite the numbers present, Jack and Henry Knott were able to join Harry Darby and a few other friends at a table by the fire, whilst Stephen Peake and his wife struggled to keep pace with the demand for ale.

"I see you've left your brother behind again," joked Darby as they ordered their drinks.

"Ah, I don't think we'll be seeing a lot more of our William down here. That's the trouble with night work. It's what you'd call a lighthouse keeper's permanent problem - difficult to avoid," replied Henry to a chorus of lubricated laughter. He supped ale from the jar that Stephen Peake had slopped down on the table and used his sleeve to wipe away the froth that had been deposited in his moustache.

"Can't say as it'd appeal to me," went on Harry with a grin, "I like my wife too much for that." Even more mirth followed.

"Give him a year or two yet Harry," joined in Jack Knott. "The lad's hardly realised what he's let himself in for. He might as well have joined a monastery as far as his love life is concerned. Besides, you can talk, Harry. With a wife like yours I'd have thought you'd have been the first to volunteer for the job."

"Now don't you be rude about my wife, Jack," returned Harry in a mock gesture of displeasure. "She comes in very useful - for scaring burglars." With that, they all collapsed in various stages of mirthful agony and John Parker spilt his beer in his lap, which only made matters worse, "I know that was a good joke, John," said Harry, "but there's no need to wet yourself."

Parker's drink was soon replaced as Bethsheba Peake handed him one from a huge dripping tray of beer.

"Thanks very much my love," said John, attempting to pinch her bottom and finding contact with her flesh quite difficult through thick layers of clothing.

"Suffering shrimps, you don't intend to let anyone take any liberties do you? What have you got on under there?"

"Never you mind, John Parker!" replied the barmaid with a grin. "If you were the man of the world you pretend to be you wouldn't need to ask questions like that, now would you?"

Parker looked crestfallen for a moment, shown up in front of the lads, and all his own fault too.

"And you a married man too," mocked Henry Knott. "I'd better have a word with your wife. She can't be treating you right. Now I know a very nice little wench who could put you straight…"

"Shut up." said Parker, slightly irritated. He had asked for all that he had got and tried to change the subject, but without success. They didn't shut up.

Meanwhile, in another part of the raucous and smoke-filled public house, William Jennings sat in a corner discussing recent events with his fellow conspirators Jake Dike, Eb Faller, Finnis Bowers and John Jale. So great was the hubbub from the rest of the clientele that they were able to converse easily without fear of being overheard. Jennings had already harangued the two Londoners for their recent foolishness, although he had not succeeded in causing them the slightest bit of regret for their actions. Bowers and Jale were uneasy at being seen in such company and were waiting for a convenient opportunity to leave the group and join other friends within the bar. They both hated and feared Faller and Dike and if they had their way would have no more to do with them. They did realise, however, that they'd really very little choice in the matter. To upset those characters, to give them so much as a hint of disloyalty, would be to sign their own execution warrants. Jennings, however, had plans.

"Now then you two, the present situation is such that we all keep a low profile for the time being. I've heard that Cooper is after us. He's absolutely no proof of our activities and so far the death is still considered to be suicide. We are safe for the moment, but Cooper and his men obviously realise that Heal must have been killed for divulging information to them. It would be too much of a coincidence for their star witness to commit suicide so soon afterwards. It's lucky for us that Heal only told them the time and place and not the people who were involved. As long as they can't prove anything we're in the clear. We won't be able to use the lighthouse again until we've persuaded the keeper that he would like to join us…"

"That's no problem," broke in Dike," we can arrange that whenever you like."

"Look, I know the way you go about 'persuading' people and we're having none of that for the moment. You two have done enough. We're not running any more operations until the summer at least to let things calm down a bit. The Frenchmen are being told about the situation - that's all been arranged. Until then, we're going to sit tight. Say and do nothing. As for you two, I think it's best if you leave the area for a while until the excitement subsides. There are too many suspicions in the air at the moment and we've got to let them settle. We've decided that you, Eb and Jake, will go and join the operation down the coast at Rye for a while until we need you again."

"And what if we don't want to go?" Jake Dike was beginning to tire of being ordered about like a tin soldier.

"Look, Jake, that's not my decision. The people in London who know more about this than we'll ever know have decided that this must happen. Besides, you're good men and we can't afford to have you out of the action for long. They need you down there. It's quite a big set-up and the preventive officers are not quite so well organised.

"We'll go, Jake," came in Eb. "I was getting fed up with this place anyhow. It's about time we got into some real action again. Nothing much has happened here for months; we've hardly made a bean."

"And what about us?" Finnis Bowers was worried. "Do we just sit here too and wait for them to catch us? We'll end up paying the price for what these two have done. I don't like it."

"No you won't," said Jennings in his most reassuring voice. Finnis was a good man really, neither he nor John Jale being capable of real violence. No-one could be in the same class as their two drinking companions. "Look, how can you possibly be accused of a crime like that? You weren't anywhere near the place and you know it. There's only one witness and she won't talk about it, not if she values her daughter."

Finnis refused to be pacified.

"What if they find out it were Eb and Jake? We'll get done too as corroborators, or whatever they call it."

"I'm sick of these moaning scum," said Jake, indicating the two fidgety fishermen with a finger of accusation as he leaned across the table. Bowers and Jale simultaneously rose to their feet and backed away from the table. Jennings, too, rose to intervene and put his hand on Dike's chest to prevent him from advancing any further. That was a mistake.

"And you can keep your filthy hands off me too," scowled Dike, grabbing Jennings at the throat so vigorously that he was half pulled across the table, knocking over several of the unfinished jars of ale. Faller by now was also standing menacingly and moving around the table to cut off the retreat of the other two. The sudden outburst attracted the attention of the landlord who was quite used to a certain amount of unruly behaviour on a Saturday night. As a matter of routine, he was soon over at the scene of the dispute, calming down his argumentative customers. No blows had been struck and Peake's swift action ensured that Dike released Jennings who immediately rearranged his clothing and began to leave. Faller relaxed from his aggressive pose. Bowers and Jale took rapid advantage of the situation and made for the door, a course of action that they wished they had followed much earlier. The rest of the customers seemed quite unperturbed by the whole affair and, apart from the turning of a few heads, together with a momentary lull in the overall level of banter, carried on with their habitual relaxation as if nothing had happened. They and the *Green Man* had seen far worse disagreements and would undoubtedly bear witness to many more in the future.

11 WILLIAM JENNINGS - 2

The month of March passed slowly. That did not mean that the March in 1730 was any different to the March in any other year, of course. England was enjoying a fragile peace with her neighbouring countries across the Channel and Sir Robert Walpole was establishing himself as a great Prime Minister, politician and Englishman, despite the efforts of the Anglo-German dynasty of monarchs to remain less Anglo than German. No, March of 1730 seemed a long month because the population of six million English people anxiously awaited the end of the winter and the arrival of more civilised temperatures and climes. The people of the Bewsborough Hundred of Kent, of which St. Margaret's was but a small part, thought about emerging from their state of pseudo-hibernation as the effects of the searing east winds died down and the sun occasionally broke through the sea of grey. To these people the April shower, the break from the grip of frost, meant that the end of the long, hard winter was surely at hand. Daylight, like the scant covering of grass over the chalk-bed, began to grow noticeably. The flotilla of small fishing craft, which had remained largely inactive through the spell of bad weather, began to venture away from the jetty down at the beach to search the depths and to deny freedom to the fish with their fiendish forays. And on the land, farmers began to organise their labourers in preparation for the growing season. The chalk and flint soil, home for a variety of wild flowers, awoke to the probing tentacles of the Campion, the St. John's Wort and the Sea Colewort, or, down in the more sheltered parts of the Bay settlement, the Marigold, the Convolvulus and the Speedwell.

The South Foreland lighthouses were in full operation, casting their dull red glow out over the cliff-top towards the ever-questing eye of the seaman. William Knott and his counterpart Saul Goldsack had been busy at their duties and looked forward to the spring and summer as much as anyone. William had found no particular difficulties in his new job other than the art of keeping awake, for, in the long hour of dark solitude, consciousness was so often elusive. A nocturnal routine was alien to him at first, and he found it hard to substitute daytime slumber for the night rest that he had always been used to. Consequently, the aggregation of noxious substances in his brain led to a numbness across his lower forehead, which threatened a betraying sleep during the silent hours. On just a couple of occasions, his eyes had given way to his duty and he had dozed for a guilty, but fortunately uneventful, hour. As the routine became established, he overcame his problems and began to enjoy thoroughly the responsibilities of the task. The workload was considerable, enough to keep him occupied, but still allowing him a certain amount of free time during the part of the day when he was not asleep.

One of the biggest problems was with the glass lantern panes. These were of poor quality and consistently became so dirty as to prevent his pyrotechnic efforts from being visible as far out at sea as the owners might have liked. Saul Goldsack (who had exactly the same problem) had remarked on the trouble to Samuel Weaver during a previous visit, and, to his surprise, the latter had been quite expecting the matter to be brought up. Complaints had been received from shipping about the efficiency of the lights in the area, North Foreland included, and Weaver had placed the matter in the hands of the Trustees who had been deliberating the topic in their own unhurried manner for several months. The options open to them, as with all lighthouse proprietors of the time, were few. Until the scientific philosophers could devise new forms of light creation other than the open fire or the candle, and make them visible at a worthwhile distance, the lighthouses were obliged to struggle on and to make use of the only luminary methods open to them.

When the Trustees of the Greenwich Hospital took over the ownership of the North and South Forelands lighthouses in 1719, the enclosure of the fires by glass had seemed a good idea. It protected the fires (and the keepers) from the elements, but, more importantly, resulted in a considerable saving of coal. However, the reduction in draught necessitated the frequent use of bellows, a distinct disadvantage to the keepers who naturally disliked any move that would lead to more work. Enclosure had also meant a reduction in the amount of light visible at sea if the lantern glass became covered with soot. The shipmasters, ever resentful of light dues they considered exorbitant and were owed in return for the somewhat dubious quality of the lights, became more and more vociferous in their complaints. On more than one occasion it was reported that rogue ships were refusing to pay the dues at all. And so the usefulness of the lighthouse to society was still the subject of argument more than two thousand years after the Egyptians recognised the need and built the Pharos at Alexandria.

It was on a visit to pay his keepers and to keep an eye on the running of the lighthouses that Samuel Weaver brought news that the owners had finally decided to remove the glass once more and, until such time as a better system was devised, revert to the old style of un-enclosed fires. William was annoyed by the plan since he had only just got used to the routine and was now faced with substantial alterations to both the lighthouse and his scheme of working. The amount of work would diminish slightly and this went some way towards mollifying the news, but the thought of being exposed to the bitter wind, not to mention the rest of the elements, would take some getting used to. The modification would not take place until the summer and would all be done by local labour under the direction of Mr Weaver. So, despite his reservations, William accepted the news in good spirit and Weaver left the South Foreland that day with the correct impression that all was well at his lighthouses and that he had two very good men in his employ.

Later the same afternoon, as William was preparing a meal before commencing his vigil, he received a surprise visitor, William Jennings. Considering the fact that he and Jennings had never before been especially good friends, Jennings seemed remarkably amiable. They had occasionally supped ale together in the *Green Man*, but only as fellow customers. Jennings travelled about the area quite a lot and, whilst he owned his own fishing boat - most other people had to share - he seemed to spend more time travelling on the land than using his boat. In fact the times when he was seen down at the Bay were usually when he was paying the *Green Man* a visit.

"Hello, William," said Jennings cordially. "I've just been down to Dover on business and since I was on my way past the lighthouse I thought I d call in to see how you were getting along in your new job. I've been taking quite an interest in the running of the lighthouses on behalf of the fishermen, Saul, of course, has always done a good job and I wondered how you were finding it."

William's meal was really only enough for one and he was reluctant to share it, especially with someone who seemed as if he'd only come to scrounge a bite to eat after an appetising walk. Therefore, William left the stew simmering in the pot and sat with Jennings around the fire, but offered him nothing.

"Yes, many 's the time I've been out fishing and seen the warning glow from these lighthouses. As you know, I occasionally go out at night so I use them a good bit. Anyway the rest of the fishermen asked me to pop in and see you and thank you for doing such a good job," he lied. "You know, it's funny how often one or both of the lights become difficult to see, even in good weather."

"Thank you for your interest and kind compliments," said William, in rather a hollow tone. "You're right. The agent has been getting quite a few complaints about the lights. It seems that they are only effective at a range of one or two miles. It's not our fault though. "We do the best we can, but it's very difficult keeping a bright light all the time with a coal fire, as I'm sure you can imagine. On top of that, the lantern glass is getting more and more opaque as time goes by. The panes are quite difficult to clean thoroughly after ten years of sooting up daily."

"Don't you find it a lonely life up here on your own? I'm not married yet but I find plenty of company by living over in the village. And I've got a young lady who I see regularly."

"Well, at the moment I'm kept fairly busy so I don't worry about it too much, but I too have a sweetheart whom I hope to marry some day. This place is big enough for a family and I don't intend to remain a bachelor all my days."

"Not like old Saul, eh? But what about money? If you're planning to get married you'll need a bit of money. Will you be able to manage on your wages?"

William, who had scented a rat at Jennings' first appearance, now got a stronger indication of the presence of vermin.

"For someone who has so far been little more to me than a drinking companion, you seem to care a lot about my welfare," said William pointedly, beginning to tire of Jennings' obvious false motives.

"The lighthouses are very important to us all, not only for our safety but our livelihood. Let's say that we in the fishing community want to make sure that our lighthouses work efficiently and that they serve the community as a whole. If that's to happen then we need to make sure the keepers are happy in their jobs."

William knew that Jennings was stringing him along and tried to play down the situation.

"I have an employer in Deal whose sole job is exactly that. I think he is more qualified to do so than you. As a matter of fact, he came to see me today, paid me my wages and enquired after my wellbeing. I told him I was very happy and content and I meant it." Jennings refused to take the hint.

"But it would be a foolish man indeed who did not take advantage of an opportunity to further himself financially for very little commitment and virtually no risk."

"Are you making me some sort of proposition? I am not a man for mincing my words so kindly say what you mean."

"Very well, my proposition is simply this. In return for one guinea I would like you to obscure the light from your lighthouse for no more than two hours on a particular night. As you have pointed out, there are so many complaints from shipping anyway, for which you receive little of the blame, that no-one will ever be aware that the light was intentionally hidden. Your fellow keeper in the other lighthouse won't know anything about it, since he cannot see your light from where he is. You will be causing virtually no risk to shipping since the upper light will still be burning and is bound to provide a warning. Since there are so many occasions when the lights cannot be seen, the increase in danger caused by your action is negligible. The only stipulation on our part is that the light must be burning brightly at the moment of obscuration which must last for two hours, as near as possible. I repeat that on each occasion you will receive one golden guinea and that the number of occasions will not exceed one per month. A quick calculation will show you that your yearly income will increase considerably for so little effort and you may of course be assured of our total confidence in this matter."

"William Knott was stunned. He was being offered about twelve guineas a year to participate in a smuggling operation - for there could be no other reason for such a bizarre request. It all seemed ludicrously easy; no-one need ever know. He could be quite well off... or dead. Jack Heal flashed into his mind as suddenly as if Jack were sending him a message from the other world. Was Jack anything to do with this? Was his death really an act of suicide? Suspicions and fears flooded his thoughts. He had only just started work in a job that he liked. Should he risk it to throw in with a gang of - who knows, thieves and murderers?

"Get out!" he said.

"Now William, I want you to think about my offer. I could even run to a higher figure if you're not happy about the risks. You..."

"Get out!" yelled William. He stood up quickly, his chair spinning back several feet and hitting the wall with a thud. Jennings said no more: he had got the message, and left immediately without closing the door. William sat down again after groping for the chair once again. He put his head in his hands and suddenly became aware that his meal was still bubbling in the pot, that the door was still open and that it was draughty.

12 JOHN COLLIER

The Surveyor General of Riding Officers in Kent sat down at the table, picked up his quill and, after dipping it into a somewhat elaborate inkpot, scribbled a few notes on the paper in front of him. William Cooper, his hand tingling slightly from the firmness of a handshake, also seated himself at the table but on the opposite side of it from his superior. Cooper had been summoned to the first floor room at the *Queen's Hotel* in Dover to report on his work for the past year. It was the first time he had had cause to meet John Collier, the latter having taken up the post in the previous year of 1734. Collier was gathering information in preparation for the yearly report on the efficiency of his officers and it was now the turn of the St. Margaret's and Dover area to come under his scrutiny. For nearly two months he had been travelling the county, meeting his men, talking to them in depth and taking copious notes on the success or otherwise of their efforts to reduce the amount of smuggling in Kent. In terms of the huge scale of the smuggling operations, success had been strictly limited. So great was the number of participants compared with the number of officers available to catch them that smugglers could go about their business with a high degree of confidence that they would not be caught. John Collier was only too well aware of the size of the task for he had himself spent twenty years doing the job over which he was now the county supervisor. It was an unpopular job for the simple reason that smuggling had never been considered to be illegal by the vast majority of the population. The only laws that made sense to people were those that concerned their moral behaviour, and, whilst smuggling was illegal, it could rarely be considered to be immoral unless violence was involved. Inevitably, people refused to obey the excise laws and viewed the Riding Officer not so much as a law officer but rather as someone who was stopping them from obtaining the few luxuries in their lives.

John Collier was a big man and had found it necessary on numerous occasions for a riding officer to be so. His excess of two yards in height was balanced by the girth of his frame which made him look powerfully proportioned and far from fat. Beneath the fashionable long black wig his thinning hair had turned to silver ten years ago, but the ageing processes had not affected the inquisitiveness of his dark eyes or the intelligent disposition of his face. Born in Broadstairs, the son of a small businessman, he had had the good fortune to receive a short but sufficient private education. This had stimulated his enquiring mind and furnished him with enough skills to enable him to show promise throughout his career such that here, at the age of 51, he was at the top of his particular branch of the tree. William Cooper had not been so lucky but was at least content with his lot in life, difficult though it was.

"Tell me about your men, Mr Cooper. Are they good at their jobs?"

"I believe them to be so, sir, as far as I can tell. Whilst they have only obtained three convictions so far this year, they go about their business as efficiently as could be expected of them."

"You say three convictions - I seem to remember hearing about only two. Who was the third?"

"John Parker of St. Margaret's, sir. Bridges caught him with two gallons of uncustomed rum hidden at his house barely two weeks ago. He has just been fined five shillings and ordered to forfeit the rum. It is a first conviction for him, but, like the rest, we're fairly sure that he is a habitual smuggler. If we had enough proof we could probably arrest two thirds of the population for possession at least."

"Yes, I know. I notice that you said that Bridges caught him. What of Tucker? Do they not go about together?"

Cooper realised that he had put his foot in it. He had not wanted to mention the recent misdemeanours of his men. Unfortunately Collier's sharp mind had picked up his slip of the tongue.

"Well, Mr Collier, I understand that recently they have parted company. They refuse to accompany each other because of some silly quarrel they have had." Collier was visibly annoyed.

"Do they not realise that it is very serious for Riding Officers to be out alone? Apart from the mutual protection which staying together gives, they also provide each other with a buffer against corruption. How can you or I be sure that they are not in league with the lawbreakers? For the moment I will accept your word that they are good officers, but you must warn them to settle their differences and ride together or I shall have them transferred."

"I will do that, sir. I think too, that there is the possibility that they are no longer in fear of being attacked. Both men have been working in the region for a number of years and know the local population quite well. I think that Tucker and Bridges know that they will not be attacked by any of these people. We have had no violence for more than five years now and on that occasion we believe that it was perpetrated by outsiders."

"Really, I know nothing of this, tell me more." Collier immediately set down his pen, fixed his eyes on Cooper and awaited his reply.

"Well, sir, back in 1730 Tucker and Bridges received information regarding a possible landing in Fan Bay..."

"Where is that?" interrupted Collier.

"It is between here and St. Margaret's Bay. It is not really a bay at all but merely a landing point at the foot of the cliffs with access to the top and away from populated areas. Anyway, as the officers were riding to investigate they were assaulted and beaten up. They were unable to identify their assailants in any way and the attack was quite out of character for the type of people living in the area. The smuggling that night ended in disaster for the French boat bringing in the contraband was wrecked in the bad weather and about a dozen lives were lost."

"Who gave Tucker and Bridges the information? It is rare to find someone prepared to co-operate with us against his neighbour."

"It was certainly most unusual to be given information and it came from a keeper at the lighthouse on the South Foreland called Jack Heal. We don't know why he chose to do it or where he acquired the information. At the time, he refused to tell us and it was only a day or two afterwards that he was found at the bottom of the cliffs battered to death. With no names to go on, and absolutely no proof, we were forced officially to accept his widow's story that he had jumped because he was depressed after a marital argument. The local people accepted the death as such because they had no reason to believe otherwise. Of course, they did not know about the information that he had given us. We are almost certain that he was murdered for his act of treachery. His widow had obviously been severely intimidated to maintain silence and we were never able to persuade her to tell any other than her original story, despite a number of interviews we had with her."

"So you have no idea who did the killing?"

"Only a guess, sir. At the time, two strangers had been seen around the area. They were believed to be Cockneys - very nasty characters. Our theory is that they were part of the smuggling operation, and had been brought down from London to help with the transport of goods back to the city. It was probably they who attacked Bridges and Tucker and who killed Heal when they found out about his involvement. We should have arrested them right away but we tried first to obtain evidence to support our theory and then after a week or so they disappeared and have not been seen since. From that day to this there has never been a hint of any violence from the locals and we remain convinced that it was they who were responsible."

"That sounds like a reasonable assumption to me, Mr Cooper. As you know, the gangs have been operating to and from London for years and only Londoners could be capable of such evil. That is a most interesting tale, which I have not heard before. However, it is all the more reason why Tucker and Bridges should continue to ride together in the execution of their duty. There is no telling if or when they will come across more of these thugs 'imported' from London for a special event. Make sure that they follow my instructions. In the mean time, I shall put in my report that you are all performing your duties to the levels required of you and I hope you will continue to do so. It is an uphill struggle but we must not relax it. I have already obtained much information about the activities in Kent as a whole and I am commissioning a gentleman to make a study of the amount of smuggling that is going on. His work must be kept a secret so that he can gain a true picture of things. In the meantime, if you should come into contact with Philemore Phillips, give him all the help you can. Should his work prove satisfactory we will be able to formulate plans to combat the smuggling in your area, which I believe to be the worst in the county. Thank you for your help, Mr Cooper and Good-day to you."

His audience obviously at an end, Cooper rose from his seat, shook hands once more and left.

"That man certainly knows how to shake a hand," he thought as he shut the door behind him.

13 JAKE DIKE

Jake Dike looked out of the small window at the stars. It had been a perfect summer night and he had spent most of it awake, enjoying it to the full. The horizon was out of sight from his viewpoint but already the glow of daybreak was beginning to show in the sky and to obliterate the faintly glimmering starlight.

He regretted none of his life. He'd been born into a tough environment and had adapted himself to suit the situation. If he'd been born anywhere other than the East End of London his life would have been quite different, of that he was sure. He'd made the best of a bad lot. He'd not gone hungry, either for food or for women, and - by Jove - he'd had some good times with the latter! Women had been the main outlets for his expenditure over the years, but they were always worth it. He'd purposely never married; he'd had no need anyway. Marriage, to Jake Dike, was a perpetual consignment to poverty and hard work. You could never trust a woman, but then, you couldn't trust anyone could you? Never in his life had he trusted a soul - except Eb. Yes, he'd trusted Eb, but Eb had been like his own brother. If there was anything in his life he regretted (and he couldn't think of anything else) it was losing Eb. They'd known each other for thirty of Dike's thirty-six tough, violent years, and now it was all over. They'd been everywhere together, done everything together; they'd even shared the same women on occasions. From the age of eight they'd begun to 'work' together as they stole their way around all the markets of London. They'd joined the Woolwich gang in their early teens and both been caught in possession of stolen goods. This had led to them serving time together, in the same prison if not in the same cell. On release from jail they'd found their last career in the smuggling business. It had been quite profitable over the eight years that they'd been involved in it and they'd travelled outside London extensively as their work took them between the capital and various points along the coast of South-East England.

Dike remembered the first time that he'd killed a man. It had never really bothered him at the time, but he'd found himself thinking about it more and more in the past few weeks. He couldn't understand why people got so upset about murder. What was so special about human life anyway? Most people were as bad as vermin, and you wouldn't think twice about killing a rat! The whole world was engaged in hatred and killing. Armies did it by the thousand and nobody punished the soldiers for it. In fact they usually got a medal. Why should it be wrong to kill a stoat like that lighthouse keeper? Dike wasn't sure what his name was but he could remember the place perfectly. He was quite pleased with the way he had done it; no-one had guessed it was murder. By the time the swine had smashed into the rocks three hundred feet below there wasn't much left of him: certainly not enough to be able to tell he'd had his face smashed beforehand. No, he didn't regret he'd killed the keeper at all. Neither did he regret the death of the dragoon. If the bastard had been stupid enough to make an enemy of Jake Dike then he deserved to have his guts spread around on the road. He'd shot Eb. He'd deserved to feel the thrust of Jake's steel into his abdomen, to feel it jerked upwards towards his chest and to watch in agony as his intestines fell out of his body. Eb had been the only real friend that Jake had ever had. Jake had had to watch, helpless, as Eb had been shot in the eye from close range and had fallen face down in the dirt. His life-blood had spurted from a hole in the back of his head where the bullet had emerged and Jake could only watch his friend die. The worst of it was that he'd actually seen the dragoon fire at Eb, but Jake had made sure the swine had not lived to tell the tale.

What had begun as a simple job of transporting 'goods' away from Rye to a secret cache had ended in total disaster. The dragoons had been waiting for them in thick undergrowth by the roadside and, greatly outnumbering the four men, had given them no chance. Once again, they'd been the victims of treachery. Someone had passed information, and in Jake's book that was the lowest of all things you could do to a fellow man. Although he was the only survivor of the episode, he'd told nothing under questioning; no names, no places, nothing. But he would not be able to exact retribution in the same way as he had done with that lousy lighthouse keeper. Yes, perhaps that was the one big regret of his life: that he would not be able to make the traitor pay.

The sound of jangling keys snapped his mind back into the present. Booted footsteps approached and stopped. After a good deal of clanking and rattling the heavy door was swung back with a shrill squeak from the rusty hinge. Three uniformed men entered the room, grabbed Dike's arms and bound them tightly behind his back; he was then hustled out without so much as a word from any of them. They didn't have to speak: he knew why they'd come. Dawn had arrived.

Figure 5: Rudyerd's Eddystone Lighthouse (1709-1755).

PART TWO

1 HENRY HALL

On a cold December night in 1755, John Hatherley handed over his duty to Henry Hall.

"All right then, Henry?"

"S'pose so," grumbled the old man, for Henry Hall was ninety-four years old. "Didn't get much sleep tonight, though. Lumpy outside i'n' it?"

"Yeh, 's bin blowin' up a fair bit since about seven, so Tom says, but tid'n gettin' no worse now. Them candles be all right for a couple o' hours but you'd best

65

look at 'em reg'lar. They 'm burnin' quick cause o' that draught from the chimley."
"Right oh, I'll see to 't. Get yersel' to bed."

John was glad to be relieved. The weather, although not unusually bad, was bad enough to require a constant watch in the lantern room. Staring into the blackness was very tiring indeed. After a while your eyes were prepared to see anything. Four hours in that lantern room without a break was as long as he could stand - Henry was welcome to it.

John climbed down the ladder into the kitchen, which was in darkness as usual except for the dull red glow from the range. Descending another level he arrived in the somewhat colder bedroom, which was almost totally dark. John knew, however, exactly where his curved bunk lay in relation to the foot of the ladder. It was not necessary to light a lamp and risk disturbing Tom who'd been asleep for about four hours. Without bothering to remove any of his clothing he lay down quietly and pulled the blanket up over his head to try to shut out the noise of the wind and the waves. Irregularly he could hear the loud 'thump' from down below as a large wave hit the base of the lighthouse. Simultaneously a short and fairly severe tremor could be felt throughout the whole structure.

John was not really afraid. After four years of keeping the most exposed lighthouse in the world, he was beginning to get used to the vibrations. He did worry occasionally - what normal man wouldn't? He worried most when he remembered how Winstanley's tower had been swept away from this very rock with its architect inside it. The present lighthouse, which had been built by John Rudyerd forty-seven years earlier, had survived far worse storms than the present inclement weather. John himself had been in the tower during some extremely bad storms and there had been times when he had thought he would never return to Plymouth alive. Always the tower held firm. That fellow Rudyerd had certainly known what he was doing when he had designed this tower. Strangely enough, Rudyerd had never once come back to see for himself how the lighthouse was standing up to the sea. In fact, he had not been to the lighthouse since the day it was completed. Everyone thought he must have died soon afterwards and John was inclined to think so too, although he could not understand why no-one knew of Rudyerd's fate.

Thud!

The tower gave another shudder as a wave expended its energy against the smooth wooden timbers. John turned over to try to make himself more comfortable and he could hear Tom shuffling in his bed. The noise of the sea and the wind and the shuddering of the lighthouse reminded him of his days at sea. It was very much like being in a boat in a storm. In fact, Rudyerd had designed the lighthouse to be more like a ship than a house. He had even employed two shipwrights to help him build it. Yes, he could just as easily be in a sloop in the Roaring Forties as in a lighthouse. He had lost track of the years he had spent plying the oceans of the world. In all that time he had been shipwrecked only once and that was an experience he was glad not to have repeated. He had come very close to giving up the seafaring life after he had been the sole survivor of the wreck of the *Prosperity*, and he would never forget the family that had saved his life. It was a pity that he had never had the chance to go back to see them. He remembered being visited by the Dover agent and how he had taken another job with George Penrice at a very good rate of pay. He had sailed all over the world - New England, Cape Horn, the Indies and the Orient, but never had he been back to Dover. Then he had been sacked. It wasn't Mr Penrice's fault - the company simply ran out of money. There was no choice but to make him redundant.

Thump!

Why could he not get to sleep?

John remembered his sixteen months back in the tin mines. How he hated it. This was a far better job than slaving his heart out in the guts of the earth. He had not come by this job easily, however. He had had to labour in Plymouth for six months doing anything that came his way. Then, quite by chance, he had met Josias Jessop in the pub on the Barbican. Josias was in charge of the upkeep of Rudyerd's lighthouse and was a regular visitor to the Eddystone together with his small team of carpenters. He knew about the vacancy for a keeper at the Eddystone and John was fortunate enough to get the job. So here he was some eight miles from the nearest land and on a small rock in the middle of a violent sea. He liked it, but he did wish that he could get to sleep.

Boom!

Yes, it was not such a bad life. Better than being at sea. He remembered the French sloop that had come close to the reef that day. They were always getting ships coming in close out of pure curiosity. The Frenchie had come for a good look at the lighthouse, but when it saw an English frigate bearing down on it, it had sailed away at full speed with every square foot of sail that it could muster.

Bang!

John Hatherley's consciousness ebbed away from him at last and carried him off to an imaginary sea battle with the French.

Boom!

The cannon roared all around him and men were dying at his feet.

"Fire!" The chief gunner was telling him to give the enemy a broadside, but his cannon would not fire.

Thump!

"Fire!" The gunner yelled at him again. Why wouldn't the damn thing fire? Then he realised that it had no barrel... his cannon had turned into a kitchen range.

"Fire, John, Fire!"

The words disturbed his subconscious. Slowly his mind twisted into reality and the shout took on a far worse proportion. He realised that it was Henry calling down the ladder from the kitchen.

"Quick lads, fer Christ's sake, the lantern's on fire... come quick please... Tom, John, fire!" Henry was frantic.

"I'm coming!" yelled John, leaping out of bed and immediately shaking Tom who was still asleep.

"Get some water as fast as you can, and hurry!" Henry had come down to the kitchen to shout into the bedroom, but began climbing back up to the lantern again when he knew that he had woken his two colleagues.

"What about the 'fresh' outside?" screamed John, as Henry was half way up the ladder.

"Used it," replied Henry. "Get some sea water and hurry." John and Tom both ran down the ladders as fast as they could for the buckets were kept in the lowest of the four rooms, along with the other general stores. John got there first and struggled to light a lantern in the dark. It seemed to take an age before the light filled the room and they could see the buckets they so badly needed. John thought it was suicidal to go out on the reef in this weather and at night, but they needed the water and there was no alternative.

"Tom, hold the lantern at the door while I fill these buckets with water," said John still panting from his exertions. Then he disappeared out of the door and down the slender wrought iron ladder onto the reef without a second thought. The feeble light from Tom's hand-held lantern, however, did not compete with the glow that was coming from the lighthouse lantern. It was not the normal light from the candles but the fire that was illuminating the rocks. Things were desperate. John filled the four buckets he had brought and passed them up to Tom, whereupon they frantically climbed back up the ladders to the lantern room. In their haste, much of the water was spilled. Even for two fit men who were used to the climb it was an exhausting effort when done at full speed and they arrived at the top to find Henry incoherent with fear. "Can't stop it... it's... I can't..."

Almost before the two breathless keepers had got into the lantern room, the buckets were snatched from their grasp by the old man and hurled upwards towards the fire. Most of the water descended on the thrower and after a loud hiss and even more clouds of steam and smoke had billowed forth, the fire continued unabated. It had obviously taken a firm hold on the lantern roof and John wondered how it could possibly have started, but there was no time for questions.

"I've used all the water from the rain tank - get some more... quick!" Henry could hardly breathe now as the smoke rapidly filled the enclosed space.

John was incredulous. A fire was raging in the roof of the lantern, and here he was having to run up and down the ladders carrying buckets of seawater. The task was obviously hopeless but it was their only chance. He and Tom did as they were bade and feverishly scrambled down the ladders once more.

Henry was helpless, crouching low on the floor for air. What could he do? The lantern room was so full of smoke that it would be impossible for him to stay there much longer, but he did not want to leave. He felt responsible for the whole thing. If only he had not gone below to the kitchen for a rest... if only he had stayed to watch the weather and the candles. He looked up into the glow. The heat was blistering now and his mouth was gasping for air. Suddenly a shaft of white-hot pain was thrust down his throat. He screamed in agony and collapsed on the floor. His lips, mouth, throat and stomach were on fire. Just at that moment Tom appeared with a bucket of seawater. Henry grabbed the receptacle and began drinking the seawater like a man possessed.

"Hey, you can't drink that," roared Tom. "What's the matter with 'e? That's fer the fire... put it on the fire."

It was too late. Most of it had been spilled on the floor and on Henry's clothes. Tom did his best to quench the fire with the other buckets that had been brought up but it was to no avail. When he had finished he knew that they would have to abandon the lantern room.

"Henry's gone mad!" he shouted above the crackling of the fire in the timber. "He just drank the seawater."

They both looked at Henry who looked desperately ill and then began to vomit vigorously as the seawater took its toll on his system. Tom rubbed his eyes as the smoke began to affect them. "Get 'im below. We'll have to abandon the fire. There's nothing else us can do."

John retreated back down the ladder to the kitchen whilst Tom tried to drag Henry to the ladder. The smoke was suffocating and Henry was being most uncooperative. Tom noticed that it seemed to be raining inside the lantern. Every so often a small stream of boiling liquid fell to the floor, scorching the wet planking and hissing loudly. Then he realised it wasn't water. It was raining molten lead.

He dragged Henry down the ladder as best he could and at last the old man seemed to have acquired the will to live once more.

"What's the matter, Henry?" asked John in the relative safety of the kitchen. Henry could say nothing but pointed at his throat. His face and lips bore the signs of superficial burns and were obviously most painful. He turned away and wretched again, making a dreadful noise. John felt ill too, but managed to keep a grip on his stomach. Meanwhile, Tom was beginning to show signs of cracking up.

"Us 've got no chance now," he jittered. "Nothing 'll stop that fire. It'll burn and burn... and us with it. There's no escape."

By the light of the lantern John could see a dreadful fear in the man's eyes. Tom turned and took a bottle of rum from a cupboard. The moment they had all dreaded had come, though in the most unexpected guise. They were facing death in the lighthouse with no hope of rescue.

Pop! Tom uncorked the rum and took a liberal swig. Henry decided that it would help his burning stomach. He grabbed the bottle and poured the liquid into his mouth, spilling a good deal into the process. The smoke was filling the kitchen now and John's lungs grew tight. His breathing became noisy as his lungs wheezed from the foreign particles lodged inside.

"Never mind the rum, you two. We must go down the tower. Come on... now." He began pushing Henry towards the ladder which led down into the bedroom. As he did so, Tom pushed in front and almost fell down the rungs into the darkness of the room below. Henry, still gasping for breath, but calmer now that he was fortified with alcohol, climbed down next, with John bringing up the rear. He groped for the lamp and lit it. Tom was in his bunk, sobbing, with his face buried in his hands. This was a nightmare they had dared not dream. They had come to terms with death from the might of the sea. Day in, day out, they thought about it but dismissed it from their minds as impossible, but to be burned alive was the fate only of the witch and the martyr. They were no martyrs - they were men, lonely perhaps with no families or homes other than this wretched tower, but they enjoyed living. Surely it could not end this way?

John pulled himself together. The air was fresher down here. His brain worked more easily. He climbed back up to the kitchen and overturned the small table off which they had eaten so many meals. Then from the top of the ladder he dragged it over the hole in the floor of the kitchen in order to prevent the smoke from encroaching down any further, for the time being, at least.

Surely the fire would be seen from the shore? It was ironic that the lighthouse was now performing its role far better than it had ever been designed to do. The feeble candles, which provided the warning light to mariners, had rarely been seen from more than a few miles away. In contrast to the skills and sheer hard work needed to build the tower, the method of lighting it was pathetic. Yet here, with the whole of the upper portion of the tower in flames it was giving a better warning than it had ever done before.

They must be rescued, thought John. If only they could hold out in the tower until daybreak they would probably see a rescue boat coming towards them. They had two more rooms below in which to shelter, but the fire was rapidly burning its way down. Having consumed the whole of the lantern the flames had now started on the kitchen. The bedroom began to get hot and, despite the table, which had been pulled across the hatch in the ceiling, the smoke began seeping through. John looked at Henry still clutching his bottle of rum. The aged fellow was breathing heavily and tears of pain filled his eyes. His lips were blistered and swollen and he was unable to speak. Tom was still prone in his bunk, mumbling away to himself. It was obvious to John that they would have to retreat down another level and he proceeded to persuade his two miserable companions to comply.

In the temporary safety of the living room they all felt better, although conditions were not good. Suddenly, John became aware of a new noise. The enormous timbers, which had been used in the construction, had now begun to burn furiously, crackling loudly as they did so. John risked opening the living room window and, after throwing back the shutter, he looked up to see the deadly inferno illuminating the sea for miles around. Flames stretched high into the sky and, above that, boundless quantities of smoke and gas billowed heavenward. Then, as one of the timbers was dislodged by its own weight, it tumbled past the window and crashed into the wall of the living room. At the same time, a shower of red-hot iron clamps and bolts chattered down from above and John had to pull his head in sharply to avoid being hit. He slammed the shutter with a bang, which startled Henry more than any of the other noises. John now became even more worried. He realised that they were well and truly trapped in the lighthouse. Even if there were room outside on the reef for shelter, and if they were not washed away by the waves, they would surely be killed beneath an avalanche of burning timbers and cauterising metal. Would the morning never come?

Slowly and steadily, the fire consumed the lighthouse and before long, the three weary and frightened keepers were compelled yet again to retreat to the room below. This was to be their last refuge inside the tower. Was there any chance of surviving outside on the reef? John knew that the tide was on the ebb and would be so for another four or five hours, but there was nowhere on the rocks big enough or far enough away from the falling timbers for them to hide. Then John had an inspired idea. In any other situation it would have been considered crazy, but it could be their last salvation. He remembered the small part of the rock known as the 'cleft' where there was a tiny ledge and some mooring rings. But, most important, there was an overhang of rock that could protect them from falling metalwork.

"Tom, Henry, I've had an idea!"

Tom did not seem to care much for ideas. He was convinced that he was going to die.

"Look, soon the cleft 'll be clear of the water. Th' over'ang 'll give us shelter against the fallin' timbers."

Tom still took no notice, but Henry forgot his stomach and began to look interested.

"An' us can tie us selves to they moorin' rings wi' the painters so 's us won' be washed away," went on John excitedly. "They 'm bound to come fer us soon. It's bin burnin' fer about four hours an' it only takes 'em three to get ye."

Suddenly the tower gave a mighty tremor as a large section of the bedroom collapsed inwards onto the ceiling of the living room. Fortunately for the three incarcerated keepers, the increasing thickness of the timbers at lower levels, combined with the fact that they were heavily impregnated with pitch, had begun to slow down the rate at which the lighthouse was burning. The pitch caused the wood to smoulder rather than burn. It was to be a further agonizing hour before the tide would be low enough to allow them to shelter on the cleft.

Finally, at the earliest possible moment, Henry abandoned his now empty rum bottle that he and Tom had used to calm their nerves. Amid a shower of sparks, he dashed down the iron entrance ladder onto the hard, red rocks of the Eddystone, to find shelter from the giant torch on the cold, wet granite of the cleft.

John had considerable trouble persuading Tom, despite his Dutch courage, to attempt the trip to shelter. Almost pushing Tom in front of him, they abandoned the lighthouse. The air was still raining all sorts of debris and their clothes were covered in small smouldering embers, which they brushed off as quickly as they could. Tom was painfully slow going down the ladder. Suddenly a huge timber came crashing down and hit the rock about ten feet from where they were. It seemed to bounce on the reef and flew off at an angle into the sea with a splash and a loud hiss of steam. After that, Tom ran down the remaining steps and across the rock to the cleft. There they bound themselves as tightly as possible to the mooring rings using the ropes that were always kept there. Tom's alcohol content prevented him from tying any knots and John had to help him before securing himself to a ring.

Although it was still dark, they could see quite clearly the immediate area surrounding them. They could not see the tower, however, because of the overhang of rock, which sheltered them. The heat from the inferno frequently swept over them with each downdraught. Then began a long and terrible wait. Though safe from falling debris, they still had to contend with the sea, which insisted on dowsing them liberally and frequently. The water was so cold that almost immediately the three men were shivering uncontrollably, despite the heat filtering down from the fire.

Dawn came, but no sign of a boat. The tide had ebbed sufficiently for them to be receiving far less frequent drenchings but the swell was still such that, even if a boat came, a rescue would be very difficult. John could not believe that no-one had seen the fire from ashore. Why were they so slow to arrive? He knew that the fishermen did not like going to the Eddystone in winter, but surely they were not afraid when men's lives were at stake? Perhaps they thought that the keepers had perished and they were not going to come until the weather improved. Though filled with despair, John managed to keep his spirits up verbally, and Henry seemed to respond by trying to talk - difficult as it was for him. Tom, however, had become little more than a gibbering idiot and was beyond all pacification. The fire seemed to be burning as well as at any time during the night. There was far more fuel for it to feed on at the base of the tower where the lighthouse was solid: the fire could go on for days.

Then John saw a sail. It was a fishing boat and heading straight for them.

"We're saved, saved… Tom… look, 't is a boat… Henry, they 'm 'ere!"

Henry and John were jubilant. Tom's eyes were vacant and his lips quivered incessantly. Very soon the boat was within striking distance of the reef. How were they to be rescued? The swell was too great for a boat to get close to the rock. John knew he could swim to a boat but he did not think Henry could manage it. Tom was not going anywhere without considerable assistance. The fishermen obviously realised their problem and for an interminable length of time stood off the rock on the lee side, apparently doing nothing. John began to lose his patience. He had waited so long, had seen his hopes of salvation rise and fall with every swell of the tide and now saw survival slipping from his grasp. He lost his temper and shouted obscenities. Still they did nothing. Had the fishermen not seen the keepers? John untied himself and stood up on an open rock waving frantically, oblivious to the fire that raged on unabated behind him.

Then he saw a small boat pull away from the fishing boat, which was obviously not going to risk coming in any closer. Joining the smaller boat with the larger larger was an umbilical that was paid out from the mother ship as the rowing boat approached the rocks. Slowly the oars pulled the tiny craft towards the foaming cauldron of the Eddystone reef. When it was within heaving distance of the cleft, one of the oarsmen threw them a line. Many years of seamanship made it a perfect throw and the line dropped within feet of where John was standing.

"Tie it round yersel'. We'll pull 'e in to the boat." The words from the rowing boat were almost lost in the extraneous noises from wind tide and fire. Henry was terrified at the thought of jumping into the sea, but he knew it was his only chance. John helped him to tie the bowline around his waist and then, with considerable hesitation and much encouragement from the men in the rowing boat, he jumped into the foam.

John watched as he surfaced, gasping for air and thrashing at the water in a crude attempt to stay afloat, for he had not swum for many years. Then he was slowly pulled towards the safety of the boat. But what had happened to Tom? The fellow would without doubt drown in the sea on his own. John realised that he would have to tie the line around Tom and swim to the boat with him. There was no other way. John was a good swimmer, but suddenly his courage deserted him. He watched as the men dragged Henry over the gunwales and was afraid.

The line was heaved with precision onto the rock once more and John retrieved it. He untied the painter securing Tom to the rock and made fast the line from the boat around Tom's waist. Tom seemed barely able to understand what was going on. John made Tom stand up and before he could protest, pushed him into the water, diving in himself at the same time. The shock of the bitterly cold water made him want to gasp for air but he dare not. He surfaced quite close to Tom who was spluttering badly, but at last seemed to know what was happening. Then he swam to join Tom and support them both as the oarsmen struggled to complete the rescue. John swam for dear life as the numbing cold tried to prevent him from moving his limbs. Even Tom was making an effort. The cold had brought him more to his senses. Several times they both went under as large waves swept in towards the rocks and Tom, caught unawares, swallowed a lot of water. Slowly but surely, spluttering and splashing, they neared the boat. Then came the final superhuman effort to climb over the sides. Even with assistance from the strong hands inside, it was completed only with considerable difficulty. It took several attempts, one of which almost succeeded in capsizing the dinghy.

The three men lay exhausted and shivering in the bottom of the boat as their saviours steadily rowed them back towards the fishing vessel. John knew that at last he was safe and a feeling he had not had since the time he had lain in the cosy bed of the Knott family swept through his soul. He summoned the energy to sit up and watched the blazing stump which had been his home grow smaller as they rowed away from the rocks. How had they survived such an ordeal? It was a miracle and he gave thanks to his God. No longer did the sight of the fire strike terror in his heart. Indeed, it seemed to be a beautiful sight in the fresh light of the morning, until the sadness of the past eight long hours returned once more.

They reached the side of the fishing vessel and John looked at Henry as he was helped into the larger boat. What a way to end ninety-four years of life! This remarkable old man should never have needed to work in such a savage place. Now he had been badly burned and ran the risk of serious illness after the long hours on that freezing rock.

And Tom would surely never be the same man again. Gone was the introspective, but kind, and often humorous, Tom he knew so well. In his place was a sad and seriously disturbed soul. John was the only one to have survived relatively unscathed, for which he was very grateful. Now he had yet another experience to add to his collection of salty sea stories. He had been shipwrecked - from a lighthouse!

2 HENRY HALL (Epilogue)

Extract from the Proceedings of the Royal Society, Volume 49, pages 477-479. Read February 5, 1756: An account of the case of a man who died of the effects of the fire at the Eddystone Lighthouse. By Mr Edward Spry, Surgeon at Plymouth.

On Thursday 4 December 1755, at three in the afternoon, Henry Hall of East Stonehouse, near Plymouth, aged 94 years, of a good constitution, and extremely active for one of that age, being one of the three unfortunate men who suffered by the fire of the lighthouse at Eddystone, nine miles from Plymouth, having been greatly hurt by that accident, with much difficulty returned to his own house. I being sent for to his assistance found him in his bed complaining of extreme pains all over his body, especially in his left side, below the short ribs, in the breast, mouth and throat. He said likewise as well as he could with a hoarse voice, fierce to be heard, that melted lead had run down his throat into his body.

Having taken the proper care of his right leg, which was much bruised and cut on the tibia, I examined his body, and found it all covered with livid spots and blisters; and the left side of the head and face, with the eye, extremely burnt; which having washed with linen dipt in an emollient fomentation, and having applied things used in cases of burning, I then inspected his throat, the root of his tongue, and the parts contiguous, as the uvula, tonsils which were greatly scorched by the melted lead. Upon this I ordered him to drink frequently of water-gruel or some such draught; and returning to my own house, sent him the oily mixture, of which he took often two or three spoonfuls.

The next day he was much worse, all the symptoms of his case being heightened, with a weak pulse; and he could now scarce swallow at all.

The day following there was no change, except that, on account of his too great costiveness, he took six drachms of manna dissolved in an ounce and a half of infusion of senna, which had no effect till the day following; when just as a clyster was going to be administered he had a very fetid discharge by stool.

That day he was better till night, when he grew very feverish.

The next day, having slept well the preceding night, and thrown up by coughing a little matter, he was much better.

He began now to speak with less difficulty, and for three or four days to recover gradually; but then suddenly grew worse; his side, which grew worse daily from the first, now reddened a little and swelled, to which I applied the emplaster of gums. But all methods proved ineffectual, for the next day being seized with cold sweats and spasms in the tendons, he soon expired.

Examining the body, and making an incision through the left abdomen, I found the diaphragmatic upper mouth of the stomach greatly inflamed and ulcerated, and the tunica in the lower part of the stomach burnt; and from the great cavity of it took out a great piece of lead of the shape and weight here described.

It will perhaps be thought difficult to explain the manner by which the lead entered the stomach, but the account which the deceased gave me, and others, was that as he was endeavouring to extinguish the flames, which were at a considerable height over his head, the head of the lanthorn dropped down, before he was aware of it, with great force into his mouth then lifted up and open, and that in such quantity as to cover not only his head but all his clothes.

Plymouth, 19 Dec., 1755.

3 JOHN SMEATON -1

"Good day to you, sir. Is this the way to the Treleven brothers quarry at Lanlivery?"

John Smeaton looked down from his saddle and questioned a middle-aged farm labourer who was skilfully using a sickle to trim the Cornish hedgerow. Smeaton had come to a crossroads about a hundred yards back up the lane and there had been no signpost. The man he was addressing had heard the sound of approaching hooves some minutes ago and from the moment Smeaton had come around a twist in the track and into view of the local, the man had intermittently glanced up at the visitor. By only the second glance he had decided that the stranger was a gentleman.

"Good day to 'e, sir. Ay, 'e just go down this yer road an' 'e 'll find yer quarry 'bout 'alf mile farther on."

"Thank you kindly," Smeaton tipped his hat.

Gently kicking his horse into motion as the local touched his forelock, Smeaton relaxed in the saddle to enjoy the beauty of Cornwall. It was a rather dull day, but there was little wind and considering that the month was April the air felt comfortably warm. At times Smeaton wanted to believe that he was back in his native Yorkshire, rather than a far-flung region of the West Country, a few miles east of St. Austell. There were, however, reasons why this was not at all like Yorkshire.

His horse gently trotted down a track that was about eight feet wide and followed a slightly descending contour through a fairly heavily wooded hillside. At the side of the lane hedges stood to the same height that the lane was wide, but Smeaton was able to see clearly over the top of these. Unfortunately the trees blocked his vision sufficiently for him not to be able to judge where the quarry might be. Smeaton noticed how well advanced Nature was for the time of year. Certainly he would not have expected to see so many wild flowers in April in his home county. Obviously this was due to the considerable difference in climate experienced in

Cornwall. The temperatures had seemed to him to be considerably warmer in the West Country than in Yorkshire. Even so, he missed his home. His employment at the Eddystone had brought him to this part of England for the first time in his life and, whilst he admired the beauty of Devon and Cornwall, he was beginning to feel homesick.

Figure 6: John Smeaton's Eddystone Lighthouse (1759-1882)

John Smeaton was a handsome, dark-haired young man of thirty-five. Born at Austhorpe Lodge, near Leeds on the eighth of June 1724, he was the only son of a successful lawyer. Apart from being brilliant at mathematics, he was interested in very little other than to work with his hands. Before he was fifteen he had constructed a lathe on which he could turn materials with considerable skill. For a brief period he had studied law in a vain effort to comply with the wishes of his father, but he soon gave it up in favour of an apprenticeship with an instrument maker. At the same time, his father's influence enabled him to gain access to the exclusive Royal Society. He was thus able to supplement the practical experience of his working hours with training in scientific and engineering theory at the regular meetings he attended. At the age of twenty-six he was in business on his own as an instrument maker, besides reading papers to the Royal Society. These covered such matters as the marine compass, an air pump and a system of pulleys that would enable a man to lift a ton weight.

Smeaton's big chance had come quite by accident. A friend in London had contacted him on behalf of a gentleman called Robert Weston of Plymouth. Weston, he said, was looking for someone to rebuild the Eddystone lighthouse, which had recently been burnt down. There was, it seemed, an urgent need for another and it was desired to start work on a new Eddystone lighthouse at the earliest opportunity. Despite a complete lack of experience in the field of building construction, Smeaton was offered the job, to his complete amazement. After some hard deliberation, he had accepted the challenge, since when, the task had completely absorbed the agile mind of the Yorkshireman. He had devoted almost every hour of his day to the design of the new tower and to preparation for the commencement of the building.

There were many problems. The first of these was to decide on the best material to use. The previous tower, built by John Rudyerd, had been destroyed by fire because of its wooden construction. Nevertheless, it had been very successful in the execution of its duty for forty-seven years. Not surprisingly, there was a considerable feeling on the part of the owners that Smeaton should rebuild the tower in wood to a design similar to that of Rudyerd. Consequently, in the early days of his discussions he had experienced strong pressure to do just that. To Smeaton, however, a wooden tower could never be regarded as a permanent structure. It would certainly weather extremely well if properly maintained - this had already been successfully demonstrated - but Smeaton was looking for something that would endure the ravages of hundreds of years. Wood could never fulfil this criterion. At some time in the future, another designer would be faced with the same task as he himself now had if wood were to be used again. No, he must use a material that would never need replacing. There was only one such material - stone. Construction of a stone lighthouse had never yet been attempted in such an isolated position. The tower must be built in the most perfect manner yet devised so that it would be an extension of the rock on which it stood. After all, the reef had been there since time immemorial, so why should not the lighthouse? In order to accomplish this facet of the design, Smeaton would not be able to rely on cement alone to hold the blocks together. He had decided to dovetail together the huge stone blocks in the same way as a carpenter joints wood. He knew that a properly fashioned wooden dovetail joint would hold two pieces together far better than nails or glue. The same would undoubtedly be true of stone. Smeaton, however, was taking no chances. He would also be using cement and special steel nails which he called 'trenails' to provide the ultimate in strength that he was looking for. His plan to dovetail stone had been met with great surprise and even disbelief when he had presented it to the owners' committee. However, he was a man of meticulous nature and had prepared his plans and his arguments in such detail as to

77

completely over-ride the mood of the meeting. By the end of a lively debate in which the eloquent scientist had removed any doubts in the mind of the committee, it was agreed that he should be allowed complete freedom to carry out his plans.

Smeaton's next problem was to find the most suitable type of stone. He had already spent considerable time visiting numerous quarries in the southwest of England. The most obvious place for him to look first had been Portland, a small island near Weymouth of about half-a-dozen square miles. The island was almost entirely devoted to quarrying and Portland stone was nationally famous having been used, in part, for Westminster Bridge.

It had taken the engineer very little time to assess the value of Portland stone. It could be quarried by fast-working expert quarrymen in unlimited quantities and there was even a convenient sheltered pier from which it could be shipped. The quarry manager, a jovial old fellow called Solomon Roper, even surprised Smeaton with a price that was much cheaper than he had expected. The visit to Portland had been most enlightening in other ways, for Smeaton recalled a startling conversation he'd had with Roper on the subject of local folklore.

Smeaton had been amazed at the enormous physical size of almost all of the Portland quarrymen, and he mentioned it to Roper.

"I do believe that in fifteen minutes your men cut as much stone as the average quarryman cuts in an hour, Mr Roper," he had said. "Where do these strongly built men come from? Is there something special about your climate on this island, or your diet perhaps?"

Roper had shrugged his broad shoulders and his face had assumed a broad grin from beneath his grey beard.

"Well, sir, there you have hit upon a very interesting subject indeed. I venture to say that you are not the first customer to have pointed that out to me. I have thought about it greatly and am sure it is due to the fact that we have no childless marriages on the island."

Smeaton had been aghast at the biological implications of Roper's remark. Perhaps here on this tiny island there was a great new anthropological discovery for him to make the subject of a paper to the Royal Society.

"Is this really so? Then you must be a race of superhuman beings. But what can be the reason for this? Be honest, Roper." He good-naturedly poked Roper in the ribs who grinned even more.

"Upon my word, sir, for I am no local and have no axe to grind. My every word is of Gospel truth. You see it is the custom on this island that no couple marries until the woman is pregnant."

A look of sudden understanding must have crossed Smeaton's face as he appreciated the real reason for this biological riddle.

"I see," he had said, knowingly nodding his head. He had then drawn near to Roper's ear lest anyone should overhear, even though they both stood in the wide-open space of a quarry cliff top. "But does this not lead to a large number of bastards? Surely your Portlanders are as fickle as the English in their romances?"

"Not a single bastard has been born in this parish since my arrival here and for a hundred and fifty years before that only one was born. Let me explain."

Roper had then taken Smeaton by the shoulder and they had walked a short distance to a point where they had a wonderful view of the bay of Weymouth.

"You see, it is customary here that a young woman does not encourage a young man unless they are to have a thorough probation. When she becomes pregnant she tells her mother, the mother tells the father, the father tells the young man's father and he tells his son that it is proper to be married."

Smeaton, however, was wise to the ways of the world.

"Ah, but what if it is a false alarm and she proves not to be with child? Do they live together without being married? Surely if they were to separate the young lady would no longer have her honour for another young man?"

"No," Roper had replied. "Marriage does not take place until the pregnancy has been well established. If a child has not been forthcoming after a reasonable length of courtship then the couple merely separate with no blemish on the ladies honour. They simply conclude that they are not destined for each other and seek another mate. The honour of the lady is not tarnished since it is the custom never to have more than one lover at any one time."

Smeaton had then remembered the time when a number of masons were imported from London for the preparation of the stone for Westminster Bridge. Roper realised that he had forgotten that occasion and apologised.

"You are right, sir. On that occasion we did have a number of pregnancies and when the men were called upon to marry they realised their mistake. Some of them fulfilled their obligations, but those who did not were very rapidly removed from the island, I can tell you."

Yes, that conversation with Roper had been quite remarkable and Smeaton had made the effort to record in his diary as much of it as he could remember.

Having decided that he could most certainly use Portland stone on the inside of the tower, for it was one of the easier types of stone to fashion, he was still left with the problem of finding the most weather-resistant stone for the main body of the lighthouse. The Portland stone would be most unsuitable for resisting the might of the Atlantic. He had already seen several types of granite, a stone more commonly called 'moorstone' because it is found on the moors of Devon and Cornwall. His enquiries had shown that granite has varying degrees of hardness and, although the harder varieties split more regularly and would weather better, they were more difficult to fashion into special shapes. Thus he had decided to find a softer stone that would be more suitable for the intricate dovetail shaping he had designed. In his quest for a quarry able to supply this type of granite, he had been recommended to visit the Treleven brothers at Lanlivery. For this purpose he had travelled in the *Eddystone Boat* to Fowey and up the river to Lostwithiel, a small, fortified town. There he had been able to hire a horse in order to complete his journey.

Smeaton was able to hear the quarry long before he reached it. Incessantly, the ring of metal on stone pierced the tranquillity of the Cornish countryside. The quarry turned out to be much smaller than he had imagined. Perhaps unfairly, he had been expecting something comparable with those at Portland, but then, almost the whole of the island was devoted to the production of stone. Surely nothing could compare with that scale of working? The Treleven quarry looked busy. From his saddle, Smeaton could see at least a dozen men working at various stages of the quarrying process. Smeaton swung his leg behind him and dismounted the well-behaved nut-brown mare in order to meet the man who now approached.

"Good day to 'e, sir. An' what can I do 'e fer?"

"Mr Treleven?" Smeaton enquired, offering his hand.

"Ay, George Treleven. An' 'e be..."

"John Smeaton. I am presently looking for a supplier of good quality soft Cornish moorstone which I understand you produce here."

"Ay, 't is so. An' fer what d' ye 'ave it in mind?" asked Treleven.

"I have been given the task of reconstructing the Eddystone lighthouse..." Treleven's eyebrows rose in surprise, "...and I shall require a large quantity of stone cut to fine specifications."

"Well I be darned. That be some task 'e got there. I be proud to show 'e round an' give 'e some idea what us can supply. Course, this stone be but the best. Come 'e over yer, sir, an' us 'll 'ave a look see."

The two men crossed a level and very dusty arena of about a hundred yards in diameter, centred amid huge walls of foreboding stone. It seemed to Smeaton as if the whole world had ceased to exist at this isolated spot. At the top of the quarried granite walls the vegetation was growing naturally, but just here, at the end of the earth, all life, except that of fifty or so human beings, had failed to survive. There were no trees, no grass or flowers - not even a weed in the barren quarry. There was no birdsong, only the perpetual "ting, ting, ting-a-ting ting..."

The two men walked towards a huge wall of stone blocks which had already been cut and which were presently being shaped and dressed by a group of masons. As they drew nearer, Smeaton found that his ears were beginning to echo quite painfully with the reverberation of the masons' hammers. He ignored the discomfort and walked straight over to inspect the stone. Treleven had to use the top of his voice to invite one of the masons to meet the visitor.

"Joe, spare this 'ere gentleman a minute, will 'e?"

Joseph Trethewey did not hear all the words spoken to him, but he had been watching as the two men approached and knew that he was wanted. Joseph was forty-two years old and despite being only average in build was as strong as any mason could be. Smeaton was able to see quite clearly that Joe's rugged hands had been cutting and handling stone for many a long year. These, together with a pair of lively, brown eyes, and a weather-beaten furrowed face beneath a dark and slightly balding head of hair, told Smeaton that there was a skilled tradesman with a profound love of his craft. Members of the Trethewey family had been masons for generations, not just labourers, but men of ability. Joseph could well remember his father and grandfather working with granite, which was the only building stone of importance in Cornwall.

Each had constructed his house, and Trethewey families had always been fortunate in having comfortable accommodation. It had been part of Joseph's education to love his work and to give his all. He believed that, in so doing, he would never be short of work for, like food, folk always needed houses. He was proud to be a craftsman and John Smeaton had the greatest respect for such a man.

Treleven introduced the two men who shook hands warmly. Having told Joe that he was already impressed with the quality of the stone, Smeaton got straight down to business and soon became engaged in a long discussion with the mason. Smeaton's brief but careful inspection of the granite had already shown it to be of a particularly high standard. The grey, porphyritic stone showed especially large feldspars set in a very fine-grained mass. Gradually, the meticulous engineer drew on Joseph's long years of hard-won experience and extracted every jot of information that might prove useful to him in his search for the perfect stone.

Meanwhile, Treleven's attention had been diverted from his guest. His foreman, John Pascoe, had approached him with news.

"We 'm ready to go, Mister Treleven."

Treleven had been expecting the report. For the past week a small team of men had been preparing to blast a large section of granite bed. It was in such a position as to necessitate the boring of horizontal blast holes into the rock. This was a task performed by three men, one holding a rod, and two delivering blows from heavy sledgehammers. The steel rods had to be held and twisted by two quarrymen after each double blow from the hammers. Three holes having been laboriously drilled in this manner, it had then been necessary to place three charges of gunpowder, the first of seven pounds, the second four pounds and the third three pounds. Then, using a wooden rod, these charges were tamped down with stone dust to within a short distance of the mouth of the hole, fuse already having been inserted into each. It was now time to light the fuses.

Treleven left Smeaton and Trethewey in conference and walked with Pascoe to the blasting site at the farthest part of the quarry. In this area the company had been pressing forward for the past two years into an enormous granite wall. The stone being produced from this point was of the highest quality that Treleven had yet seen in his quarry. All efforts had been channelled in this direction, leaving the remainder of the quarry walls unworked at the moment. Once blasted, the huge slabs were then moved to other parts of the quarry where they were fashioned and stored, as required. In this way, blasting was able to continue at the original site with the minimum of delay.

Briefly, Treleven inspected the week's work. All appeared to be in order. He instructed the men to take shelter and then returned to his visitor as a shrill whistle was sounded to denote that blasting was imminent.

"Mr Smeaton, I's goin' to 'ave to ask 'e to join us in the shelter over yer, for we 'm about to blast a bed o' moorstone."

Joseph Trethewey was by now giving Smeaton details of the range of sizes they could handle and Smeaton was engrossed in the information he received. Nevertheless, he acknowledged the warning offered by Treleven.

"I got yer 'orse took care of, so if 'e like to come over yer, please…"

Treleven had thought of everything, which was a good thing because Smeaton had completely forgotten about his horse. He noticed how silent the quarry had become. No longer did the sound of hammers prevail. It was a strange, eerie silence - a foreboding quietness.

The shelter turned out to be a small, dark cave at some distance from where the blast was about to take place. The men filed inside and stood in the cave, their faces showing a little excitement even though they had seen it all before. Carefully, each man was counted by a charge-hand, and, when all of their number was accounted for, Pascoe returned to the blasting area to light the fuses. Within a minute he came running back to the shelter. An explosion such as this was a fairly regular occurrence at any quarry, but it never failed to arouse a deal of excitement amongst the men. In silence they awaited the blast. To Smeaton, it seemed to take a very long time. He found that, unconsciously, he was tensed up, holding his breath. For the moment, all ears were anticipating the explosion. When it finally occurred, Smeaton thought that it seemed surprisingly quiet and something of an anti-climax. The men seemed to think so too and began to murmur, mildly disgruntled at the feeble result of a week's strenuous effort.

Pascoe and several others left the shelter first in order to investigate the results of their work, while Smeaton, Treleven and Trethewey followed behind, engaged once more in technical discussion. As they rounded a corner, Smeaton was able to see Pascoe inspecting a section of rock, which, it seemed, had been left untouched by the blast. Suddenly, to his horror, there was a terrific explosion. Before Smeaton's very eyes, the body of John Pascoe disintegrated in a minute fraction of a second before an enormous cloud of smoke from the gunpowder obliterated all sight. Half a second later, Smeaton and his companions were bowled backwards by the shock wave and only just managed to remain standing. Smeaton could not take his horrified eyes from the scene. John Pascoe had been blown to pieces as surely as if he had stood in front of a cannon.

Then, seemingly ages after the blast, a huge section of granite became detached from the rock face and collapsed to the ground in a smothering cloud of dust. From out of the cloud of dust, several men came staggering. The remainder of the men had been transfixed by the startling tragedy that had befallen them. Then one man began to run towards the dust, and soon everyone, including Smeaton, was running frantically to the scene of the tragedy. At first it was difficult to be of much help, for the dust was blinding and clogged Smeaton's lungs. He coughed and covered his eyes with his hand, peering between his fingers to see, like a child playing peek-a-boo. The suffocating dust seemed to take an age to clear, for there was little wind to blow it away. Finally, as it began to settle, the horrible event began to unfold once again in lurid detail.

William Symons was found lying with his head in a pool of blood, his eyes and forehead having been badly injured by flying debris. He was, fortunately, still alive and several men gently removed him to a place of safety for such treatment as might be available. Many of the men wept openly as they manhandled huge slabs of moorstone to look for the remains of poor Pascoe. His limbs, trunk and head were gradually recovered from several widely scattered points in the quarry. Miraculously, apart from Symons, all the other men who had gone with Pascoe had escaped serious injury. Workmates comforted them as they tried to regain their composure.

Smeaton was dumbfounded. Never had he witnessed such carnage of a human being. Involuntarily, the event replayed itself over and over again in his subconscious and Smeaton was forced to walk behind a stone to be sick. Joseph Trethewey and Treleven tried to re-organise themselves and to maintain a state of order in the quarry. It was quite apparent, however, that there would be no more work here for some time. Eventually, George Treleven found Smeaton looking very pale and apologised unnecessarily as his eyes were filled with tears for his lost foreman.

"My dear fellow," said Smeaton, "I shall go immediately and leave you to your grief. Thank you sincerely for your help and be sure that I will contact you again."

Treleven led Smeaton to where his horse waited nervously and the two men said a brief farewell. Then Treleven went quickly back to his men, while Smeaton had a little trouble in gaining his saddle. Even at such a distance from the scene of the blast, the mare had been quite disturbed by the noise and was not keen to receive Smeaton's weight. Even though he liked the animal very much, Smeaton was far from concerned about the state of health of his horse. A human being had been killed before his very eyes and, as he rode away from the quarry it was likely that a wife, a child, was waiting eagerly for John Pascoe to come home from work. The child would wait for its daddy in vain.

Smeaton vowed to do all in his power to avoid fatal accidents during the building of the Eddystone lighthouse - a job that was to prove the most challenging in the history of human achievement.

4 JOHN SMEATON -2

For John Hatherley, his harrowing experiences in the fire that burned down Rudyerd's lighthouse were soon overshadowed by the problems of unemployment. The winter of 1755-6 proved to be a difficult time and Hatherley was grateful that he had no family to support. There were few opportunities for a 51-year-old unemployed lighthouse keeper, but his friendship with Josias Jessop was to come to his rescue.

Jessop too, had had to realise a drastic change in his employment, for the lighthouse had been his total responsibility for a great number of years. However, as a fully qualified foreman shipwright, he was able to return to his old duties in the naval dockyard of Devonport during the winter months. Then, in March 1756, John Smeaton contacted Jessop and asked him to help build the new lighthouse. Jessop had heard rumours that the Eddystone lighthouse was to be rebuilt and he was delighted to be offered the job, which he accepted at once.

The first task was to find a shore-based work-site. It had to be at the water's edge with good access for a variety of shipping. A sheltered position was also desirable so that the weather would not influence the ship movements more than was necessary. Smeaton and Jessop visited many sites and finally selected one in Millbay, a distance of two miles from the town of Plymouth.

With the shore site chosen, Jessop reviewed the craft that would be necessary to carry the materials and the workforce back and forth. The most obvious choice was the *Eddystone Boat*, a ten-ton sloop which could be rowed or sailed, and which was big enough to take a sizeable number of men in a modicum of comfort. Jessop, who was acquainted with Hatherley's plight, humanely invited the keeper to be the mate of the *Eddystone Boat*. It was a rational decision because, not only did Hatherley have a background as a seaman, but he had a thorough working knowledge of every part of the Eddystone reef, knowledge which would be fully tested on every visit to the dangerous swirling waters which gave the reef its name.

It was early April and just prior to his visit to the Lanlivery quarry when Smeaton and Jessop first attempted to make a landing on the rocks. By the end of May they had made ten attempts, only four of which had been successful. On several occasions they had rowed the twelve miles from Millbay and got to within a few hundred yards, only to be turned back by a sudden change in the wind, tide or weather. Occasionally, they had been unable to return to Millbay, and were forced to sail to Fowey. Journeys to the reef were taking two or three days at a time, only to be unsuccessful. On the few occasions when a landing was possible, a matter of two hours at most could be spent in useful work before it was time to return.

It was during the interminable hours spent plying fruitlessly between Millbay and the rocks that Smeaton decided to use a floating 'inn' moored close to the Eddystone to accommodate his workforce. They would then be on site and instantly available for work whenever the weather and tide permitted.

When he had finally completed his survey, Smeaton returned to London for most of June and July to finalise his drawings. During his absence, Jessop acquired an eighty-ton herring boat that was to become the floating accommodation. Its name was the *Neptune Buss*. This vessel, which everyone was to grow to hate on account of its devilish handling problems, was taken to within a quarter of a mile of the reef and anchored firmly. By the time Smeaton returned to Plymouth, all was ready to begin.

Jessop had signed on the workforce, which consisted of two teams of twelve men. A foreman was in charge of each team, which, in turn, was made up of six stonemasons and six Cornish tin miners. The stonemasons would be required to have the highest degree of skill in order to cut the intricate stone shapes in the exact sizes required. The tinners, renowned for their stamina and strength, were to carry out the labouring tasks.

On 6 August work began. The first company of men had arrived on board the *Buss*. Their immediate task had been to cut six steps into the immensely hard red granite that had been so much trouble for Winstanley, builder of the original lighthouse. Day or night became irrelevant, only the state of the tide mattered and work continued throughout the night by torchlight whenever the tide was favourable. It took until 22 November to complete the steps, by which time it was necessary to cast off from the buoy and bring the *Neptune Buss* back to Millbay for the winter.

The twelve-mile journey home took rather longer than expected. The weather deteriorated quite quickly and before long they were in the grip of a nasty storm. The handling of the *Buss* was appalling, and with the wind at gale force from the east-southeast, there was no chance of getting into Plymouth Sound. Although they tried to make for Fowey, they became hopelessly lost, and throughout that Monday night they rode out the storm as best they could. The storm continued in full flight for two further days, during which time the storm-tossed but unsinkable *Buss* was blown steadily farther and farther west. Smeaton and Jessop, in company with sixteen other soaked and shivering men, feared that they must be into the Bay of Biscay and resolved to try to cross it, thus making landfall in Spain. Mercifully, on Thursday morning, the wind changed direction. A gentle northwesterly enabled them to make blissful contact with the Cornish coastline and, at long last, to sail back to Plymouth where they arrived on Friday morning. The end of the first summer season of work on Smeaton's new tower had almost ended in disaster.

With the arrival of winter, work continued at a breathtaking pace - not upon the reef, but in Millbay. The consignments of moorstone began to arrive on the quay and the masons worked hard to shape them into interlocking building blocks. The aim was to produce horizontal circles of stones which fitted together in a complicated jigsaw arrangement and which were known as courses. Dovetail joints in the rock would be used for the first time to hold them together, but Smeaton also planned to use oak wedges between the blocks, and oak trenails that passed through one course and into the one below. Furthermore, Smeaton had formulated his own quick-setting cement to be laid between the courses. Each stone was uniquely numbered and had its own position and identity within the three-dimensional jigsaw.

It was not until June that the weather was sufficiently settled for work to begin again on the reef and early in the month the *Buss* was once more sailed to its mooring. Smeaton erected on the rocks his own design of lifting gear for use with the blocks, some of which weighed over two tons. He decided to test it by lifting onto the rocks a longboat, together with its ten sailors, much to their dismay. The act was accomplished flawlessly, but all aboard the longboat were most relieved when the boat was back in the water once more.

The topography of the rock on which the tower was to be built, and the steps that had been cut the previous year, meant that there were only four stones in the first course, but thirteen in the second. Part way through the laying of the second, five of the unique stones were washed away before they could be properly fixed and a valuable week was wasted while Smeaton's overworked masons hastily made duplicates. By the end of June the second course was finished. As the third course of twenty-five stones progressed, other problems occurred. Just as two boats were about to bring stones out to the rocks, both crews, Hatherley included, were captured by Press gangs. Smeaton had already anticipated this event. He had made an arrangement with the naval authorities that men working on the project were exempt from the Press. To that end, he had minted a special medallion in silver for the men to carry as proof, but on this occasion their exemption was ignored. Smeaton himself was forced to petition the Port Admiral for their release and more of his valuable time was wasted.

By 11 August the sixth course was complete and this brought the base of the tower to the top of the rock. From this point, the courses would be laid on a flat, circular base. Furthermore, progress would be faster because they were getting farther above the level of the tides and thus less affected by them. By mid-October, nine courses were finished and everything was back in Millbay for the winter. A substantial portion of the base had been completed.

The winter of 1757-8 saw the completion of all the stonework in the yard, under Jessop's supervision. Smeaton, meanwhile, had returned to London. The work on the reef in 1758 did not commence until 2 July and by 8 August the next five courses up to level fourteen were finished. This was the top of the solid base of the lighthouse. The next ten courses would allow an entrance door and a central staircase five feet in diameter and, by 28 August, this too was finished. The next levels would comprise the accommodation, which was to be a storeroom, and fixing a temporary light above its ceiling. He found two volunteers prepared to spend the winter in the single room for twice their normal wages and the plan to light the Eddystone a year ahead of schedule looked set to go ahead. He applied to Trinity House for permission to exhibit the light and in the meantime pressed on to complete the storeroom. Quite unpredictably, the Corporation refused to allow him to show the light until the tower was completely finished, a remarkably shortsighted decision under the circumstances.

And so, in the spring of 1759, the partly built lighthouse had survived the winter with only the uppermost levels to be assembled. While Smeaton in London and Jessop in Plymouth waited impatiently for the arrival of the calm summer weather, dramatic events were about to unfold at the South Foreland lighthouse.

5 LIZZIE KNOTT

In the spring of 1759, life at St. Margaret's proceeded undisturbed along its usual course as yet another war between England and France entered its third year. It was quite possible to be unaware of the war for most of the time, although occasionally news of a battle in some distant land arrived in the village. Periodically, one or two young men from the village disappeared suddenly after a visit from the press gang, but this sort of event came to be recognised by the local inhabitants as something of an occupational hazard and it was simply bad luck on those unfortunate enough to be caught.

Rather sadder, however, were the occasions when grief visited the household of a loved one who had been killed in the service of his country. Yet the international quarrels lay far beyond the ken of village folk. The supreme sacrifice of an individual was recognised only in terms of government statistics. Hundreds, sometimes thousands, of miles away from their homes soldiers faced bullet and bayonet. Starved and frozen heroes marched to ignominious death in the mud and stench of the battlefield. Sailors lived for months on end in dark, disease-filled floating pig sties and diced with any one of a hundred degrading forms of death.

Why? A rich, new land was ready for raping and governments were not prepared to share. And the families of dead young men were consoled by the fact that they had given their lives in glory for the good of their country.

The Knott family had no cause to be sad. With a steady income and the permanent roof of the South Foreland lighthouse over their heads, they were one of the more fortunate local families. Though the numerical size of William and Elizabeth's family had ceased to increase, the physical size of its members had not. The parents had been blessed with five, fast-growing and healthy children and offered up thanks for them at Reverend Marsh's Sunday services.

Eldest was Elizabeth, or Lizzie, as she had always been known. Though she could not be described as beautiful, her dark features, long dark hair and soft, loving eyes held a youthful freshness which more than one local lad was beginning to admire. She knew no hatred and went about life with an earnest desire to make everyone like her. As eldest daughter at seventeen, she dutifully and uncomplainingly assisted her mother in the many tedious chores associated with a growing family. In stature, Lizzie was becoming the image of her mother and although she was two years older than her eldest brother, she was two inches shorter than he.

Will adored her - much more than many a lad of fifteen cared for an elder sister. To boys, big sisters could only ever be looked upon as mother substitutes without the necessary wisdom. Consequently they were resented because of the authority they possessed and the lack of discretion with which they used it. Indeed, to the three younger Knott children, Lizzie was certainly a mother substitute (though they little needed one) and they abused her for her caring dutifulness. To them, the innocent desire for play overcame any sense of family responsibility. Lizzie accepted them as but children and was rarely annoyed. That was partly what Will loved so much about her. Despite the hardships of Lizzie's day, she was always cheerful and never a cross word passed betwixt brother and sister.

Of all the womanly duties expected of growing young women, Lizzie took most readily to the skills of the needle. By the time she was ten years old she had been able to make dresses. As is often the way, proficiency led to deficiency. Desire to sew led to lack of interest in cookery and, much to her mother's disappointment, Lizzie was distinctly awkward in the culinary art. Naturally enough, this led to many a jest from the rest of the family when her efforts at baking went slightly astray. True to character, she always took the jokes in good part without recourse to smart rejoinders.

And so it was in the spring of 1759 that Lizzie began to attract attention from outside the family circle. In church one Sunday morning, Lizzie became aware that she was attracting the gaze of a good-looking young man. At first, she was uncomfortable under the unremitting pressure of his eyes, for this was quite a new experience for her.

Edward Gibbon was a member of the Gibbon family of Wallet's court. The Gibbons had occupied the manor house of Westcliffe since 1627 when it was acquired and renovated by one of Edward's ancestors. The whole village knew that they were a wealthy family although no-one knew or even bothered to ask where that wealth had originally been obtained. Wealth was hereditary: the Gibbons had always had money. They would always have money. They were gentlefolk.

Normally Edward would not have noticed Lizzie, for the Knotts usually attended St. Margaret's church rather than St. Peter's at Westcliffe. Periodically, however, they worshipped in the church of the Gibbon family. It mattered little to the Knotts, especially since Reverend Marsh was the vicar of both churches.

On this particular morning Edward's seat in the family pew at the front was empty. He had arrived late for the service and rather than cause a disturbance he slipped quietly into a pew at the back of the church. It was not long before he noticed Lizzie in one of those head-turning Sunday dresses that she had made herself.

Intermittently through the hymns and psalm, continuously through the lessons and sermon, an invisible beam of masculine desire burdened Lizzie. No matter how hard she tried she could not ignore it. On more than one occasion their eyes actually intercepted each other as she summoned the courage to look at the source of her embarrassment, but each time she quickly turned her head forward once more with increased uneasiness and a distinct flush in her cheeks. Her self-consciousness was so overwhelming that hardly a word of the service entered Lizzie's head. Even an uncharacteristic feeling of anger swept briefly into her mind as a reaction to the invasion of her privacy. Gradually, however, it subsided. He certainly was good-looking.

After the service Lizzie hurried homeward lest she should cross paths with her admirer, but once relieved of the pressure of his stare she soon found it easy to forget Edward and immersed herself in housework. It was not until a few more days had elapsed that Edward's existence became important to Lizzie.

As she was walking to the village she saw Edward ambling apparently aimlessly along the path towards her. She could not avoid him, for to do so would have meant a diversion across a muddy field, neither could she ignore him when once she was in speaking distance - that would have violated the code of common decency. Though she might be a mere working girl she had sufficient breeding to be appalled by incivility. So, although she was mildly annoyed at meeting him (for she suspected his ulterior motive) she was nevertheless quite polite in her greeting as she attempted to hurry past.

"Good day, Master Edward," she said with a smile, but without changing her speed along the track.

"Good day to you, Elizabeth," replied Edward, raising his hat and stopping to talk. Unfortunately he found his quarry less desirous of conversation, and he was forced to backtrack lest he lose the opportunity he had been seeking for days.

"Will you not stop and pass the time of day, Elizabeth?" queried Edward, almost falling over his own feet in what had become a peculiar sideways motion.

"Most certainly, sir, though it is not my place to be seen with you for long."

Lizzie stopped, aware once again that she was blushing. She could not find it in her heart to tell Edward to leave her alone, much as she wanted it - or thought she did.

"To be seen with me, perhaps," replied Edward, but who can see us? I see no one else in the vicinity. Do talk to me."

"What would you like me to talk about, Master Edward?" enquired Lizzie, realising that he was right. She had no excuse to walk on other than her female prerogative, which she had no intention of using.

"Oh, anything, Elizabeth. I just want to hear the sound of your sweet voice, to admire your beautiful dress and your fine looks." Now he was getting too *gallante*, but he certainly was good-looking.

"I do not think I should…" Lizzie began, but changed her mind and started slowly on her way once more. Edward grasped her gently by the arm.

"Please don't go, Elizabeth, not yet. Look, I know you think me rude, but my intentions are really quite honourable. Will you walk with me one afternoon? Along the cliffs to Dover, perhaps… anywhere… please say you will. No-one shall see us, I promise."

That was a bit rash. Lizzie was confused. She could not deny an attraction to Edward. He surely was a gentleman, but that was the trouble. For a gentleman to publicly court a working girl was not the done thing. This was not the first time that she had been asked to walk with an unrelated male, but the other times had been merely pleasant afternoons out with boys. Lizzie felt that this could be quite different. Edward was not a boy. The relationship would not be between children. To be found out risked becoming the talk of the village, to say nothing of upsetting her parents, which was an event, she would do anything to avoid. Why, oh why, was he so good looking?

"How about Sunday afternoon?" pressed Edward. He could sense her weakening. "Please say you will. I will meet you here at half-past-two… no, don't say no. I will be here at half-past two on Sunday afternoon. If you decide not to come I shall understand. Please come Elizabeth. No harm shall come of our relationship, I promise. Until Sunday then…"

Offering Lizzie no further opportunity in which to decline his invitation, he left her bewildered and speechless. Of course, Lizzie's character was such that she would not disappoint Edward. So when Sunday afternoon came she kept the appointment. It wasn't unusual for her to take a stroll along the cliffs on her own so her parents were not at all suspicious. The weather thoroughly befitted such a big occasion in her life, the fresh spring sunshine mirroring the love she believed herself capable of.

Lizzie and Edward took a quiet path in the direction of Dover and ambled along together, carefree and falling in love. Eventually, they found what they thought was a private and sheltered corner of the field adjacent to the path. There they slid into the long and slightly damp grass. Soon, Lizzie was being held in a tight and tender embrace. The proximity of his lips was too great to ignore. Secretly she had been longing for Edward to kiss her and when the moment arrived she plunged headlong into it, quite unaware that at least three pairs of eyes were watching her.

A grey-brown field mouse skittered along the roughly built wall of matching stones not more than a dozen hops from where Lizzie lay clutching her man. The mouse, refreshed after its hibernation, was eager to retrace its buried store of sustenance. Strange noise. It stopped and stood still like a stone as the couple rolled in the grass. Then, lest its presence should attract attention, it sought refuge amid the stones of the wall.

At least two other pairs of eyes saw Edward's hands slip gently between the layers of Lizzie's clothing to explore uncharted regions of the warm and soft female body. The field mouse became alarmed as its predators made more noise. It found a secret and draughty staircase, steps of moss, fern and cold sandstone, down through the inner reaches of the wall. At ground level the external vegetation of nettles and dandelions provided even greater shelter. From there the mouse proceeded at top speed away from the corner of the field where Lizzie lay, oblivious to the world, abandoning herself to an irresistible urge, drowning in the superb sensations surging through her body, surrendering maidenhood.

From a vantage point high in the clear blue sky the tunnel vision of a kestrel had already spotted what looked like a human body lying face down in the field. The kestrel could hardly have been less interested, for that particular pair of eyes had also pinpointed the minute grey-brown speck as it darted through the long blades.

The shafts of life and death were swift. The field mouse had given up its life to the unseen enemy in the sky. Lizzie lay exhausted. She too had given up something that, like life itself, could be lost but once. And at least one other pair of eyes continued to watch from behind a shrub.

Lizzie became conscious of a tear on her cheek. Suddenly the world had become a stark reality once more, and although Edward had kissed her gently before lying back in the dampness, he had become strangely silent. She wriggled to adjust her clothing, loathe to sit up until she was decent, but tears filled her eyes and she found it difficult to get dressed. Edward said nothing. He had seen it all before. They usually cried the first time, but they soon got over it. He gave her a consoling smile, a soft touch on the cheek to wipe away the tears. Then he sat up to see if anyone was near. The eyes crouched low in the shelter of the foliage and then, when Edward looked in the opposite direction, the human body that housed them crept cautiously away, smugly successful in its dirty deed.

6 WILL KNOTT

Young Will was pleased with himself for the fishing had been good. He often spent a Sunday afternoon fishing from the beach and this time had caught half a dozen small mackerel - enough for a tasty breakfast next morning. He walked along the cliff top and watched the fiery ball that had brought warmth and happiness to the day slide slowly behind the tower of the lighthouse that was his home.

As he approached closer he suddenly had a feeling that all was not well... Raised voices from inside... Crying - someone was crying. He laid his fish quickly on the stone slab outside the house and burst into the living room. Immediately he saw Lizzie huddled in the corner of the room. She was crying inconsolably into her favourite Sunday dress, which now looked fit only for wiping dishes. Her mother stood close by with bloodshot eyes and a look of anguish on her face the like of which Will had never seen before. Father was pacing the room in a terrible rage. From the small bedroom next door came more sounds of heartbreak from Will's brothers and sisters who had been sent to bed prematurely.

"Dear God, what has happened?" Will looked pleadingly at his mother and father, waiting for one of them to explain the meaning of all the distress.

"Your sister has taken to the life of a common whore. She has disgraced us all." William senior was extremely angry.

"Have a care, William," sobbed his wife, "she does not deserve that name."

"A whore I said and a whore I mean. There's no place for such immorality in this household. She must leave tomorrow. Let her go to live in the brothel in Dover, that's all she's fit for."

Young Will was speechless. Never before had he heard such strong and ill-considered words from his father who was normally a sweet-tempered and understanding man. Another crescendo of sobbing arose from the corner where Lizzie lay, convulsing with sorrow.

"You'll not turn her out, William, I won't have it."

"What has she done father? Lizzie can't be bad. I don't believe what you say. She wouldn't do such things." Will's own strength of character was beginning to leave him as his own eyes filled with tears.

"I'll have no bastard of hers in this house." William was so angry that he could nothing except pace the floor, taking great care not to let his eyes rest on another member of his family, least of all, Lizzie.

"Father, what are you saying? What has she done? Tell me... tell me..."

"Everyone will know what she has done. We shall all be laughed out of the village." William was in no mood for explanations.

His son was desperate to know the cause of the trouble, but he was afraid to ask his father any more questions in case he provoked violence. There had never been any violence in the family before but such was his father's wrath that Will was afraid for his sister's safety. Then, fortunately, William remembered his responsibilities. It was growing dark outside and he had not lit the light in the lighthouse. He was already late. William senior left the family in their misery and went about his work, not just to carry out his duty, but to give himself time to think. Young Will crossed the room to where Lizzie lay. Kneeling down he lifted her head and lovingly caressed her face against her chest. He ran his fingers through sticky strands of tear-soaked hair and kissed her forehead.

91

"Your sister has disgraced us all," said mother, sitting down to try to compose herself. "She gave herself to Edward Gibbon this afternoon in Edgar Pilcher's field."

"How do you know that, mother? Did she tell you?"

"No, we didn't learn of it from her, although she admitted it when her father accused her. He came home from the village just now and knew all about it - I've no idea how he found out. Someone must have seen her with Mr Edward and told father about it."

"But what is so wrong with what she did?"

"Oh, William, you know as well as I do." His mother was scolding him now, and Will wished he had not made that last remark. Of course he knew why his parents were upset. In saying the words he'd been somehow hoping that the offence would seem trivial and that his parents would forgive Lizzie here and now and that they could all get back to the normal, idyllic existence they had know such a short time ago. But no. The Gibbon family were one of the noble families of the district. It was not Lizzie's place even to socialise with them, least of all to do what she did. Besides, members of the Knott family were always brought up strictly in accordance with the Christian Commandments and hanky-panky of that sort was greatly frowned upon.

For several minutes William was silent. There seemed nothing more to say. So great was the apparent tragedy that had occurred in the household, that he needed time to mull it over in his mind. He crouched low, cuddled Lizzie's pathetic form, and listened to the last, tired sobs emanating from his family. William's whole world seemed to have ended. His father had threatened to cast Lizzie out, but what had she done? One mistake, one slip: that was all she had made. Anyone could have done the same. Poor Lizzie. She had never hurt anyone in her whole life. How did his father find out? That was a puzzling question. Had someone really seen her with Edward Gibbon? Who could be mean enough to tell father? There was much to be discovered about the whole business.

"I'm going to speak to father," said Will suddenly. He looked across at his mother's face. She had ignored his last remark and simply sat staring into an imaginary void across the room, too shaken by the events of the last hour to do anything else. Will half rose, slid an arm under Lizzie's thighs and hoisted her to his chest with all his young strength. Then he laid her on the bed and covered her with a blanket. He kissed her tear-stained cheek and tasted the salt of sorrow. Her eyes were closed beneath red, swollen lids. She seemed to be asleep. Then Will left the room and climbed resolutely up the stairs to where his father had at last succeeded in raising the lighthouse fire to the required level.

The night was clear and fine. The moon shone full and low across a silver sea and William's lighthouse cast its brilliance in poor competition to its heavenly counterpart.

"Father, Lizzie is sorry for what she has done. Please forgive her."

"It is too late, son. You can't turn back the time. The seed is sown and can't be poisoned."

"What do you mean, it's too late? It's never too late to forgive, father. Lizzie is my sister and I love her dearly. Surely you can forget her one and only mistake?"

"You don't understand, son," said his father tersely and obviously still very upset, still very angry.

"I do understand - I understand that you are too mean to forgive Lizzie. All that you think about is yourself and what people think..."

"Mind your language, son."

"I want us to be happy again and not to argue like this for ever. You can't throw her out of the house for a careless moment of passion. It was her one and only error in all those years. Who cares what people think - who gives a damn what people say. The only thing that matters is our family and that we all love each other."

"I care what people say. We have always been able to hold our heads high in this community and now we'll be the laughing stock."

"So what! What if they laugh? What if they talk amongst themselves? Does that justify treating your own daughter this way?

His father had had enough cheek and uncharacteristically raised his had to strike Will.

"Get downstairs and to bed before I give you what for."

"No! I won't let you treat us like this. I've had enough."

Will had felt his own outrage growing with every word. The last action by his father was enough to make him dash from the lantern room, down the stairs and out into the open. His exit disturbed a host of buzzing, black blowflies that were enjoying his abandoned mackerel. Then, not knowing where he was going or what he was doing, Will set off running along the cliffs until his breath was short and he had to slow down to a walking pace. But he did not stop. He walked and walked. The world around him had ceased to exist, except for the hard ground that reverberated up through his bones as he trod his path with leaden feet. His mind could think only of his father's anger, his mother's anguish, poor Lizzie's tear-soaked skin and his own misery. He felt no cold, noticed no dampness around his feet as he strode through the dew-laden cliff top grass. He simply walked on into the night, never once considering turning back for home. Why should he? There was no home - just misery.

After an hour, he realised that he was almost into Dover. He had walked about three miles and was descending the steep hill by the castle and down into the town. Although it was still early evening there were few signs of life as he entered the first street - just the occasional dog lurking in the shadows or a few flickering lights behind the windows. Soon he was quite close to the harbour and he saw the fishing boats in their rows against the quayside, the rhythm of the waves rocking them gently.

"'Allo, young sir, lookin' fer a good time are ye?"

"Will was startled and swung around to see a middle-aged woman smiling evilly at him from a doorway. Facially, the woman might have been attractive twenty years ago, but the passage of men through her life showed in her bedraggled greying hair and drawn features. Quite apart from any verbal intimation, her rather large and, no doubt, pliable bust left William in no doubt as to her ulterior motive in conversing with him.

"Yer a fine lookin' young fella, sir. Come along wi' me an' 'ave a bit o' fun, eh?"

Will did not reply but turned again and broke into a trot to get away from the old hag.

"A whore... your sister's a common whore..." The words of his father rang in his ears and William felt sick. How could his father compare dear Lizzie to the foul creature he had just seen? Will wondered how any woman ever got into such a situation. Was she mentally sick? Or perhaps she had been widowed at an early age, left without family or friends and forced to make a living the best way she could. If Lizzie were turned out onto the streets, would she become one of these prostitutes, forced into sexual slavery by the need to survive? His stomach was churning out of control. He stopped and vomited against a wall. He felt terrible. He'd eaten nothing for six or seven hours and his stomach was now empty. He looked around and saw what looked like a tavern at some distance along the road by the harbour. There was a good amount of light from the full moon and he could detect considerable activity. All he could think about was food. As he approached the entrance to the tavern, a nautical-looking fellow came over to speak to him.

"Here's a fine looking gentleman. Step right this way young man and have a drink." He patted Will on the back and seemed extremely pleased to see him almost as if he had been a long lost friend. Will's hunger was so overwhelming that he had no hesitation in walking straight into the tavern. In so doing he failed to notice the large bill posted outside that advertised the true nature of the tavern on this occasion.

There was considerable hullabaloo inside the tavern with more people than Will had seen in the past month. He was taken aback for a moment until his newfound friend grasped him by the arm and pulled him through the throng of people to where a uniformed man sat at a table.

"Give the fellow a drink, Marker," said the man with a voice of authority. Then Will realised that he had no money.

"I have no money, sir, I can't pay you."

"Pay me? You don't have to pay me for a drink, lad. What's it to be?"

"Actually, sir, I'd be very grateful for some bread or soup. I've not eaten for hours."

"Will did not have to try hard to convince the officer. He looked as bad as he felt.

"You heard the man. Marker, off you goes then. Now young fellow, sit down here." He indicated a stool alongside the table and Will sat on it eager to listen.

"How would you like to make a fortune in gold, be a hero, visit parts of the world you never even dreamed about, and do your country a great service besides?"

"I don't think there's a man in this room that would not," replied Will, "but I would be very wary of a man who promised so much to a perfect stranger. I presume, from your words and your uniform, you are the Press officer?"

"I see I'm talking to a sharp, quick-witted lad. Welcome to the Rondy. You're quite correct, but I ask you not to dismiss my words as those of a fool. There are many in the ranks of the Service who have found it possible to become rich. The war with France promises many prizes for the brave seaman. I am recruiting brave men to join His Majesty's Navy. Your country is in need of young men like you to save us from the French invasion."

"Marker came back, pushing his way through the crowd. In his hands were a plate of bread and a tankard of ale. He placed them in front of Will and the boy began to devour the bread as though it were to be his last.

"My name is Lieutenant Ivey. What's yours?"

"William Knott," mumbled Will as best he could with a mouthful of bread.

"And how old are you, William?"

"Seventeen, sir," Will lied.

"Well then, let us get down to business. Have you been to sea before?"

"Only to fish from a small boat."

"That makes you a landsman then, but there is a three pound bounty, as well as your lawful shilling, if you decide to sign here."

Will was still hungrily attacking his free supper and his mouth was too full to say much. Ivey brandished the roll of parchment that had been resting on the table and on which were written many other names of volunteers. Presumably the bounties were larger for experienced seamen, but three pounds was a handsome sum. He had never seen so much money before, and as for joining up - well it couldn't be that bad. He didn't want to go home anyway... not tonight. He didn't feel part of a family any more. Here was food, warmth and good company. Why should he return to the upset and ill will at the lighthouse? After all, if his father had wanted him back, wouldn't he have chased after him? It didn't occur to Will that he'd left his dear Lizzie undefended, and, for that reason alone, he should go home. The promise of seeing the world, not to mention the possibility of wealth, appealed to him.

Just then, Marker, who had disappeared again after bringing Will his supper, suddenly reappeared with another two more volunteers for the Lieutenant's parchment, two more disillusioned young landsmen, eager for adventure, travel and instant wealth.

"Thank you, Marker... oh, and Marker, more beer for the lad here, his mug's dry."

The officer despatched his subordinate for more alcohol after Will drained the last malty dregs from his tankard. As he waited for Marker to return, he watched the eagerness with which the two newcomers made their marks on the register. They seemed to have no doubts about their actions. As they did so, Ivey drew a large bag of gold pieces from his pocket and paid the men their bounties. Then he ordered more beer to keep them happy while they waited to be taken to the tender.

Marker returned with a tray of ale and distributed a tankard to each man.

"Well, lad, have you made up your mind yet?" asked Ivey as Will sat back watching all the activity.

"Yes, sir, I have," said Will, the ale beginning to give him a feeling of contentment and confidence. "I'll sign your paper, though I am unable to write my name."

"That is of no consequence, young fellow. Simply put your mark here where I have written your name - William Knott you said, didn't you?" He thrust the paper in front of Will and indicated the place where Will was to sign. William took a quill and made an ill-disciplined mark on the paper.

"That's right, and now I believe I owe you three pounds and one shilling." The silver shilling was still the legally binding contract of entry into the Navy, although in addition the three golden coins had been offered recently to tempt more men into the Service. The coins felt cold and hard in William's hand as he clutched more wealth than he had ever possessed in his life. Quickly he put them into a small pocket in his breeches for safety.

"Right lad, Marker will take you off to the fleet tender at closing time, but until then have some more beer and enjoy yourself. You are about to start a new life. Have yourself a celebration."

"…About to start a new life…" The words suddenly seemed a bit serious and a fleeting doubt entered Will's mind that he had made a mistake, but the other fellows who had signed up had soon pulled him into their company, thrust more beer into his mind and Will allowed the soothing liquid to dispel his worries, to eradicate the family feud from his thoughts, so that all that remained was a pleasant, warm, confident feeling. Beer was a very potent substance in more ways than one and the Navy was using it to its best advantage. Unfortunately, Will would have to wait to discover the truth.

The rest of the evening passed quickly for the Navy's newest recruit. His stomach felt much better for the food, and the alcohol began to take effect on an unhardened consciousness. When it was time to leave for the fleet tender Will had hardly a care in the world. He had left the troubles of the lighthouse far behind him.

It was not far to the tender. That was a good thing, for Marker was having trouble with some of the others who had taken the celebrations a little too seriously. The *Medway Lady* was a small vessel of about a hundred tons used for transporting new recruits to the Navy. Though Will did not know it, this time the men were to be taken to the naval dockyard at Chatham where they would join ships sailing to meet Admiral Sir Edward Hawke's fleet at Plymouth. As Will boarded the vessel he could never have imagined the experiences that were in store for him.

Several lanterns lit the gangway as the ragged band staggered past the quartermaster. Once aboard, they were led forward to a large hold where they were impolitely told to "get below." Will began to have second thoughts about his decision. Access to the hold was by means of a rope ladder, a fiendish device at the best of times, but Will's co-ordination had been upset by alcohol and he found it almost impossible to find a footing. His hands grew tired of supporting his weight and he fell headlong into the dark and very unpleasant smelling hole. He was rather more fortunate than some of the other fellows in his group who were pushed into the hold without any ceremony whatsoever. Men were piling into the hold on top of one another like sacks of coal pitched into a coalhole. Some were hurt as they hit the deck. Others were injured as their shipmates were pitched on top of them. All were so inebriated that they knew little of it, except to groan with pain or wretch with booze, and tumble away from the danger zone into the background. It was totally dark and Will had to grope his way amongst many stinking and apparently sleeping bodies before he could find space on the deck to lie down. He was filled with consternation as he realised that he might have made a mistake in joining the Navy, but the money in his pocket reassured him, and the beer, which addled his brain, told him to sleep. He winced as several other drunkards stepped on him in their efforts to find sleeping space and he was frequently kicked by his neighbour who was obviously having a bad dream. Will kicked him in return and tried to make more room on the other side by pushing the unconscious body away from him. Having partially succeeded he did his best to relax, but he was constantly aware of the ship rocking... side to side... to and fro...

They were at sea. At last he was a real sailor. A familiar voice spoke to him out of the darkness.

"Well lad, you've made it then, eh?"

He remembered the voice. It was Lieutenant Ivey.

"Where would you like to go then? Trinidad, India... the Horn? You name it and we'll go there."

"What about my job, sir? What am I to do?" asked Will.

"How would you like to navigate, lad? I'll teach you. I'll show you how to take bearings, how to read charts. We'll sail the seven seas together. How's that? I can't make a better offer can I?"

Will could not believe his ears. It was too good to be true. Suddenly he felt a cool breeze in his hair. It was light and they were cruising off the coast somewhere.

"I'd love to learn navigation, sir. Please teach me."

"Just one thing, lad. If you want to be an apprentice navigator there's a small fee... three pounds and one shilling. I know you've got it in your pocket."

The officer came towards Will and thrust his hand into Will's breeches.

"Come on, now, pay up. It's cheap at the price."

"I've changed my mind," said Will, pushing the hand away. "I don't want to navigate."

"We'll soon see about that. Hand over the money or I'll have you clapped in irons and flogged around the fleet."

The hand was back in his pocket. He fought it. His money... he must save his money. Then his arms were grasped firmly by an unseen force and his money was gone... he was being pushed towards the ship side... over... they pushed him over... wetness... swimming... drowning...

Thin light filtered through a grating in the roof as Will's eyelids opened. He was still on board the tender and lying amidst many other male bodies, all of which seemed to be asleep. His breeches were wet. He had wet himself. Will felt ashamed and uncomfortable. So he had had a dream... that beer... what a fool he had been to drink so much. He felt for his money. Gone. That, at least, had been real. He had been robbed when he was least able to defend himself. He smiled grimly as he realised the clever plan executed by those in control. Sign up a lot of gullible youths, offer them money, get them drunk and rob them blind later when they can do nothing about it. Will choked and realised that the stench was dreadful. Obviously he was not the only one who had disgraced himself. He was so uncomfortable he wanted to scream, but there was nothing he could do. He had no other clothes to change into. He might as well be in prison, yet he'd done nothing wrong. He remembered the previous night. He had been paid good money to join the Navy, along with many others far keener than he. Why was he being treated like this? Surely life in His Majesty's Navy could not be worse than that of a convict? By now his eyes had adjusted to the low light level. He could see the rope ladder hanging down from the hatch over which the grating had been placed. He struggled to get up, cursed his wet, clammy breeches and picked his way between the sleeping bodies to the foot of the ladder. The dreadful smell was beginning to turn his stomach again and he just wanted to get out as quickly as possible.

With extreme difficulty he managed to pull himself up the ladder to the level of the grating and pushed it with what little leverage he could summon. It did not move. He put his hands through the holes and his shoulder underneath it, but it was held fast.

"Whadaya want?"

A gruff voice rasped out from above.

"Why are we locked in here like this?"

"Yer in the Navy now ye scurvy landlubber. Git back down that bleedin' ladder an' stop complainin' ye mutinous dog."

"But I've been robbed," complained Will bitterly. "Someone has stolen my bounty money."

"Didun you 'ear wot I say you son of a 'ore... now git away from that 'atch."

At the end of the sentence a mouthful of vile dissolved tobacco was squirted from the speaker's lips through the grating into Will's face. So great was Will's revulsion that he lost his hold on the ladder and fell into the heap of human flesh below. Shouts filled the air as the owners of the bodies were crushed beneath his weight. Will could hold his stomach no longer. He vomited... from the very bottom of his stomach he retched over several unfortunate shipmates. Other bodies stirred in the hold and pandemonium erupted. Voices protested that they had been robbed. Punches were thrown, eyes were blacked, but the beery hangovers put paid to any enthusiasm for pugilism and soon the sore heads laid down once more and slept off their pain. The *Medway Lady* would not make land until she reached Chatham. Will's baptism into the Navy had begun.

7 JOHN JENNINGS

It had been a very long night. Lighthouse keepers were not often bothered by the length of the dark hours, but William Knott had found every minute of his last vigil a trial. First his family life had been shattered by the dishonourable deeds of his daughter and now his son had run off into the night. His wife and remaining children had cried themselves to sleep, whilst he had fulfilled his duty and tended the fire of the lighthouse as usual. Hour after hour, William had stared into the darkness and expected to see young Will emerge from the void. He had stared as if some yet undeveloped mental power could draw his son home. He had stared as if he could communicate with his son that he would forgive Lizzie and continue to love his family as he had done in the past. But his son did not appear. When young Will had run away from him, his paternal pride had forbidden him to chase after the lad. He felt that Will must return, after all, where could he go? He had gone off in the direction of Dover, but William couldn't think of anyone they knew well enough to give Will a bed for the night.

During the early hours of the watch he had been very angry. His thoughts were full of blame for the children. Then, as the night passed, his anger had turned to remorse as he remembered the anxiety in the faces of his family. Only then did the blame pass to him. He had never been so angry and had never thought he could be. Gradually he felt ashamed. His mind turned towards the real culprit. The Jennings family always seemed the source of trouble for him. First it had been that business, years ago, over the smuggling. William Jennings had never forgiven him for the way he had been humiliated, and now his son, John Jennings, had been spying on Lizzie. Surely it must be this wretch who was really to blame. So, even as the first strains of morning filtered through the grey shrouds of cumulus, William still awaited his son's arrival. The lad must be very hungry indeed for William recalled that he'd had nothing to eat since midday on the preceding day. His stomach, if not his pride, must drive him home soon.

William extinguished the fire and descended the tower to the cottage below. His wife was up and about her normal routine, but her appearance disturbed William. He could see that she hadn't changed a single item of clothing since yesterday morning and concluded that she must have spent the night sleeping fitfully in her favourite chair. He knew Elizabeth too well. She could not have gone to bed having been so upset. Her eyes bore witness to this theory for they looked red, swollen and very tired. Her uncombed hair slopped untidily across her cheeks, its greyness suddenly making her look much older. She was obviously not at all inclined to commence a conversation, for instead of greeting him with a kiss, as was normal, she ignored him and hunched herself over a pot of oats to avoid eye-to-eye contact.

There was no sign of the younger children, which was also unusual. Mary, William and Elizabeth's second daughter, was often Lizzie's apprentice around the cottage and both girls would have been assisting in the kitchen. The boys, Henry, aged ten, and Joseph, nine, were invariably getting in the way and chattering incessantly as the women did their best to feed all the hungry mouths. This morning it was silent. Either the traumas of the previous night had caused them to oversleep or they were diplomatically staying out of the way until they had ascertained that the mood of the household was calmer.

"Will's not back," said William. No answer. Elizabeth continued to stir the glutinous steaming mass as if she were stone deaf. She realised that she had made her usual quantity of porridge without thinking that Will was not there to eat it, but she would keep it warm for him. He would be hungry now. William did not take offence at Elizabeth's continued silence. He did not feel like talking either, but someone had to make the first move. Then after a further minute or two of silence, Elizabeth suddenly reached for a bowl, ladled two spoons full of porridge into it, and laid it on the table for William to eat. She stole a quick glance at him to try to gauge her husband's mood more accurately, but when he looked back at her she instantly diverted her gaze back to her cooking.

"He'll be back shortly," said William again, trying hard to break the deadlock, but his effort was again ignored. He began half-heartedly to eat his breakfast. It was not long before the sound of spoon on bowl succeeded in convincing three hungry children that lying in bed was no longer the order of the day, but there was still no sign of Lizzie. Elizabeth, having served her younger children with food, then filled a fourth bowl and made steps toward the door of the room where Lizzie lay. William knew where she was going and instantly dropped his spoon, jumped up and flung himself towards his wife. Elizabeth feared another outburst of retribution and broke the silence.

"The poor girl has suffered enough, William. Let me take her this…"

She need not have worried. William laid a hand comfortingly on her shoulder and reached for the steaming bowl.

"Let me take it," he said. "I am responsible for all this. I must repair the damage I've done… if it's not too late."

In the gloom of the bedroom, he struggled at first to see Lizzie's face, but as his eyes grew accustomed to the dimness he discerned the pathetic form of his daughter, motionless and face to the wall. He placed the bowl on the cold stone floor and crouched to put his arms under Lizzie's shoulders. As he turned her over he realised that tears were blurring his sight and dripping down onto his daughter's head. His heart was suddenly filled with grief for the grave, spiritual injuries he had caused this young girl. Lizzie was slow to awaken. As her father roused her from unconsciousness, her nightmares did not dissipate but simply blended into the new living nightmare that was to be her life from now on. Her painfully swollen eyes finally opened and gazed into the face of the father she thought had disowned her for ever. Suddenly she could see his eyes too were filled with tears and she knew he had forgiven her. They embraced so tightly that Lizzie felt she would suffocate, but somehow it didn't matter. Her father was apologising without words, for there was no need to speak to make his feelings known. She adored him and instantly forgave him, though her eyes were terribly sore and her soul ached.

"I'm sorry father," she said, bursting into tears again and kissing his face. They embraced for several more minutes until William remembered the bowl of not so hot porridge and, pulling himself from his daughter's grasp, gave her the food.

By the time that the early May sunshine had chased the cumulus away and evaporated the last drop of dew from the cliff tops, William had completed his routine chores at the lighthouse. His family had forgiven him for his tirade and he left the lighthouse walking briskly and purposefully towards St. Margaret's. He would find young Jennings, the cause of all his family sorrow. Yesterday it hadn't occurred to him that the fellow was nothing more than a treacherous swine who deserved a punch in the mouth. William had been too upset by what Jennings had told him. His first reaction had been to punish Lizzie, but in the light of a new day and with the benefit of retrospect, he decided to pay Jennings a return compliment. His dear daughter had suffered enough. William dared not think what had happened to his son. If only he had not reacted so angrily, Will would still be with him.

He crossed a field that formed a small part of Wanstone farm and joined a track that led past Reach Court and into the village. He knew that Jennings often worked in the churchyard and William wasted no time in seeking out the villain there. He was lucky. The youngster was stretched out on his back on a gently sloping sward between two gravestones, fast asleep. The revitalising sunshine would have tempted anyone to soak up its warmth, given the time to do so. Jennings was obviously making the time. A mud-covered spade lay in the grass beside him. A few yards away a pile of turf and a small area of disturbed topsoil showed where a grave might eventually be if Jennings ever got around to digging it. William stood over the slumbering youth and gazed at the peaceful face below. He found it difficult to reconcile the look of innocence with the vile act Jennings had committed the day before. The sleeper awoke instantly as William's boot contacted Jennings' right kidney. Jennings rolled over onto his side and brought his knees up to his chest with a scream of pain. Then, half crouching as the throbbing around his middle slowly subsided, he staggered to his feet.

"I should have done that yesterday, you evil little swine." William was in no mood for trifles. Jennings had substituted shock, pain and surprise with anger and, remembering the spade, snatched it for his own offence. He swung the tool at William's left side, but the move was predictable and William was able to grasp the shaft. With superior strength, he wrenched it from Jennings' grasp and without a break in the movement, hurled it behind him. Meanwhile, Jennings had decided that he did not fancy his chances against the well-built lighthouse keeper. He bolted for the lych gate, but William was able to cut him off amongst the gravestones. He caught Jennings and both fell to the ground. For about a minute they wrestled and grunted in deadlock, each struggling to obtain a controlling grip on the other. Suddenly William felt Jennings' knee come up sharply between his legs. The blow was incapacitating and he knew that he had lost his opponent.

Jennings scrambled up from the grass and ran towards the gate, but was stopped short by a man far bigger and stronger than the man he had just fought. He realised that in the tussle on the ground he had not noticed a group of men encircling them. Another man was soon on hand to ensure that there was no chance of Jennings' escape. William was still recovering in the grass from his misfortune when he looked up and saw four large sailors bearing down on him. To his right he could see Jennings remonstrating with his captors. Furthermore, on the other side of the lych gate, a man in the uniform of a naval officer had just dismounted from his horse, tied it to the gate, and entered the graveyard where William and Jennings had been so neatly trapped.

"The Press gang," uttered William in surprise.

"Right first time," came the reply.

Jennings was having none of it. No-one was going to deprive him of his freedom. Taking the first sailor by surprise, he wrenched a hand free and landed his fist firmly on the nose of the second sailor who instantly let go of Jennings and reeled backwards. Before Jennings was able to take advantage of his sudden release, two more seamen, who were in no mood for arguments, caught him. A solid fist was plunged into his soft abdomen with a sickening thud, followed by another to the jaw that removed Jennings front teeth. The two debilitating blows were quite sufficient to eliminate the youth's resistance and he was rapidly ushered out of the churchyard semi-conscious and with his feet only occasionally touching the ground. Once outside he was poured into a waiting cart where another two men stood guard over John Davys and George Writtle, who had also been conscripted.

By this time the remaining men had closed in on William. He was surely in trouble unless he acted quickly.

"You can't take me," he mumbled uselessly.

"That's what they all say."

"No, really, I have an important job, I swear."

"Oh, yes, and what might that be? Don't tell me... let me guess. You're an Admiral of the Blue? No? Well, what about Chancellor of England... or perhaps you're the Archbishop of Canterbury?" The man with the horse was obviously not impressed by William's plea. The sailors, however, enjoyed their officer's cynicism and smiled to each other. William was desperate. How could he persuade these men of his importance in the lighthouse? How could he prevent them from carting him away to sea?

By pure chance, it was then that the Reverend Marsh turned the corner of the church.

"Reverend Marsh, help me," shouted William as the sailors began to march him too towards the lych gate. The vicar hurried over to where the men were holding William in close custody.

"Vicar, tell the Press gang officer that he must not take me, please."

"You still haven't given me a good reason," grumbled the officer, annoyed at all the time wasting.

"The gentleman is quite correct, sir," proclaimed Reverend Marsh without hesitation. "I can vouch for this man. He is William Knott, keeper of the South Foreland upper lighthouse that you must have seen with confidence from your ships

102

more than once, for he keeps it as well as any keeper should. If you take him with you now, perhaps many of your friends lives will be lost until a new keeper is found."

The mood of the officer changed perceptibly.

"Is this so?" He rather foolishly asked William, for the latter would hardly have denied it if it were untrue.

"I would have told you myself in another few seconds, though I doubt that you would have believed me," replied William. The officer paused in thought for a moment. "You're right. I would not have believed you but for the word of a man of the cloth here. Release him. We do not take lighthouse keepers. Good day, gentlemen."

Without wasting any more time, he turned and walked back to his horse. His men left the churchyard and joined the cart where the others were still captive. Reverend Marsh hurried along behind them so that he could sympathise with the trapped men. He would probably visit their families later.

The officer untied his horse, mounted and was about to ride off when he seemed to have second thoughts and restrained his horse. "By the way, I signed up a lad by the name of William Knott last night. Any relation of yours is he?" Without waiting for a reply, he twitched his spurs and was gone up the road.

8 SAMUEL GRAVES - 1

Chatham dockyard could not have been busier. Its wharves were filled with sailors and storemen, carrying boxes, pushing barrows, pulling carts, struggling with kit bags. Men sweated. They shouted and swore. Some tripped over ropes or other unseen hazards. One or two relieved themselves into the Medway. Ships must sail. Wars could not wait.

Secure alongside the stone wharf lay HMS *Duke*, HMS *Swiftsure* and HMS *Intrepid*. Ships-of-the-line and proud, they waited patiently for their companies to complete their sailing preparations. Close by in the single dock a new sister ship would soon be born. Another mighty ship had been laid down and someday would join them. She would be bigger than any of them: more powerful, more beautiful, more deadly. She would be christened Victory.

Unlike his ship, Captain Samuel Graves was waiting impatiently on board the *Duke*. He was an old man and his time was running out. He could not wait forever. The Graves family were naval and had always been. Samuel's brother, Thomas, had risen to the rank of Rear Admiral in 1747, having first taken command of the *Dulwich* in 1713. Samuel's nephew was presently in command of the frigate *Antelope*, whilst he himself had commanded *Barfleur*, *Scorpion* and *Venus*, as well as his present ship. HMS *Duke* was a first-rate ship-of-the-line of ninety guns, but she had seen hardly any action in the first three years of the war. Graves' orders were to sail to Plymouth to join Admiral Hawke's fleet, which had been assembled in response to a French invasion threat. Graves was sure a major battle was imminent. It had taken a week to store ship, however, and he was becoming restless.

"*Medway Lady* a comin', sir."

"Very good. Stand by to receive pressed men, Mister Pethen."

"Aye aye, sir."

The *Medway Lady* was one of the last things detaining Captain Graves. Hawke's fleet needed men and the arrival of the *Medway Lady* was to provide the last part of the contribution from Kent. During the journey to Plymouth, *Duke* was to be a ship both for training and transport.

The small tender eased slowly up to the towering side of the *Duke*. Lines were heaved and made secure. Graves watched as her holds were opened. A hundred or so filthy, scruffy human beings began to emerge from within. They seemed to be unaware of where they were, but were obviously glad to be in the fresh air at last. They were made to scramble up five rope ladders which had been let down from the main deck. This proved to be a slow process for many of the men had been considerably weakened by their recent experiences. Once aboard the *Duke* they were mustered in a long line for registration by the bosun. Samuel Graves was rather happier. They would soon be at sea.

The journey to Chatham had seemed interminable to Will, for conditions on board the wretched boat were so bad that he thought he would never escape the embrace of the *Medway Whore* as he had re-christened her. Whilst some of the men had been allowed out of the hold occasionally, it was only to put them to work on another part of the vessel. The passage had been rough and many of the men who had never been to sea in their lives had been vilely sick. The filth and stench were not cleaned up and the fifteen-year-old lad had found it so abhorrent at first that he had cried to himself on many occasions. As the time went on, however, he found that he was almost getting used to the stench of a hundred caged and noxious human animals. Worse even than the smell was the food. The water was mud-brown, evil smelling and nauseating to drink. The only solid food available was biscuit that was alive with white, wriggling weevils. Although he had refused to eat initially, it was inevitable that he would be forced to try to digest some of the vile material.

During the three days in which he had been imprisoned, the strong-willed, clean and decent young lad had been reduced to a state of human existence lower than any farm animal. It was thus a dirty, untidy and malodorous young man who arrived alongside the immaculate *Duke* as Captain Graves paced his quarterdeck.

Will found the climb up the rope ladder to be almost more than he could manage. He was weak and tired through lack of food and sleep, and just managed to make it to the top, spurred on by the realisation that he was finally escaping from the *Medway Lady*. Surely, life on board a ship, as big, and as beautiful as this, could not be as bad?

Once at the top of the rope ladder, a firm pair of hands bundled him unceremoniously over the side and onto the spotlessly clean wooden planking of the main deck. There he joined the queue which was registering with the bosun under the sharp eyes of his mate who continuously brandished (and sometimes wielded) a fierce looking cane which Will would soon discover was called a rattan.

After Will had given his name he was allocated a station by the bosun and, together with several others at the same station, he was led off by a regular seaman. Just as he was passing the point where other poor devils were being brought on board, he suddenly found himself staring into the familiar, but fist-damaged, face of John Jennings. Will had no reason to bear the youth any malice, but he saw Jennings' eyes immediately fill with hatred. Dried blood and vomit were caked down the front of Jennings' clothes and Will noticed that his lips and mouth were swollen and purple with bruising. It was only when Jennings opened his mouth to curse Will that he saw that Jennings had lost his front teeth. Neither had known of the other's presence on board the *Medway Lady*, a fact that Will found surprising at first, yet when he considered further, it had been dark and amongst nearly a hundred men they had not noticed each other.

The Jennings family had never been friends of the Knotts. Will's father had always told his family that the Jennings were scoundrels, but Will had not had much to do with them and had been unable to form his own opinion. Will did not know that it had been John Jennings who had spied so cruelly on Lizzie, or of the events that had caused Jennings to be on board the *Medway Lady*. Consequently, he was unprepared for the demonstration of malice towards him.

"Gunna kill thee, Knott bastard."

Jennings looked menacing and was about to strike Will when one of the regular seamen who was engaged in ushering the conscripts on board restrained his arm and pulled Jennings back from a confrontation.

"Now then, young fella, tha won't git far 'board this ship actin' like that. Tha 'll be thrashed afore the week's out."

Jennings ignored the sound advice. His right foot lashed up towards Will's groin. Will tried to turn away but caught the force of his kick on his thigh. Jennings was smothered by the grip of the seaman already holding him and was unable to do any further violence to Will, but the bosun's mate had witnessed the disturbance and was on the scene in a flash. His rattan whistled through the air and fell heavily and painfully on Jennings' legs. He crumpled towards the deck in severe pain, despite the hold of his captor.

"Tha' 'll larn ye. Na git below, ye mutinous scum."

"What is going on down there, Mister Blomer?"

Captain Graves had noticed the skirmish from his lofty perch.

"One o' the new 'uns givin' trouble, sir. 'T is naught us can't 'andle," replied the mate as order was rapidly restored to the registration procedure. Will was led below to his station.

It took a little more than an hour to complete the induction of the new men and Captain Graves was confident of sailing with the next high tide. The *Duke* had been successfully stored at last and, now that she was manned too, they could soon be under way to Plymouth where they would lose many of these troublesome pressed men to the other ships of Hawke's fleet. Graves would be glad to see them go.

9 JOSIAS JESSOP

"Another inch and a quarter towards your left hand... that's it. Fix it there please, Josias."

The test was a crucial one for John Smeaton. He was about to make a measurement that would confirm or deny the craftsmanship of his workmen, as well as his own success as the supervising engineer of the New Eddystone Lighthouse. The measurement in question involved the hanging of a plumb line from the very centre of the topmost manhole in the floor of what was to be the lantern room, down through the centre of the tower to the solid base. There it would be matched with a mark already carefully measured out by Smeaton as at the very centre. A small nail had been hammered into the stone at that point. The distance of the plumb bob from the nail would then measure just how far the new tower deviated from the vertical. So, as Smeaton carefully held the measure in exactly the correct position at the top of the uncapped tower, his colleague, Josias Jessop, was fixing the plumb line at the central point by a neat reef knot around the wooden support.

It was the sixteenth day of August. After only forty-four days of the working season of 1759, which had begun on the 5th July, the stone part of the tower had been completed. Only the lantern and balcony rails were yet to be erected and it was now a race against the weather to complete the lighthouse before the season deteriorated. Smeaton was hoping to exhibit a light for the first time during October, but there was still a lot to be done before he would be able to confirm his plan with Trinity House.

The plumb line was in position.

"If you would stay here, Josias, and keep your eye on the line, I will go below and check the deviation."

Smeaton looked into the rugged Cornishman's dark eyes and received an approving nod. As Smeaton began to make his way carefully down the ladders, Jessop relaxed on the cold, hard, ice-smooth finish of the lantern room floor to watch his knot. The Eddystone Lighthouse had been Jessop's life for over twenty years now, and only Smeaton himself could have been prouder than Jessop to see the new Phoenix rise from the ashes of Rudyerd's tower.

Born into a very ordinary working family, Jessop had been gifted in handicraft. At the age of twelve he had become apprenticed as a shipwright in the Dockyard at Devonport and had rapidly proven his ability by rising to the level of foreman of shipwrights at the early age of twenty-nine. Soon afterwards he had been recommended to the proprietors of the Eddystone Lighthouse as a suitable man to supervise the maintenance of Rudyerd's tower and that had been his job until the fateful fire of 1755. Since then, he had been Smeaton's deputy, working harder than ever before on the reconstruction.

He remembered clearly the first day that he had met Smeaton. After twenty years of living with the Eddystone and its lighthouse, Jessop had been very suspicious about the appointment of an instrument-making Yorkshireman to build a new tower. How could such a man have any idea of the sort of problem he would face? Certainly, he could have no notion of the fickleness of the sea in the region of the reef and Jessop was quite convinced that Smeaton was going to fail. He'd had no experience of any type of building construction, let alone the very specialised field of lighthouses, and the fellow had never even been to Devon before. There was no doubt that Jessop had been quite jealous of Smeaton's position and would be hard to convince of his ability. That first meeting had been very cool, but Jessop had been forced to admit that he liked Smeaton's personality. The young thirty-year-old had a persuasive yet polite manner and was openly meticulous in his methods. Gradually he had drawn on Jessop's wealth of knowledge and experience without his knowing it and it was only in retrospect that Jessop had realised just how much he had been talking and how precisely Smeaton had been taking notes. He remembered too how Smeaton had first told him that the tower was to be of stone. He had been most surprised, for the previous tower had been so successful that he'd naturally assumed the same material would be used. Foolishly he'd asked Smeaton how they were going to fit the timbers to the outside of the tower. He soon realised it had been a ridiculous question as Smeaton gently explained there were to be none. Now, having finished the tower, it was patently obvious how much better was a stone tower than a wooden one. After all, the essence of a brilliant idea is that it is so simple that no-one else has thought of it. Jessop was now quite convinced that the tower that had taken just over three years to build was the finest construction of its kind in the world and would last for ever.

Momentarily, Jessop's eyes tired from watching the stationary knot and he bent his balding grey head forward to see that Smeaton had carefully made his way down to the next level and was still descending. He sat back on his heels and absorbed the cool breeze as remained on his perch, a bare platform some seventy feet above the waves. The tower was quiet for the men had taken a well-earned meal break on board the *Neptune Buss* while Smeaton carried out his critical measurement unimpeded. The weather was perfect. The sky was blue and cloudless, the sea azure and crystalline. He could see the *Neptune Buss* quite clearly as she rode at anchor a quarter of a mile from the reef. Much farther away he could see the coast of the mainland with perfect clarity from the Prawle to the Lizard, a distance that occupied about a third of the horizon.

The *Neptune Buss*, if she could have talked, would have had many a tale to tell. An eighty-ton herring boats at the end of her useful life, she was due for scrap, but had been bought by the proprietors of the Eddystone lighthouse for conversion and use as a floating light whilst the new tower was being built, an eminently sensible idea to all concerned – except to Trinity House. At first agreeing the suggestion and allowing Mr Weston to spend a considerable sum of money converting the *Buss*, the wise Brethren later reversed their decision and said that they would provide their own floating light. Much ill-feeling was generated and considerable delay in setting up the light resulted. Meanwhile, however, Smeaton had deemed the *Neptune Buss* to be ideal for a floating hotel and workshop for his craftsmen. By accommodating them so near to the reef, much time would be saved by not having to make the long journey from the mainland and back each day. The men would travel from the *Buss* to the reef in a yawl, whilst a shuttle of smaller craft would ply night and day between Plymouth, the sloop and the rocks. By this means, blunted tools could be replaced, provisions and relief crews ferried out, besides the vital supplies of building materials and the beautifully dovetailed granite blocks themselves.

The *Buss* was an appalling ship to navigate and mooring it to its two forty fathom chains, each weighing two and a half tons, had scared the experienced seamen who were to carry out the task. However, Smeaton was an expert with pulleys and had designed a block and tackle especially for the task. Everything went smoothly and at the end of the day Jessop had watched amazed as hardened sea dogs had applauded the landlubber in accomplishing a task they had deemed impossible. From that time onwards the *Neptune Buss* had been loved like a favourite woman as the men, exhausted after a gruelling session on the reef, sought relief within her comforting embrace. She had also been hated with the fierceness of a man who would gladly murder his worst enemy for she was regularly transformed into a pitching, sodden hell as she rode out the storms at the Eddystone. Stonemasons were not used to the vicious motion of her bowels. On many occasions men would gladly have ended their lives rather than suffer a minute more of the debilitating sickness of the sea. Even Jessop, who had a good pair of sea legs, found a rough night on board the *Buss* to be an appointment in hell. How he hated her, the bitch.

Jessop cast his eyes inside the tower again. Smeaton was now at the middle level. Josias could honestly say that Smeaton was the most remarkable man he had ever met. There seemed no end to the man's abilities. Intellectually, he was brilliant. His mathematics were astounding and the calculations which Jessop had observed among Smeaton's notes were unintelligible. The whole concept of the tower had been unique. No-one had thought of the possibility of constructing a tower in such a way. In the style of a true idea of genius, many had scoffed at it. Almost all Smeaton's personal tools and measuring equipment he had made himself, a direct result of his early apprenticeship as an instrument maker. The models of his new tower showed an aspect of his skill that Jessop, himself an expert woodworker, admired most. There was little Jessop could even begin to criticise. Everywhere Jessop cast his mind, he found innovation by Smeaton. Oak nails called trenails and marble blocks known as joggles had been used to hold the beautifully dovetailed structure together. Special cranes and lifting gear had been designed to transfer huge blocks weighing a ton and a half each from the moving seaborne platform onto the tower itself. Not least was Smeaton's own formula for cement. His building site was continually drenched in rain and sea spray. This had necessitated the creation of a new form of cement that would stick to moist surfaces and harden without first drying completely. After an exhaustive series of tests, just the right mixture of lime and volcanic ash from the region of Vesuvius seemed to provide all the necessary properties. Another success was under Smeaton's belt.

There had been yet another vexing problem with a simple solution. From the first occasion that work had begun on the reef, all the workmen had been plagued by the attention of the Press gangs. England was at war again and it fell upon the men of the Press to conscript almost every able-bodied man they set eyes on. Each time a group of workers had been seized, or a ship crew taken captive, Smeaton became embroiled in major negotiations to secure their release. He was usually successful, but long delays were sometimes incurred. Smeaton's solution was stunningly simple again. He gained authorization from the Admiralty to mint a special medallion giving the bearer immunity from the Press. His problem was eliminated at a stroke. Jessop was proud to work with such a man.

One more level to go. Jessop made a minute adjustment to the line, which had not moved at all.

Another thing that Jessop admired about Smeaton was that he had never been concerned for his own safety above that of his men. He always personally supervised every operation, no matter how dangerous. Of course, he'd always taken the greatest care never to allow his workers to experience an unreasonable level of danger. He had earned, however, the highest level of admiration from his men by being prepared to do himself anything he asked of them. Inevitably, there'd been accidents. On one occasion, after allowing his concentration to wander, Smeaton had stepped into one of the joggle holes, stumbled and fallen down the sloping construction onto the rock below. Fortunately, he received no more than a dislocated thumb and some bruises. Then, rather than waste a great deal of time by sailing back to Plymouth to find a doctor, he'd closed his eyes and agonizingly relocated his own thumb. The hand had been badly inflamed and quite useless for a month, but not once had he complained or allowed it to interfere with his duties on the reef.

On another occasion, Jessop remembered how Smeaton had been heating metal bars in the upper storeroom and was overcome by fumes from a charcoal fire. Workmen had found him unconscious on the floor and were convinced he was dead, but after half an hour he came around and was soon none the worse for his experience.

Jessop and Smeaton had become firm friends, the sort of friends who instinctively know that the friendship will remain close for the rest of their lives, whatever might happen in the future.

"Josias." He heard a shout from below and quickly saw that Smeaton had finally reached the base level. "Is the line still in position?" Smeaton called.

"Spot on." Jessop suddenly realised he was feeling tense. He knew how disappointed Smeaton would be if the measurement proved to be a good distance out from the centre. There was nothing they could do about it now, he thought. If the tower were much out of the vertical it would just have to stay that way - it could hardly be rebuilt. It had been Smeaton's intention that the stones, once set in place, could never be dismantled. He leaned well forward and saw the figure of Smeaton crouched over the nail some thirty-five feet below. He was carefully measuring the deviation.

"Well, what's it like?" asked Jessop, impatiently.

"Not too good. It's a fair distance out," replied Smeaton, his voice carrying all the flat, droll intonation that was a typical trait of men from Yorkshire. Jessop felt a wave of disappointment sweep over him.

"How far?" Jessop felt he didn't really want to know the bad news, but he asked anyway.

"An eighth."

"An eighth? An eighth of what?" Surely he didn't mean an eighth of a foot, or an eighth of a yard?

"Why, an eighth of an inch, of course," answered Smeaton clinically.

Jessop took a deep breath, sat back on his heels and hit the stone hard with his clenched fist. He said nothing.

10 NEPTUNE

In a small area ten miles due south of Rame Head the steel blue waters of the English Channel were disturbed. It was here that at least a million tons of rusty red gneiss scarred the breathless seascape. The Eddystone reef, like a deadly iceberg, gave but the merest hint of its presence on the surface, but below the tireless waves lurked the real menace. Graveyard to countless ships, it was a constant thorn in the side of Neptune and his desire for total domination. Now the situation had been exacerbated. Neptune had always been supreme champion, but here on the Eddystone reef, the human race had claimed a small victory. The reef had been colonised by man who, until now, had been totally subjugated. A region which had always been under the jurisdiction of the sea, the more so for the impudence with which the reef was despoiling its structured lines, was now lost to a small group of people representing man's seafaring interests.

Old Man Neptune was not amused by the smooth, grey, artificial monolith of mismatching granite that now adorned the reef. He had been involved with periodic skirmishes with the human race. More than a century earlier, he had been forced to vent his wrath on the first puny attempt to erect a building in his kingdom. It had not been difficult to erase from existence the offending article, together with its creator. Unfortunately, it seemed that his adversaries had learned by their mistakes, for the next structure had been much more difficult to deal with. Its smooth boat-like construction resisted some minor attacks, but Neptune had been confident that an ultimate show of force would have dealt it the final blow.

Surprisingly, he had been offered assistance from an old ally. Vulcan was a strange bedfellow at times, but this was, after all, a special case and Neptune had been grateful to be spared the effort. Vulcan was almost (but not quite) as successful with the second incursion as Neptune had been with the first.

Now there was a new monstrosity to deal with and it would cause problems. Man had returned in force with an even bigger and stronger building. Would he never admit defeat? Like its predecessor, it had been designed to deflect Neptune's advances rather than try to absorb them. Even his mightiest efforts merely slithered threateningly up the smooth pinnacle, only to be turned outwards at the last moment by a cunningly placed lip at the top. With the energy of the attack expended, the edifice seemed to smile impudently through the spray as each wave collapsed in fragments around it, but Neptune would not be dismayed. He would change his line of attack. Perhaps a weakness could be found and exploited - a chink in the armour. There was no hurry, for Neptune had all the time in the world. And besides, he had an idea. He had found the Achilles heel and he was going to tread on it...

11 JACOB EVANS

The voyage of HMS *Duke* from Chatham to Plymouth Sound proved to be a busy one for Will. He had been told that when the ship arrived at Plymouth all new recruits would be sent to any of the other ships of the fleet that were undermanned. The *Duke* would therefore not be his home for more than a few days. Will soon realised that this was a good thing for the ship was full to bursting with newly pressed men in addition to its normal complement. Conditions were exceedingly cramped and with so many men on board, Captain Graves realised that they would need plenty to keep them occupied if they were not to cause trouble. Consequently, he ordered a very busy training schedule that made the usual daily routines seem like a holiday. The majority of the new recruits had never been to sea before and there was much to learn, not only about their duties, but also about the countless naval ways and customs which were as alien to them as any foreign language. The period of transit was thus so demanding for young Will that he had little time even to think about home.

It had been obvious to Will from the start that he was about to embark upon a lengthy sojourn in the Navy, whether he liked it or not, and he reconciled himself to making the best of whatever good or bad fortune came his way. He was wise enough to realise that the more work he did the less time he would have to think of home. That way, he might be able to avoid feeling too homesick. In the meantime, he would apply himself wholeheartedly to his training and try to further his new career as much as possible. After all, conditions on board the *Duke* were comfortable compared to the *Medway Lady*. After such a horrendous beginning to his Naval career, his luck could only improve.

As soon as the *Duke* arrived in Plymouth Sound on May 10th, her surplus bodies were mustered on the fo'c'sle. There the bosun read out in hallowed tones the long list of drafts which would influence the lives and perhaps the deaths of everyone of those unlucky enough to have been plucked from the safety of civilian life and thrust into the scenario of an international war.

Some months before, it had been learned by their Lordships at the Admiralty that the French were preparing to mount an invasion of England. As a countermeasure, at Plymouth, Admiral Hawke assembled a large fleet of twenty-three ships-of-the-line. Ports along the south coast had been scoured for every available man to bring the fleet up to strength. HMS *Duke* was the last ship to arrive. Thus, with his fleet fully stored and manned, Hawke planned to sail as soon as possible. His strategy was to blockade the French ports, trapping the enemy fleet within them. Then, at a convenient moment, he would apparently withdraw and encourage the fleet to emerge. It could then be attacked when all the conditions were favourable to the English.

Within two hours of dropping the anchor amid the forest of masts that filled the Sound, Will was sitting in a long boat rowing himself and eleven others towards HMS *Resolution*, for this mighty vessel of 100 guns was to be his new ship. Once on board he was given a hammock space on the orlop deck, a dark and dingy hole close to the bilge and below the waterline. It was clean, however, and, apart from the darkness and a musty smell, which he would soon get used to, it was home. It was here in the close confines of his mess that he met Jacob Evans, a quiet, seasoned old salt with thick grey hair and warm eyes. Each new recruit had been assigned to a regular sailor who would take the new boy in hand. Jacob was to be Will's 'Sea Daddy' and would show him all the duties and routines of the ship. He would also be responsible for training him in seamanship and gun drills.

As a landsman, Will had been given a place on the larboard watchbill and his place of duty was in the afterguard, as well as being part of the crew of number five gun on the middle deck. Apart from the times when he was asleep or eating, his whole world consisted of work. There was no opportunity to survey the outside world, the disposition of the other ships or the proximity of land. He had been incarcerated within a wooden box for an unspecified term. All else had ceased to exist.

On May 15, the fleet weighed anchor and sailed in line ahead out of Plymouth Sound, past the deserted, partly built tower that would soon become the new Eddystone lighthouse. Will saw nothing of it as he polished his gun barrel on the middle deck, at the same time keeping his eye cautiously on the bosun's mate and his rattan. During the weeks that followed, Will worked all the hours his aching body would permit. HMS *Resolution* remained at sea, sailing he knew not where.

The working day was long and arduous. It began at half-past-four in the morning with the piercing bosun's pipe and the uncompromising bawl of the piper. It frequently took a good deal of effort to ensure that 'all hands' actually were 'on deck'. The bosun's mates were liberal in their use of the rattan, three sturdy canes bound tightly together. Swiftly wielded, this caused a severe stinging sensation for the rest of the day and often drew blood. The mates needed no excuse to inflict such pain upon the crew, and it was a very fortunate seaman who did not find himself at least once a week on the end of the rattan's travel.

The first task of each day was to scrub the deck with a holystone or scraper. Next was to wash the paintwork and clean the guns. At half-past seven the men were allowed five minutes to lash up their hammocks. At eight o'clock was the first meal of the day. There was usually plenty of food and the diet was substantial, but very often the quality of the meat and biscuits was poor. Occasionally a biscuit, impregnated with large, black-headed maggots, was found, but the food was usually palatable and provided a welcome respite from the energy-sapping routines. Will always welcomed mealtimes. Beer was plentiful soon after the ship was provisioned, but it quickly went bad and was substituted by the ever-popular grog. This was a mixture of half a pint of rum and a quarter pint of water, and despite the dilution still tasted like liquid fire. The sailors adored it, and the twice-daily issue at noon and six in the evening was not to be missed.

After breakfast came the order to 'clear lower deck', upon which all hands went to their quarters. The routines varied according to the day of the week; one day it might be cutlass and musket drill, another it might be training in reefing, furling and shifting sails. Through all this training, Jacob cast a fatherly eye over Will's efforts, encouraging him if he became frustrated, chastising him if he became over-confident. Gun practices always seemed to be held too often and were extremely repetitive. The ship's company was summoned to action stations by the beating of drums. On the middle deck were a hundred and eighty men under the orders of two lieutenants and five midshipmen. Each pair of twenty-four pounder guns had two captains, one for starboard and the other for larboard if the ship were fighting both sides at once. Boarding parties stood ready with cutlasses and pikes whilst lantern and firemen held buckets and swabs. Young boys known as powder monkeys ran to fetch gunpowder and cartridges from the magazines. Gun crews were poised to sponge, worm, load, and run out the heavy guns, each captain holding a smouldering match over the touchhole. Every man had his duty to perform and as a complete fighting unit each gun crew constituted a severe menace to enemy ships. With constant repetition, the actions became instinctive and the fighting unit became ever more efficient. Will could not help but be impressed as he thought of this repeated throughout all the ships of Hawke's fleet. The French stood no chance.

On Thursdays, the crew were allowed a 'make and mend'. This was a vital period for many men as it was an opportunity to make or mend their clothes. The sailors were initially non-uniformed and sometimes in rags. Those who had been pressed had no chance to bring spare clothing or personal possessions with them and hence the only clothes they had were the ones they stood up in. The onerous duties soon reduced these to tatters and the 'make and mend' was thus essential. For those who could afford them, the purser sold slops, which included grey kersey jackets lined with brass buttons and red breeches with leather pockets. There were also red waistcoats of welsh flannel, grey stockings, linen shirts, leather or woollen caps and buckled shoes. Working dress for the majority, however, was usually a canvas frock with baggy breeches and no shoes. Will found this dress most odd at first, but soon adapted to it, and by the end of his first week at sea he felt as if he had been a seaman for years.

At eight in the evening, hands were piped down to their hammocks whence they would hang like bats from the deckhead at the regulation spacing of fourteen inches. It was here that such social discourse as was possible occurred. Those who did not fall immediately asleep, exhausted by their efforts, chatted quietly to their close friends. Others sung shanties in hushed tones. All relaxed and offered up thanks that another day had passed safely.

As the weeks became months, Will found that the routines became instinctive. Under the guiding of Jacob, Will soon became a competent seaman and gunner, but as the time passed other difficulties arose, for the men became restless the longer they were at sea. With no enemy action to dissipate their emotions they became tense and inclined to vent their anger on each other. But by far the biggest problem for Will was John Jennings.

After the confrontation with Jennings on board the *Duke*, which had resulted in Jennings being very forcibly put down, the malicious Kentish man had retreated from the limelight to lick his wounds. This might have helped if their ways had parted in Plymouth, but it was not to be so. Perhaps because they had been recruited at a similar time and place and their names were therefore close together on the ship's books, Will and Jennings found themselves both transferred to *Resolution*. Jennings' hatred of Will fermented for a few more weeks until he had gained sufficient confidence to be in control of the situation. From that point on, life for Will became an irregular series of disturbing incidents, each exacerbated by every meeting of the two men. On a number of occasions, Will had been subjected to painful retribution from the bosun's mates after minor scuffles with Jennings, and no matter what Will did or said, Jennings was totally unswerving in his malice. Will could foresee no end to the problem other than the removal of one of them from the ship.

By the end of October, after five continuous months at sea, the crew were regularly being punished for fighting amongst themselves. The tension of living for so long under the constant threat of enemy action reached such a pitch that the only way to relieve it was in violence towards each other. Captain Speke was well aware of the problem and clamped down hard on the offenders, but there was little he could do to help the men. The French had been successfully pinned down in their ports and dare not put to sea. The English had spent the months simply keeping station along the French coast and preventing all movement of French warships.

As October came to a close, the autumn weather turned into winter and grew so bad that the fleet was forced to return to the shelter of Torbay and Plymouth. For the men, this proved to be a god-send, for no sooner had *Resolution* dropped anchor in Plymouth Sound than boatloads of prostitutes were allowed to come alongside. These 'pleasure boats' had been organised by enterprising businessmen in return for a sizeable share of the proceeds. Each boatman carried as many ladies as the boat would take and once these boats were alongside the seamen were allowed into them to take their pick at a cost of one or two shillings payable to the boatman. Will had heard stories about such happenings from the more experienced seamen, but he could never have imagined the extent of the debauchery.

The sailors selected their women in the same fashion as Will remembered watching farmers select a pig or a sheep on Market Day. Having chosen their 'wives' the sailors brought the women back on board. Each was examined at the gangway for smuggled liquor and then escorted below by her 'husband.' As Will made his way through the ship he could not comprehend the range of human activity that greeted his eyes. Everywhere was the disgusting language and conversation as men made open propositions with their business partners. Everywhere, bare breasts and buttocks writhed uncomfortably between guns, or precariously within the regulation fourteen inches of the hammock. Suddenly the whole ship had acquired a look of filth, a stench of debauchery. The glorious *Resolution* had become a floating whorehouse.

Will's upbringing in the sleepy Kent village had shielded him from such crudity and he could not help but find this entire episode disgusting. There was no escape. His mess-deck was the scene of an orgy. Its stifling darkness overwhelmed him and he sought refuge in the only place possible - the upper deck. Even here, couples copulated in every available space, but eventually Will found a tiny corner where he could sit and watch the sea. The cool breeze cleansed his nostrils and he stared disconsolately into the distance. Suddenly he was so alone, even in such a densely populated area. He felt friendless and deserted by the human race. Then it began to get colder and he snuggled up close to a bulkhead for shelter. As he stared into the distance he saw an object on the horizon. He concentrated his focus on it and saw that it was a lighthouse. But no, it was not just any lighthouse: it was the Eddystone lighthouse. Many of the sailors had talked about the new tower being built of stone. Immediately his thoughts passed to the only lighthouse that mattered to him - the one on South Foreland. He wondered how his family were. What of poor Lizzie? How silly he had been to leave them all. How would all this end?

Will cried long into the night and when all the whores had gone he went below to his hammock and cried there too.

12 TAR

Bleedin' Navy. You 'ates it or you loves it. Well, p'raps not - I aint sure. Bin in it so long reckon I 'ates it, but then why've I bin in it so long? Must be sixteen year now, damn near. P'raps I loves it wi'out realisin' it, I dunno. Love-'ate i'n't, 'owever you looks at it? Bleedin' mis'rable life reely. Five in the mornin' they gets you up an' if you aint sharp at it you gets a stripe from the mate. Scum! They comes round wi' a lantern in one 'and an' a rattan in t' other, cuttin' away right an' left. Them wi' beds on t' deck gets it first an' they falls out o' bed an' runs fer the 'atchways like rats wi' terriers after 'em.

Where them boats got to? They must be comin' sometime, they usually do.

Five month we bin on this soddin' ship an' where's it got us? No further than bleedin' Brit'ny. I'm sick o' Bisky. Nowt but bloody oggin 'eavin round all year. When I gets up top (if I ever do) what's I goin' to say to 'im... God? Able Seaman Pigshit reportin' fer duty in the afterlife, Sir. 'underd an' seventy years in 'is Majesty's Navy, scrubbin' decks, swiggin' grog and shaggin' 'ores... not necessarily in that order. Bugger me, 'e's goin' to be 'ard pressed to find me a job in 'eaven. Reckon I'd best stay put down 'ere. Mind you, I dos a better job than a lot of these bastards. 'alf of 'em aint even seen a ship like *Resolution* afore. Must be four year I bin on 'er now. Knows every inch of the decks I do, every canvas, every 'alyard an' every damn job too. These bleedin' pressed men - most of 'em are scum. They don't care like I do. I might 'ate it but at least I cares. She aint so bad I s'pose. Just like a bleedin' woman - you 'ates 'em but you can't do wi'out 'em.

Where the bleedin' 'ell's they damn boats? Us bin 'ere two an' 'alf days now. They 'm all behind. Ha! Just like some o' the 'ores... all behind!

No. These pressed men comes 'ere lookin' like bloody scarecrows. They 'ardly got a pair o' breeches to keep 'em decent. Make 'n mend Thursdays they 'm stitchin' and mendin' for all they 'm worth. They aint got no money to buy nowt from the slops - old Pusser sells some pretty decent stuff really but these new buggers can't afford 'alf o' it and they bloody well ought to. Five months they bin at sea, no runs ashore, nowt to spend it on. They ought to be able to get somethin' decent to wear.

There's a boat... what only one? Where's the rest got to? Dozens of 'em come out to us at Portsmouth. We must 'ave 'ad five 'underd women aboard one time... 'angin' from the gunn'ls they was. They watermen 's tight bastards. They 'm out for every farthin' they can get. You 'ave to pay 'em two bob to get an 'ore off a boat. When they 'm aboard though 't is all right. You can 'ave 'em anywhere. Don't matter anyways as you aint got no privacy. You screws 'em where you can find room. Tis funny, bangin' away with another five 'underd 'eavin' asses goin' up and down alongside. It's dark down on the orlop deck so 'taint too bad for privacy 'cept you can 'ardly see a tit in front of your nose. 'T is understandable though, in it? I mean, after five month like we just 'ad, 't aint surprisin' you can't walk nowhere for shaggin'. Biggest problem's tryin' to 'ang on to the one you got and paid for, cause there's always some bastard spent all 'is money on ale and wants yours wi'out payin'. I've 'ad to leave the job several times to thump some bastard and then get back to it again. Tis every man for 'iself.

Well, I aint goin' to be lucky this time I reckons, even though I's first in the line. Reckons the officers 'll get any that's on this boat.

Navy's not so bad I s'pose. Just this trip's bin bad. Sorted the men out from the lads though, din it? Plenty of sea time, lots of rough weather. They 'ad plenty of time to learn their selves seamanship and some of 'em still 'aven't. Soon learn 'ow to get pissed though, don't they? Swigs their grog like seasoned salts they dos. Next thing they 'm 'onkin' all over you and pissin' their pants and you 'ave to sleep with the smelly bastards. 'T aint even as strong as the neaters we used to get. Bleedin' Admiral Vernon, I remembers you well, sir. 'Old Grog' we called 'im. Made all the neaters watered down, one barrel to three o' water. My ass, probably couldn't take it 'iself. Come visitin' a ship I were in once and a real mean old fart 'e looked too. Old Grog... huh... Old Shit, more like.

That boat don't look like it's got many women aboard. Praps it's a vittler. Can't see what tis yet. If there's one on that boat I'm goin' to be the first aboard the bastard... after the officers 'ave 'ad theirs o' course. I'll maim any other bugger tries to get in afore me.

Now that young pressed lad... Will... on our gun. Soon learned 'is tricks. Old Jacob showed 'im well. Not a bad lad at all. Now 'e 'd make a decent tar if 'e stuck to it. Too nice, though. You got to be a fine upstandin' man of breedin' like me to get on in this man's Navy. Bleedin' laugh, everybody's thievin' and robbin' and killin'. Thievin' gets you flogged but don't seem to matter. You gets flogged for bein' groggy. A floggin' at Jacob's Ladder... I 'ad it meself when I were young. I were rude to the Cap'n... didn't know no better then... two dozen I got. The officers come out on the spar-deck, marines on the quarterdeck and the people on the main deck. That cat must've bin an inch thick and two foot long. Stripped me to the waist they did, tied me wrists to a grating and give me twelve all over. Then another mate come 'cause the first were tired and not doin' it well enough, poor bastard, and I got another twelve. Sometimes they keep on until the Cap'n tells them to stop. That's what I 'ad any'ow. Pissed blood for a month after, I did. They say as 'ow you aint s'posed to get more 'n a dozen, but there aint many Cap'ns stick to that rule. I seen a bloke flogged round the fleet once. The poor bastard were tied to a scaffold in the ships boat. They took that boat - with four drummers in it playin' the Rougue's March - alongside every ship in the fleet wi' their companies watchin'. 'E 'ad six lashes alongside each ship wi' a different bosun's mate each time... every ship between Rochester and Gillingham... over a 'underd lashes 'e 'ad. Poor bugger was maimed for life after that. Can't remember what 'e done. Rather be 'ung from the yardarm meself.

Course, you always gets a few funny buggers aboard. Man tries to touch me I'll finish 'is sex-life permanent, that's for sure. Trouble is wi' 'ammocks fourteen inch apart you 'ave to pretty choosy 'bout your shipmates. And it's so dark you can't see what they 'm up to 'ardly. First thing's when you feel something pokin' you in the back and it's not 'is finger.

Shipmate you'd better not try to push in front of me or you goin' to find your ass danglin' from the bowsprit. I bin 'ere first and you'd best remember it. It's bin a long time since May... actually 'er name were Annie... I think. Real Barbican scrubber but she knew 'er business. Showed me a trick or two. Trouble is when you gets used to gettin' it every night and then nothin' for months. It's bloody 'ard. Just let me get at 'em. What's takin' so long for bugger's sake? Still, looks like we'll be lucky to get 'em at all. Tis a bit unusual not 'avin 'ore boats out when we 'm in Plymouth Sound. This Cap'n 's all right though really. Tries to look after us best 'e can. Lumme 'avin' seen 'is misses aint surprised le wants a 'ore. Don't go for women wi' no tits meself. Course 'e don't come out to choose for 'iself. 'Alf a dozen of the best gets took down the officers quarters. We gets the poxy ones that's left.

I aint sure that boat's comin' 'ere anyway. Looks like a bleedin' vittler. Could be she's 'eaded away towards the *Union*. What's 'er name? *Weston*. Aint seen 'er before. No she aint comin' for any of us. Looks like she's off out to sea. Bloody fishin' boat I s'pose. Oh well, looks like I'll just 'ave to go back to doin' it meself.

13 ZACHARIAH MUDGE

The immaculately groomed grey and white seagull paddled tirelessly on the stiff swell, totally disinterested in the yawl that was tacking past it in a series of hesitant, lurching paces. On board the *Weston* stood three passengers, their eyes eagerly fixed upon a thin column of stone as it drew imperceptibly nearer. The atmosphere was so crisp that, but for the curvature of the Earth, they would have been able to see America. Instead, they had to be content with the purplish-tinged lines of the Lizard peninsula in the west and the green-brown of the Prawle in the east. To the north, the direction from which they had just come, a jumble of naked masts marked the position of Hawke's fleet as it took shelter within the maternal embrace of Plymouth Sound.

Southward bound, the *Weston*, named after her Eddystone sponsor, was heading for the very newest Eddystone lighthouse, and amongst its three important passengers was the creator of the tower, John Smeaton. Alongside him stood his assistant, Josias Jessop and his friend the Reverend Zachariah Mudge who was the vicar of St. Andrew's Church in Plymouth. Only an even chance would decide whether the three men would be able to make a landing on the westerly limb of the cluster of rocks upon which the slender lighthouse was built. Passage of the tiny rowing boat into the Gut would be tricky in such a swell but there were none more able to perform the task than the men who made up the crew of the *Weston*.

During the past four years, Josias Jessop had seen the waters of the Eddystone reef in all their moods and his seamen had negotiated the dangers of the rocks on countless occasions without incident. Of course, there were many times when it was not possible to land, but this was invariably obvious to the trained eye even before the ship left its mooring. If it had been Jessop's decision he would have stayed at home today, but Mr Smeaton was anxious to visit his lighthouse. Two days earlier, on the sixteenth of October, its twenty-four candles had been lit for the first time but the weather recently had been quite tempestuous and had prevented Smeaton from being present at the very climax of his greatest achievement. It was only now that a journey to the lighthouse had been considered possible and, despite his friend Jessop's doubts, Smeaton had made the decision to sail.

A further deciding factor in his choice was that he had invited his friend, the vicar of St. Andrew's Church in Plymouth, to accompany him to the tower. John Smeaton was a humble and god-fearing man. He had refused to heed the advice of others to carve his own name on his creation, but had preferred instead two religious inscriptions. The first he had ordered to be cut into the wall of the upper storeroom. Quoting the 127th Psalm it said, "Except the Lord build the house they labour in vain that build it." The second was carved on the very last stone to be set and proclaimed simply, "*Laus Deo*." Smeaton had planned to worship the glory of God at a short religious ceremony in the lantern room to coincide with the lighting of the lighthouse, but bad weather had made it impossible. Instead, he asked the Reverend Zachariah Mudge to accompany him to the tower as soon as the weather improved so that they might give thanks to God.

Zachariah Mudge was a rotund sixty-nine year old with a bulbous shock of white hair both on his head and his face. A priest and a high Tory, Mudge was a classical scholar with a vigorous intellect and a racy humour. Earlier in his life he had been a second master at Plympton Grammar School. Headmaster at that time had been the grandfather of young Joshua Reynolds and Mudge had formed a deep and lasting friendship with the painter. In 1731 the Corporation had elected him as vicar of St. Andrew's where he built up a well publicised and deserved reputation for his preaching. In all those years he had not once set foot upon the rocks of the Eddystone,

118

although they were part of his parish. Upon striking up a friendship with John Smeaton during the engineer's frequent stays in Plymouth, he had resolved to correct his omission and at Smeaton's invitation he was about to fulfil his promise. Thus it was that the three passengers aboard the *Weston* awaited a chancy landing on the dangerous Eddystone Rocks.

The herring gull became aware of the wooden wanderer and wondered if it might be a source of food. Stretching its wafer thin wings, it pulled itself out of the water with two beats and into a westerly airstream on which it glided and circled the small ship. Soon it was joined by a number of its relations that had been reconnoitring the outer rocks of the reef. A piercing cry of welcome rent the busy westerly wind but passed unnoticed on board the *Weston* where all hands were now preparing for the passenger transfer to the reef.

From the comparative comfort of the tower, two of its keepers had been aware of the approaching visitors for some time. The third keeper, Henry Edwards, was still sleeping soundly after his middle watch. Henry Carter had spotted the familiar lines of the *Weston* through the telescope a couple of hours before as it wove a delicate pattern amid the multitude of ships in Plymouth Sound. Now both he and John Hatherley watched cautiously from the open door of the lighthouse as the yawl was brought skilfully alongside the landing area within the Gut itself. At the appropriate moment that the boat and the rock achieved the correct relative level, first Smeaton and then Jessop jumped onto the rock. The elderly priest was naturally quite reticent to follow his juniors, for he had not made such a perilous step in his life before. However, with the aid of a long arm and a short prayer, Zachariah Mudge was finally welcomed ashore on the infamous Eddystone Rocks. Crossing himself in salute to his safety and in respect for the thousands of poor unfortunates whose lives had not been spared on the reef, he hurried up the few steps and into the bowels of the lighthouse that had made news throughout the civilised world. It had been totally unthinkable that such a construction of stone could be built on a wild and desolate wave-swept reef, but John Smeaton had accomplished the impossible, a feat for which they would soon give thanks to the Almighty.

It was in the storeroom some thirty feet above the swell that five men came face to face. Only a brief introduction was necessary for the benefit of the reverend visitor, the other four men being well acquainted, and they immediately climbed the ladder to the kitchen for a warming drink. Already Mudge was almost speechless, for he found himself so comfortable in the circular quarter that he was totally unaware of the sea in which he stood so isolated. He stepped up to the small window and gasped as he looked down upon the minuscule *Weston* which was now standing off the reef about a hundred yards away. The waves were breaking in snowy cascades about the jagged rocks, but apart from the occasional distant thump he was merely aware of the gentle crackling of the fire and the hissing from the pot which was about to boil on the range. Smeaton, on the other hand, was more anxious to ascertain the state of the lighthouse and the way the keepers had conducted themselves. He had introduced a new method of victualling the keepers and was keen to find out what they thought of it. In the past, keepers had complained either that there had not been enough food, or that food had gone bad and they had been obliged to ditch it. It had even been claimed that they had been forced to eat candles in order to survive until the relief boat came. Smeaton had always doubted this claim for he had heard rumours that some keepers liked rather too much alcohol and that they often exchanged their victuals for drink with visiting fishing boats. After much consideration he had concluded that one way around this was to ensure that the lighthouse was well stocked with food. An inventory would be taken at specified periods and the food which the keepers had consumed they would pay for (at wholesale prices) out of their wages, generously fixed at £25 per annum. The food stocks would then be replenished until the next occasion. It seemed the only way to avoid embezzlement was to make the men responsible for provisioning themselves.

Smeaton found that the three men were reasonably satisfied with this state of affairs, but that they would be more ready to comment when the system had been in operation for a longer period. By the time Mudge was ready to enjoin conversation, having satiated his curiosity with the tower, Smeaton had already questioned the keepers to his satisfaction.

"John, my warmest congratulations to you. This is a truly magnificent achievement." Mudge was enthusiastic in his praise.

"Thank you, vicar," replied Smeaton, trying not to sound annoyed, for his modesty forbade him to enjoy self-adulation. "Perhaps when you have finished your tea you would like to come up with me to the lantern."

"I would be delighted, John. Perhaps these two gentlemen" - he indicated the keepers - "would like to join us in a short service of thanksgiving?" John Hatherley gave a quick knowing glance at Henry Carter as the vicar awaited a reply. He knew that both his colleagues actively avoided church, but not only that, Carter could be a little indiscreet at times and he was anxious to reply before Henry said something he should not. Henry kept silent, fortunately.

"Us be glad to offer us thanks to the Lord with 'e sir," replied Hatherley. "In fact, 't is time old Edwards disturbed 'eself. 'E's slept long enough so 'e can join us. I'll go get 'un up."

By the time the visitors had warmed their digestive systems with a bracing brew, Henry Edwards had been reclaimed from the brink of unconsciousness and was cursing his colleague for spoiling a good dream.

" 'Ush up now 'Enry, the vicar 'll 'ear thee, You 'm comin' up top for a prayer with Mr Smeaton and Reverend Mudge so look sharp now." The small curtain, which was permanently drawn, was flung aside and Edwards squinted for a few seconds to avoid the bright light. Unfortunately in so doing he did not notice the head of Reverend Mudge appear through the hole in the floor.

"Bugger thee, 'Atherley, I'll 'ang your ass from the gallery tonight."

"Not only hast thou a foul tongue, Edwards, but the execution of violence on thy neighbour is not in accordance with the teachings of the Lord Jesus Christ." Mudge rebuked him.

"Oh, I be most sorry, sir, I didn't see 'e there, sir." Edwards blushed,

"Come with us up to the lantern, my good fellow, and make thy peace with God."

"Right away, sir." Suddenly Henry Edwards was keen to be religious.

In the shadow of twenty-four candles mounted in two concentric rings and hanging from the pinnacle of the lighthouse, the six men stood in prayer. Zachariah Mudge was in his element as he invented suitable words of thanksgiving, his eyes tightly closed, his head raised toward the candles, his hands gesturing reverently heavenward. Beside him stood Josiah Jessop with head bowed.

"Oh Lord, our heavenly Father, we thank thee for thy guidance in the building of this lighthouse, and beseech thee to take into thy care the brave guardians of this light..." John Smeaton felt a tingling in his spine as his soul became refreshed. The priest's words were well chosen, if somewhat longwinded. John's achievement was now complete, both physically and spiritually.

John Hatherley listened to the words of the preacher and although he did not understand all of them, he felt sure that he agreed with them. As Henry Carter looked down vacantly at the metal grating upon which they were standing, he was unaware that Henry Edwards was covertly watching the spectacle of a ship-of-the-line passing the tower and was thus completely ignoring the preacher. Edwards noticed that the wind had changed. Mudge continued regardless and invited them all to sing Psalm one hundred.

"Acclaim the Lord all men on Earth,
Worship the Lord in all gladness;
Enter his presence with songs of exultation,
Give thanks to Him and bless His name
For the Lord is good and His love is everlasting.
His constancy endures to all generations."

His voice was loud and flat.

John Smeaton recognised the tune and did his best to drag the notes out of the others. Hatherley and Jessop joined in, stumbling over the words, whilst the others mumbled discordantly. By the time that Mudge had begun on the Grace, the other five men, including Smeaton, had become aware of the display outside, and were so completely enthralled by the spectacle of sail that now surrounded them, that they completely ignored the incantations emanating from their effusive friend. It seemed that the whole of the English fleet was encircling the lighthouse in salute, perhaps, to the ultimate engineering achievement. Mudge, as if by divine communication, sensed that his congregation was being inattentive and, opening his eyes, saw the amazing sight as Admiral Hawke's fleet slowly passed the sentinel and glided southward to continue its blockade of the French port of Brest. John Hatherley counted a dozen ships-of-the-line and five frigates, all with full sail and looking immaculate in the October sunshine. He could hardly believe the closeness with which the ships were approaching the reef, as if in a gesture of supreme confidence in the architect and constructor of the new Eddystone lighthouse. One ship, the *Duke*, was so close to the

121

reef that he could see the faces of some of the sailors. They seemed to be tired; young faces with so much to look forward to, but which seemed not to care. He wondered how many pressed young boys were dreading the weeks ahead and how many of them would not return. Even if they survived the battle that the whole of England was predicting, they might not survive the food, the filthy conditions, the punishments and the disease. Yet how fine the ships looked... so glamorous yet so inhospitable...

Mudge, almost in an act of defiance to win back his audience, burst forth into yet another prayer committing the fleet and its sailors into the care of the Lord and beseeching that He allow them to banish the threat of the enemy forever and to return each and every one of them home safely - a plea which he knew to be impossible. It nevertheless drew a loud "Amen" from the assembled men and the vicar decided to call it a day as far as religion was concerned. The view of the ships was so startling from their lofty position that they continued to watch in silence until the sails had diminished to mere specks on the horizon. At last Smeaton broke the silence.

"Well, gentlemen, I fear that we must take our leave once more before the tide makes our departure impossible."

"I hasten to add, John, that I would not be sorry to be forced to spend a few nights in this place. I cannot think of a more peaceful and restful place in which to contemplate the joys of life than in this wonderful tower." Mudge was still enthusiastic in his praise for the lighthouse.

"I am most pleased to hear that, vicar," replied Smeaton, "but I fear that if we do not leave now it is more than possible that you could be marooned here until the spring. I do not think that your parishioners would be too pleased, would they?"

"Can't say as I would either," mumbled Henry Carter. Hatherley kicked him and Carter restrained a curse only with great difficulty. Fortunately the vicar did not hear him.

"I believe that you are right, John. What a pity that there is no time for another cup of your wonderful tea, Henry Carter. Come, let us depart now before I decide to change my vocation and become a lighthouse keeper."

The party broke up and withdrew down the tower, floor by floor, until they once again stood in the entrance door. Jessop made a signal for the *Weston* to make its approach. The change of wind from southwesterly to northwesterly had caused a considerable easing of the swell in the Gut and the embarking procedure was accomplished without mishap.

As the three men waved farewell to the keepers, Smeaton had a strange feeling that he might be making a last farewell to his beloved tower. Winter was closing in and he had to return to London to commence other work. He recalled that Rudyerd, his predecessor, had waved farewell to his wooden tower and never been heard of again. Smeaton hoped desperately that the peculiar premonition he was experiencing would be wrong. He promised himself that he would return.

Back in the comfort of the living room, John Hatherley was sad that the visitors had gone. He had nothing but admiration and respect for Mr Smeaton, and now all that lay ahead were months of solitude on the lighthouse. Meanwhile, Henry

Carter was imitating in his most reverend voice the vicar's parting words to a grinning Henry Edwards.

" 'I would not be sorry to be forced to spend a few nights in this place,' 'e says. Pompous old bugger. Let un try eatin' a few candles. 'T wouldn't be so keen to stay then."

John smiled and put another pot of water on to boil.

14 SIR EDWARD HAWKE

In the solitude of his cabin on board the wave-tossed HMS *Royal George*, Admiral Sir Edward Hawke poured himself a glass of his favourite Madeira and then sat back in his chair to contemplate his plan of action. Surely the game of cat and mouse would be ended tomorrow? For five months his fleet had been blockading Brest where the remains of the French fleet under the command of Admiral Conflans had been waiting for an opportunity to set sail. Louis XV was anxious to launch an invasion of England and in order to do so had assembled his army in transport ships at Morbihan. But this armada needed the support of the fleet at Brest to escort it through the English defences. Thus Hawke, by means of his superior force, had delayed indefinitely Louis' plans by preventing the French from leaving Brest. Apart from two short spells when he had been forced to take shelter from gales in Plymouth and Torbay, Hawke's fleet had continuously patrolled the Brest roads since May. His seamen, who at first had been an ill-disciplined, untrained crew, were now amongst the finest ever. Five months of continuous instruction in seamanship during testing weather conditions had produced a fine crew in each of the twenty-three ships, and now they were keen for some real action to relieve the monotony and end the campaign.

In contrast, Conflans' men had been port-bound and Hawke knew what that meant. They would be entirely Breton conscripts trained only in the art of consuming alcoholic beverages in the local taverns. They would have had no opportunity to learn how to sail or fight a ship-of-the-line.

It was mid-November and winter was fast approaching. For the past few days Hawke's fleet had been sheltering in Plymouth and Torbay from a severe southwesterly gale. Hawke was confident that the same gale would prevent the French from setting sail. Then on the fourteenth the wind had veered northwest and Hawke had sped back towards Ushant with urgency. He felt sure that this time his adversary would leave port and sail to Morbihan to meet the transport ships. As a contingency for this, he had stationed Commodore Duff with a few frigates near Quiberon Bay to keep an eye on things. On the sixteenth he had sent the Fortune sloop to warn Duff that the French were likely to break out. Two hours afterwards he had been proved right for the *Royal George* came upon a housebound victualler, the *Love and Unity*. Her master told him that he had sighted the French fleet on the previous day only sixty miles or so from Belle Isle. The news had caused Hawke to make for Quiberon Bay at the utmost speed, not just to attack the French but to go to Duff's aid.

Hawke sipped his wine and closed his eyes in order to savour the exquisite taste. Someone knocked on his cabin door and, having gained permission to enter, did so. It was Hawke's Captain, James Campbell.

"Yes, James? How are things?"

"We're making good time, sir. There is still a good north-westerly blowing and we should be off Belle Isle during tomorrow forenoon," replied Campbell confidently.

Hawke was pleased but not surprised. "Excellent. Let us hope that Duff manages to keep his distance. Tomorrow could well be the day for which we have waited so long."

"The men are bursting for a fight. We've had a lot of minor incidents between decks recently. The strain of all the sea-time is beginning to tell on them. They need some action now to get it out of their systems. You know, sometimes I think we do them a favour by having wars. They do not seem to have any idea of how to get on with their fellow men - always fighting and squabbling amongst themselves. It does them good to have a pitched battle occasionally."

"You do not appear to have a lot of respect for the common man, James," said Hawke with a smile as he rose from his seat. "Madeira?"

"Thank you. Oh, don't get me wrong, sir, they are a superb crew at present. Their seamanship has never been better. No, it's just that they behave like animals when they have nothing to do."

"Yes, I think you may be right, James. Well, it will not be long now." He handed his Captain a crystal glass of the finest Madeira wine that money could buy and indicated to Campbell to take a seat. "If all goes to plan they will be able to relieve their tensions tomorrow in the proper manner." For a moment both men were silent as they contemplated the probability of a battle. Campbell sipped his drink and complimented his Admiral on the choice. He had known Hawke for a long time; they had served together in the past and Hawke often invited Campbell to join him for dinner during which they exchanged sea stories over a favourite glass.

"How many ships does Conflans have, sir?" Campbell wanted to remind himself of the odds.

"The master of the *Love and Unity* said he had counted twenty-one ships. That is about the number that I had expected," said Hawke, finishing his drink and putting the glass down. He made it a rule never to drink more than one glass. Campbell knew this only too well and did not expect to be offered another.

"That makes us fairly even then - twenty-one to our twenty-three..."

"Don't forget Duff, " interrupted Hawke, "... Twenty-four."

"Of course," replied Campbell nodding his head in satisfaction at the overwhelming superiority of his own fleet. "That should be enough to ensure victory."

"You mean you are not certain, James?" quizzed Hawke mockingly. "I will wager a cask of port on it," he said, goading Campbell for his uncertainty.

"Then it is a certainty that I, for one, shall not bet on, said Campbell laughing. "I have never known you risk your best Madeira on anything other than stone cold fact. And besides, how would you pay me if you lost the bet?" The two men smiled at each other. "Well, sir, I must go to bed. We could well have a busy day ahead of us."

"Goodnight, James. Our long spell at sea will soon be over."

Campbell paused in the doorway. "I hope so. Goodnight."

The cabin door closed behind the Captain leaving Hawke to contemplate the moving shadows being cast by the suspended oil lamp. His gaze wandered and came to rest on the wine decanter. The lingering memory of its taste tempted him. He decided that he was going to break his rule. After all, it would be a big day tomorrow.

Through the night the fleet sped on across the heavy Atlantic swell. Twenty-three officers-of-the-watch, twenty-three helmsmen and twenty-three groups of duty hands went about their work. All felt deep inside that the end of the voyage was nigh the voyage that had kept them from their families and had taken them nowhere farther than the coast of Brittany. At two o' clock in the morning of November 20th., Hawke was awakened from a fitful slumber in his armchair. It was Campbell.

"Sir, the wind has turned; it is now from the west-south-west and very squally."

"Time for a starboard tack then, James," replied Hawke as he rubbed his eyes still heavy with sleep. "Make a signal to the rest of the squadron and wake me if there are any developments."

"Aye aye, sir," replied Campbell dutifully.

In the crisp moonlight of the piercingly cold November night the duty watch clambered more than a hundred feet up amid lurching masts to get down the topgallant yards. With unresponsive fingers they struggled to reef the topsails so the fleet could begin the final passage around the southern coast of Belle Isle and into Quiberon Bay. Onward into the night surged the British force.

At first light Hawke was on the upper deck and fully prepared psychologically for the fray. He signalled to *Magnanime* to go ahead as fast as possible in order to make landfall. Meanwhile the rest of the fleet were to follow behind with a large spread of canvas despite the ferocity of the weather, which was mostly astern. Hawke needed speed if he was to rendezvous with the French on time. Months of seamanship training combined with the new sense of urgency to enable the fleet to dash in for the kill at a pace rarely achieved before. Every canvas strained at every lashing as the vicious gale sped them along.

Hawke scrutinised the horizon with his telescope, as also did a dozen other lookouts around the flagship. There, almost on the horizon and some six or seven miles ahead, he could see the Maidstone and the Coventry. It was an intermittent sighting as the Atlantic swell elevated his viewing platform on the crest of a wave and then plunged it flippantly down into a trough. *Magnanime* lay about two miles away on the port bow. Suddenly a burst of shouting rang out from some of the other ships nearby. He looked again at Maidstone. To his delight he could clearly see her topgallant sheets flying out in the wind - the signal that she had sighted French ships. As the news spread amongst his crew, they too became exuberant, and the sighting was fast communicated to the rest of the fleet. It took a further hour and a quarter before *Magnanime* made a similar signal. They were catching Conflans.

Soon Hawke caught his own glimpse of the enemy ships.

"They have changed course towards the Bay, James," he declared after closely studying their disposition. "The fox is running for his lair, damn him. I'll wager that Conflans is hoping we will not dare to follow him into the Bay."

Two dangerous reefs guarded the entrance to Quiberon Bay. On the port side were the *Cardinals* and on the starboard side *Le Four* Shoal. Entry into the Bay in fine weather could be dangerous to those unfamiliar with the waters, but in such fierce conditions it could only be described as suicidal. Hawke clenched his jaw with sheer stubbornness.

"He is wrong, James, he is wrong. Make a signal to Hardy. The van shall give chase. Meanwhile I want every bloody square foot of sail you can give me. I mean to catch them before they reach the safety of the Morbihan. Oh, and tell the Chaplain to pray for a change of wind."

Campbell executed the Admiral's orders at once. Vice Admiral Sir Charles Hardy aboard his ninety-gun flagship Union led the van in pursuit. Meanwhile the *Royal George* groaned in every timber as the forty mile-an-hour winds urged her towards her quarry. The Chaplain, Robert English, kept his diary with every new event and offered up a short prayer, as ordered. Suddenly there was a cry from one of the starboard lookouts.

"Ships on the starboard bow." Hawke swung round in a trice.

"It's Duff," said Campbell in excitement. "He's coming to join us."

Soon the crew were cheering once more as the eleven magnificent British ships headed towards them in line astern, their sails straining to breaking point, their bows punctuated with snow-white mantles. Hawke felt his spine tingle with excitement.

"Sir, may I ask if you still intend to follow Conflans into the Bay?" Campbell seemed to be anxious.

"That is correct, James. Why do you ask?" replied Hawke without taking his eye off the magnificent array of ships under his command.

"May I be so bold as to suggest, sir, that we could find ourselves in considerable difficulty within its confines. There is not enough room to accommodate two large fleets and we could lose many of our ships."

"But do you not see, James, that is the very reason why we are going in? I have the finest seamen it has ever been an Admiral's privilege to command. Conflans has shiploads of Breton conscripts whose total training in seamanship began three days ago. They do not know a main topgallant from a capstan. Conflans knows it only too well. He would not dare to remain in the open sea where he knows that we would overhaul him and annihilate him. He is gambling that fear such as yours will save him…"

"I'm not afraid, sir," interrupted Campbell.

126

"I know that, James, but do I make myself clear? It is they who will come to grief, my friend, not we."

Campbell, though not totally convinced, felt better for having aired his views. Not daring to protract the argument, he said no more. As the distance between the two fleets closed rapidly Hawke could see that Conflans was leading his ships in line ahead into Quiberon Bay. Under these conditions the rules of war permitted Hawke to attack.

"Hoist the general chase." he commanded. At the foretop masthead of the *Royal George* the flag of St. George was the signal for the hounds to move in for the kill. Being nearest, Hardy's seven ships began to close in on the prey as the signal gun was sounded three times. At exactly half-past two the dull thump of cannon fire was heard briefly before the pathetic vibrations were engulfed by the howling gale. Hawke could see smoke swirling around the gun ports of *Dorsetshire* and *Torbay*. They had attacked the trailing ships of the French fleet as they approached the *Cardinals*. Seconds later, the cannon boomed out from Hardy's division, and cheers rose from the British seamen as they realised that the French gunners were no match for them. Their accuracy was very poor and reloading was obviously a painstaking procedure.

Campbell, at Hawke's side on the quarterdeck, suddenly knew that his Admiral was right again. It was plain that the British van was inflicting heavy casualties on the French rearguard. He looked up into the rigging and a broad smile broke out on his face.

"Sir, the wind has changed - it has gone west of north-west. He is trapped... Conflans cannot get to Morbihan now."

"By God, you're right. Mention the Chaplain in the despatches. Conflans is stuck in the Bay. Now we've got him."

In the distance, Hawke was able to discern the change of direction that the obliging wind had enforced upon the French. His ability to observe the progress of the battle, however, was fast diminishing, not only because of the fading light of a winter's day, but because of the increasing amount of smoke emanating from the action ahead.

"About two miles to the entrance by my reckoning, sir" informed Campbell.

"Put us right in the middle, James."

"Aye aye, sir."

Hawke looked ahead to the *Formidable*, flagship of the French Rear Admiral du Verger. She had come to a halt on the port bow of the *Royal George* and Hawke could see that she had been terribly damaged. As he watched, her flag was pulled down rapidly - the sign of surrender. Her officers must have been killed; du Verger would certainly not have surrendered if he had been alive.

"French ship dead ahead," called a lookout. Hawke ran to the ship's side. He could just make out the name on the stern of the vessel: *Thésée*. To starboard, *Torbay* under the command of Keppel was preparing to attack her.

"He's going to use his main batteries. He will be swamped!" Campbell was aghast. Keppel was indeed in serious risk of losing his ship in such heavy seas by turning into such a dangerous heading. But he knew what he was doing. Just as the sea began to burst in through his gun ports, Keppel brought his ship around into the wind. Captain Kersaint on board *Thésée* was busy preparing his ship to return an expected broadside and was not so quick to respond to Keppel's sudden manoeuvre. *Thésée* gave a mighty lurch as water poured into her. The crew tried in vain to rectify the problem but *Thésée* came to a dead stop and sank in less than a minute. Those Englishmen who witnessed the sight were struck dumb by the rapidity of the sinking. It was not an event to celebrate for each man knew that the same could happen to him. Some terrified Frenchmen were able to jump into the bitterly cold seas, but most stood no chance of saving themselves. *Thésée's* complement of six hundred and fifty had been drowned in one minute.

The *Royal George* had by now come very close to the scene of the drama and Campbell was forced to make a rapid alteration of course.

"Do you wish to look for survivors sir?" he asked his Admiral.

"I doubt if there will be more than a few, James.

Leave them for Keppel. Press on. I want Conflans." Hawke was becoming a little impatient. The *Royal George* sped past a screaming human being as he clutched desperately one of the few pieces of flotsam to survive the sinking. The wash from the ship upset him from his precious perch and he drowned.

"The French have turned about, sir. They're making straight for us." informed a lookout. Hawke wasted no time sorrowing for *Thésée* and turned his attention to the forthcoming engagement. At last the French flagship, the *Soleil Royal*, together with twelve other ships-of-the-line were on a collision course with the *Royal George*.

"Prepare for action, Captain," bellowed Hawke formally.

"Prepare for action," echoed Campbell to his men.

The ships closed at an astonishing pace, for Hawke was still carrying a press of sail. Just as the two giants were drawing alongside, Hawke stared as *Soleil Royal* was momentarily engulfed in a smother of hushed grey smoke. He braced himself for the impact, and, as he did so, the thunder of fifty cannon, fired in near unison, tormented the air. Hundredweight of shot whistled overhead but amazingly there was no damage. The French had been far too hasty and inaccurate besides. Seizing on a sudden idea, Hawke ordered his men to hold fire while *Royal George* cut in astern of *Soleil Royal* so that he could give her a broadside with impunity. But before Hawke could execute his plan, he was faced broadside-on by *Intrepide*, which had also cut in astern of her flagship in order to prevent just such a manoeuvre as Hawke had intentioned. The two ships let fly with everything at their disposal, but only one broadside could be fired before the ships were past each other. Again, the French had missed the *Royal George* almost entirely whilst the English gunners had punished the audacity of the *Intrepide* by demolishing a good deal of her superstructure. Still the rest of the French fleet plunged headlong towards the British.

"I want two rapid broadsides this time," yelled Hawke as the clouds of smoke still swirled about him and the choking gases dried the back of his mouth. Almost before he'd had time to plan his next manoeuvre the *Superbe* was upon them. This time, the French seemed to delay the vital order to fire and Hawke got his in first. *Royal George* despatched a terrible wall of iron straight into the port side of *Superbe* who had no reply ready. The British gunners reloaded faster than they had ever done before and a second mortal missive drilled along the complete length of the hull of *Superbe*. The result of the brilliant English gunnery was even more dramatic than it had been on *Thésée*. *Superbe* was converted instantly into scrap wood. Disintegration was total. Six hundred and thirty souls, many of whom were conscripted peasants who had never been to sea before, prayed for mercy. It was not to be granted to them. There were no survivors.

By now, the other ships in Conflans' procession had either voluntarily altered course to avoid close action with their superiors, or had been scattered by marauding English vessels. Hawke brought his ship around hoping that he might be able to tackle *Soleil Royal* once more, but his chance was gone. *Intrepide* had done her duty and protected her flagship. As Hawke wondered whether he would be able to swoop down on stragglers from behind he suddenly realised how dark it had become. It was very difficult to ascertain the state of the battle, which seemed to have spread out over the whole of Quiberon Bay. He ordered that the signal for close engagement be brought down and took his ship almost to the entrance of the Bay. Even Hawke dared not risk his ship in such dangerous waters at night. He made a signal to anchor and the mother hen with the remnants of her brood came to roost for the night in fifteen fathoms of troubled water. Gradually the sound of human conflict faded with the light. Hawke's men lay to rest on the tarred timbers next to their guns.

As the night passed slowly and sleeplessly, Sir Edward Hawke pulled the blanket closer around him and listened to the distress calls from the void. The wind shrieked over the dark desolation of water and swept away the forlorn call of those in trouble. In such conditions the signal of the cannon was in vain for no-one, not even the brilliant English seamen, could aid the needy. All on board the *Royal George* were restless at the thought that other English ships might be in difficulty. One of them was.

On board *Resolution*, all the skills that Will had acquired over the previous five months had finally been valuable. For the whole of the afternoon he and the rest of his gun crew had been extremely busy loading and reloading their gun. On several occasions they had completed the evolution in less time than they had ever done it before. This was not necessarily that the men had become more skilful than they were at the last drill, although the practice had helped, but that they all knew the urgency of the situation. Every man knew that if they did not get in the first shot they might not get a chance to shoot at all. To be once beaten by an accurate French broadside would be enough to kill many if not all of them.

From his action station on the middle deck, Will could see nothing at all of the action outside the ship and little of it inside. The smoke was copious and filled the whole of the deck for about a minute after each broadside. Nonetheless, the achievements of the gun crews were remarkable and it seemed that the French must be very poor gunners for the *Resolution* suffered no damage at all that Will knew of. By the end of the afternoon the pace had slackened and the tired men were able to rest by their guns for short periods. Although few of the men could see what was going on, word spread around the deck that the French were being hard pressed. By all accounts their gunnery was very poor and few of the English ships had been hit.

As the daylight receded so also did the sounds of battle. The gun crews were stood down but told to rest beside their guns so as to be ready at short notice. The rumour was spread around the deck that the Captain was looking for somewhere to anchor. It was said that they were in a small bay with little room to manoeuvre and it was safer to anchor lest they run aground on one of the many shoals.

About half an hour after dark, as the men lay against their weapons and sipped a mug of grog, *Resolution* instantly stopped dead in the water with a lurch that sent every man who was on his feet flying across the deck. Jacob Evans was one of these and, in his fall, injured his ankle against a gun wheel. At once all discipline broke down. A great shout went up from the crew and every man made a panic-stricken dash for the nearest ladder. To a man, they all thought that the ship would sink within minutes, and since they had all heard stories of French ships going down that very afternoon in less than a minute, the panic was inevitable. Men fought for positions on the ladder and succeeded only in delaying their exit onto the upper deck. Will too was caught up in the rush to escape, but it took a long time for several hundred scared seamen to evacuate onto the upper deck and as Will patiently waited his turn he plainly felt the strange new movements of the ship. The smooth pitch and roll of the open sea that Will had grown used to had been replaced by a faltering sway and a periodic shudder. The ship seemed to have a list to starboard, which varied from the barely noticeable to the severe. Will guessed that the *Resolution* was still in one piece but what damage had been done to the hull by such a colossal blow he dared not to imagine. His first thoughts were that a broadside had hit them, but he soon realised that he was wrong. No ship was firing in anger at night. Although it was possible that *Resolution* had collided with another ship in the darkness and confines of the Bay, he thought it more probable that she had struck one of the reefs.

As the son of a lighthouse keeper, Will was well aware of the dangers that lurked amid the waves. If *Resolution* had run aground on a reef there was a good chance that she would not sink quickly. It was far more likely that the ship would be battered and broken up slowly. The panic that had overwhelmed the crew was thus quite unjustified.

Now that Will was part of the crush to escape it was far easier for him to go along with the crowd than to try to extricate himself from a jostling, impatient smelly mass of frightened flesh. Slowly and steadily the men filed upward deck by deck until they reached the bracing chill of the November gale. As Will emerged onto the upper deck he found complete chaos. The pandemonium that had existed below seemed like a children's tea party in comparison. The ship had been dismasted and the once pristine and tidy deck was littered with tangled rigging and smashed woodwork. Around the wreckage, the whole ship's company was milling about and occupying every available space. Men were pushing each other from pillar to post with no apparent idea of what they should be doing. If they were trying to save themselves from drowning then they had little hope of achieving it. Furthermore in the darkness it was difficult to see what was happening. The feeble light shed from the few lanterns was largely obscured by the scores of bodies buzzing about like bees round a biscuit barrel. The mates were struggling in vain to regain control of the crew but the situation was delicately balanced between simple disorder and bloody combat. Will looked to the quarterdeck, which seemed to be relatively undamaged. He could just discern Captain Speke nervously pacing about his elevated position. Every so often he would stop and appear to bark an order to a subordinate, though he could not be heard above the hubbub. Speke was obviously an angry man.

The sailors too were angry. They were being ordered to remain on board: there was no need to panic. The men, however, would not be forcibly held on board while the ship was reduced to driftwood. There was a terrific commotion as the large gathering of frightened men fragmented into smaller groups. Some of these groups were hell-bent on abandoning ship despite the orders of the mates who were grossly outnumbered but barely maintaining command of the ugly scene. Other groups were nervously watching each other and wondering whether they should take the advice of the militants or obey orders. There was no doubt that before long the Captain would have ordered his armed marines to take control. Men would be shot dead if they did not comply with instructions.

It was impossible for Will to follow all the events that were taking place in such a short space of time and amid such chaos. He managed to get close enough to the ship's side to look overboard, but all he could see was white water up to about fifty feet from the ship. He had no idea how close the ship was to the shore or how badly the hull had been damaged. His instinct, however told him that the ship would surely remain afloat until the morning. When daylight came, the other English vessels in the vicinity would surely rescue them.

Meanwhile, the situation on board had become extremely unpleasant. Many of the men had already begun to lash together crude rafts using the plentiful supply of materials that surrounded them. Several of the ringleaders were loudly berating the other men for being so indecisive. Everyone, they said, should be building rafts before they were all drowned. Will decided that he did not want to be found with the militants when the marines arrived in force. Then, as he was moving to a position of more neutral ground, he came face to face with John Jennings who, together with several others, was in the process of getting a raft over the side of the ship. Jennings had obviously decided to join those escaping the clutches of the Navy. Jennings immediately released his hold on the raft and, with a snarl from his clenched jaw, leapt upon a surprised Will. The area of deck in the immediate vicinity of the conflict, though crammed solid with seamen, suddenly found enough space to accommodate the duel. Will tried to defend himself from Jennings' lunge, but before he could brace himself he was flat on his back and his face was being arraigned with blows. By this time Captain Speke had managed to muster a squad of marines in front of the quarterdeck. A volley was fired into the air in an attempt to restore order, but there were so many men between the marines and the for'ard areas where most of the dissent was occurring, that it had no immediate effect. Jennings' companions had already begun to disappear over the side to embark upon their crudely built life raft. No-one in authority was in any position to stop them and the remainder of the men merely watched the proceedings.

Will, his face bloodied and sore, struggled to fight back. With all his strength he managed to roll over onto his side and pushed Jennings off. The two enemies instantly jumped to their feet and charged. Will was just the stronger of the two and pushed Jennings towards the ship's side where the others had been climbing overboard. Jennings crashed against the side-rail and at once brought his knee hard up into Will's groin. Young Will was poleaxed; bent double, he was helpless... unable to counter Jennings' continued assault. Then he felt himself being lifted up into the air. He knew he was going overboard and there was nothing he could do to stop it...

At the moment that he hit the water, the extreme coldness took away what breath remained in his lungs. Will surfaced very close to the ship. He coughed up the water he had inhaled and wheezed for breath. Frantically he looked about him to find a way of getting out of the freezing water. Suddenly he realised that he had fallen into a gap between the ship and the life raft that Jennings' mates were riding. He caught sight of Jennings descending a rope that had been thrown over the side, but the raft, which was about fifteen feet away, had been taken up by a wave and was headed straight towards him. He tried desperately to swim away, but within seconds one of the timbers of the raft closed in on him, crushing him against the ship. The pain in his chest was unbearable...

Jennings let go his hold on the rope and fell the final eight feet onto the raft. He nearly fell overboard at once, but retained his grip and shouted at the others to get the raft away from the ship as quickly as possible. He did not know the exact fate of his adversary - Jennings could not see Will - but when he reached the safety of the shore he would be well pleased that he had finally put an end to William Knott.

15 REGIS DU PLESSIX

On the morning that followed the great battle of Quiberon Bay, there was to be little further fighting. Plenty of action remained, however, for as the first strains of daylight converted the blackness into a foggy grey, sailors in the two opposing fleets awoke uneasily at their emergency moorings and found their ships interspersed, each within the clutches of the other. By this time, one fleet had been proved superior and the inferior contestants were in for a shock.

Ashore, the scavengers were arriving in considerable numbers on the snow-white beaches near Le Croisic. As the first debris of battle was being washed ashore, any man in possession of a cart took it to the beach to help carry away the spoils of his own personal war of survival. With so many ships sunk, wrecked or merely damaged each successive high tide would bring a fresh harvest of useful items. It would be days, perhaps even weeks before the sea finally gave up all its trophies. The greater proportion of the mass of the sunken ships would never be released for popular consumption, but there would still be a bountiful crop of flotsam and jetsam ready for the reaping. To the peasant farmers and fisher-folk of Le Croisic, any item that could possibly be of use was fair game. Many of them that could not be used immediately might be valuable in an exchange. Always, it was a question of 'finders keepers'.

Many of those who had come to the seashore at first light in search of booty had also witnessed the ambivalent action of the day before. Despite the poor visibility, it was obvious to all that the French losses were severe. However, the sight of so many vessels being wrecked or damaged had ensured rich pickings at the time of year when they were most likely to be of advantage. Inevitably, personal gain outweighed national loss.

By the time that daylight had secured a hold on the fragile, windy morning, Regis du Plessix and his daughter Isabelle had almost finished their forage along the beach. The horizon was littered with the masts of scores of vessels even now attempting to bring the action to finality, but, to the du Plessix couple, the action on the beach was of far greater significance. Their small cart had acquired an assortment of items, mostly timbers of various sizes. Besides these, there were two flagons of rum, some small cartons of foodstuffs, and a number of packets of unused clothing. The most disquieting of the finds however were the bodies.

Isabelle, a gentle dark-haired seventeen year old, was very distressed by the sight of so many young men lying dead in the sand. It had been an impulse that had brought her to the beach in company with her father. Although he had advised against it, she had been keen to help her father and he was glad of it. Neither had expected to find such a sad spectacle awaiting them. The bodies, some untouched in their deaths, others with hideous injuries, lay scattered along the length of the beach in large numbers, frozen soulless corpses intertwined with seaweed.

Regis du Plessix, though shocked and sad at the sight of the dead, examined all the bodies as a matter of course. In the first place he was ensuring that the men were indeed dead and in the second there might be a ring, a pocketed coin or a gold watch. He did not consider his actions to be immoral. Such items could never be returned to relatives for there was no way of doing so. Rather than stealing from the dead, it was more a redistribution of assets to those who had need of them. In any case, if he did not help himself he knew full well that others would do so. Regis did not distinguish English from French - all were treated alike.

He came to yet another body lying close beside a large piece of driftwood. From the style of dress he could see that it was an Englishman. The trunk was face down in the sand so he turned the body over in order to examine it more closely. As he did so he heard a faint groan and detected the tiny movement of an arm.

"Isabelle, viens ici, vite."

Isabelle had found the sight of the dead too distressing. Consequently, she had avoided the bodies and had concentrated her search among the other items. When she heard her father shout, she ran to his side.

"Il vive," said Regis briefly, but with an air of excitement. Isabelle knelt down in the wet sand and thrust her ear to the man's chest. After a few moments listening intently she turned to her father.

"Oui, c'est ça, papa," she said, her eyes sparkling with anticipation.

"Ce n'est pas un homme, mais un enfant," said Regis studying the seaman's face. It was a young face, dark haired, smooth skinned and innocent. Regis had wanted a son, but although his wife had produced a baby boy, she had died painfully in childbirth. The infant, deprived of its mother's breast, also failed to survive. Regis had been left alone to bring up his daughter, the toddling two-year-old Isabelle. Now, the sight of this lad lying gravely ill on a foreign shore touched his heart. Regis could not tell the extent of the boy's injuries, but he would surely die if he were left on the beach. By a miracle God had preserved the boy's life and brought him ashore. They must not leave him to die.

Without even discussing the matter, Regis and Isabelle decided there and then that they would take the boy home. Neither was influenced by the fact that he was English or that he was a prisoner-of-war. Their duty was to care for another human being, this victim of the politicians, the son and brother that they had never had. Even with two pairs of hands it was difficult to get the patient from the beach into the cart. They tried to be as gentle as they could, but with unknown injuries it was a mercy that he was unconscious for he would have otherwise suffered agonies in the move and during the subsequent journey back to the cottage du Plessix.

Le Croisic was a small village with a population of four hundred and sixty. It was situated at the tip of a headland and just inside the entrance to a natural harbour from which a large proportion of the inhabitants operated fishing boats. Around the headland the coast was largely comprised of sandy beaches punctuated by the occasional gneissic outcrop, whilst the land inshore was sparsely populated with trees and used mainly for pasture. In random locations on the gentle hillsides, numerous small dwellings looked down upon the troubled waters of Le Four shoal. Their occupants were almost entirely poor farmers with a small number of animals. It was to one of these cottages about two miles from the village and a few hundred yards from the beach that Regis and Isabelle took the injured seaman. Soon he was resting peacefully in a warm bed with dry clothing and as many spare blankets as Isabelle could find. Then Regis climbed aboard his cart once more and set off to the village to fetch the doctor. As he drove along the meandering cliff road he began to ponder the consequences of having taken an Englishman into his home.

There was a good chance that the authorities would not discover that the boy was English for Regis had removed the patient's clothing and given him his own clothes. At present the boy was unconscious and thus his tongue would not give him away. Regis guessed that the doctor would not realise that he was treating a potential prisoner-of-war, at least for the time being. Regis was well aware of his responsibility to report the enemy seaman to the militia, but he was not prepared to do so at present. Lieutenant Rodier would be in no sympathetic mood after the defeat of the French fleet and would quite likely shoot the boy rather than suffer the problem of transporting a badly injured prisoner to gaol.

The doctor was an enormous Breton with little hair, glazed eyes and a liking for gin. He was, however, competent and not averse to visiting the sick, in contravention of what seemed to be the doctors' unwritten code of ethics. Lastly, he rarely overcharged his clients, another facet of his character that Regis liked. Claude Dixneuf was at home eating breakfast when Regis knocked, and within minutes of explaining the situation, Regis was driving the doctor back to the cottage on the cliffs. No sooner were they on the move when, to Regis' despair, the doctor asked about the nationality of the survivor. Regis thought quickly, but his hesitation was enough to give the game away. He replied that he thought the boy was English, though he had not yet uttered a syllable. The doctor smiled knowingly, touched the end of his nose with his forefinger and asked no more questions.

The rough track along which they travelled led uphill out of the village and then contoured along the seaward side of the headland. The gales of the day before had continued all night and were still giving rise to hazardous conditions for those at sea. With the full force of the wind beating against the side of the cart it proved quite difficult to navigate the vehicle around the numerous obstacles along the route. The whole business of returning to the cottage with medical assistance took half an hour and by the time the daylight was two hours old Monsieur Dixneuf had arrived at the bed of the immensely lucky survivor. He conducted his examination with Isabelle in anxious attendance. Apart from broken ribs, which, he said, would give the lad a lot of pain for a month or so, and considerable bruising around the chest, arms and face, there was nothing seriously wrong. The big man prescribed warmth, prolonged rest and attentive nursing for a complete cure and with a suggestive wink he intimated his confidence that Isabelle could handle it. She shook his hand in delight and smiled at her father.

As Regis and the doctor left the cottage to begin the return journey they witnessed a spectacle in the bay the like of which neither had seen before. There, but a few miles from the shore, two French men-of-war appeared to be running for the safety of Le Croisic harbour. With the gale astern of them their speed was remarkable. In pursuit were two smaller English ships, and from the courses being followed it became increasingly obvious to the spectators that the French were not going to make safety. Regis, knowing little of sailing matters, could not understand the tactics of the situation. As the French approached nearer and nearer to part of the rock-strewn coast he was amazed that his countrymen could not come up with a better plan of action than to run aground.

At the very best they might be beached on the sand farther north. At the worst the ships would have their bowels torn open by the razor-sharp protuberances close inshore. In line astern, the two vessels were heading for certain destruction. The two men watched, helpless and incredulous. They could only watch and await the end whilst the two ships seemed unable or unwilling to manoeuvre in the restricted space available. With the English so close behind it may have been that the two captains had decided upon beaching as the only available option.

With two ships about to smash themselves to pieces, it was obvious that the doctor would soon be the busiest man in the area and so he and Regis quickly climbed aboard the cart and set off at speed. Regis hurried the horse as well as he could, whilst trying to keep abreast of the events below. The doctor became most restive at the sight of such deliberate disregard for human life, and began to complain to Regis. He resented the way those in authority always gambled with the lives of others as if they were but insignificant coins. Too often it was the medical profession that had to clear up the mess and carnage caused by the military.

The leading French ship actually increased her sail as she neared the shore, whilst by now the English had begun to turn around into the wind, a dangerous manoeuvre in the prevailing conditions. The leading ship sped on rapidly and then, when it came to within a cable of the beach, it was lifted up into the air as if it were a toy. At that moment all navigation was over. The masts and most of the rigging seemed to disintegrate, collapsing into a bedraggled mass on the upper deck. Much of it hung over the ship's side and became caught up in the waves that were sweeping in towards the beach. Then, apparently from nowhere, swarms of dark ant-like creatures began to leap into the sea and swim ashore for there were still a good many yards of angry foam between the ship and dry land. Within minutes, the second ship suffered an identical fate and the number of men who were struggling for their lives was doubled. Amazingly, this was not the end of the drama for, just as the second ship began to topple over on her starboard beam, there was a puff of smoke from one of the English ships followed by the time-delayed blast of a broadside fired in anger. The accuracy was deadly. The shot ripped into the magazine of the first stricken vessel and the resulting explosion reduced her to an inferno of blazing timbers that was unrecognisable as a ship. The horse took fright and began to bolt down the road. Regis and the doctor bounced in their seats like hares escaping from a pack, and while Regis struggled to regain control of the frightened stallion the good doctor cursed the English. There was no further firing and the attackers sailed away making heavy going as they beat into the gale-force winds.

Meanwhile Isabelle remained at the bedside of the young man. Time and again she adjusted the position of his blankets and between times caressed his forehead whilst checking his temperature. Isabelle was able to discern a gradual return from being bitterly cold and corpse-like to a normal temperature, as well as a restoration of a lively colour to the lad's handsome complexion. But still he remained unconscious. Isabelle did not worry unduly for the doctor had indicated that it could be a day or more before the boy regained consciousness.

The day passed slowly for Isabelle. Regis, on the other hand, could hardly have been busier as he did all he could to help the survivors of the beachings. By mid afternoon the first French ship was heavily consumed by the fires that still raged inside her, but furthermore the second was also on fire, this time without the help of the English. Regis subsequently discovered that her crew had set her on fire before

136

abandoning ship. The doctor was kept extremely busy on the beach, though there was no shortage of help, and by late in the afternoon Regis returned exhausted and hungry to his cottage. There he found his daughter still tending to her newfound friend who still showed no signs of consciousness.

There had been several moments during the day when Regis had seriously questioned his own wisdom in bringing the Englishman into his home. The sight of his countrymen with agonising powder burns, their limbs puffed into grotesque balloons, was sickening enough, but the fact that they had been caused directly by English egression against a helpless wreck made it intolerable. The sailors themselves, however, were not so much mad at the English as they were at their captain and officers for running them ashore in the way that they did. There could be no excuse for such bad tactics and management and Regis knew at once why his nation had lost the battle. There could be no doubting the superiority of the English in all departments: gunnery, seamanship, equipment and, above all, leadership. This last, he suspected, was the real reason for the ignominy of the French defeat.

By the time that Regis had returned to stare down in expectation at the young English face in his bed, he had quite overcome his feelings of animosity towards Englishmen. There was the face of a boy who might have been his son had his wife and child lived. It took no conversation between father and daughter to tell that Isabelle felt the same way. Indeed she seemed to have become obsessed with the health of her patient and could turn her attention to other things only briefly before returning to the bedside vigil. That night, the healthy young girl slept very badly in comparison to the sick sailor who was enjoying perfect mental rest. On several occasions during the night Isabelle rose from her rummaged, uncomfortable bedclothes in order to check the condition of her charge, but with no positive response. The little sleep she did fall into was punctuated by unpleasant dreams of grotesque bodies rising from the wind-swept beaches and prowling the cliff paths in search of her. Thus by the time that the light of a new day percolated through the tiny windows of the cottage, she was extremely relieved to find the situation exactly as it had been the day before. Fortunately, Isabelle had acquired a far more sensible order of priorities. Paying only fleeting visits to her patient, she focused her attention on her father's appetite and her household chores, both of which had been neglected on the previous day.

Regis awoke early. Refreshed from a deep, dreamless slumber, he breakfasted leisurely on bread and jam. Then he set off to the beach once more in search of any more useful items that might have come ashore in the night. On the beach, the smouldering skeletal remains of the once proud men-of-war lay shamefully where they had fallen. There was no sign of their crews. Many of those who had been uninjured and who were no more than illiterate and inexperienced landsmen had deserted back to their homes. Others who were more responsible to discipline had been mustered on the sand and marched off towards St. Nazaire, the nearest naval port.

137

As Regis gazed in bewilderment at the surf-pounded hulks he noticed that the local militia were approaching. The small platoon was in the charge of Lieutenant Rodier and was responsible for the maintenance of law and order in the area. Now that the beach had become a focal point for village life it was obviously a checkpoint on the patrol route. Regis guessed that they would not allow any of the locals near the ships until all surviving official documents and valuables had been recovered. He set off in the opposite direction to join the dozen other beachcombers in what was to be a daily ritual for the next two weeks.

As the eve of the second day drew to a close and the du Plessix were about to retire, Isabelle heard a faint moan from her patient. In a flash she was at his bedside, just in time to witness the raising of the youth's heavy eyelids. There beneath was a pair of anguished and quizzical brown eyes. Isabelle guessed that his anguish was caused by the pains from his injuries, and she soothed his cheek with a delicate touch of her fingers. Then the youth seemed to relax after the initial tension of his re-awakening though his gaze, almost of disbelief, asked a hundred questions. His lips, parched from hours of immersion in cold salt water, could manage but one.

"Who are you?" he said.

"Papa, papa, il se reveille." Isabelle addressed her father. Regis hurried into the room and stood alongside his daughter. The brown eyes passed only fleetingly to the newcomer and then returned to the perfect vision of loveliness that was Isabelle.

"Please may I have some water?" The lips were swollen and sore.

"Qu'est-ce qu'il dit?" questioned Regis, shrugging his shoulders. Isabelle shook her head.

"Je ne sais pas, papa," she replied.

16 TOM ELIOT

The escape of John Jennings from the stricken HMS *Resolution* proved to be more of an ordeal than remaining on board. No sooner had Jennings and his cohorts pushed their crude raft away from the ship's side, and out of the lee, than white-crested breakers swept up the fragile craft. Even in the middle of the night, they seemed to glow with a macabre, blue-green luminescence. Jennings, who, minutes earlier, had been desperate to leave what he thought was a sinking ship, was terrified. The raft had been hurriedly put together and was barely able to support the weight of the three men aboard it. Surely it could never survive regular immersion below the surface of the sea as the enormous rolling waves swept in from the Bay of Biscay. The water was so cold and the gale force wind so chilling that Jennings had lost the feeling of his extremities from the moment he boarded the raft. There was nothing more he could do now than to hold on to the timbers and pray that the force of the waves would not sweep him off to certain death. They could not return to the *Resolution*, even if they tried, for the elements had separated the two platforms to too great a distance. Even the strongest swimmer could not have made the return journey in such conditions, and Jennings was not a strong swimmer.

Jennings found a loose end of rope where one of the fixings had been finished off hurriedly. This he tied around his wrist in the hope that if he were swept off the raft he would be able to pull himself back onto it. He glanced at the faces of Eliot and Dobbs and saw that they looked as frightened as he himself felt. Before tonight he had known them only superficially. Now their lives lay balanced on the fulcrum of fate. At any moment they might perish; survival was their only concern. An invisible bond of destiny now linked the men more firmly than they could ever have imagined.

In the darkness, the only things visible were several flickering lights aboard the *Resolution*, although these were rapidly becoming fainter. This was their only means of gauging their distance from the ship. They had no idea how far they were from the mainland and Jennings bitterly regretted his actions that had now proved to be foolhardy in the extreme. His only consolation was that he had finally settled the score with his enemy. He gained considerable satisfaction from the lingering memory of Knott being crushed between the raft and the ship, the look of agony as his chest was pulped, and his subsequent disappearance into the hissing foam. Jennings must survive.

The three men did not speak at all; they were far too cold and miserable to bother with the trivialities of conversation. All felt wretched. All were trying to cling to the flimsy raft with a desperation that only condemned men can muster. They had no doubt that they were travelling somewhere for the lights on the ship had receded into the gloom and the fluorescent water was still sweeping past them, driving them away from the ship in the direction of the gale. Jennings was unable to guess how long they had been on the raft, but after a seemingly endless period in which he wrestled with his consciousness, he became convinced that he could hear a different sound from that of the open sea. He guessed that the sound was the rumble of the enormous surf upon a beach. Furthermore, the waves he could see around him had become much more like the breakers which sweep in towards shallow waters.

Jennings was jubilant and vented his feelings to the others, who, realising that he was right, suddenly became revitalised. Pathetically they all strived to paddle the raft with their hands as if to speed themselves along, but in the grip of such vast elemental forces it was totally ineffective. Ten minutes later they were close to the shore. Jennings caught sight of the waves breaking on the beach. He released his bond to the raft and slid into the sea, confident that he would be able to swim such a short distance. Once immersed in the sea he was surprised to find that it seemed warm, but he did not know why and was not concerned about it. The only thing that mattered to him was to stroke to safety. For once, he had made a good decision.

Jennings made faster progress than the raft and within a minute he felt the delicious support of sand beneath his frozen feet. With every last measure of energy he struggled out of the vicious breakers that burst down upon him, occasionally knocking him over. Finally, he collapsed gratefully into a large clump of warm grass at the base of a sand dune. In the luxury of his field bed he fell asleep instantly…

Jennings awoke, startled. Something was tickling his body. Then he realised that a pair of hands was feeling his clothing and rifling his pockets. Quickly he rolled over and came face to face with an elderly man. For a moment each stared at the other, bemused, scared. It was the elderly man who backed down. He ran off along the beach, shouting at the top of his voice. Jennings could make no sense of the man's exclamations and then realised that it was because the man was speaking a foreign language. It was daylight, but the weather was much the same as it had been during the night. Jennings staggered to his feet, which were still numb, but tingling painfully as the nerve ends recovered from their ill treatment in the freezing water. Awkwardly, Jennings began to stumble through the soft sand in the opposite direction to that of his finder. He soon came across Dobbs and Eliot, lying prone in a rather more protected position. The old chap must have missed them for they were still asleep. He shook them into consciousness and quickly acquainted them with the situation. Then Jennings led his compatriots away at best speed, though he had not the faintest idea where he was going. As he looked over his shoulder he could make out numerous distant figures, which he took to be soldiers, apparently patrolling the coastline. Fortunately there were none that could be seen in the direction ahead of them so Jennings judged that they should continue their flight that way.

After several hundred yards of painful, lumbering effort, the three men collapsed in a sand hollow to recover their breath and debate their plan of action. There was very little else they could do but escape from the area as quickly as they could, now their presence had been publicised. But they were weak, hungry, and had no conception of the best direction in which to travel. This was France and she was at war with England. They knew only that they were somewhere on the coast of Brittany, which Eliot happened to know was close to the Bay of Biscay.

"We'll steal a ship somewhere, that's what we'll do. We're all seamen, we can manage." That was Dobbs' idea.

"And where the hell are we going to find a ship, flea brain?" asked Jennings, disgustedly. "We're at war with these buggers. You don't just walk onto a ship and steal it, even if you know where there's one to steal."

Elias Dobbs resented being dubbed a flea brain, but said nothing for he realised that it had been a stupid suggestion. He could already tell that Jennings was not going to be easy to get on with.

"First things first," led Jennings. "Let's get some transport away from this area where they are going to be looking for us. North is the direction to go, but there's one problem with that."

"What's that?" asked Tom Eliot.

Jennings pointed with his hand. "That's north, and to get there we've got to go in the very direction we don't want to go." He was pointing to the direction in which the old man had run off along the beach. "We'll head east as fast as we can, and if we can pinch transport on the way, so much the better." There was no time for lengthy discussions: they had to be on the move.

They set off to climb up the gentle hillside away from the sea. The going was quite easy, but it was across open land and they were all very tired. They kept close to the hedgerows that lined the fields and sought whatever cover they could. Although they tried to run at first, this pace soon relaxed to a brisk walk with fairly frequent stops for rest and observation. As they climbed and gained more height they saw the spectacle of opposing warships in pursuit of each other, heading towards the shore. It was obvious that the English were still giving the French lessons in seamanship, and the three fugitives would have loved to lie on the cliffs and watch the events at their leisure. However, escape was far more important.

Higher and higher up the slopes they climbed until they came to a track that led along the hillside to a cottage. There, outside the cottage a man was standing quite still, engrossed in the events at sea. It was fortunate that he was so busy watching the imminent downfall of his own nation's ships that he had no knowledge of the proximity of the three Englishmen as they crossed the track and hid behind a convenient shrub. To the interest of the seamen, there was a horse and cart already waiting outside the cottage.

"We'll have that cart," said Jennings eagerly. It was the answer to his prayers. "I'll go around the back and you two keep an eye on this side. When I give a whistle, get him.

"That's incredible," said Dobbs.

"What is?" asked Jennings, irritated by the remark. He looked at Dobbs, who in turn was gazing out to sea. The sight of the men-of-war bewitched Dobbs as - suicidally - they flew towards the shore.

"You cunt!" exclaimed Jennings. "Did you hear what I said?"

"Course I did," said Dobbs indignantly. "Did you see the size of him?" He nodded towards the cottage, but did not take his eyes off the ships. A satisfied smirk appeared on his face at the thought of getting one over on Jennings. There were now two men standing outside the cottage and watching the drama. The second man was of frightening proportions and looked as if he could beat off the three of them single-handed. The Englishmen little suspected that he was a man of medicine and as gentle as a baby.

"I'm not fighting him," said Dobbs, even if there are three of us."

"And what about you?" Jennings asked Eliot.

"I don't think it would be wise," said Eliot, patronisingly.

"You bastards." Jennings made a decision. "Come on."

They pressed on to the top of the escarpment. Regis du Plessix would never know how fortunate he was that John Jennings had not come to call.

Once at the top of the hill, the whole geographical layout of the area could be seen. Beneath them lay a small bay around which they must pass in order to proceed north. Beyond that lay grey rolling hills very similar to the one that they had just climbed. Apart from a few scattered homesteads, there was little indication that they were likely to encounter vast hordes of Frenchmen. There seemed to be a village at the end of the headland on which they were standing, but they would be travelling away from it.

"We'll get as far as we can around the bay and then look for a nice quiet cottage to spend the night," said Jennings. "I could do with a good feed and a sleep." The others nodded their agreement. About a hundred yards below their position was another track that seemed to lead in the right direction. So, temporarily refreshed, they ran down the slope, crossed two hedges, and, with some relief, joined the track.

"Keep your eyes open for Frogs," ordered Jennings. He had assumed his role as leader without any opposition from the other two. After the incident at the cottage he knew that they were both weak characters. "Tom, you watch behind."

The track meandered down the hillside towards the edge of the bay. There, it appeared to run level with the waterside for some distance before it turned uphill once more to the north. Progress was much quicker once they were on the track, and even though it was rough there were no other hurdles to slow them down.

"Look out, someone coming." Dobbs had spotted a lone peasant about a quarter of a mile down the track leading a horse and cart towards them. They all leapt off the track and lay flat behind whatever cover was available.

"Can you see any soldiers, anyone?" quizzed Jennings.

"Not a soul," replied Eliot.

"No," confirmed Dobbs, scanning the landscape.

"Right, he's our man." Jennings' eyes half closed in anticipation. Slowly the unsuspecting peasant ambled his animal towards his village and his home. He had been away from his family since early yesterday morning and was quite unaware of the naval battle or, more importantly to him, of its ramifications ashore. He was taken completely by surprise as Jennings jumped up from his cover and thrust his arm around the man's throat from behind. Then the peasant was dragged behind the bush that Jennings had been using for a hide-away. Tom Eliot ran out to grab the horse's reins lest the animal run away. Elias Dobbs was a spare part. There was a brief groan from the rear of the greenery and then Jennings appeared wiping blood from the blade of a long glistening knife. Dobbs who had nothing else to do spotted it at once.

"You fool, you absolute bloody fool. What did you do that for?" Elias went berserk, screaming at Jennings. "We've no chance now. We didn't have much of one before, but when they catch us now we're up for murder." Elias was crimson with rage. For a man of diminutive proportions he had a foul temper when roused. Jennings had treated him badly enough without this. "You know what they do in this country, don't you? They don't hang you... oh, no. They chop your bloody head off. Well thanks very much, pal, you've just said goodbye to ours. You stupid, bloodthirsty, murderous cunt!"

Jennings remained quite unaffected by the tirade; even Eliot was surprised by the ferocity of Dobbs verbal attack on Jennings. Eliot was a worried man also, but hurling abuse at Jennings was still far from his mind. Jennings walked to where Dobbs was standing. The Kentish man's face was a picture of innocence.

"Don't worry Elias, old friend," he said soothingly, as if to make up for all the things he had said about Dobbs in the past. "You should trust me, you know. I won't let you down." He put his left arm around Dobbs' neck and swung the still bloody knife with a jerk, deep into the man's bowels. There he left it, embedded to the hilt, while his victim instinctively clutched the handle with both hands and staggered several paces backwards. An expression of ultimate horror appeared briefly on the face of the dying man before his eyes closed for the last time. Jennings dragged him off to the same place as the peasant lay. Dobbs did not die at once. The trauma of the attack had caused him to lose consciousness, but the wound was a fatal one and it was fortunate that he did not suffer.

Eliot collapsed at the roadside with his head in his hands. For a full ten minutes he sat motionless, disbelieving and adrift from reality. Even the thought of his own safety in the company of this butcher did not enter his head. It was not until Jennings approached him wearing the peasant's clothes that Eliot gathered his presence of mind.

"Did you have to do that?" he asked forlornly.

"He was asking for it. Nobody talks to me like that." Jennings was still outwardly relaxed, but inside, his hatred was only now beginning to subside. "There's no problem now. Over there lie the bodies of two men dressed in English seamen's clothes. Dead men have no French accents. Even if they do discover that one of them 's a Frog, it's quite simple - one of them killed the other. The knife is there to prove it. We don't know anything about it, do we?" Jennings looked at Eliot knowingly. Eliot thought quietly to himself for a few minutes. He could not quite understand his countryman's logic, but he was not inclined to disagree. He said nothing. Jennings continued. "Right, let's get as much space between us and these corpses as possible."

Jennings leapt into the cart and turned it around so that it faced in the direction from which it had just come. Then he shook the reins and the horse broke into a trot even as Eliot was still debating whether he should jump aboard. He soon made up his mind, however, and ran after the cart to jump up beside Jennings.

"Now then, since you've decided to join me, get down underneath the sheet in the back," ordered Jennings. "I look French but you don't." Eliot could see the logic of complying with the instruction. With luck, they would be able to travel a good distance and be questioned by nobody. Besides, after what had just happened to Dobbs, Eliot would do whatever Jennings told him to. The fact that Jennings had left the knife sticking out of Dobbs' guts did not make him any less dangerous. Even in hand-to-hand combat Eliot did not fancy his chances against his travelling companion.

At present, Jennings had no reason to dislike him, but Eliot now knew only too well that if the time ever came when Jennings had no use for him, his life was as good as over. Indeed, in his English clothes he was already something of a liability to Jennings. This man was the cruellest, evil mind that Eliot had ever met and arguments were to be avoided at all costs.

Eliot lay in the back of the cart and pulled a rather foul smelling rain sheet over him, whilst Jennings drove onwards. It was the most uncomfortable ride Eliot had ever had in his life. He remembered vividly the first day he had gone to sea. As a landsman he had been badly sick and it had seemed as if it would last for the rest of his life. Once at sea, there was no escape from seasickness. Fortunately, he did eventually get used to it. He was now in a similar position for he was being bruised and battered with every wearisome yard they travelled, but he dared not complain or ask to stop for a rest.

The cart descended from the escarpment and followed the track at sea level around the edge of the bay. On the left was a small beach upon which an incessant succession of sizeable waves was breaking. At the far end of the bay and the northern extremity of the headland from which they had come, Jennings could see more clearly the village with its fleet of fishing boats moored close inshore. It was obvious that the site of the village had been well chosen to be in the lee of the weather. Then he noticed a number of people walking along the track towards him. He kept cool knowing that he would not be recognised if he kept silent. It was too late to hide for he must have been spotted. As the people drew nearer he counted five men who all looked like farming folk. He did not slow the cart, which was travelling at quite a speed. As he went past, one man had to jump aside rather more quickly than he had thought. There was a shout of annoyance at Jennings after the cart had gone past, but he did not look back. Only when he was a considerable distance away did he, through curiosity, look to see if there was anyone following. There was not.

Having rounded the southern side of the bay they travelled for several hours more, occasionally meeting people, but never stopping. When the track began to climb steadily upwards the pace slackened considerably and even Jennings was beginning to tire. Eliot had almost passed out with pain, but he did not complain. Both men had not eaten for over a day and finally Jennings decided that before the daylight began to recede he should look around for somewhere to get a meal and a bed for the night. He shouted his plan to Eliot and received a feeble reply. Eliot tried to sit up with his back against the seat, but it was more than he could manage. His back was so stiff and sore that he could hardly bend. However, after much discomfort he finally succeeded and as he looked away from the back of the cart he could see they had come a considerable distance. Way beneath them was the bay and the headland, the other side of which was the place that they had come ashore. How far they would have to travel he had no notion. He could not contemplate another day of travelling in such a manner, and the whole escapade began to seem pointless. They would never be able to leave the country even if they did find a port. They had no money or food, nothing except the clothes they wore - and of those, Eliot's were English. He wished he had stayed on board the *Resolution*. At the time he had been convinced that he must escape from the ship in order to survive. Since then, his future had looked progressively gloomier. First he had risked his life on that ridiculous raft in suicidal seas. Now here he was in enemy country with a travelling companion who would kill him for the slightest reason. Tom Eliot was at his lowest ebb. Life on the ship had never been easy, but there was always a bed, food and good shipmates. They lived as a team and fought as a team. They shared the same perils and the same luxuries. It was a wonderful life compared to the living hell which he was now experiencing. When he had first discovered himself on the beach, the feeling of elation was unbelievable, for he had survived a terrible ordeal. Since then, matters had become even worse than being adrift on a raft. He preferred drowning to any sort of death that Jennings might put him to. Eliot was convinced that, whatever Jennings was planning, he would not be able to stay with that man for much longer. Somehow he would have to escape; he would even give himself up to the soldiers. They would not execute him: he had done nothing wrong. Nothing - not even a French prison - could be as bad as this.

Eventually, as the afternoon began to fade and the gloom of the short winter evening fast approached, Jennings drove the cart off the road and stopped. He got down and ordered Eliot out of the cart. By now, Eliot was so stiff that movement of any kind was painful, but he forced himself to do what Jennings wanted. He must not become a burden.

"There's a cottage up there." Jennings pointed to a small building made of grey stone about two hundred yards from where they stood. It was obviously inhabited, for a swirling column of smoke rose from its squat chimney only to be swept away by the wind, which still gusted in from the west. Jennings went on. "I don't think there are any other places nearby. "We'll watch it and see what happens. I doubt whether there's more than a single family live there, in which case there'll be a man, a woman and some kids, maybe less. There'll have to be a bloody army in there to stop us eating and sleeping here tonight."

Eliot and Jennings found a concealed position from where they could watch the door of the cottage. It was a crudely built dwelling of probably two rooms. At the back there appeared to be a kitchen garden, which looked well stocked.

During the half hour that they watched the house, they were able to deduce that there was just an elderly couple living inside. The wife could be seen at the window from time to time, and on one occasion came out of the door to dispose of a pail of hot water. It seemed that the Englishmen had arrived just in time for supper. The man was visible to them only once, but it was enough for Jennings to be able to gauge the level of threat from the occupants.

"Time to go," he ordered suddenly. Eliot, who had been lying quietly beside Jennings, was surprised, but he stood up and wondered what violence his companion was planning for this helpless and unsuspecting couple.

"How are we going in?" he asked.

"Through the front door, dumb-head. How else?" said Jennings scornfully. So saying, he stood up, walked into the open and began to approach the house. It was a matter of yards to the door, and having reached it, he walked into the house as if it were his own.

The French couple were sat at a small table enjoying a simple meal. Both were startled and jumped from their seats. The old man adopted a threatening posture, but when it came to threats Jennings was the master. His facial contours said more than a hundred words of local dialect could have. For a moment Jennings and the Frenchman stood still, glaring at each other. Eliot, who had followed his leader into

145

the room, waited for a reaction. The Frenchman grabbed a knife from the table and his wife ran to the corner of the room farthest from the door. There she turned to face the intruders. In a flash, Jennings had grabbed a chair, raised it to waist height with the legs facing his armed opponent, and then with a bloodcurdling scream, had run at the old man. In a second, the Breton was pinned against the wall with his weapon waving in the air. Eliot disarmed him. The poor man had never stood a chance against Jennings and this move was sufficient for him to give up all hope of offering any resistance. The wife covered her mouth with her hand and began to sob. Eliot put the knife back on the table and, grabbing a piece of bread, began to devour it as if it were the first he had ever tasted.

"Get some rope, and be quick about it," ordered Jennings. Eliot stuffed the bread into his mouth and began to look around inside the cottage. When he could find nothing suitable, he remembered that there had been a length of rope in the cart.

"There's some in the cart." he said, pleased with himself. Jennings, however, was not so delighted. Without taking his eyes off the terrified Frenchman, he cursed.

"You stupid mutt. Why didn't you bring it with you? Hurry up. I don't want to be here all night."

With all the speed he could summon from his aching limbs Eliot ran the distance to the cart to fetch the rope. The horse was contentedly chewing at a patch of fresh grass. Eliot leapt into the cart, gathered up the reins and drove it quickly to the cottage door. There he jumped down and took the rope into the house.

"Give me that knife," said Jennings, and having received it he dropped the chair and ordered Eliot to tie up the old man. As Eliot duly pulled the man's arms behind his back and wrapped the rope around his wrists, the woman tried to protest. Jennings grabbed her at once and used the same rope to tie her to her husband. The two unfortunates were then forcibly seated in the corner of the room while Jennings and Eliot tucked into the food that they had so long awaited.

By this time it had become quite dark and Jennings lit an oil lamp that stood on a shelf beside the fire. Eliot was feeling very tired indeed. The events of the last two days had caught him up and now that he was able to relax somewhat his brain was beginning to fail. Jennings was also ready for sleep. Having finished his meal he made sure that the couple were securely tied together, back to back. As an extra precaution he forced them to accept gags in their mouths, not that there was much chance of them attracting attention by shouting. The house was two hundred yards from the track and on a cold November night there would surely be nobody about.

When he was satisfied with the prisoners' security, Jennings went to the bed in the other room only to find that Eliot was already preparing to sleep on it.

"Clear off," said Jennings to Eliot. "I'm on here tonight. You have the floor by the fire. That way you can keep an eye on our friends as well."

"But there's plenty of room for both of us," protested Eliot. He was very tired and the lure of the bed was causing him to forget the danger of upsetting Jennings. The Kentish man made no reply except to give Eliot such a glare that Eliot retreated at once. As he left the room the bedroom door was slammed behind him.

In the living room, Eliot looked around for something to sleep on. There was only a mat by the fire. He examined the mat and found that it was made of coarse fibre. It would probably be most uncomfortable, but in comparison to the hard, cold stone floor it would at least form a crude mattress. He found a cushion on a chair and used it for a pillow. Then he stoked the fire with several neatly cut logs that stood beside the grate. In the dim light of the room he could see the old folk sitting uncomfortably and watching his every move. He guessed that their sad faces were wondering what their fate would be.

Eliot turned down the lamp and lay on his horsehair bed, but the recent events were too fresh in his mind for him to sleep. In the darkness, as he lay with his eyes closed, he could see incessant images of waves on the seashore, of running across cliffs and fields, and of two brutal murders. He saw the death agonies of two men not unlike himself and felt his own life slipping away into the consuming, bottomless, black void of eternity. He remembered the hours of agony as he lay daring not to move in the back of the cart. Then he remembered the frightened, pleading looks on the faces of the captives, as he was about to extinguish the flame of the oil lamp. Would Jennings extinguish their lives too, just as carelessly? The old folk would be unable to move for hours now. They would be hungry, cold and uncomfortable, just like he was in that cart. Their limbs, frail and bruised would be getting more and more numb. The shock alone might even kill one or both of them. Then Eliot thought again about his chances of survival with Jennings. He knew deep down that they would never escape the country and the thought of a journey, however short, with that madman appalled him. He considered his chances in the hands of the French authorities. Surely, they must take prisoners? There was no reason to execute him, Tom Eliot, ordinary seaman, who had done nothing wrong. He had harmed no-one except these poor folk. Again, their faces materialised in his mind's eye. He must release them. He must surrender to the soldiers. It was his only chance. Jennings had become aggressive towards him too, and would probably kill him tomorrow. If he released the old couple they would go and fetch the soldiers. All he had to do was to remain in the cottage and pretend to be asleep. He could tell Jennings that they had broken loose on their own - perhaps the man had a concealed knife.

Eliot opened his eyes and stared at the ceiling, which was glowing orange with reflected light from the log fire. He made his decision and stood up silently. In the glow from the fire he could see the prisoners in the corner, still wide-awake with fear. He fetched the knife that lay on the table and approached the couple. The fear in their eyes intensified to wild panic and they both struggled with their bonds as they anticipated their own imminent murder. They could hardly have expected that the man who had broken into their home and had tied them up was about to release them unharmed. Eliot was as quiet in his movements as he could possibly be, knowing that Jennings was a matter of feet away from him. He held his finger to his lips in a gesture that he hoped would encourage silence from the captives as he severed their bonds. Fortunately, they quickly realised that he was releasing them and they kept quiet. Dumbfounded, they sat on the floor and rubbed their limbs to restore the stifled circulation. The man quickly hugged his wife, kissed her cheek and rose quietly. He stared at Eliot in puzzlement. What was he to do now? Eliot indicated the door. The man was free to go. For a moment the Frenchman was reluctant to leave. He seemed either incredulous or mistrustful. Was it a trick? He looked at his wife and then at Eliot who repeated the gesture, this time trying to include the woman.

They needed no further invitation. The man took his wife's hand to lead her to the door. Unfortunately, after being tied up for so long in an awkward, uncomfortable position, the woman's legs were not quite ready to obey her. She stumbled and fell against the table, knocking a piece of crockery onto the floor. For an instant the three people stood motionless. Then Eliot heard a sound from the adjacent room.

"Go, go... now... quickly," he urged them. They spoke no English, but they understood. Just as they had left the house and were climbing onto the cart to escape, Jennings burst into the room where Eliot was standing indecisively.

"Where are they?" he snarled.

"Gone," said Eliot smugly, as he stood between Jennings and the door. Jennings looked past Eliot to the open doorway where he could see nothing but darkness, but the sounds informed him of the situation. Eliot was so pleased because he had something for himself that he quite forgot about the knife that he still held in his right hand. Suddenly the fire, which had been burning contentedly, spat an ember into the room as if it were a pistol shot. For Eliot, it would have been better if it were. He was disturbed and turned his face away from Jennings for a moment, which, though brief, was sufficient for Jennings to pounce on him and knock him to the floor. His knife hand was held firmly to the ground by Jennings' left, and before he could summon the energy to rally against the attack, Jennings had seized a metal poker that stood alongside the grate. In the seconds before he lost consciousness forever, Eliot was aware that he had thwarted Jennings and was pleased.

17 ELIZABETH KNOTT

In the immediate aftermath of the events that had so divided the Knott family Lizzie had been, quite naturally, a destroyed personality. At a stroke she had lost not one but two of the men in her life. She had never intended to love Edward Gibbon, but love had grown within her and she had given him everything. Now she had nothing: the affair was over. Not only had her man been forbidden to her, but Edward too, fearing a scandal, had stayed well away from Lizzie and there was rumour of another woman. Lizzie had also lost young Will whom she loved dearly as a brother, friend and past playmate. Unlike a lost sweetheart a brother could never be replaced and she could not shake off even the slightest feeling of responsibility for Will's absence.

William soon forgave her for her indiscretions, but Lizzie had been struck two mortal blows in the deep recesses of her heart. In return for her father's forgiveness she did her best to appear normal to her parents, but inevitably she found herself struggling to hold back the tears a dozen times each day. Indeed there were many occasions when Lizzie and her mother, clamped tightly in each other's embrace, wept unashamedly for the welfare of young Will.

On the day after Will's departure their only information of his whereabouts had been the casual but devastating remark from the Press Officer that Will had been signed on by the Navy as a volunteer. After that meeting with the officer in the graveyard William had proceeded to Dover without delay and had done his utmost to secure his son's release. There was never any hope of that, however. Even if Will had not signed a contract, he would still have been held amongst the pressed men. William lacked the financial resources necessary to bribe the appropriate people and was forced to leave Dover without his son and in despair for the boy's safety. His earnest enquiries had nonetheless born even the tiniest fruit for he had discovered that Will would probably join Admiral Hawke's fleet from which he would not return until either he had earned some leave or the Navy had no further need of him. Either way, he was unlikely to return for a very long time.

William was only too familiar with the conditions of service within the fleet and these, together with the risks if Will were to see active service against the French, weighed heavily against the lad ever returning alive. Thus it was a very despondent lightkeeper who returned to the small cottage on the South Foreland that evening.

William and Elizabeth did all they could to help Lizzie overcome the traumas she had been caused, but there was little to be done. Only the passage of time could heal the grievous wounds, or so it seemed, for, as attractive, impressionable young girls are wont to do, Lizzie recovered almost overnight. A chance meeting with a handsome young man admirably achieved what her parents had been praying for. It was one summer Sunday afternoon whilst walking with her younger brothers along the cliffs that Lizzie met James. The first sight of his broad labourer's shoulders his manly gait and his admiring smile had been sufficient to diminish her problems tenfold. Now, six months later and two days before Christmas, she was to be married to the most important man in her rejuvenated world.

Elizabeth had never been so busy. Far outweighing the onerous but pleasant seasonal preparations were those for the wedding of her firstborn. If only she might have some word of Will to hear that he would be home for Christmas, or just that he were alive and well, would make Elizabeth the happiest woman in the county. The wedding had been intentionally arranged to a date close to Christmas in the hope that Will might come home for the holiday, but there had been no word from him since the day he had left home. Even though they believed that he had been sent to Hawke's fleet, its size was such that he could have joined any one of a score of ships. The Knott family had countless times digested all news of the war that reached the village, but Hawke's fleet seemed to be doing little and the news was scant. Elizabeth was consoled by the thought that since there had been little combat her son was probably safe, at the very least. Then, at the beginning of December came news of a great victory at Quiberon Bay, wherever that might be. The British had lost several ships, but casualties were light and the Knotts could only pray that Will was not among them.

Meanwhile, the plans for the wedding proceeded normally. Though she sorely missed her brother, Lizzie brought back to the household some of the family sparkle that had been missing for so long. Her renewed zest for life and her family was overtaken only by her incessant womanly banter about seemingly trivial details of marriage. Elizabeth absorbed it all and contributed almost as much in return, for her daughter's wedding was to be the most important event in her life since her own marriage to William nearly twenty years ago. Young Henry found the female excitement too hard to bear and gave his father even more help in the lighthouse than he usually did. Mary and Joseph were still too young to be bothered by it and continued to play tirelessly around the lighthouse.

William, in the meantime, had had the most difficult task of all, as he coped, on the one hand, with his conscience, and endeavoured, on the other, to restore his family's coherence and morale. At first he had felt completely responsible for all that had happened. In one brief moment he had cloven the spirit of his dear Lizzie and, through driving his son from the family home, had committed him into the uncaring grasp of the Royal Navy. On at least one occasion William had considered ending his own life, but fortunately his powers of reasoning had averted what would have been the final blow to his loved ones. Nevertheless, the full weight of the burden rested squarely on his shoulders, and it was only by continual self-examination during his lonely nocturnal watches that he found the mental strength to support his family in the way that they deserved. It would have been so easy to slump into a morass of self-pity, hopelessly encompassed by the Slough of Despond. From such a position the only road led towards suicide. Only the constant struggle against his conscience had finally born fruit in the rebirth of Lizzie. In a matter of days he had watched her revert to her usual carefree and cheerful manner, this time with the added bonus that there was an undeniable look of love for a man deep within her eyes...

William had unreservedly welcomed James into his home, not only because he was a most pleasant and acceptable suitor for Lizzie and that he was obviously making her very happy, but also because half of William's burden had been suddenly released. The anguish he had caused Lizzie suddenly seemed to be so far in the past; all that remained was for Will to return... how they all longed for Will to come home.

And so the day of the wedding had arrived. The weeks of tittle-tattle, the planning, the cooking and the sewing were over as the eve of Christmas Eve dawned crisp and bright. The tiny lighthouse cottage was splitting at the joints as Knotts, little and large, struggled into their Sunday best, mislaid cravats, knotted bootlaces, spilled the milk, stood on the bride's freshly bathed toes and otherwise enjoyed every minute of the excitement. Elizabeth tried her utmost to remain calm amid the cacophony of childish banter and bridal panic. As the appointed hour drew near, Lizzie was forced to barricade herself in the bedroom in order to find the freedom to prepare herself for her finest moment. There she made last-minute adjustments to the face in the looking glass and smoothed out invisible creases in her gown. An accomplished seamstress, Lizzie had surely surpassed herself with a magnificently embroidered white and pink gown bordered with the finest lace she could afford. Suddenly she found herself in tears. Why was Will not here to share her joy? If only she knew where he was…

Just then Elizabeth overcame the barricades and opened the door as her daughter broke down. Immediately she rushed to her daughter and began to comfort her.

"There, there love, you mustn't cry on your wedding day."

"Oh, mummy, why isn't Will here? I miss him so much. I just want to know that he's all right, that's all." Lizzie tried to control herself.

"Yes, love, we all want that, and by the grace of God he is fit and well somewhere… a long way away perhaps. We must be patient, Lizzie dear. News will come… soon… you'll see. Now you must straighten your hair and be ready to go. Your dress is absolutely beautiful. You'll make your father a proud man today. He has suffered more than any of us, though he rarely showed it, even to me. Today, we're both very happy parents."

Lizzie gave her mother a fond hug and kissed her cheek. Then, without another glance in her looking glass, she wiped away the last trace of her tears and proudly strode into the living room to greet the rest of her family. Henry still had a crooked tie, but it was an admirable effort since he had tied it without assistance, and as Lizzie entered he cheered and applauded his sister. The bride was quite unable to avoid blushing as the rest of her family followed suit. After a half-minute of admiration they girded up their coats for the short walk to St. Margaret's church.

The service was due to commence at midday, so it was with twenty minutes to spare that they marched in stately procession along the cliff path towards the village. Mary and Joseph on their best Sunday behaviour were in the van, closely followed by Henry who dutifully escorted his mother. At the rear William with a broad smile proudly escorted his daughter and cared not the slightest as she tip-toed here and skipped there, picking her way carefully between even the tiniest areas of mud lest she dirty her shoes. As they approached the church and entered the village, some of the inhabitants stood in their doorways and applauded the bride as she walked by. The womenfolk politely gasped when they saw the bride's dress and even the men were forced to admit that Lizzie looked quite stunning. As the Knotts entered the churchyard itself they found a small crowd awaiting them. Many of these good people filed quickly into the church to witness the service and, while they did so, William and Lizzie waited outside in the sharp atmosphere. Though she was slightly chilled by the walk, Lizzie's heart was as warm as the villagers' welcome. She was glad that she had not warn a coat which would have obscured her dress from the envious looks of the spectators. When all had gone in, William led her through the church door. The organist, whose keyboard fingering had until then paralleled Lizzie's meandering footsteps along the muddy footpath, suddenly burst into a majestic march which Lizzie associated with weddings. Its inspiring notes sent a shiver down Lizzie's spine and she began to feel cold for a moment. Then the involuntary muscle spasm turned to a tremble and Lizzie became afraid. All this was for her… the music, the ceremony, and the pomp. So many people had come to witness her marriage to James, but was she doing the right thing? Would James be the sort of man who would love her as her father had loved her mother? She felt so sad that she could not give up her virginity to her lover; she was paying the price for her earlier indiscretion with Edward. She had told James that he would not be marrying a virgin, for he was sure to find out. Then, like a true gentleman, he had sworn solemnly that it made no difference to him as long as the affair was truly over. Lizzie, however, could not restrain her guilt and sorrow that she could not give James everything a man deserved. Perhaps he would grow to hate her for it. Perhaps he would turn into an ale-swilling wife-beater, like several other men she knew.

Suddenly Lizzie saw James peeking expectedly over his shoulder at her. The sight of his smile was enough to dispel all doubts from her mind. Her confidence returned and her love bubbled up inside her. With the firmest of steps and her head held high she marched toward the altar in slow, regal time to the music. Here was Lizzie Knott, princess for a day.

The church was rather more than half full and as she passed the filled pews Lizzie was conscious of the stares of admiration emanating therefrom. Staring straight ahead, her eyes fell upon the friendly smile of the Reverend Marsh who was delighted to be officiating at the ceremony. As a caring and conscientious pastor he had been only too aware of the sorrow felt by the family when Will had disappeared and, although Will was still missing, this marriage was to be an occasion of deserved happiness for the Knotts. He had known Lizzie since the day she was born, had baptised her into the Christian faith and had watched her grow into a fine young woman. There was a fond place in his heart for the girl. He had known James for only a short time since the Banns had been published, but he had formed a good impression of the young man. Marsh felt that James was very lucky to be engaged to Lizzie and he had made his thoughts abundantly clear to James in a private interview before the wedding.

Now, as the young couple stood before him at the crossroads of their lives, Geoffrey Archibald Marsh opened the hearts of the congregation and joined Lizzie and James in holy wedlock until death did them part. In the second pew Elizabeth cried to herself, William beamed and Henry fidgeted. At the end the row Mary and Joseph played quietly with two marbles which Joseph had eagerly fished out of his top pocket when the service had become boring. In the remaining pews some folks watched patiently whilst a few even slept, but in the place that mattered Lizzie and James exchanged rings and vows and became man and wife.

With the service over, Lizzie retraced her steps down the aisle with her new husband at her side. She tried very hard not to shout for joy; now she was a married lady with new responsibilities. Nonetheless she had never been so happy and the smiles on the faces of the congregation made her want to burst with joy. She clutched her man's arm so tightly that James had to loosen her grip for fear of losing the circulation.

The organ was by now in full flight as the bride and groom stepped from the reverend atmosphere inside the church into the chilled December air. There they were met by a deafening peal of bells ringing out their congratulations. Additionally, a good-humoured mob awaited them. This was comprised of all those not sufficiently motivated to enter the House of the Lord, but well lubricated by the proximity of the festive season. Their wish was to join in the happy occasion, and, as James and Lizzie emerged, the crowd proceeded to deluge the pair with cheers and good wishes. Lizzie succumbed to the emotion and threw herself into the arms of her man amid even greater cheers from the crowd. This was what they had waited to see: not a prurient, starchy curtain call but an unrestrained public exhibition of the love everyone felt for the couple.

Of the older ones present, each individual remembered his or her own wedding day. In particular, William and Elizabeth, who had joined the celebrations outside, clasped hands tightly. In her mind's eye, Elizabeth substituted herself for Lizzie, the beautiful bride revelling in this her greatest moment. Elizabeth knew that, for Lizzie, no other occasion would ever be comparable. Even the groom stood in the shadow of this, the most beautiful girl in the world... for one day. Every young girl who witnessed the scene yearned for the day when they too would stand thus, lost in the embrace of her Prince Charming.

It was a joyful procession that made the return journey to the lighthouse for the celebrations that were to follow. As many people as Elizabeth could possibly accommodate in her small home had been invited to follow the bride and groom. Lizzie found herself being carried for the last half of the journey lest she muddy her dress. It was a feat that the gallant James was only too happy to perform, though he felt the strain of it towards the end. Although offered assistance by William, he gamely refused. The last few staggering yards were distinctly painful for the poor chap, but a warming tot from a special pitcher that William produced soon restored his strength. The rejoicing, which had taken on a new dimension because of the proximity of Christmas, was conducted at fever pitch, and went on late into the afternoon. Thus, by the time a number of guests had begun to take on the appearance of sailors strutting the decks in a storm, it was time for the newlyweds to leave the lighthouse. They waited until William had stoked the fire; then, as he came down the stairs, they began to say farewell to the guests. Lizzie, still immaculate in her wedding dress, hugged and kissed everyone.

Good-bye Uncle Henry... thank you for coming... good-bye Aunt Mary, my, that's a lovely hat you have on... yes, of course we'll come to visit you..."

Then to her brothers and sister she said, "Good-bye little Joe. Be a good boy for mummy. Good-bye John, I'll see you again soon. Good-bye Henry."

Her father clutched her tightly to his chest. They said nothing except good-bye, for there was nothing to say which would have been suitable. Lizzie and her father had a special understanding. It had grown out of the terrible ordeal they had suffered together. Now they stood together closer in spirit than ever before.

The biggest hug of all was reserved for Elizabeth. The tears flowed freely from the corner of Lizzie's brown eyes. Both Elizabeths, senior and junior, choked up so much that they could hardly talk.

"Why isn't Will here, mummy?" Lizzie sobbed. "It has been such a beautiful day but it would have been so much better if he'd been here."

"There now, child," comforted Elizabeth, in almost as bad a state as Lizzie. "It wasn't meant to be. Try not to dwell on it, love. Just now, Will is probably thinking of us and waiting to come home whenever he can. And you... you've got a wonderful husband and a new home to go to. Love him, Lizzie, with all your heart and you'll be as happy as your father and I are. God bless you, child. Now be on your way."

With impeccable timing, the door of the cottage suddenly burst open, and there in the doorway stood Saul Goldsack.

"Lady... Sir," he proclaimed in courtly style, "Your carriage awaits."

Lizzie was taken aback. She had not expected to ride to her new home. She looked at her father who stood silently, but a huge wink said as much as a hundred words. Saul had obviously been persuaded to offer his services as coachman, and would take them all the way to their new cottage in East Langdon.

"Did you know about this?" Lizzie scolded James. The grin on the face of her husband was enough to tell her that he was indeed a party to the plot. "Why didn't you tell me?" she screamed excitedly as, to a huge cheer, she chased her husband through the door.

Darkness had fallen. The air, though crisp and cold, was still and the half-moon beamed down its best wishes to the happy pair. The lighthouse shone brightly and cast a warm glow all around the cottage. As the guests poured out into the garden with every lantern they could find the whole area around the front of the cottage seemed as bright as day. A few yards distant from the front door stood Saul Goldsack's 'carriage'. Lizzie stood in amazement.

"It's beautiful she gasped. It was really the waggon on which Saul delivered coal to the lighthouse, but by the light of the lanterns, Lizzie could see that it was scrupulously clean. Saul must have spent the whole day scrubbing off the coal dust. Furthermore, the whole of the cart had been decorated with ribbon and streamers and was almost unrecognisable as a coal waggon. In the back Saul had even put down a rug for the passengers to sit on. At the front stood Ramsgate, a good-tempered old workhorse who had hauled coal around the locality for fifteen years. Lizzie skipped up to him and stroked his nose.

"Hello, old fellow. What a surprise to see you here. Why, how beautiful you look!" Lizzie saw that he had been superbly groomed and there were a number of rosettes made from fancy ribbon tied to his harness. Ramsgate licked her hand in recognition of her friendship." Go steady, Ramsgate, old chap... I know you will." Then with a golden twinkle in her eye from the warm lantern light, she ran to James and flung herself into his arms. "Take me away, husband," she said. James was only too glad to lift her onto the back of the cart; then he seated himself beside his wife. As Saul mounted the driving seat and shook the reins, the cries of "Good-bye, Lizzie... good-bye, James," resounded for many minutes into the blanket of silence surrounding the lighthouse.

154

It was only when the cart had finally disappeared from view into the darkness that the guests returned to see if there really was any bottom to William Knott's pitcher of rum.

18 REVEREND GEOFFREY MARSH

In the library of the vicarage of the parish of St. Margaret's-at-Cliffe the Reverend Geoffrey Marsh MA (Cantab) sat in his favourite leather chair beside a roaring log fire and mused quietly to himself. On his lap a copy of the "Gentleman" magazine lay open at the page that carried a particularly vivid account of the recent British action with the French at Quiberon Bay. A great victory for the British, it had been received with great jubilation in every corner of the nation. To the vicar, however, it was merely another milestone along the long hard road of war with France. Even the well-informed Marsh had begun to wonder what it was all about. It had occurred to him on more than one occasion that the politicians might have themselves forgotten the reasons for their enmity. Perhaps war had become a habit? The two nations had hated each other for centuries so why should they not fight now?

It was Christmas Eve. Tomorrow would be the high spot of the Christian calendar, but for England and France there would be no peace and goodwill. Maybe the armies and navies would put away their guns for the day? Perhaps the day would pass without a death on either side? There would surely be no fighting on Christmas Day? But on the day after it would be business as usual. War was business. Huge profits were to be made by those with their money in the right places. The untapped wealth of a new continent lay maturing in the keg, waiting for the rival innkeepers to decide on its ownership. As always it was the ordinary people who paid the price of the political ambitions: a fee of blood and misery. How could he preach the word of love and joy without being hypocritical? He picked up the journal and scanned it once more.

HMS Royal George
at Quiberon Bay
November 25, 1759
To the Editor,
"Gentlemen's Magazine"

Sir,
I write to you so that you may acquaint your readers forthwith of a magnificent victory for the Royal Navy in our war with France. Notwithstanding this letter, please find enclosed a map as well as lists of the British and, French vessels involved. Taken together I trust that you will find it convenient to publish this account, if not in whole, then in part.
On the 14th. of November inst., Sir Edward Hawke hoisted his flag on board the Royal George in Torbay, where the fleet had put in a few days before through

stress of weather.(His most reluctant removal from the Royal George to the Ramilies was made necessary since that ship became waterlogged whenever it blowed hard.) The same evening we stood out to sea with twenty-three ships of the line and two frigates, and on the 16th. were within eight or nine leagues of the isle of Ushant. As you are aware, no doubt, we have been off Brest since May, without break except for that enforced by inclement weather. In this position we have been able to blockade the French fleet who are under the command of Admiral Conflans, and thus to prevent them from joining with Louis' invasion force stationed in the Morbihan district. In the afternoon of the 14th. we fell in with some English transports returning from Quiberon who gave the Admiral the information that they saw the French fleet the day before, consisting of twenty-four sail, standing to the south-east, and were at that time twenty-four leagues west of Belle Isle. The intelligence received from the master of the Love and Unity was received with universal acclamations and every ship prepared for action. The Admiral lost not a minute of time but pursued with the utmost alertness. After six months of unbroken training in seamanship, our crews were most ready for an altercation with the French, besides possessing a greater degree of skill than many an Admiral has been fortunate enough to command. In the evening of the 18th. the wind came on fresh from the westward and we spread all our canvas to court the prosperous gale. In the crisp moonlight of the piercingly cold November night, the duty watch clambered more than a hundred feet up amid lurching masts to get down the topgallant masts, and with unresponsive fingers they struggled to reef the topsails.

On the morning of the 20th., as the first strains of daylight trickled over the troubled horizon, Hawke, like a master of the hounds, led his ships in full cry after the vulpine Conflans. He signalled to Captain Howe on the Magnanime to go on ahead at greatest speed to make landfall. The rest of the squadron were to bear away before the wind and, regardless of the ferocity of the weather, to unreef their topsails. The canvas billowed out powerfully as the vigorous gale sped the ships from astern, the bows driving hard and deep into the grey torrent like a school of dolphins riding the surf.

About half an hour after eight, the Maidstone frigate let fly her topgallant sheets which was a signal for discovering a fleet. At nine not a doubt was left of the happy hour being arrived which we had six months been patiently expecting. We ascertained them to be the French squadron of twenty-one sail of the line and three smaller ships. It was further apparent that they were then chasing Captain Duff's frigates, the destruction of which was one object of their destination. (I should make clear at this point that Captain Duff's squadron had been deployed to patrol the area of Quiberon Bay lest the French should slip unnoticed from Brest in Hawkers absence.) Upon their having a distincter view of our ships they gave over the chase and appeared to be forming a line to receive us. From the equality of the combatants we concluded that the action would be very great and general, but I may venture to assert there was not an Englishman from high to low who did not assure himself of victory. Upon our advancing, Marshal Conflans changed his plans and put right before the wind towards the shore, seeking safety in his flight to the Morbihan.

At this critical time, Sir Edward paid no regard to lines of battle, but every ship was directed to make the best of her way towards the enemy. The Admiral told his officers he was for the old way of fighting to make downright work with them. At noon our headmost ships were pretty well near them, and between one and two of the clock the Warspite and Dorsetshire began to fire. They were then abreast of the Cardinal rocks, being a most dangerous shoal guarding the entrance to the Bay of Quiberon. Presently after, Revenge, Resolution, Torbay, Magnanime, Swiftsure, Montagu and Defiance came into action. The firing now became very alert on both sides and there was no distinguishing any longer English colours from French. M. du Verger, the French Rear-Admiral in the Formidable bore a very fierce cannonade from the Resolution, but upon the Royal George's coming up, they hauled down their flag and struck to Sir Edward Hawke. This was only a point of honour, the Resolution having the merit of subduing them. The Royal George continued advancing and Sir Edward gave orders to his master to carry him close alongside of M. Conflans in Soleil Royal. The French Admiral seemed to have the same ambition on his part and it was a glorious sight to behold the blue and white flags both at the maintopmasthead, bearing down on each other. As they did so, the Royal George passed the Torbay which was closely engaged with the Thésée of seventy-four guns. Both captains decided at first to use their main batteries, which procedure was most hazardous in such heavy sea conditions. However, Captain Keppel brought Torbay around into the wind at the moment when the sea began to burst into his gun ports. Captain Kersaint in Thésée was not so expeditious as his opponent. Water rushed into the ship so quickly that the unfortunate vessel gave a sudden lurch and sank as rapidly as if she had been constructed of lead. In less than a minute Thésée's complement of six hundred and fifty men were exterminated almost entirely.

On the other side was Magnanime who kept up an incessant fire on one of the largest of the French ships, Héros, and in the end obliged her to strike. The two commanders-in-chief were now very near and M. Conflans gave the English Admiral his broadside. The Royal George returned the uncivil salutation, but after two or three exchanges of this kind, the Marshal of France declined the combat and steered off. Immediately the French Vice-Admiral de Beaufremont in Le Tonnant likewise gave Sir Edward his broadside and soon followed the example of his superior. Another and another acted the same part.

The fifth ship, Superbe, escaped not so well. It should be mentioned that in all this the shooting of the French gunners left much to be desired, both in terms of speed and accuracy. Likewise, the gunners on the Superbe were very slow and wild in their aim. The Royal George sent a first fusillade of destruction across the intervening void, so intense in its magnitude that the French seemed to have no reply. Almost at once a second blade scythed into the hull of the wretched vessel as the English gunners proved their superiority. The effect was cataclysmic. In a fraction of a minute a beautiful and graceful ship of the line was reduced to random assemblage of timber. Six hundred and thirty souls, many of whom must have been pressed peasants possessing little knowledge of the ways of the sea, were dispatched to the Almighty.

157

Not a man on board the Superbe survived that callous minute of the encounter, at the end of which the hulk was engulfed by the sea for ever. The Royal George's people gave a cheer, but it was a faint one. The honest sailors were touched at the miserable state of so many hundreds of poor creatures.

The blue flag of Sir Edward was now encountered with seven ships all at the same time and appeared in the very centre of the French rear. Every observer must have pitied the Royal George to see her singly engaged against so many of the enemy. It seems indeed a kind of degradation to so noble a ship to be pitied, but really her situation would have been lamentable if the enemy had preserved any degree of composure or fired with any sort of direction. Their confusion was so great that of many hundreds of shot I do not believe that more than thirty or forty struck the ship.

Sir Charles Hardy in the Union, with Mars and Hero and several other ships were crowding to the Admiral's assistance when the retreat of the French covered by the obscurity of the evening put an end to the engagement. Happy circumstance for the enemy, as an hour's daylight more would have brought on their total ruin. The battle was fought so near the coast of Brittany that ten thousand persons on the shore were sad witnesses of the white flag's disgrace.

When I sat down to write, I intended to have given only a general account, but upon such an animating occasion as this there is no possibility of leaving off whilst a margin remains unoccupied.

As daylight ebbed away, Sir Edward gave signal to anchor, for it must be remembered that the presence of the British fleet in such hostile waters and weather conditions without a pilot was dangerous in the extreme at night. Royal George came to anchor in fifteen fathoms at a point close to the Cardinals with such other of her flock as had seen the signal. As the men lay to rest beside their guns they could hear distress calls from the void, but the wind still shrieked over the dark desolation and swept away the forlorn call of those in distress. In such conditions the signal of the cannon was quite meaningless and simply an expression of helplessness and terror. There could be no aid to the needy.

On the morrow we discovered to our surprise that M. Conflans had been anchored in our midst without our knowledge, but in seeing his precarious position, he ordered that the cable be cut. Soleil Royal made an escape towards the harbour at Le Croisic, together with Héros, but in so doing both ran ashore a matter of yards from safety and were afterwards burnt.

Besides these, we have thus sunk the Thésée of seventy-four, and the Superbe of seventy; we have driven the Juste of seventy guns upon the rocks where she overset, and have taken the Formidable of eighty, sixty-two of whose guns are brass. Ten or eleven other ships were aground in the mouth of the river Vilaine, but got off again by throwing their guns and stores overboard. They are now crept well into the entrance of the river where we do not despair of setting them on fire. Whether we succeed in this or not, we have room to believe they have undergone so much damage that few of them will be able to put to sea any more. The rest made their escape the night after the engagement, under the command of the Vice-Admiral M. Beaufremont and stretched away for Rochefort.

We have had the misfortune to lose the victorious Resolution of seventy-four guns and the Essex of sixty-four. The former struck upon a sand called Le Four the night after the battle, and next morning the Essex going down to her relief unhappily ran upon the same shoal. Our endeavours to get them off were unsuccessful but we have the consolation that almost all their people are saved and are embarked on board the Formidable.

Our loss by the enemy is not considerable. In the ships which are now with us we have only one lieutenant and fifty seamen and marines killed, with about two hundred and twenty wounded.

It gives me a most sensible pleasure to assure you that Sir Edward has been very liberal in his praises without a single imputation to cast a shade upon the triumph of the day. The glory of the British flag has been nobly supported, while that of the enemy is vanished into empty air.

> *I am, sir,*
> *Your most obedient servant,*
> *Robert English,*
> *Chaplain, Royal Navy.*

Marsh closed the magazine and set it down beside him. He cast his mind once more over the ideas for his morning sermon. In an adjacent chair sat his wife, engrossed in the making of a rug. It was nearly finished and, enveloping her knees, it fell onto the floor in an untidy heap. Mary Marsh spent as much time as she could spare at this activity, its intricate and varied skills having captured her imagination for the past ten years.

The library in which the priest and his wife rested was on the ground floor of the vicarage and positioned between the lounge at the front of the house and the dining room at the rear. It was the room that the vicar preferred most in the house, especially on cold December nights such as this when the only thing worth doing was to stay at home in front of a good fire. That morning the weather had turned much colder as the wind had swung around to the east and the vicar predicted that there would be a sharp frost on Christmas morning.

Not being one for spending time in the kitchen, Mary had left the preparation of the festive food to her cook, Emily. Although Emily was by no means expert, Mary was unable. She much preferred to direct her energies in the maturing of her talent for rug making. Besides, cooking had not been part of her education as a child. Folks from her social background were able to employ others to perform such tasks. The spacious vicarage had proved ideal for a rug-maker, however. Its numerous empty rooms needed her rugs. Her present work was destined to fill a large area of cold stone floor in the dining room and, when finished, would be a mixture of cream and brown lambs wool with a delicate floral pattern which she had designed entirely herself.

Apart from her skills in handicraft, Mary Marsh was also a good vicar's wife. After all, a learned man such as her husband needed the strength of personality of a wife such as she in his dealings with the gentlefolk. Mary was on extremely good social terms with everyone who mattered in the locality, not that there were too many. She fulfilled all her duties as the wife of the parish priest and professed more than a passing respect for the ordinary people. Her only problem was that as the daughter of a wealthy lawyer and landowner she had little in common with them and preferred to mix with those who were more in keeping with her own station in society.

Geoffrey Marsh was everything to everybody. A magnificent brain in a diminutive but chubby body, he possessed a ready wit, as those of ample proportions are wont to do. As a vicar's son himself he had been educated at public school and had gone up to King's College Cambridge as a scholar in divinity. There he had chosen the middle path of the extremes of study and self-abuse, but had still come down with a first class honours degree. After his entry into the holy orders at the age of 24 he had spent a number of years working as curate at St. Peter's, Canterbury, before coming to St. Margaret's.

Reverend Marsh was without ambition and sought none of the glory of high office. He had remained content with his position and enjoyed the privilege of detachment from social class that his cloth allowed him. On the one hand he could mix readily with the gentry at the local coming-out ball; on the other he was at home consoling a grief-stricken farm labourers widow. During his thirty-one years at St. Margaret's he had become genuinely fond of his parishioners and had always done his best to solve their problems, welfare as well as spiritual. Consequently he had been able to cast a fatherly eye over a huge Christian family that lived in an area covering twenty square miles. He also considered it his responsibility to look after those who felt that they were not part of his faith. Most of these usually respected him, but a few families would have no truck with the church at all, except when they betrayed their atheism for a baptism or funeral service. Geoffrey Marsh never refused them; it was not for him to decide on entry into his Lord's house.

His perception of human failing extended to his wife too. He was fully aware of his wife's preferred role in their marriage. Whenever she felt disposed to prattle on about the crudeness of one person or another he simply reminded her that they were all children of God. Quietly, he prayed for her forgiveness and continued to love her for all her faults. He would not forget that whatever her shortcomings she had remained loyal to him for over thirty years with only minor complaints that he had not made sufficient effort to further his career.

The vicar roused himself from his thoughts and rose from his chair. The fire had died down and he added another log to the grate. Using a brass poker that had been standing in a corner of the fireplace, he carefully prodded the partly burned wood into a suitable position. Then he added another log so that there was a good draught of air circulating between the cold and the red-hot fuel. Just as he was completing this calorific manoeuvre there was a pronounced double knock on the front door of the vicarage. Marsh left the room at once to ascertain the nature of the call. It was not unusual to receive calls at such a time and Mary continued with her craft without looking up. At the door, the vicar found a very weary visitor in the distinctive dress of the Royal Navy.

"Good evening, sir. I understand that you are the vicar of this parish." The seaman addressed Reverend Marsh with a confident and polite tone to which the priest instantly responded.

"That is correct, my good man. You look as if you have travelled a good distance today. Do come inside." He stood aside and invited the stranger into his home.

"Aye, sir, I've come from Chatham today. It has been a long journey." Once inside the hall of the great vicarage and with the door closed behind him, the visitor introduced himself. "My name is Sam Millichamp, sir."

"Geoffrey Marsh - pleased to meet you, Mr Millichamp." They shook hands.

"I'm off the *Formidable*" began the seaman." We've just brung her back as a prize from the battle with the French. I live down Dover really, sir, and I'm on my way home for a bit of leave for Christmas... but, well sir... the reason I come to see you is that I've brung you a letter. Well, it's not actually for you, sir, it's for William Knott at the South Foreland lighthouse, but the thing is, sir... it's got bad news in it. I didn't know whether any of his family would be able to read it so I thought it were best if I brung it to you, sir. Then not only can you break the news to them, gentle like, but you can read the letter to them as well. I can't read it meself and I don't know all what's in it... I didn't write it see? It's from another bloke on board what knew Mr Knott's son."

The vicar's face was by now showing great concern. "My dear fellow, how good of you to think in this way. Come with me into the kitchen. Emily will get you something hot to eat and drink."

Reverend Marsh accepted the sealed letter from Sam and, without looking at it, led the weary seaman into the kitchen where Emily was putting the finishing touches to a cake. The room was delightfully warm and cosy despite its functional capacity and the sailor began to feel much more at home.

"Emily, would you please find some sustenance for a tired traveller?"

"Really, don't bother too much about me," he protested half-heartedly, for he was really very hungry and the months just spent living on Pusser's rations had left him with a craving for a good, home-cooked meal. Emily did not disappoint him.

"Of course, Reverend Marsh. I've a little lamb stew left over from dinner, sir. It'll only take a moment to warm through." Emily busied herself with the task and the vicar offered Mr Millichamp a seat at the table. He himself began to study the letter that had arrived from afar.

"I'll say naught until you've read it right through, sir. I think it speaks for itself," said Sam, eagerly eyeing the pot of stew that Emily had placed on the range. The vicar read the letter twice in order to make sure he fully understood its implications. With every minute that passed, his face assumed a firmer, more serious expression. The letter was very badly written, but had been a labour of love on the part of the author. It was perhaps fortunate that the letter had been written at all in view of

161

the low literacy level of sailors in general. As the vicar reached the end of his second reading Emily was spooning a sizeable serving of steaming stew for a hungry man. Sam began to devour the food with gusto and considerable lower deck slurping. Reverend Marsh said nothing, as the feeding process got under way. Then he asked deliberately,

"Would you tell me of your role in this affair Sam - may I call you by your Christian name?"

"Yes, of course. Oh, I'm only the messenger, sir. I was a shipmate of Jacob Evans. He knew I lived in Dover and he asked me to deliver the letter for him. He was most keen that the Knotts should hear from him personally. That's why he got the letter wrote. I think he'd have come himself if he'd had the chance but he wasn't allowed no leave like me. I owed Jacob a favour so I was glad to come. It wasn't far out of my way to come over here, but if you wouldn't mind sir I'd like to get away off home when I've finished this. I can't say more than is in the letter. I didn't know the lad concerned and I was in a different part of the ship when it all happened." He stopped talking for a while to take a few more gulps of his manna. Then he continued, though his words were garbled as he tried to cope with concurrent mastication and explanation. "I heard about it after the event, sir, but I was too busy elsewhere at the time. We run aground on this reef and we all thought we were going under but we all stayed put on board. A few idiots got away from the ship on rafts, but it wasn't many. The next day they took us off *Resolution* and put us on the *Formidable*, which we had won. We had to sail it back here and that's what we done."

He continued with his meal. The vicar said nothing more for a time, but looked at Emily who was by now most concerned and wondering what the bad news was all about. In bemusement she returned the vicar's stare, though her good manners forbade her to pry by asking him directly.

"Is there any chance that this information is inaccurate? Could he have survived?" asked the vicar in the forlorn hope that there might still be some facet of the story, which Sam had forgotten.

"I doubt it, sir. 'T were a terrible rough night and bitter cold," came the brief reply. The vicar fetched his overcoat and hat from the hall while the visitor finished his meal. Then he looked around the door into the library where his wife was still engrossed.

"I have to go out for an hour or so, my dear. Don't wait up for me if you wish to go to bed." Mary Marsh did not enquire about her husband's business. She was well used to these occurrences and, besides, was too near the end of her own little task.

Sam had finished his stew and was a revitalised man. He thanked the vicar sincerely for his hospitality and complimented Emily on her cooking - the best meal he'd had in nine months.

"You're very welcome, Sam. Leave it all to me. Take this for your trouble." Reverend Marsh took a coin from his pocket and tried to insert it into the palm of the sailor's hand.

162

"No thank you, sir... much obliged, but I'll not take a penny for a shipmate's favour." The vicar smiled and returned the money to his pocket.

"You're a fine fellow, Sam. Go home, have a blessed Christmas and thank the Lord for your deliverance."

"Aye, sir, I'll do that." The vicar slapped the man on the back as they left the house and parted at the gate, the sailor to take the back road through the village to Dover and the vicar to take the cliff path towards the lonely lighthouses on the South Foreland.

The night was cold and the easterly wind tugged at the vicar's coat as he strode purposefully along the dark path. He needed no lantern for, although there was little moonlight, he knew the path extremely well. The task which he was now to perform was one of the most unsavoury he had ever known. He had no intention of flinching from his duty and as a result his resolve was transformed into an increased firmness of gait. His face was set solidly into an illustration of his intention and his heart, though filled with sorrow, coaxed his limbs to speed up their work. The sooner he were at the lighthouse the sooner he would be able to help a stricken family.

For the whole of the short walk to the lighthouse, he fixed his eyes upon the comforting glow from the top of the tower that was William Knott's. Saul Goldsack's light shone brightly too, but it was only the lower of the two that the vicar studied. The closer he got to the tower the more light was available until, when he was about a hundred feet from the cottage, he could see quite clearly. It was getting late. He knocked gently on the door of the small cottage. It was opened sharply by Elizabeth with an expectant air, which vanished instantly when she recognised the priest. For a few moments she had prayed that it might be Will at her door. What a wonderful Christmas present it would have made.

"Good evening, vicar," she smiled warmly. "What brings you over to see us at this time of night?"

"Elizabeth, I am sorry to trouble you at this late hour. May I speak with you and your husband for a while?" Elizabeth's eyes suddenly lost their warmth. She sensed from the vicar's tone that all was not well. He was looking drawn and severe. Her heart began to pump vigorously.

"Y-yes, vicar... come in... er...William is in the tower. I'll call him." She knew that he was the bringer of bad news, but she did not ask, partly in fear and partly so as not to pre-empt William's right to be present. She showed the priest to a chair and dashed up the tower to fetch her husband. Reverend Marsh braced himself as he sat alongside the small but cosy fire. He removed the letter from his pocket and fingered it rather nervously. He realised that there was no sign of the younger Knotts and guessed that they had retired to bed early in anticipation of the feast day tomorrow. His heart became heavy. The poor children...

Elizabeth returned, out of breath after her exertions, and was closely followed by William who was rather more used to the climb up and down the tower.

"Is it Will? You've heard from Will haven't you?" pleaded Elizabeth, her face twisted in anguish. The vicar rose from his seat, took Elizabeth physically by the arm and placed her in a sitting position. William was at once by his wife's side, his arm around her shoulders.

"My dear friends, I have received a letter which concerns Will. I will read it to you."

The letter was indeed badly written and it was with considerable difficulty that the vicar interpreted the message, his delivery punctuated with numerous stops and stammers as he stumbled either on the poor handwriting or the grammar.

le formidable november 1759
to mister william knott
sir it must be your utmost intrest to no the reson for gettin a lettr from an inglish sailor you never met. praps of more intrest that it be rit from a french ship o the line i should mak it clear that this lettr be dew only to the kindly eforts of a shipmat for i meself is unable to writ. my name is jacob evans and sins early may i forgets the exact dayte i am honerd to be akwainted with your son will. twere then they brung him abord - us was in reserlution then - as us layed at anker in cawsand bay which be ner plymouth reserlution were one of a flete of twenty or so ships o the line undr admral awke who wer on bord ramilees now as i sed erlier your boy wer brung on bord by bote from plymouth in cumpny of saylers newly presad he wer put in my charge by the mayte so as ow i cud lern im the skils of gunnry. wen he ferst com with me he wer fed up lyke all presad men but as the days com and went us got good maytes corse he tolld me the resons wot got him in the navy and expectin you nos all abowt it i shal not spek of it i must say he always spok well of his famly and soon was sory for joynin up. mist you all that he did. wot relly roted things up was that roge jennins did i tell you he wer brung on bord same tyme as will they took im abot the sayme tyme as will. you no ion jennins come from your vilage must have been a flook they both ended up with us anyhow ther was othrs from kent so they was not the only ones. us was prepring to sayl and gettin men from all over afore us left from therl til now us bin at sea five months all tolld. the crew is fed up of it ther neve semed no rime nor reson for all the ils us suffrd. us spent most of the tyme practisin us semanship and lernin the new boys all us new. i can tel you sir by the beginin of this month us was the fynest ships cumpany that evr sayld the seas and your will tok in all i lernd im always intristd and qwick with it he wer for a lad of his ayge he never shod no frite wen he wer up aloft and as for gunry well he pikt up all that stuf in no tyme a grand lad he wer sir. wel i am gettin away from the poynt this jennins skowndrl wer always pikin on will semes he rekond yourself was to blaym for his gettin prest thow i dont no how. in all my tym abord ships i met som derty cracters but i aint neve met one so ful of ate and evl as jennins. he mayd will rely angry cause he new abot wills sister lizzy and will said to me he had tolld you and you was angry with lizzy that be non o my bisniss sir but it wer rely upsetin will they was always at each othrs throts and i oftn had to get betwixt em. course it upset will to be within ayt cabl of the scurvy swyn and the pore lad wer homsik enuff with out this othr upsetin im. best i cood i kept will away from jennins but as always appens ther wer one tym i wernt abl to stop im startin a fite

164

will wer not urt exept for a few bruses but the capn got to ere of itand had both of em punisht hed had a lot of fites cause the men was fed up of bein at sea and he deciderd to set an exampl of em six lashes on the spot they got i cood not bring meself to wotch but you can rest ashurd i lokd aftr im sir he com threw it all riyt did will an tho he had a fare of payn twernt oftn as ow he complaynd. jennins wer madr than evr at will but minderd his one bisniss so as not to get iself in trobl with the capn agayn. id lik to remynd you sir that all this tym us bin boncin up an down in the bryny lyk a rowin bot in a ronn forty us neve had no chans to get ashor and ferget us problums will was not the only one to get the cat lods of othr men got it to. this story is a bit long so il get on with it. erly this month us wer forsd to sheltr in torbay to eskap a bad westrly in bisky we vitlld and waterd but ther wernt no shor leveand us thawt as how usd iievr- get of this dam ship sir. soon we was undr way again and eddin bak towords frans this tym word was we was goin to mete the french this got evryone werkd up well sir us adn done nowt for for month and some dont get me rong sir us dont normaly lok for fites but it were a way of gettin us bak home qwik. well for days sins us met up with em frayd i cant tel you nowt abot the battl cawse i dont no how many was killd or owt us wer bisy lettn frogy ave it threw the gun port. us coodn see much cawse of the smok but sumtyms us cood see the od ship her and ther. they didn seme much good for us had ardly any wonded and not much damag. on the othr hand us ammed em with all we had and must hav kild a fair few som of our crew got hit with timbr splintrs but most of us was all rite viell sir the battl turnd out nawt wen i thinks of wot appnd next it soon got dark and the capn was lookin fer a saf plays to anker for the nite then she struk i think its cald for shoal my ther was a comoshun most of us thawt the ship wood sink and panik was evrywer. reserlution gav a mitey shuddr from stem to stern i wer flung agaynst a gun and twisterd me ankl bad. werd soon com as us wer saf and whil she wernt sinkin she wer fast on the ref the inen was upset tho for it wer bittr cold and raynin cats and dogs. they wantd to bild rafts to get away and evn tho tha capn ordrs them not to and as us shood stay put til mornin wen us be reskewd many was perswadr by this argymint but i thinks they was afeard of gettin on a tidly ole raft in the middl o wintr and the wethr so bad. stil ther was a lot wat didn want to stay jennins inkludrd obsesd they was with eskapin and bildin rafts with old bits of timbr wat was rekag. capn didn do nowt to stop em an after a few howrs they was goin ovrbord into a bittr sea evil twas wen jennins was goin he tryd to get yung will to go with im sed he was goin to setle the skor ons and fer all jennins puld a nife and thretend to kil your son will pownsd on im and thay struglld hitin each othr they was i coodn do nowt caws of me bad ankl but even afor i cood a done awt they was ovr the syd and fel in the sea rite next to the raft. i got to the edj and saw will swimmin twards the ship syd for a rop wich hung for the desrtrs jennins got on the raft with help from they alredy abord but it got took up on a big rollr and swept in twards the ship with will in between it braks my art to tell'esir no chans he had at all i didn see will agayn us lokd ard but he wer gon then desrtrs all clerd of and us didn see em agayn ether us got tok of next day and they giv us the formidable a french ship us capturd. so thats how i com to rit to'esir and i am so sory i had to giv you such bad news abot your son

a grand lad he wer sir i was prowd to no him. i hope us can met one day so as i can tel
you to your fase i dont rekon jennins cood ave livd wethr was so bad

i am sir your honorabl servnt
by jacob evans and rit by his mayt john exworthy

Before the vicar had reached the end of the first page, Elizabeth, sensing the terrible news that was about to be revealed to her, had burst into silent tears. William, round-shouldered and pale, held her tightly in a vain attempt to console her. By the time that the vicar had uttered the dreadful words to the effect that their son was dead, William too was wiping the tears away from his eyes.

To the Reverend Marsh, death was always a time of terrible family tragedy and the utter finality of it shocked even him. Nevertheless, when faced with the relatives of the dead person the circumstances were always different; the long-awaited passing of a bed-ridden elderly burden, the loss in childbirth of a newly born babe and its mother, the death of a husband and breadwinner in a farm accident, were all scenes of tragedy in degree. But here, with a marriage one day and a death the next, was an unusual combination of events that seemed to be bad enough, without the added pain of occurring at Christmas. Furthermore, it appeared from the letter that John Jennings had been involved in Will's death.

There was no doubt in the vicar's mind that William senior would assume for himself a large share of the blame for the death of his eldest son. Geoffrey Marsh had known all about William's personal suffering at the time when Will had left home. At the moment of his deepest despair William had requested a confidential talk with the vicar. After a detailed briefing on the subject of Lizzie's extra-marital relationship, Marsh had done his best to diminish William's feeling of guilt by agreeing wholeheartedly with William's tough stand. Now the net had been cast on his side of the boat once more and he would have to work very hard to convince William of his innocence in the matter.

William, Elizabeth, your grief is natural and you must surely mourn your loss. Young Will was a fine young man who should be with us today. The workings of the Lord are most strange to mere mortals. You must find it in your hearts to offer up thanksgiving for the pleasure his life has given you, short though it may have been. Be assured that your son will rest in heaven for evermore."

The vicar's words did not help a great deal. Elizabeth sobbed unremittingly and William could do nothing but kneel beside her and clutch her to his breast. Reverend Marsh bowed his head.

"Almighty and most merciful Father, Whose eternal love for His family outlives mere mortality; enter into the house of these Thy children and comfort them in their grief at the loss of their loved one. Release them from the burden of their sins and show them the paths to true happiness in the kingdom of Heaven. Take the spirit of William Knott junior into Thy care, and may Your peace rest among his family for evermore. In the name of the Father, the Son and the Holy Ghost, Amen."

William Knott had begun to compose himself. He rose and persuaded his wife to lie down in the next room where the children still slept. Then William thanked the vicar for his kindness, for his prayers and for coming out on such a cold night.

"Dear friend," said the vicar, "I must leave you to your grief now. You will be in my prayers tomorrow at Thanksgiving. God bless all of you."

Despite his own considerable pain at the events of the evening, the Reverend Marsh had sufficient presence of mind to call on Saul Goldsack at the upper lighthouse. William would surely be unable to stoke the fires of his tower for the rest of the night? Then, as the vicar stepped out briskly on his homeward journey and left the Knotts to gather up the pieces of their shattered lives for the second time in a year, he discovered that he had been quite correct. It was not yet Christmas morning, but there was already a particularly heavy frost.

19 JANE HEAL

In a corner of the dark and damp room a large female rat emerged from a dusty hole in the loose brickwork and scampered hungrily along the floor. She was closely followed by six greedy offspring, just a few weeks old, and being taught to find their own food rather than to suckle. White whiskers twitched constantly as seven wet, pink noses sought and analysed odours from every direction, searching for any sign that would relieve their hunger. The search for food was endless, for the fulfilment of the insatiable appetites of six tiny young was the mother rat's single-most priority in life apart from self-preservation. She could smell the presence of a human being, but was not disturbed by it. The human was motionless and there was no food in that direction to interest the rat family. The human body odour was much stronger than usual in this room. The rat ignored it, however, and continued to sense in every direction. She reached a corner of the room and scampered off at right angles, keeping close by the adjacent wall, looking for a way out of the room. No food here, she thought. Wait a minute... yes... something straight ahead. Her babies followed behind her, as if linked by an invisible thread. In an even darker corner of the room the mother rat had detected a cache of boiled potato on the cold floor, spilt by a cook in a careless moment and now forgotten and mildewed.

The human stirred. The rats froze, hidden in the shadows. Another human was coming. Take care.

There was a gentle knock on the door of the cold, two-room cottage and, without waiting for an answer, Lizzie Knott entered quietly.

"How are you, love?" she asked the invalid.

Jane Heal was too weak to say much. She raised a hand feebly and a faint smile of recognition crossed her face, but she remained silent. Lizzie crossed the room to her bedside and sat next to Jane on the stool that Jane also used as a little table.

"You're ever so cold, love. Here, let me tuck you in."

Lizzie tried hard not to breathe through her nose as she adjusted the bedclothes that smelt of urine.

"Didn't you manage to light the fire this morning?"

Lizzie looked at the grate and saw a charred pile of unburnt fuel. It seemed as if the fire might have been lit first thing in the morning, but had gone out soon afterwards. Jane had not got out of bed to tend to it. Lizzie left the stool and spent ten minutes rekindling the fire, which soon crackled healthily, and cast its flickering warmth around the room.

The rat family had almost finished its meal.

Lizzie could see that Jane's condition was worse today. Normally, Jane could find just enough energy to climb out of bed to keep her fire alive and to respect nature. Today the fire was out and the bedding stank. Lizzie had not seen her so ill as this.

Jane's life had been wasted throughout almost its entirety. Of her fifty-two years, only five had brought her any pleasure. The third child in a family of eight, only she and her brother Thomas had survived to reach the age of maturity. Her parents had always been very poor, mainly because her father was too interested in gin to care much for the welfare of his family. The cottage in which they lived was too small for such a family and the extreme dampness had been largely responsible for the deaths by consumption of Jane's siblings.

The two ground floor rooms were always dark because of tiny windows, which were to help retain what little heat was produced from the fire. Since there was rarely much fuel in the cottage, the fires were poor and the rooms became bitterly cold. This, in turn, brought a penetrating dampness that left clothes and bedding uncomfortable and unhealthy, but on top of these misfortunes came the misery of life with an aggressive, drunken head of the household. In fits of drunkenness, Jane's father regularly beat up Jane, her mother, and the rest of the family. Although Jane never suffered more than bruising, the continual arguments and physical punishments meant that life within the four walls was mostly miserable. Despite the violence, however, Jane loved her parents, for what other kind of childhood did she know? With the perfect innocence of a child she forgave all. She made the best of a bad lot in life and found as much happiness as a young girl could amongst the company of her sickly brothers and sisters. It was only her relationship with Jack that brought her to realise the meaning of true happiness.

For a brief and wonderful time Jane fell in love with her handsome Jack, the lighthouse keeper on the South Foreland. She had loved Jack with all her heart and soul, for, in total contrast to her bullying father, Jack was gentle and caring towards her. For the first time in her life she knew of real love. Thus it did not take Jane long to decide on marriage to Jack rather than her pathetic existence with her parents. Soon the misery of East Langdon was left far behind when, after her wedding, she had gone to live in comparative comfort in the lighthouse. Their intense lovemaking quickly bore fruit. Jane gave birth to a pretty little girl with green eyes and brown hair whom they had called Alice and in whom both Jane and her husband had delighted. Alice was always kept dressed in the prettiest clothes that Jane could provide. Jane was blissfully happy at last in the bosom of her own family. Then, just as she was beginning to get used to her newfound happiness, one brief hour of terror in the

168

middle of a night had put an end to all that she had held so dear. It was a night that she had spent the next thirty years trying to forget. Her world had been devastated, her husband brutally murdered, her home lost; her whole life lay in ruins. There was no escape from the nightmare that was reality.

Jack's death had caused Jane's eviction from the lighthouse for the management did not allow it to be looked after by a woman alone. Whilst many keepers' wives performed duties at lights where there were families in occupation, nowhere was there a lighthouse under the sole care of a woman. In any case, Jane would not have been able to cope with some of the heavy manual work, carry out night watchkeeping and be a mother to Alice without assistance. Inevitably and unwillingly, Jane had unwillingly returned to live with her parents in East Langdon.

The village was about four miles from the coastline and about three-quarters of a mile from its twin, West Langdon. Both villages had originally grown up around an Abbey founded in the reign of Richard Coeur de Lion by Sir William de Auberville for a group of Premonstatensian Canons from Leyston in Suffolk. With the dissolution of the monasteries however, it had been eventually converted into Abbey farm.

Meanwhile, the villages continued, although West Langdon was but a cluster of half a dozen houses. East Langdon, on the other hand, had fared rather better and its draughty stone cottages now housed about a hundred souls, most of whom rarely visited the coast. Thus, whilst St. Margaret's contained a good proportion of fishermen, East Langdon's inhabitants were almost exclusively farm labourers.

All agricultural work was poorly paid. Much of the time it was not available. The people, however, always managed to cope, eking out their existence in the most admirable ways. In common with the other villages in the area, East Langdon had its share of poor folk, who, for one reason or another, were unable to support themselves. Under the auspices of the village church, the charity of those who were able to afford it was regularly distributed among those officially regarded as being 'poor'. In addition to alms, a benefactor to the poor had donated a small plot of land so that they might grow vegetables. It was, however, understood that the poor folk who were in receipt of alms could not use the land. The reverse was also true. Nevertheless, both of these aids to the unfortunates of the village proved sufficient to keep them alive.

Jane's family were not able to receive alms because the vicar considered Jane's father to be able to work, even though he usually did not and, more often, would not. It was therefore left to the rest of the family to obtain what food they could and it was by cultivating tiny portions of the 'poor' land that some of them survived. Six of Jane's brothers and sisters died.

Soon after Jane had returned to the misery of her family home, little Alice became ill. Her cough seemed to be incessant and to emanate from the very depths of her lungs. Her pretty dresses became dirty and torn and soon began to fall from her body as her weight diminished to just a few stones. Her hair ribbons had long since gone and her hair hung filthily and uncombed, for her mother had completely lost interest in the welfare of her child. Alice missed her father mortally. She cried herself to sleep every night, the sobs punctuated only by the remorseless coughing. The shock of being locked in the dark coal store to listen to the screams of her mother being raped and her father being murdered had made her terrified of the darkness. Regularly, the peace of the night was shattered by the piercing screams of the child's nightmares. There seemed to be nothing anyone could do. There was a doctor in the village but his time was spent mostly in climbing the social ladders among the wealthier members of the community. Eventually when Jane had saved enough money to persuade him to visit poor Alice, he gave her a cursory inspection and declared that the child should be kept warm and given plenty of hot food. Jane could provide neither. The doctor charged two shillings and left. Alice died in Jane's arms two days later having lost the desire to live. The tiny bones of the once happy little four year old with green eyes and brown hair lay forgotten and unmarked in the paupers' corner of East Langdon churchyard.

A few years later, Jane's mother had died in great pain after two enormous lumps grew on her left breast. Jane was never able to forget the agony those flaming red cancerous sores caused her mother. Her father seemed able to cope only from behind the protective screen of an alcoholic haze. Progressively, he drank more and more until he was only sober when there was no money in the house and he could not beg steal or borrow drink from any of his many sources. He had long since stopped beating Jane, for, not only did he rarely have the strength, but he had almost ceased to recognise her existence. Dutifully, Jane did what she could for her father, but ultimately the old fellow had drunk so much that his liver had stopped functioning. After three days during which his body turned green with the build up of poisonous body waste, he died painlessly in the oblivion of his last alcoholic stupor. Jane had finally grown to hate him, for it seemed so cruel that the one person who had caused her much misery had died so peacefully and in such contrast to her mother, her husband and her daughter, who had all deserved better. Was there no justice in the world?

Since then, ten years ago, she had been alone. The cold and damp were unremitting. Jane could not stand it. Her wizened fingers were rigid and painful with rheumatics. They were bleached white with cold. Her breathing had become harsh and her chest always felt tight. She too had gained a nagging cough, which caused her much pain, and her weight was now declining daily.

Lizzie returned to the stool and gently gripped Jane's icy fingers as the flickering flames of the fire cast cheery shadows in the room, but Jane seemed not to care. Lizzie and her husband, James, had moved into the next cottage to Jane after their marriage three months ago. James was a hard-working farm labourer and had so far managed to keep his wife in modest comfort. They both eagerly anticipated the birth of their first child for Lizzie was already pregnant. Lizzie had always done what she could for Jane, but her help was limited by her own circumstances. It was almost unimportant now, however, for Jane's health had deteriorated drastically.

"How do you feel, love?" asked Lizzie, trying to restore the circulation to the frozen limbs of her patient.

"Not so good today, my dear," said Jane in a whisper, her eyes becoming more vacant with each minute that passed.

"Are you feeling warmer now that I've lit the fire? Can I get you another blanket?"

"It's all right, Lizzie. I haven't got any more blankets," said Jane.

"I'll get you one of ours - just a minute…"

She half rose, but Jane's hand clutched hers and weakly prevented her from leaving.

"It's all right dear. There's no need. I'm warming up now." With great effort she smiled at Lizzie who sat once more.

The one thing that Lizzie was able to provide in abundance was love and friendship. This she had done willingly, but her love had come too late and had not been sufficient to improve Jane's health. It was in the long and peaceful sojourns at Jane's bedside while James was at work that Lizzie had learned the horrible truth about Jane's past.

Jane had always been careful not to tell of the murder of her husband. The terrible threats of his killer to return to rape and murder little Alice had forced Jane to remain silent. She had accounted for Jack's death with the story that he had committed suicide. Untruthfully, she had told that she had been the culprit who had caused her husband's misery. This was an obvious lie to anyone who knew the couple for their marriage had been a happy one. Soon after the death of Jack, however, the murderers had left the area and no-one had seen them since. Furthermore, her daughter had died and there had been no need to perpetuate the secret. On the other hand, there had, until now, been no need for her to tell the truth. Jane had few friends and the only villagers with whom she ever had contact had long since accepted her original story. In deference to Jane, it was no longer talked about.

Then Lizzie came along. Their long talks had resulted in Lizzie learning the full story. Lizzie had tried at first to stop Jane from telling it, for it obviously caused her much pain. Jane, however, insisted that it would make her feel better. Indeed, since Jane had relieved herself of the hideous secret, she had felt as if a great burden had been lifted from her shoulders. Lizzie thought that Jane seemed to be much more at peace.

Jack's death had, of course, resulted in Lizzie's father becoming the lighthouse keeper. The lighthouse had been Lizzie's home all her life and it was doubtful if her childhood would have been as happy if her father had not been so fortunately employed. Perhaps Lizzie would not even have been born. Lizzie was not sure if William, her father, knew the full circumstances that had led up to his appointment. She doubted it and resolved never to tell him: there seemed little to be gained from it.

Lizzie sat with Jane for a time until she heard the sound of James arriving home. She then tucked up the peacefully sleeping patient, made sure that the fire was well stoked and left quietly to make James his supper.

The following day, after James had gone to the farm once more, Lizzie decided to take Jane a hot drink. Holding the cup in her left hand and a small bundle of her own dry kindling wood under her arm, she knocked on the door of Jane's cottage with her free hand and quietly slipped the latch. The room within was in its usual dark state, but Lizzie could just make out the bed and Jane looked to be asleep. She crept over to the fireplace and placed the wood in the grate. She noticed that there seemed to be a strange smell. There had always been an unpleasant smell in the cottage. It was mostly caused by the dampness, but recently Jane's incontinence had added to it. Today the smell was worse and quite different.

Still carrying the hot cup, she approached the bed. Something seemed to move on the pillow. Jane was facing the wall.

"Jane, love, I've brought you a nice hot drink."

She placed the cup on the stool on which she had sat yesterday and which still stood beside the bed. Then she placed a hand on Jane's shoulder and gently shook her as she turned Jane over. As Jane's head turned to face Lizzie a large female rat ran up Lizzie's arm towards her face. Instantly she gasped and knocked it off. At the same time, half a dozen other much smaller rats scampered in every direction, disappearing into the gloom in a split second. Then, to Lizzie's horror, she realised that she was staring into the face of death... a horrible, bloody, eyeless face... an unrecognizable face. The rats had begun to eat Jane. Lizzie screamed from the pit of her stomach and ran from the room leaving the door open.

20 ISABELLE DU PLESSIX

It took a long time for William Knott to recover from the injuries that he sustained on the dreadful night in November. Because of his broken ribs, any sudden breathing motion or the slightest awkward movement was excruciatingly painful. Fortunately there was no pressure from Regis and Isabelle du Plessix for him to leave their home. Generously and without prompting they encouraged him to stay as long as was necessary for his wounds to heal. As time passed however a far more serious problem arose: Will fell in love with Isabelle.

Isabelle's fondness for Will had been kindled at the beach on the morning when she had discovered him unconscious and barely alive. She had wanted to save his life and it was quite inconsequential that Will was an Englishman. The fact that her own government had decided to make all Englishmen Isabelle's enemy had not the slightest effect on her. Thus, when faced with the responsibility of caring for a badly injured human being, Isabelle and Regis together had grasped the nettle and taken Will into their home as if he had been a blood relative. The arousal of the mother instinct in the seventeen-year-old girl resulted in Will being given undivided attention for weeks after the rescue.

Each day Isabelle gently bathed his wounds as a mother might tend to the needs of her helpless child. The facial injuries sustained during the fisticuffs with Jennings came out as extensive swelling and bruising of the cheekbones. His eyes blackened and his nose was choked with dried blood. For many days therefore, Isabelle was unaware of Will's natural good looks and her affection for Will was born of compassion rather than physical attraction. However, as the days passed and his countenance healed, so Isabelle gradually became captivated by the Englishman who was also her enemy.

The care and attention necessary to facilitate Will's recovery was problem enough for Isabelle, but there was another problem. At the moment when Will regained consciousness to be met by Isabelle's anxious, caring blue eyes, he and she were unable to communicate. Neither Will nor Isabelle had heard even a single word of the other's language in their entire lives, and to be faced with the problem of explaining urgent physical needs without the advantage of verbal intercourse was most frustrating. Both were forced to learn basic words and phrases in a matter of days and their many mistakes provided them with endless fun. The monotony of Will's recuperation had become a pleasantry. Each revelled in the novelty of learning the language of the other, and before very long they delighted in their newfound past-time. Will, being severely restricted in his movements, would have been exceedingly bored by an extended period of recovery had it not been for the extra dimension of learning to talk to such a delightful female friend. Furthermore, the fun of teaching her his own language and sharing the fun of each other's silly mistakes made each day a joy.

Will found Isabelle's personality quite magnetic. In many ways it paralleled that of his dear sister Lizzie, and although they were facially quite different, Will could not help feeling that they were temperamentally quite similar. Both shared a deep sense of caring and compassion; Lizzie too would have taken an injured Frenchman into her home at the drop of a hat. Both girls had a sense of fun that was second to none, and with a smile had a happy greeting whatever the weather. Isabelle's jollity was always an asset, especially when Will was in pain. However, by degrees, the joviality of life was transformed into a more serious, profound relationship as each of them came to acknowledge the love that was maturing between them.

Isabelle was much more attractive than Lizzie, her dark Breton features being set in a seemingly flawless complexion of silk-soft skin. A pair of the most delicate ears could just be seen beneath her shoulder length dark hair, which itself served to emphasise Isabelle's long and graceful neck. Her dresses, for a working girl, always successfully exhibited her figure in its best light, without ever becoming too demonstrative.

Soon Isabelle and Will were deeply in love. Regis began to have mixed feelings about Will's presence in his house. He had been quite happy to take the Englishman home because the urgency of the situation demanded an instant decision. The vacuum in his life created by the death of his own son had caused him to act spontaneously in a way that would save the life of the boy, even though he knew that problems would ensue because of the war between England and France. However, when Isabelle began to spend almost every minute of the day with the newcomer, Regis naturally became a little disturbed. The chores of the house were not getting done as efficiently as in the past, but most of all, the wedge had been driven between him and his daughter. No longer was he the most important person in her life. There were other problems too, for although they lived in a cottage a good distance from their nearest neighbours, they were being forced to conduct a masque of deception in order that Will's presence would not be detected. There was no doubt that if Lieutenant Rodier were to be informed of Will's presence by a villager acting out of national interest, the seaman would be arrested immediately. Furthermore, what would be the fate of Regis and his daughter? The garrison commander was sometimes friendly, often officious, and always rigid in his application of the law. There was no telling how he would react to the sort of situation in which Regis now found himself. English sailors who were shipwrecked on the Brittany coast were usually helped, as were any nationalities; the seafarer always looked after his own folk. War, however, introduced other complications.

The biggest problem of all was caused by the aftermath of the two murders. Two bodies were found on the road that led out of Le Croisic. Both bodies were dressed in clothes that were associated with English seamen, but one of the men was identified as a villager. Both men seemed to have been killed with the same knife and the circumstances of the episode were most puzzling. It led to much speculation amongst the villagers and made the English even more unpopular than they were after the battle in the Bay. In addition, a number of other English seamen were rounded up in the surrounding countryside. Rumours were spread that they had come ashore on rafts from one of the English ships that had struck *Le Four* shoal. For a number of days afterwards the local people went to considerable lengths to secure their homes against intruders. Fortunately, none were reported.

Thus it was even more vital that Will's presence in the du Plessix household be kept secret. If it had been the responsibility of himself and Isabelle alone, Regis would not have worried, but the fact that Doctor Dixneuf was also party to the secret had caused Regis to lose sleep. The Doctor was as good as his word, however, and the secret was kept.

As for the language barrier with Will, Regis flatly refused to learn English. He declared himself far too long in the tooth to change his way of life and left Isabelle to translate his feelings on the matter to Will. Regis was most surprised and gladdened by the speed with which Will learned to speak French. Had Regis possessed the cool analytical brain of his daughter he would have put forward three explanations for such remarkable progress. Firstly, a young mind was well known for its enormous learning capacity, and, secondly, Will was getting a considerable amount of practice each day. Thirdly, and perhaps most important of all, was the desire to cultivate the rapidly blossoming romance between the two youngsters.

Though at first Regis became quite unhappy when he realised that his daughter was falling in love with the Englishman, a few days of careful thought established his position. Regis was a kind man. It would not be easy to give up the attention he had enjoyed from Isabelle over the years, but in her best interests he must. If not Will, his daughter would fall in love with somebody else sooner or later. Now that time had apparently arrived he must surrender her with dignity or else risk losing her for ever. Isabelle would not be the first daughter to desert her father in favour of a forbidden lover. If, on the other hand, he were to openly condone the affair, he would surely retain her love, whilst sharing her affections. Regis could find no hate in his heart for the English; they had caused him no trouble. Furthermore, Will was making excellent progress towards becoming a French speaker and that was an important point in his favour. Regis resolved that, rather than create trouble between himself and Isabelle, he would allow the romance to continue under his paternal eye. This necessitated extracting an oath from his daughter that she would not take advantage of Will's presence in the house for although Regis was happy to bless the match he would not countenance any dishonourable conduct behind his back. Isabelle was so pleased with her father when he made his position clear that she kissed him eagerly and promised to retain her honour. From that point onward the du Plessix household was even more relaxed and contented. Only the vagaries of the future and Will's legal position as an enemy of France remained to cloud the horizon.

As each day passed Isabelle found Will more and more desirable, and in return he worshipped her. On one very special occasion when Regis was away in the village, the youngsters found themselves tired of exchanging small talk. With their bodies close but discreetly distanced, Isabelle absorbed his gaze and found that intimate, inner smile that is given only through the eyes of love. There was no doubt of Will's attraction to her. No eyes she had ever seen had contained such affection and desire. The translation of these emotions, which they both recognised, into words that were understandable to both parties was only partly successful. A physical act alone could compensate for their inadequate powers of expression. Inexorably their faces drew closer and they kissed. First a furtive, timid contact of lips from afar, then a lush, unashamed show of emotion, the kiss lasted forever. Even without an embrace, which would have caused Will too much pain, the couple had finally crossed the chasm which divided friends from lovers. Their lives would never be the same again.

As with all those in love, the problems of life passed high above the heads of Will and Isabelle, whilst to Regis they remained a stern reality which would have to be dealt with at some stage. It would not be possible for the three adults to exist for an extended period on the food that his household was presently able to provide.

With Christmas but days away, Will was out of bed and able to move around the cottage in slow, measured movements so as to protect his ribs. His face had completely healed and he was beginning to feel like a whole man again. The du Plessix' cottage was well stocked up with food for the winter, but the increased consumption caused by the third hungry mouth was beginning to make an impact on the stores. Regis began to consider the options available to him. If Will were to remain he would eventually be arrested and sent to the big military prison at St. Nazaire. If the couple wanted to marry, there was no real possibility of them making a home in France, at least until the war was over. Alternatively, if Regis helped Will to escape back to England it was unlikely that he would want to leave Isabelle behind. Regis decided to allow the youngsters to enjoy Christmas together before attempting to plan the best course of action.

Christmas Day came, and with it a bitterly cold snap which froze the ponds and small streams. The wind blew strongly from the east and penetrated every layer of clothing. Everyone was persuaded that the only good place to be was indoors beside a log fire. The du Plessix were well prepared with traditional French festive foods and Will spent the day in a cosy chair with a log fire on his right side and the feminine form of Isabelle on his left. The three ate heartily and chatted the day away without a care in the world, as if they were all of the same family. Only occasionally during the day did Will spend time in meditation for his real family. Did they believe him dead? How were his brothers and sisters? And what of dear Lizzie? Surely she had recovered from the affair with Edward by now. How trivial the row with his father had been.

Brief mental images of the family he had not seen for months flashed through his mind, but the fleshy, sensual presence of Isabelle in her flouncy lace-trimmed dress quickly dispelled any anguish he felt. Just a trace of perfume pervaded the festive air, so that even with his eyes closed Will was aware of her reality. Here was a true woman. The flickering firelight cast ever-changing hues over her graceful form. Her long black hair glistened with golden gossamer while her soft, dark eyes radiated warmth, gaiety and love. Her cutaway neckline exposed the most perfect neck and shoulders and the bodice projected her figure neatly, emphasising her bosom in just the right manner. Her waistline was trim, her hips supportive, and, beneath the extended hemline, Will could see dainty, shapely feet. His physical attraction could not have been stronger. To have spent more than six months entombed in a ship without sight of the female form was a most unnatural experience, which he cared not to repeat. Then, to find himself in the company of such a beauty as Isabelle, was surely the most amazing turnabout. He had been spellbound from the moment when he had first set eyes on her. That vision, which at the time he had thought was of an angel in the afterlife, he would remember forever. He had felt certain that he must be dead, but of course he was not. Will could hardly believe his luck. Isabelle was the sort of girl that every young man dreamed he would marry one day. What was even more remarkable was that she loved him too. The dream must go on and on forever; he would not let it end. He must marry Isabelle. Unfortunately, the problems were not as clear to Will as they were to Regis.

After the perfection of Will's Christmas Day with his beloved, the snows came, and caused Regis to postpone the day on which he would try to decide Will's future. The snow lay for six weeks and no sooner did one fall thaw than another layer arrived to prolong the freeze. By the end of that time Will had almost completely recovered and Regis was becoming anxious to plan the future. Their food stocks had taken a sharp fall during their enforced isolation and the time was nigh to settle the problems.

Will too had had sufficient time to contemplate a prognosis to his predicament, and was becoming restive. He had been hidden away in the cottage for more than two months and although the weather had been discouraging he was keen to get out and about. He would have been delighted to stay in France with Isabelle if it had not been for two important considerations. Firstly, he was an alien in the country with which he was at war. Secondly, he had become obsessed by the need to let his family know that he was safe and well. There was no way to convey a message to them other than by his own hand.

Regis had tentatively suggested that Will could try to escape the country by sea from St Nazaire, but even he had been forced to agree that he was being optimistic. All the boats belonging to the villagers were too small to attempt a journey of such a distance but there was a slight chance that a friend might be able to arrange a passage from St. Nazaire to a neutral country such as Ireland or Holland. The journey to England could not be arranged from France, and once he was in a neutral country Will would have to fend for himself.

21 JULES PAULIN

John Jennings' capture by the French militia was inevitable. Once the soldiers had been alerted to the presence of an English fugitive in the vicinity of the elderly couple's cottage they were soon on the scene where they began a thorough search of the surrounding countryside. They had to wait until daylight in order to find him hiding in a small copse about two kilometres from the house where he had held the French folk captive. Jennings surrendered without resistance for he'd had two complete nights without sleep and had eaten very little in two days. Even Jennings knew when he was beaten.

Once caught, his wrists were bound tightly behind his back and he was marched several kilometres to a farm cottage that Lieutenant Guy Rodier was using as a search centre. The officer would have liked to interrogate Jennings on the spot, but there was no means of communicating with the prisoner. Rodier's only course of action was to send Jennings to the regional military gaol at Rennes. There would be an English-speaking intelligence officer who would ascertain the truth by whatever means was necessary. Usually, by the time this had been done, the information was virtually useless. Rodier eagerly wanted information about the murders that had occurred just outside Le Croisic. The satisfaction of his curiosity would alone have been sufficient, but if he could discover the perpetrator he would be delighted.

Rodier wrote a report for despatch, along with Jennings, to the Rennes gaol so that the questioner would be adequately acquainted. Then Jennings was put in a cart with two guards and sent on his way. The long, arduous journey took three days, at the end of which Jennings was actually quite glad to see the towering city walls that were to hold him prisoner. If he had possessed any foresight of the trials that lay ahead of him, however, he would have been mortified at the sight.

Once inside the walls of the fortress he was taken deep into the basement of the gaol where his bonds were removed and he was thrown into a pitch black, stinking cell. The total darkness did not prevent him from discovering the constraints of his situation for, apart from the dimensions of the cell, there was nothing to find. By touch he could tell that the cell was about four feet square and six feet high. It had been evilly designed so that an inmate could never sleep outstretched. There was in one corner a vile smelling hole in the floor, which was obviously the toilet. There was no bed or blanket and no furniture of any kind, just bare, cold, unsympathetic stone and suffocating darkness.

Jennings remained in the cell for a very long time. Day and night were indistinguishable and consequently he had no conception of the length of time that he was in the tomb. Initially he was very tired and able to gain sufficient sleep to recover some of his strength, but after a time he became so uncomfortable that he could not rest at all. His posterior became painful to sit on and his knees ached relentlessly through being so long in a bent position. The greater proportion of the time spent in the black hole was in a sitting position. It seemed more natural to close his eyes than to keep them open, constantly straining to detect a chink in the Stygian armour. He prayed constantly for sleep to take away the stultifying boredom of the endless detention, but it did not. Soon he began to hallucinate, for in the darkness his brain projected images of such reality that he cried out, over and over again. The cries became screams, pleas for mercy, pitiful petitions for pardon. All passed unheeded. It was as if he were totally alone in the vacuum of existence, his being suspended in immortality.

Then there were footsteps and the sound of heavy bolts being moved outside the door. As the cell was opened, even the dim light from the dungeon passage blinded Jennings for a time. A heavy hand was placed upon his clothing and he was dragged out of the cell and thrust towards the end of the passage. He found that he had almost forgotten how to walk and adopted an awkward, gangly gait in response to the urgent demands of his captors. Three flights of steps, new passageways, two doors, more steps. Where was he being taken?

Finally he was pushed into a sunny room and the heavy oak door slammed shut behind him. For some time he felt disorientated and his eyes squinted to cope with the bright light. The room was about fifty feet long and ten feet wide. Along one side four narrow windows were let into the thick, stone wall, and through them the weak, winter sun streamed to form three-dimensional blocks of golden presence. The walls were of bare grey stone and the floor of wooden planks. The room was completely unfurnished except for a table with two chairs facing each other across it. One chair was empty. The other contained a man wearing an immaculate white uniform trimmed with blue. Jennings was startled briefly, for he had taken a minute or two to realise that the man was there at all.

"Welcome," said the soldier in a friendly tone. He spoke in English and smiled at Jennings as if he really meant what he said. "Would you like to sit down?" He indicated the vacant chair.

"Yes," replied Jennings, still dazed and feeling wretched, but relieved after his ordeal in the cell. He occupied the chair.

"Are you hungry?" said the voice, again in a most inviting tone. Jennings nodded; he could hardly remember his last meal. The man rose and walked to the door

178

which he opened. He shouted a string of incomprehensible syllables and then returned to his seat from which position he said nothing. The two men studied each other for several minutes when a sudden bang on the door was succeeded by its squeaky opening. Another soldier entered and laid before Jennings a large brown earthenware bowl of piping hot stew and a loaf of bread. The second man then left without a word. Jennings needed no invitation to dine. He eagerly devoured every morsel and burned his tongue with the soup. When he had finished he sat back in the chair and rested in contentment. A piece of meat was lodged uncomfortably between his teeth and he picked at it with his tongue. Then the second soldier returned and removed the crockery. As soon as he had done so, the first soldier, whom Jennings took to be an officer because of the impressive looking insignia on his uniform, began to speak again.

"What is your name?"

"John Jennings."

"Which English ship do you come from?"

"*Resolution.*"

"How many men were travelling with you?"

Jennings hesitated. He must be careful. Suddenly the seriousness of his position materialised in his mind. Until now, there had always been something else of more importance. First it had been avoiding capture, then the physical and mental survival in that cell. He had not really considered that he would be questioned in this way and he was angry with himself for not expecting it. If only he had planned his story better.

The officer leaned forward and repeated his question.

"How many men were travelling with you?" The voice was still polite, but Jennings hesitation had introduced the first hint of suspicion.

"Just one other," replied Jennings. He must not tell the officer about Dobbs or he would be effectively confessing to the murder of the French peasant as well. His course of action was plain: he must pretend that he and Eliot had been travelling independently. "There was just me and another bloke, that's all."

"Who was that?"

"You know who it was."

"Who was it?" The voice became more insistent.

"Tom Eliot, the one whose skull I beat in at the old people's cottage."

"Why did you kill him?"

"He made me mad."

"Why did he make you mad?"

"Because he let the old people go. They escaped and raised the alarm."

"You didn't need to kill him."

"He was rubbish… scum." Jennings was angry.

"But you did not need to kill him." The tone of the voice was becoming sterner with every question.

"No."

179

"This man, Eliot, was he your only companion?"

"I told you he was… there were just two of us."

"How did you come ashore from your ship?"

"We built a raft from wreckage after the ship struck the rocks. We floated ashore at night."

"Just the three of you…

"Two, I said, two."

"Why did you leave the ship?"

"We thought it was going to sink. We thought we were going to die."

"But it did not sink?'

"We thought it would."

"So you deserted your ship?"

"We did not desert, we escaped to save our lives."

"Who was on the raft with you?"

"Just Eliot."

"No-one else?"

"No." Jennings was rapidly losing his temper. He rose from his chair but the officer sat motionless and continued to gaze at him with an air of total control over the situation. He was almost gloating and Jennings guessed that the officer was trying to annoy him purposely. Jennings considered attacking him: it was one against one. He changed his mind when he remembered the fortress into which he had been taken. There could be no escape from such a place without detailed plans. He must keep cool. He calmed himself and sat rather uneasily in the chair once more. He wondered how long the interview would continue. The officer rose and went to the door. More shouts. Immediately three soldiers came into the room and walked straight to the chair in which Jennings rested. His arms were seized and each wrist was bound firmly to the respective horizontal arm of the chair. The officer seated himself once more to face Jennings who by now was in fear of what was to come.

"I shall ask you some more questions and if I do not like the answers, my men will give you a - how do you say? A manicure? Ça va!"

At the French instruction two of the soldiers took up positions, one each side of Jennings, who pulled hard at his bonds, to no effect. He hardly dared to think what they were going to do to his hands.

"How many men travelled with you?"

Jennings was terrified. He knew that the officer believed he had killed the Frenchman and all he could think of were Dobbs' last words about them all having their heads chopped off. If he were to admit that he had killed the frog he would surely lose his head. If he continued to lie he would have to suffer pain.

"There were only two of us."

"Ça va!"

One of the soldiers produced a tiny blade that had been concealed in his hand. He grasped Jennings' right hand and selected the forefinger. Jennings struggled with all his might, but he was immobile. The soldier thrust the blade right up underneath his fingernail and with a well-practised flick of the wrist completely removed the protective shell from his finger. Jennings vision was obliterated by a scalding sensation, which passed through the whole of his arm to the front of his brain. His eyes filled with the tears of ultimate pain and he screamed with all the capacity of his lungs and throat, but it failed to reduce the pain even by a fraction. When Jennings sight was restored he saw his forefinger swathed in blood and a steady stream of drips onto the wooden floor. Since leaving St. Margaret's, Jennings had become familiar with the sight of blood, but until now it had always been that of others. The sight of his own caused him to feel faint.

"How many men travelled with you?" That damned question, the one he could not answer, stood between death and agony. The choice was appalling.

"Just Eliot... only Eliot," he pleaded. "Please believe me, I didn't kill the Frenchman..."

The officer sat up sharply. "Which Frenchman? I did not mention a Frenchman." Jennings knew that he had given the game away. Perhaps they would stop hurting him now. They did not.

"Ça va!"

The second blade underneath Jennings middle finger nail seemed marginally more bearable than the first, but within seconds caused him to pass out. For many hours afterwards his subconscious mind coalesced with his consciousness until he was quite unable to distinguish reality from illusion. His pain was relived time and again blade after blade stabbing into his fingers, his toes, his face... Eventually Jennings was reborn into the real, consistent world and found that he was back in the cell once more.

The darkness, the cold seemed somehow friendly now, for they were not the source of such pain. He could not bear to touch his fingers that still throbbed painfully. This time there was not long to wait before he was once more being taken along the same passageways, up the same steps and through the same doors. Stupidly, he tried to make an escape at one point, but a soldier's rifle butt quickly clubbed him to the floor. It hurt his shoulders badly and diverted his attention from his fingers. Then he was dragged to his feet and frog-marched towards that room where he would doubtless be tortured further.

The chair was still there, as was the table and the officer. The sunshine was not, neither were the soldiers. Jennings tried to summon all the courage he possessed; he was determined not to be afraid.

"Please sit down, Monsieur Jennings." It was the friendly tone again.

"As you saw in my earlier demonstration I can make your life very unpleasant and there is very little chance of your failing to tell me what I want to hear. When I ask you questions I want you to tell me the truth. If you do not then you must suffer pain. There is one thing of which I want you to be absolutely sure. The pain you felt yesterday is but a token example of the most hideous pain that you can imagine. I have methods of making you writhe in agony, the like of which you never dreamed possible. I can cause you to suffer the ultimate torment of Hell itself. Against that, I want you to balance the thought of a... reasonably comfortable cell in the company of other prisoners. You will have food and some recreation. When the war is over you can return to your own country. Is that an unreasonable offer in return for your co-operation?"

Jennings was incredulous. He had been offered his life. He could keep his head. It was too good to be true.

"You mean... if I tell you everything I know... you won't execute me?"

"Mon Dieu... of course not, monsieur. Whatever gave you that impression?"

Jennings bit his lip. Had he suffered for nothing? Who had given him the idea that he would be executed for what he had done? It had been that stupid fool Dobbs. He had no reason to say it. What did he know about France anyway? Jennings was very glad that he had opened Dobbs' guts for him. Then the thought occurred that the officer could easily be lying. After getting the information he wanted there would be no further use for Jennings.

"What do you want to know?" he said.

"How many men came ashore with you?"

"Two others," he replied. He had to take a gamble and trust this man. He could suffer no more torture.

"What were their names?"

"Dobbs and Eliot."

"Was Dobbs one of the two murdered men near Le Croisic?"

"Where?" asked Jennings.

"The village where you came ashore."

"Oh, yes," confirmed Jennings.

"Who killed the French peasant?"

"Eliot killed him... I told him not to, but he ignored me..."

"Come, come, monsieur, remember those little razors. Monsieur Eliot was a man with a conscience. He allowed the old couple to escape. He would not have done such a terrible thing, would he?"

"All right, I killed him. That's what you wanted to know... I killed him... me!" Jennings defiantly stabbed his chest with the forefinger of his left hand.

"That, monsieur, is all I wanted to know." The officer rose and left the room. Within moments Jennings was being taken away, this time along a different set of passageways and down different stairs... down and down... Where this time? He had no idea whether the officer would be true to his word or whether he was being taken to some unimaginable hell-house to have his limbs amputated one by one before his very eyes. After the pain they had given him already he would believe anything possible.

When he arrived in his new cell he could hardly believe his luck. It was large and contained quite a number of other men, all of whom eyed him suspiciously as the heavy metal door clanged shut behind him. Compared to his previous cell, this one was luxurious. There was plenty of space in which to move about. There were people to talk to, and, above all there was light. A very dim light it was that pervaded the cell, but Jennings found it more than adequate after the total blackness of the tomb in which he had first suffered. There were about thirty other men in the cell, some of whom were filthy and ragged, most of whom were very malodorous, and all of whom spoke French. There were no beds or furniture of any kind, but there was straw on the floor, which gave the dungeon a degree of warmth. Each prisoner was allowed one blanket, a mug and a bowl, and all wore steel anklets with eighteen inches of sturdy chain joining them. It was a matter of minutes after Jennings had been pushed into the cell before the man who Jennings decided must be the jailor returned with blanket, mug, dish and anklets for the new inmate.

Jennings' first illusion about being able to talk to fellow prisoners was quickly shattered.

"Hello, I'm John Jennings. Do any of you speak English?"

No response.

Jennings shrugged his shoulders, and then, spotting an area of floor space that was vacant, he settled himself down to sleep. Once again, however, he could not find peace of mind. Though he did manage to fall asleep, his dreams tormented him and caused him to wake in tears. Sometimes the other inmates, who were obviously angry with him, kicked him, though he knew not why.

Three days passed during which Jennings began to settle in to the routine of the cell. No-one spoke to him, or indeed, even approached him and as time passed he became more and more upset by it. It seemed unnatural to him that he should be ignored whilst in the company of thirty other human beings, even if they did not speak his language. He realised that if he was going to survive for a long time in this foreign country, he had better learn to speak French. Then, just as he was beginning to despair of his predicament his luck changed again. A middle-aged man with an untidy, grey beard and long, straggling hair approached him.

"The others are angry with you because you shout in your sleep and wake them," said the newcomer. Jennings was so pleased to discover another person who spoke English that the significance of the sentence was lost.

"You speak English! Why did you not speak to me before?"

"Why should I want to know you, monsieur? You are nothing to me. I just wanted to tell you that you are keeping us all awake with your - how do you say it? - nighthorses?"

"Nightmares, you mean."

"Ça va! Yes."

"Where did you learn to speak English so well?"

"I was fortunate enough to be able to go to school."

"Ah, an educated man, I should have known. What is your name?"

"Jules Paulin."

"How do you do, Jules. Mine is John Jennings. What's a man of learning doing in a hell-hole like this?"

"It is quite simple, monsieur. I am born into the wrong religion. To be a Protestant in a Catholic country is a worse crime than murder."

Jennings was surprised. For many months he had devoted his life to violence, and recently had killed four men. To be imprisoned under such circumstances was natural, but to be locked up for believing in God seemed odd. Jennings did not truly believe in God anyway. He had heard of Papists, but had never met one and, though he had never really thought about it, he had assumed that everybody was Protestant.

"How long will you be here, do you know?" asked John.

"Who knows, monsieur? One day they will come for me." The significance of Paulin's remark was lost on Jennings, not for the first time. The latter's mind was already spinning off at a tangent now that he had found someone to talk to.

"Will you teach me to speak French, Jules?"

"Of course, if that is what you want. I'm surprised you feel the need." Jennings was surprised.

"Why not? There is nothing else to do, is there? I shall be kept here until the end of the war and that could be years away. I can probably learn quite a lot from you until they move one or other of us."

Jennings and Paulin became firm friends during the weeks that followed. Paulin was a natural speaker; even in a foreign language he was obviously at home with words. Although, at first, Paulin was reluctant to say too much about himself, his affinity for conversation got the better of him and gradually, during the course of their long language lessons together, he told Jennings his life story.

Jules had been born the son of a wealthy landowner and farmer whose family had been brought up in the Protestant faith. His parents' wealth had ensured a good education for Jules and his three brothers, but the problems of actively pursuing a religion different from that which had been the norm for centuries had grown considerably. Jules had carried on his father's farming when the old man died, but found that he was being harassed in his business.

Other farmers and businessmen refused to deal with him and Catholic peasant folk refused to work for him for fear of retaliatory action. The farm became so difficult to manage that he and his family had been forced to abandon home. Soon, their money began to run out and they were reduced to a pitiful state. Finding so much difficulty in a Catholic land, Jules began to associate with other Protestants and to use his powers of oratory in order to mould them into effective units of opposition to the ruling parties. There had been two demonstrations in the regional capital. The second had ended in violence when several of the more unruly minorities began attacking the shopkeepers and stealing food. Jules had done his best to dissuade them from their actions, but discovered that even his lyrical leadership had no effect on a mob. As soon as the disturbance had been quelled the authorities had come after Jules and arrested him for inciting a riot. There was no defence against such a charge when it was rooted in religious difference. Inevitably, Paulin had been found guilty.

Jennings was amazed that his relationship with Paulin could develop despite their profoundly different backgrounds. To Paulin, however, it was quite natural, for so much of his recent life had been spent pursuing the cause of Protestantism and supporting the underdog. Jennings, besides being born a Protestant, was also an underdog, an English lamb who had strayed into the lair of the French wolf.

That Paulin had befriended an evil murderer, however, remained unknown to the Frenchman, who assumed, because the sailor told him so, that Jennings was being held only as a prisoner-of-war. Jennings, for his part, considered it necessary to conceal his recent misdemeanours on the thesis that the humanitarian Paulin might not be so kindly disposed to someone such as he if the true facts were known.

The daily routine of cell life soon became the norm to Jennings. The company of his English-speaking friend made the hard life tolerable. To his credit, Jennings made a workmanlike attempt at learning French. The other prisoners had formed their own friendships and mostly associated in small, exclusive groups. None made any attempt to approach Jennings once his contact with the Huguenot had been established. Only occasionally were glances of disapproval cast in Jennings' direction when the muttering and repetition of the parrot-fashion teaching methods continued after an unacceptable hour. Apart from the addition of one other French prisoner to the cell, its complement remained the same for seven weeks after Jennings' arrival, by which time his French was becoming quite useful. He could express himself slowly, to Jules' satisfaction, and could understand much of the French that Jules spoke. He had difficulty, however, in understanding many of the conversations that took place in colloquial Breton in other corners of the cell. Jules did his best at first to explain some of the phrases used, but there were so many that he confined himself to the King's French most of the time.

Just when Jennings had begun to reconcile himself to an existence in the cell until the end of the war, an event suddenly changed his whole outlook on life.

As a Thursday, the day was quite undistinguishable from any other to the prisoners, but it was to be a significant one for six of them. Breakfast of bread and soup was served as usual at first light and the morning passed uneventfully, as ever. Then, at about midday, the door of the cell was flung open and the jailer entered, accompanied by a dozen soldiers. One soldier produced a parchment and read aloud the names of six of the assembled audience. As each name was announced there was a cry of despair from among the prisoners. Jennings was bemused. It was as if each man knew the reason for his summons. In view of the reaction of the men it was obviously not their release that they were expecting.

On completion of the reading, the soldiers rounded up the six men, whilst four others stood guard with muskets aimed at the remainder of the captives. Five of the nominated men submitted to their summons, but the sixth tried to resist the attentions of his keepers. Two soldiers immediately raised the butts of their weapons and without hesitation brought them viciously down on the skull of the screaming prisoner. Then, bleeding and semi-conscious, he was dragged unceremoniously from the cell by two particularly large soldiers. A single soldier searched the cell and collected the men's accoutrements, whilst the sullen five had their anklets removed and their hands tied behind their backs. Then they were marched outside leaving behind a very subdued and anxious band of prisoners who stood gazing at each other in silence. Gradually, each returned to his own pitch on the floor of the cell to contemplate his fate. Jennings was aghast. He grabbed Paulin by the arm.

"Where are they going?" he said in French, now that he had become well versed in his new language. His air was urgent.

"To be executed, of course. This is the death cell, after all. We are all due to meet the same fate eventually, though none of us knows when."

"Death cell?" Jennings was almost in tears. "Me, in the death cell?"

"What is it, mon ami? You mean you did not know you were to be executed? I assumed that you did not wish to talk about it since you did not bring the subject up."

Jennings was in no mood for explanations or excuses. The revelation had come as if it were a blow to the head from an assailant in a dark alleyway. That officer had promised to release him at the end of the war and Jennings had believed him. The cell had seemed so much better than the one he had been in before. How could it be the death cell? Tears flowed freely from his eyes and he turned to the wall in shame. His legs were weak and he collapsed in a feeble convulsing shambles, clutching his straw pile for comfort like a baby seeking solace from a sucker. After an hour his misery turned to rage. He leapt up and rushed to the cell door. There, he hammered on it with his fists and screamed in English, for he was too upset to remember his French. All sounds from the cell were ignored by those outside, as they always had been. The prisoners could commit mass suicide for all the captors cared; the authorities would probably prefer it if they did, for it would surely save them the trouble of organising executions. The prisoners could do whatever they wished within the confines of the cell, but there would never be a response to a disturbance within the death cell. Jennings gave up the protest, his hands bruised and sore. He soon realised that there could be no reaction from the guards: so many men, condemned to death in the near future, could be very dangerous indeed.

Paulin chose to leave Jennings to his misery. He felt guilty that he had not discussed the subject with Jennings and was therefore partly responsible for his friend's misery. He had had no reason to do so, however, for he had assumed that Jennings was aware of his fate. Paulin was amazed that Jennings had not guessed, even if he had never been told. Perhaps Jennings was more stupid than Paulin had imagined. When Jennings seemed to have regained his composure, Paulin approached him once more and tried to commiserate with him. Jennings, however, felt nothing but bitterness, not only towards that interrogator, but to all Frenchmen. He swore at Paulin and refused to listen to the Frenchman's apologies.

The brief event which took place on the Thursday in early February and occupied a mere five minutes out of the enormous amount of time that they had spent in the dungeon, had a profound effect upon the inmates. Although they had known about their ultimate fate, the long period of endless confinement had induced a mood of lethargy and of carelessness about the future. Then, though they knew no detail about the execution of the Thursday six, the chilling reality of death pervaded every cubic inch of the cell like a bad smell. Conversations, which had been briskly conducted before, now occurred far less frequently and in a more serious tone.

186

Jennings was a destroyed man. His interest in learning French had evaporated, as had his interest in anything but himself. He refused to talk to Jules for days on end, preferring to spend his time prostrate on his hay pile where he agonised over the details of his execution. For many hours he tried to plan an escape, but he had no knowledge of the fortress or the town, and could think of no feasible method. The door was never opened except to take prisoners to their deaths: it was that simple.

Then, one night, the inevitable sexual approach was made. The inner tensions that drive men to distraction, if not released, made it a statistical certainty that out of twenty-five male human beings left caged for months, at least a few would relieve the pressures in the company of each other. When Jennings awoke to the affectionate embrace of another man he was instantly reviled and leapt to his feet as he screamed with rage. Complaints from the other prisoners disturbed from their slumbers filled the air. In the darkness he could just make out the shape of a body creeping away across the stone floor. Jennings pounced on it and rained blows into the place where he judged the man's face to be. He beat the man senseless and stopped only when his hands were excruciatingly sore. Then he returned to his hay pile, but slept for not an instant that night.

Three more weeks passed. Jennings had still barely spoken to Jules when without warning the cell door was flung open once more. Everyone sprang to their feet to face the open doorway where a line of armed soldiers stood with muskets at the ready. The tension was high between the two groups of men. Jennings felt that it was time to make a break for freedom. There were twenty-five prisoners in the cell, all certain to die. They could lose nothing by attacking now and seeking escape. If he were to die now in the invisible path of a musket ball, at least he would have made a stand. He did not deserve to be executed - the officer had promised...

Somehow, Jennings did not manage to find the spark that would lead the revolt against the row of cocked weapons, and even while he was considering the best option to take, the soldier in charge emerged from behind the row of guards with the vital piece of parchment. In a moment he had unrolled it and, holding it high and close to his eyeballs, read aloud.

"Attendez!"

Jennings listened intently to the list. He did not hear his own name, though Paulin's was included. He felt no sadness for the imminent demise of the man with whom he had once been a friend. Only his own fate concerned him. The initial relief that Jennings felt when he did not hear his own name called dispelled an escape bid from his mind, but before he could fall back on his straw heap the soldier in charge became agitated.

"Jennings, Jennings, qui est-ce que Jennings?"

The soldiers began rounding up the wretched prisoners concerned. Suddenly, the Englishman recognised his name. The Frenchman, knowing no English, had chosen a completely unrecognisable pronunciation for Jennings' surname. He was going to be executed now.

He fought the guards when they came for him, but he was knocked to the floor and held firmly face down while his anklets were removed and his arms bound behind him. Then he was on his feet and being marched quickly out of the cell with the others. Death was but moments away.

22 GUY RODIER

Lieutenant Guy Rodier was visiting Le Croisic on routine official business. He always found it by far the most boring part of his work but it was not his job to write the rules, merely to carry them out. As he left the last port of call and walked towards his horse it began to snow quite heavily. The easterly wind, which had been the carrier of so much snow in recent weeks, was still gusting between the houses and causing the snow to pile up along sheltered walls. Brittany had had far more than its usual quota of snow this year and Guy grimaced at the thought of another fall. Whilst other folks stayed at home and watched the snow from the comfort of their living rooms, it was his duty, as far as was possible, to continue with his official rounds according to the regulations which had been laid down in his terms of reference. Snow was, to him, a major hindrance and he wished it would stop.

He reached his horse and was just about to mount it when he saw Isabelle du Plessix walking up the main street with a basket of provisions in her hand. She was warmly dressed and had tucked her head well down into her cloak to shelter as much as possible from the driving snow. The officer knew her fairly well, for, although he was a married man, he always kept a weather eye open for a pretty girl. At once he knew that she had a considerable distance to walk, which would be hazardous in the present weather conditions. He knew how quickly the wind built up drifts along the cliff path, for he had experienced them many times before. He shouted to her, causing her to raise her head sharply in surprise.

"Mademoiselle Isabelle, are you planning to walk all the way home in this blizzard?" Isabelle was caught unawares. She had not noticed him in her desire to shelter her face.

"Yes, monsieur, I have no transport today," she replied factually. She feared his next question.

"Then I must insist that I take you home."

"Oh no, monsieur. I shall be quite all right." The worst had happened. "It will not take me long to get home and the snow has only just started." In the circumstances the words rang hollow. By now she had approached within ten feet of where the officer stood.

"Mademoiselle, it is at least half an hour's walk when the weather is fine. You shall ride with me and that is an order."

Isabelle was most concerned. She knew there was no way out. Once Lieutenant Rodier had made up his mind, he would not allow his opinion to be changed except by a superior officer. She dared not argue any more in case he should become suspicious. She had no alternative but to allow the officer to give her a leg up

188

onto his tall black stallion on which she sat side-saddle. The Lieutenant then climbed up himself and with Isabelle between his arms spurred his horse to walk unhurriedly in the direction of the du Plessix cottage. She turned the situation over and over in her mind as she tried to conceive of a way by which Will's presence in her home could be kept a secret. Perhaps Will would stay in the cottage when he saw them coming... if he saw them coming. On no account could she invite the Lieutenant inside. She could jump down before they got to the house and thank him there. It would be very rude not to invite him inside after being so considerate, but she must accept that. Besides, she was a woman and women were allowed to be rude to men. She began to pray hard that Will would see them coming and hide in the house. So engaged in mental activity was she that she said not a word for the first ten minutes of the ride.

"You are very quiet, Isabelle," said Guy as the horse plodded reliably onward. "You usually have plenty of conversation."

"Oh I'm very tired and cold, monsieur," she replied, thinking that he'd noticed she was worried.

"Don't worry, we'll soon be home," he said kindly and reassuringly. He had no idea that the last thing she needed was reassurance.

The snow was getting quite deep and Isabelle could see that Guy had been quite right to bring her home. It would have taken her hours to make the journey on foot. How she wished that she had not left the cottage that morning! Her seat on the horse was rather uncomfortable and so tightly was she held between Guy's strong arms that she was not able to adjust her position. Rather than create a fuss she preferred to remain uncomfortable. By degrees they approached the cottage, and although she recognised several of the local landmarks along the route, the snow was falling so densely that she could not see her house even when she judged that they were within fifty yards of it,

"We are nearly there now," she said. "You can drop me here, if you like. You have got to go back through all this." She made as if to get off the horse, but Guy held her firm.

"We shall go to your front door and I shall deliver you to your father, mademoiselle." Isabelle's heart began to beat vigorously and she could feel herself beginning to sweat despite the cold. She must get down before they came in sight of the house. She pushed his arm aside and fell off the horse into the soft, dry snow.

"Isabelle, are you all right?" Guy dismounted in an instant to ensure that she had not hurt herself, but she was on her feet at once.

"I am unhurt, monsieur. Thank you for the ride home. You are very kind. Now you must go before it gets any worse." She turned and tramped through the snow towards her house. She knew that she had been abrupt, but there had been no other way. Fortunately Guy accepted the situation. He shrugged his shoulders and shouted after her.

"You are most welcome. Give my regards to your father," and then to himself, "Women!"

189

He turned to remount his horse and Isabelle walked the remaining few yards to the cottage. Just as the Lieutenant was putting his foot in the stirrup he heard the sound of a voice. It was not Isabelle's father welcoming her home. Funny. Guy did not recognise what was said. At first he thought it was because he had not heard properly. Then he realised that the reason was simple: the language was foreign. Guy recognised its tones. There was an Englishman in the house. Suddenly he understood Isabelle's strange behaviour. He knew why she had been so reluctant a passenger. He drew his pistol in an instant and marched towards the cottage. As he emerged through the blizzard into the view of the house, a startled young man wearing badly fitting clothes faced him. Isabelle burst into tears and ran into the house.

"Stand where you are, monsieur," said the officer. He guessed that the Englishman would not understand, but the pistol and the firm intonation of his voice would surely be unambiguous. To Guy's utter amazement the Englishman replied in very good French.

"I am your prisoner, don't shoot."

"Go inside," ordered Guy. The Englishman raised his hands high in the air, warily turned his back on the pistol and walked slowly back into the warmth of the living room. There he saw Isabelle in considerable tears with her head buried in her father's lap. The soldier followed Will into the house and ordered Will to sit down. Guy closed the door and sat on a chair where he could see Will quite clearly. The pistol remained cocked and pointed at Will's chest. Lieutenant Rodier was in his full official capacity as an army officer faced by a member of the enemy's armed forces.

"What is your name?" he asked sternly.

"William Knott." Will had decided to co-operate fully rather than be difficult. To behave otherwise would merely serve to compound his problems and create even greater trouble for Regis and Isabelle.

"How do you come to be here?" questioned the officer. He could hardly believe his luck as Will began to recount in good French his experiences since leaving home all those months ago. Regis took Isabelle into the bedroom while the story was being told so that he could try to quell her unhappiness. The officer sat in silence while Will told his tale, although, when Will occasionally stumbled over vocabulary deficiency, Guy offered up possible words to help him along. The story took a considerable time to tell and Guy listened attentively and with much interest. He had never been able to question an English prisoner before because of the language problem and was eager to make the most of this opportunity.

Will, for his part, had to make the decision to tell the truth. He judged that if he told lies about the involvement of Regis and Isabelle the officer would easily be able to disprove them.

This man, Will decided, whilst firm and decisive in his duty, would at least be fair and honest to him and the du Plessix. This man had a kind face and an unswerving eye. All such people that Will had come across in the past had been men of honour. He told of his quarrels with Jennings and of the battle they fought on board *Resolution*. Then he told how the ship had run aground and a number of the men had

190

deserted. The officer was visibly moved when he told how he had been pitched overboard and crushed against the ship's side. Then Will noticed how the officer nodded as the story of Isabelle's lifesaving care was related. Not once did the officer take his eye from Will's own. Will found it quite nerve-wracking, especially as he was telling everything in French and trying to make as few mistakes as possible.

"What do you know about the murder of two people on the road out of Le Croisic?" asked the Lieutenant.

"Absolutely nothing, monsieur. I was seriously ill in bed in this house. I have not been outside at all except in the past week, and then only briefly. My friends here will confirm that, if you will believe them. Oh, and the doctor can, too. He treated me a couple of times when I first arrived here." The Lieutenant's eyebrows rose.

"Doctor Dixneuf is involved in this too, is he?" Will could have kicked himself. He need not have mentioned the doctor.

"Yes, he is."

"And what happened to this fellow - what did you call him? Jennings?"

"Yes - I never saw him again after I was injured, but he must have come ashore on a raft somewhere around here, assuming he survived the journey, that is."

The officer nodded again, thoughtfully.

"How many men left your ship that night?"

"I don't know, monsieur. I saw three go before I went overboard. Then there were three on the raft, including Jennings. That's six. How many left after I did, I couldn't say, but it could not have been many because the Captain had got the marines mustered by that time and they were firing on the mutineers."

"I see," replied the officer. Will felt that the interview would soon be over. He wondered what the officer would do next. Rodier then said, without blinking or averting his piercing stare, "Why should I believe that you are honest when you say that you were thrown overboard? You could easily be a deserter; you have certainly had plenty of time in which to have made up this story."

"Because it is the truth, monsieur," said Will with conviction, though he feared that Rodier might not believe him after all. The officer, who had barely moved throughout the story and subsequent questioning, continued to hold his pistol pointed at Will. For a few minutes he said nothing, but many thoughts passed between the eyes of the two men. Then, at last, Rodier said, "I believe you. The truth usually seems to have a strange air about it." Will took a deep breath and rubbed his eyes with his hand.

"What are you going to do with me?" he asked.

"Why, send you to prison of course," replied the soldier in a tone which cast stupidity upon anyone who might have thought otherwise. Will bit his lip: he should have known the answer to the question. Then he thought for a second and told himself to be pleased that the response had not been one of execution.

"And what of my friends, Regis and Isabelle?" He hardly dared to ask the question.

191

"They have done nothing seriously wrong. I will ignore it this once, monsieur, though I hope that they will not make a habit of harbouring English fugitives for I shall have to treat them as enemy collaborators."

Will was relieved at the reply. "Thank you", he said, gratefully.

"Where will you send me?"

"To my headquarters at St. Nazaire. You will be held there until the end of the war."

"But that could be twenty years or more!" Will cried out in desperation.

"Perhaps they will put you out of your misery, like a sick animal, in that case," said the Lieutenant, stiffly. Will cupped his head into his hands. "A joke, monsieur!" said Rodier showing just a trace of a smile. So the man was really human, after all, thought Will. "You should feel lucky, mon ami. I have questioned you myself because you were able to speak in my own language, for I do not speak yours. If you had not been able to speak French then I would have sent you to Rennes where they have interrogators who speak English. The last poor devil I caught was sent there."

"You speak as if it is worse than the gaol at St. Nazaire," Will asked pointedly.

"Let us say that the interrogators in Rennes are not as easily convinced as I am." Will fell silent for a minute and gave thanks to God that this man was being so reasonable with him. Then, quite out of the blue, an idea entered his head. The sudden inspiration was inexplicable but inspired.

"The man you sent to Rennes... what did he look like?" Lieutenant Rodier gave an exact description of Jennings. Will nodded severely. "Then he did survive, after all."

The Lieutenant's curiosity was aroused. He asked Will to describe the two men who had gone with Jennings on the raft. Will proceeded to describe two of the three dead men that Rodier had had to deal with.

"It is beginning to look, monsieur, as if your friend Jennings killed all three," said the officer, delighted with his afternoon's work.

"I think it is quite likely," said Will, in fear that his worst enemy had now become a brutal killer.

"Monsieur Knott, you have been most helpful," said the Lieutenant with a smile that seemed to end all the animosity that might ever have separated them. He put the gun down, released the mechanism and put it back in its holder. For a brief moment Will thought that the Lieutenant was going to let him go free, and he beamed at the officer in return. "I will ask them to treat you well in St. Nazaire." Will's face was crestfallen. Guy saw his disappointment and guessed why. "Ah, monsieur, you must not think that I have the power to release you. I do not write the orders, but merely carry them out. In the meantime I do not think that we shall be going very far today." He nodded to the window. They looked outside. The snow was very deep and the day was drawing to a close. "I must ask you for your word of honour that you will not try to escape. If you do I shall not tie you up. I think you would be very foolish to try to escape, don't you?"

192

Will shrugged. "I have nowhere to go, have I? I agree to your conditions."

"Good. I shall tend to my horse." The officer stood up and went outside, quite suddenly.

Will could hardly believe how circumstances had changed during the course of the day. When he had awakened he had not had a care in the world. By midday he had made a decision to try to escape to England, and by evening he had been captured by a French officer who might have shot him on sight, but who was actually going to commit Will to prison for an indefinite period. By dark, he was on very good terms with his captor who would soon lead him away from Isabelle.

He remembered poor Isabelle and went to her room. She had recovered her composure, though her eyes were puffed. Will had never seen her so upset and he recalled vividly the dreadful night at South Foreland when Lizzie's argument with father had caused Will to leave home. As Will entered the room, Isabelle rose and threw herself into his embrace.

"My darling, I tried... oh, how I tried not to bring him here. He insisted on bringing me home. Oh, it's all my fault." She began to cry once more. Will tried his best to comfort her but she was very upset. Regis patted Will on the shoulder, just as Will's father would have done. He said simply, "I'm sorry, Will."

"You have saved my life," replied Will. "You have nothing to apologise for." There was a sudden draught and the door banged shut. It was Guy. His anxious face appeared in the bedroom doorway.

"Ah, there you are. I thought for a moment that you had decided to do something foolish." He smiled. Will and Regis smiled back, and Isabelle's tears subsided. "I am afraid that my prisoner and I shall be staying the night, Monsieur du Plessix."

"Of course," said Regis. "I will find us some food."

"No, let me," protested Isabelle. "I have been little enough use today. You shall not starve because of me." She visibly pulled herself together and set about making the meal.

The snow caused the Lieutenant to hold his prisoner under open arrest for three days until finally it was time for them to leave. There was never any alternative course open to Guy Rodier, other than to send Will to Rennes. Isabelle was heartbroken when the moment came for Guy to tie Will's hands behind his back and march him back to the village from where he would have Will sent on to St. Nazaire by cart. The two lovers had no idea whether they would ever see each other again.

"My darling, Will," said Isabelle in their last moments together, "I shall wait until you are released, no matter how long it takes, and we shall marry that very day, I promise you. Never believe anything else. I love you." They kissed with every last grain of passion they possessed.

"I love you too," said Will. He studied her face in order to make in his mind's eye a final imprint that would last him for evermore. Will realised that he was trembling and feared that Isabelle would detect it. He could not let her think that he was afraid. He embraced her vigorously and squeezed the breath out of her lungs. They kissed for the last time.

"Time to go, monsieur," said Guy. He tied Will's hands and mounted his horse. Spurring it, he ordered Will to walk ahead of him.

"I'll visit you!" shouted Isabelle. Then, as an afterthought she added, "Is it allowed, Lieutenant?" The officer shook his head.

"No visitors," he said sternly. He pulled up his horse and looked back at Isabelle whose face was filled with dismay. "I do not make the rules, but merely carry them out, mademoiselle," he said coldly. Then he smiled a big, disarming smile and kicked his horse.

"But in your case…"

23 MARIE d'ARRANDA de DARRAX

The six condemned men were led in single file from their cell by a heavy guard of armed soldiers. Jennings was the last of the line, with Paulin immediately in front of him. The exit from the deep recesses of the fortress to the open air was even more complicated than Jennings' walk from his black hole to the interrogation room. The long, solemn procession weaved its way along bare, stone corridors, up steps, through archways, around corners, down steps. As he walked Jennings became more and more aware of a strange noise which at first sounded like the February wind moaning in the empty caverns of the castle, but, the further they walked, was identified as the excitement of a large crowd of people. Sure enough, as Jennings walked down the final flight of steps into a bright, cold open-air environment, he found himself one of the major attractions in a vast square surrounded on all sides by tall, seemingly fortified buildings and filled to overflowing with people. The crowd let out a mighty shout as the file of prisoners appeared before them and as the unfortunate captives were led forward the noise, rather than abating, became even more deafening. Jennings had never in his life seen so many people in one place and, compared to the somewhat claustrophobic cell with its quiet, morbid air, the atmosphere he now found himself in was greatly charged with excitement.

The way ahead was guarded by a double column of soldiers who dutifully kept the crowd at bay as the party marched along the path toward the place where Jennings could see a large elevated platform. He blinked quickly, his eyes still not fully accustomed to the brightness. Then, having confirmed his first impressions, his heart began to beat furiously causing tightness in his chest and a shortage of breath. There on the platform stood a man in black clothes with an enormous, double-edged axe at his left side. To his right was what looked like a large wooden block on which Jennings presumed he would soon be invited to rest his fragile neck. He felt himself begin to shake, his legs threatened to give way beneath him, but still the party marched on. At first, Jennings had not appreciated the reason for such a gathering, for such an event was quite new to him, but it soon became obvious that all these people - thousands of them - had come to see him lose his head. Doubtless they would all cheer loudly as it dropped neatly into the basket. Probably they would push forward to see the blood from his still functioning main arteries spew all over the scaffold until his heart, too weak to pump any more, beat for the last time.

The crowd was in uproar. There was no question of a silent majority revering the awesome spectacle, as might happen at a funeral. These bloodthirsty peasants positively slavered at the thought of the executions. As Jennings passed along the narrow avenue that precariously divided the mob, he was intimidated by a torrent of shouting from those at the front of the crowd. He could not understand why such hatred should be directed towards him in particular. Perhaps the English were more disliked than he thought.

When the execution party had got to within thirty feet of the scaffold the men were brought to a halt and the first of the condemned was prodded towards the steps of the stage on which he was about to perform the last act in his own personal tragedy. Jennings knew the man as Old Pierre. He had been convicted of the murder of a soldier who had tried to rape his wife. Jennings had never talked with him but Jules had related the story in detail. As Jennings stood helplessly watching the climactic sequence of events as if he were a spectator rather than a sacrifice in a peculiar human ritual, many things passed through his mind, but not one was to escape. How could there be an escape from such a vast number of enemies? Suddenly his fear dissolved as surely as if it had been the morning's frost directly irradiated by the weak February sun. He was no longer afraid to die. The inevitability of what was to follow made fear quite pointless. Suddenly he was reconciled with death and became divorced from the proceedings. He stared around him as if in a dream. He felt like a peeping Tom squinting through a glass pane to catch a glimpse of some evil, satanic rite. His mind had played such tricks on him lately that he felt that he would be immune to all pain. Even that interrogator's little shiny razors could not hurt him now.

The crowd seemed to have worked itself up into a frenzy. The shouting in French washed completely over Jennings, until suddenly his lessons with Paulin flooded into his memory. All that French he had learned in the hope that it would prove useful. Alas! He had wasted his time. Jennings listened to the shouts and tried to translate the obscenities that were surely being hurled at him. Then he was able to make sense of a rather surprising remark from the crowd, "It's all right Jules, it won't be long now."

He dismissed it at first as a piece of sarcasm directed at his friend, although he found it strange that the speaker should use Jules' Christian name. Even as Jennings was still analysing the situation from within his own invisible glass capsule, the crowd closest to Jules burst forward screaming and shouting through the line of sentries as if to attack the prisoners.

Jennings was taken completely by surprise and snapped out of his dream. Before he had time to react and defend himself the guards standing nearby began to turn and face the mob. The angry peasants however were so fast in coming forward that by the time the guards were levelling their muskets to fire the crowd had swarmed into them. A few shots rang out harmlessly over the heads of the people Jennings was helpless and undefended. The soldiers had no answer to such a large riotous gathering and most of them were struck to the ground and trampled underfoot. Then in a moment the crowd was upon Jennings and he felt many strong hands upon his body. He noticed a particularly large ring of people around Paulin but the panic was so great by now that he had lost sight of the other prisoners. The noise was painfully loud, but one quiet sentence reached Jennings' ears and made him wonder if his mind had once again deserted him. He translated it. It could not be true.

"It's all right, you're with friends."

Then the most remarkable thing began to happen. In an instant, the bonds which still held his arms behind his back, vanished, and, within the tight confines of the huddle, he was able to wriggle his shoulders a little to restore the circulation. From then on it was as if he were surrounded by a ring of his own personal guards who this time were ushering him through the mob to a destination unknown. As his circle pushed forward in a predetermined direction it seemed as if the crowd parted to let them through and then closed up again behind them. Although he was not religious, Jennings remembered a particularly amazing Bible story about Moses crossing the Red Sea. He managed to construct a question in French for his 'friends'.

"Where are we going?" The answer, if there was one, was lost in the pandemonium. He felt sure that the army would soon start to shoot and could not believe that they would give up six prisoners without a battle. Progress through the crowd was remarkably rapid in view of the enormous number of people gathered in the square. Soon Jennings' group was approaching what looked like a gateway, which presumably led away from the vicinity. He tried to look backwards to the place where the scaffold stood and thought he could discern fighting between soldiers and civilians. Then, moments later, he was passing through the arched gateway and out of the square.

The crowd began to disperse as soon as it reached the relative openness beyond the gate. Men and women were running in all directions. They all knew that the military would not allow mob rule to prevail for very long before taking severe steps to remedy the situation. Suddenly Jennings band of bodyguards seemed to melt away. The dozen or so strong men who moments ago had saved his life seemed to care about him no longer. Jennings was left on the cobbles of the street where he looked around in bewilderment and wondered what the devil was going on.

One young man who looked about the same age as Jennings was last to leave him. Jennings grabbed him firmly by the arm. Quickly he tried to remember his French.

"Where are you going," he asked urgently.

"Anywhere, away from here as quickly as we can," was the reply. The youth was about eighteen years old with light brown hair and calm brown eyes. He could so easily have been English.

"Why did you help me like that?" asked Jennings still holding the youth's arm and determined to extract as much information as he could.

196

"We came to save our leader, Jules Paulin. You were about to be executed with him and the others so we helped you all to escape at the same time."

"Then you are Huguenots?" asked Jennings, knowing the answer.

"Yes. Now come, we must not stay here any longer." The young man smiled briefly at Jennings and then pulled his arm free from the grip that the Englishman continued to exert. Then the two men began to run. The guide led Jennings down a narrow street lined with small, dingy, dirty-looking houses and small shops. They weaved a zigzag path through the maze of peasant hovels until they reached the outskirts of the town. By this time, they had become part of a large exodus of people of all ages travelling in the same direction - out of town. Jennings was quite breathless and the pace had long since deteriorated to a stuttering rapid walking pace which occasionally became a slow jog. Jennings tried to ask some of the scores of questions that entered his mind continually, but his shortness of breath made it difficult and he gave up.

As they reached the open countryside, they passed long lines of carts at the roadside. Their owners, who tried to turn in the narrow thoroughfare, were unhitching many. The stream of human traffic that was escaping from the wrath of the army, which was sure to follow soon, made this task even more difficult. Jennings found the whole event completely incomprehensible. Every waggon, cart or vehicle for miles around must have been brought to the execution. With youth on their side, the two travellers sidestepped the slower folk and sped along quite quickly through the fleeing crowds.

"Where do you come from?" Jennings finally made the effort to satisfy at least some of his curiosity.

"Saint Malo," came the brief reply. Jennings had never heard of it and was none the wiser.

"How did you get here?"

"I walked with my father and brothers."

"Where are they now?" asked Jennings stupidly.

"How should I know? We'll meet again soon, I expect." The youth suddenly stopped and took Jennings to the side of the road. "Look, mon ami, the soldiers will be after you. There will be roadblocks and searches. They'll have the cavalry on the road by now. You've got to hide somewhere until it all quietens down. I'd rather not be with you when they come. We all came to Rennes to help Monsieur Paulin. I think we've done that. We've also saved you from the axe. I can't help you any more."

"I understand," said Jennings." I won't stay with you any longer, but please answer a few more questions. Were all those people Huguenots?"

"Mon Dieu, no, but no-one likes the army. We all work too hard and pay too much tax to love the authorities. Most of them came to see you die, but when we started the riot they all joined in. They like to make a protest from time to time. Now I must go. Good luck."

In a moment he was gone, skipping through the weary crowd like a young deer amid the forest. For a time Jennings looked about. He wondered what to do next.

197

The road was no more than a dirt track with open fields on either side. There was a fresh wind blowing that he had only just become aware of, for he had been too hot from his physical exertions to notice it before. By now it was mid afternoon and would soon be getting dark. Still the crowds swarmed down the road. Some people hurried as fast as they could; others seemed more relaxed. Many looked anxious as they worried about the outcome of the riot, but most looked very weary. The flow of carts and waggons had begun to speed up as those with farther to travel urged their horses along. Jennings considered trying to get a lift, but the carts were all overloaded with tired individuals who could walk no farther. Jennings followed along on foot for some time. He had decided that there was little else to do and he might see somewhere suitable to hide on the way. He guessed that he must have travelled about five miles by the soreness of his feet. He looked at the sky. Although the clouds were almost unbroken he could see the direction in which the sun would soon be setting and was able to judge that he was travelling north. That was a bonus: he did know that England was to the north of France.

As he walked on alone, though in the company of a diminishing number of refugees, he noticed a physical shape that he recognised walking ahead of him. The ill-fitting trousers that clung precariously to a starved waistline, the uneven bandy gait and the round shoulders - all belonged to Old Pierre. Jennings was delighted to see someone he knew in the midst of so many strangers. He ran up to Old Pierre and put his arm around him. The older man, though startled at first, was also pleased, and they exchanged greetings. Although they had never spoken to each other during the whole of their confinement, they were now firm friends by virtue of their common experiences.

"Are you alone too?" asked Pierre.

"Yes. Shall we stay together?"

"If you like, but what are we going to do?"

"They are hunting for us now, but it will soon be dark; that will help. We'll look for the nearest cover and hide." said Jennings optimistically. After another half an hour the light began to fade, but they were able to make out a large area of woodland ahead. With hopes raised they stepped up the pace, though Jennings had to keep stopping for Old Pierre to catch up. Just for once, however, Jennings was so glad of the company that he was prepared to put himself out in order to stay with Pierre. Besides, the old chap might be useful in other ways later.

When they were within a mile of the trees Jennings noticed the sound of hooves in rapid contact with the road. The army was coming up from behind and would soon be upon them. There was much shouting too, as the waggoners and other fugitives impeded the progress of the hunters.

"Take cover," urged Jennings.

"But where?" asked Pierre. He sounded desperate for there was nowhere to hide. The ground was flat and treeless; there was hardly any vegetation substantial enough to conceal them.

"Run!" yelled Jennings. They did so, pushing past stragglers who were in their path. Perhaps they could cover the mile to the woods before the horsemen reached them, thought Jennings. Soon they caught up with a particularly bulky waggon that had lumbered past minutes before. It was crammed full with tired peasants returning home to their village somewhere in the Breton countryside. An idea came to Jennings in a flash.

"Jump on the waggon," he shouted to Pierre.

"But there's no room, replied puzzled Pierre.

"That doesn't matter - jump!"

Both men in turn jumped, not onto the waggon, but onto another human being already lying in the cart. Neither person was pleased at being used for a mattress, but they were old and too tired to complain by violence. Amazingly, space for the two newcomers seemed to materialise from nowhere as Jennings and Pierre adjusted their limbs between those of the other passengers. Indeed, the two fugitives lay very low in the cart and actually encouraged the others to sit on them, so that they were then virtually hidden. Jennings hoped that the sound of the cavalry would not mean a full-scale search at this stage. It seemed likely to be an attempt to get ahead of the escaped prisoners by making speed along the roads. They would probably stop and search the carts thoroughly at roadblocks, but by then Jennings and Pierre would be hiding in the woods.

As Jennings lay prone on the rough and uncomfortable boards of the cart, he heard the sound of approaching hooves get louder, rising to a deafening intensity as fifty or so horsemen brutally pushed their way past the traffic. There was screaming as several travellers were knocked aside by the riders, and several young children, who were terrified by the level of noise and the vigorous movements, added their own screams to the cacophony. Jennings half expected to be spotted, but his fears were groundless for, as he had guessed, the army was in too much of a hurry to give more than a cursory examination of the people at this stage. The crowds who had come to watch Jennings die had actually helped him survive, for, without them, the prisoners would surely have been caught long ago. Both men were relieved as the horses passed and began to move some distance ahead. After waiting a few more minutes Jennings and Pierre pushed their way off the back of the waggon to the further annoyance of their fellow passengers who did not understand what was going on but were nevertheless glad of the extra space in which to continue their journey home.

Their point of disembarkation from the weary waggon left them with only a short distance to travel before they were able to dissolve from view amid the thick undergrowth of the copse. In any case it was now virtually dark and there was little chance of their detection for fifteen hours at the very least. Pierre was all for collapsing into the first available sheltered hideaway, but Jennings was too jealous of his freedom and insisted that they penetrate deep within the trees first. Eventually, when they could no longer see the branches before crashing painfully into them, Jennings allowed the old fellow to sink exhausted to the ground in a cold, damp, but soft pile of decaying leaves. There they spent an extremely uncomfortable and uneventful night. Sleep was fitful and dominated by ghoulish nightmares in which headless soldiers chased them through endless overgrown footpaths, but whenever Jennings became depressed he reminded himself that in comparison to that cell in Rennes prison, it was like paradise. He was alive and free and he would do all in his power to ensure that he stayed that way. Even the complete lack of food did not bother him unduly. His stomach ached in protest, but Jennings body had suffered so much that such deprivations were trivial.

When the new day dawned cloudy and bright the two men were eager to continue on their travels. As quietly as they could they picked their way through the undergrowth and followed a narrow badger run until they came to a road. Neither man was able to recognise it as the road on which they had travelled the day before. They had completely lost their bearings in the woods, but Jennings was sure this was a different road and had no idea which way they should travel; there was no sign of the sun to assist the choice. Pierre was beginning to complain. The efforts of the previous day during which he had walked and often run for miles in old, worn out shoes, had given him blisters which were giving him severe pain. Furthermore, the cold and dampness of their forest bed had caused a return of the old fellow's rheumatic hip pains. He was in considerable difficulty and would not be able to travel far, at least on his feet. Jennings was not pleased with this latest threat to his progress.

"You stupid old sod. I knew I should have left you yesterday. You're bloody useless to me," he grumbled.

"Leave me then, you don't have to stay. I can manage," protested the elderly Frenchman. For once in his life Jennings actually hesitated in the pursuance of his own consuming self-interest. His tone softened.

"I've got a long way to go and I can't walk all of it. We'll wait here and get some transport when it comes along."

"Where are you trying to get to, then?"

"England, of course, stupid. Haven't you any brains in that bald shiny head of yours?" Pierre was unimpressed by the insults and came back at Jennings.

"Huh, the only transport you need is a magic carpet. Looks like we'll have a long wait," he quipped. Jennings, on the other hand, was not one to be belittled.

"If I want jokes from you I'll ask, you bandy old Frog.

Until then, shut up and sit there beside the road. Look as if you're about to die and I'll flag down the next vehicle that comes along. Make it look real or I'll fix it so that you really do look like death in a shirt."

They waited a long time; it was, after all, very early in the morning. During their long wait Jennings' temper abated as he enjoyed the forgotten pleasures of a fresh, spring morning. He found a small stream nearby in which he had an invigorating wash and a very long drink. Then he told Pierre to do the same. Afterwards it was but a half hour more before a coach and four horses could be seen approaching at considerable speed. Jennings was prepared: he had to make the driver stop, though from the rate at which the coach was covering the ground he wondered if it would. Pierre began to appear very sick in a sitting position by the roadside, whilst

Jennings ran down the middle of the road, furiously waving his arms in the air. To run directly towards a coach and four travelling at top speed was rather like a boy on a donkey jousting with a knight in full battle armour. The desired effect was achieved, however, for the driver slowed the team and came to a halt just as Jennings finally stepped out of its path. Jennings looked at the roof of the coach, which was heavily laden down with luggage of various shapes and sizes. The passengers were obviously making a considerable journey. A Frenchman looked down from on high and pointed a pistol at Jennings.

"What's the matter?" said the driver sternly.

"It's my friend," replied Jennings, pointing to the pathetic heap of human flesh that was Pierre. "I think he's going to die. He needs help.

"We can't stop, stand clear." The driver was about to whip the team into motion when a lady's face appeared through a window that had been opened in the side of the carriage.

"What is the delay, Albert?"

"Madame, there appears to be a sick fellow by the side of the road," said the driver in a completely different tone which reflected the change in status of the addressee.

"Then let us help him," replied the lady.

"Very well, Madame, but we are already behind time…"

"That is not a valid excuse, Albert. Now see if you can help the man, will you?" The face withdrew to the privacy of the vehicle and the window closed. The driver, still clutching his pistol but no longer aiming it, turned his back on Jennings in order to descend from his seat. It was a mistake for, just as he was about to place his foot on the surface of the road, he was struck by a rabbit punch in the neck. As he fell his pistol was snatched from his grasp and into the grip of a far more aggressive owner.

"Right, Pierre, over here… quick." The wizened old Frenchman suddenly came to life as the coach driver began rubbing his neck and struggled to regain his feet. Jennings, his confidence boosted tenfold by the feel of the smooth round handle of the flintlock in his palm, strode up to the carriage and flung open the door. It was perfectly timed with a projected exit from the interior of a middle-aged man in an immaculate suit of clothes. The two men came face to face. Jennings with surprise on his side thrust the pistol under the man's nose.

"Get out and stand over there," he said sharply, pointing to the place where the driver now stood dejectedly. The man did as he was told. Jennings could now see that the carriage was empty except for the flowing dress of a beautiful woman. The lady made as if to get out, but Jennings anticipated her action.

"No, Madame, please remain seated. You will be on your way again very shortly." The lady's face took on an air of puzzlement. Surely this brigand was not going to release her and her husband? Jennings very quickly answered her unspoken questions.

"You!" He indicated to the driver. "Get up there again. No tricks or I'll blow your brains out of your head. Pierre get up beside him and watch him." Jennings then climbed into the carriage, shut the door and wound the window down.

"What about me, monsieur?" pleaded the lady's husband. "You can't leave me here." Jennings took no notice of him.

"Driver, move this cart."

"Where to monsieur? Where do you want to go?"

"Calais," snapped Jennings and closed the window. He took a deep breath and relaxed in the soft seat facing his travelling companion. The coach jerked into motion. He was pleased with the way he had handled the whole business. The lady was shaking with fright. He smiled and laid the pistol beside him to allay her fears. "Don't worry, Madame, I don't hurt beautiful ladies."

"My husband, what about my husband. Can we not take him?" she protested, wiping a tear from her face. Jennings pulled a face as a schoolboy might to a play-friend.

"Oh, two's company, but three... we'll have more fun without him here." The lady failed to notice the malevolence of the remark in her concern for her husband.

"But it's such a long way to Calais."

"Madame, your husband can sell that ridiculous suit he's wearing and buy a ticket to Highgate on the proceeds." The lady, being French, had never heard of Highgate.

Jennings sat still for a time, gazing at the lovely creature opposite. She was terrified but had so far managed to control her fear very successfully. Her initial panic-stricken visage had been transformed into a calm one. It was her eyes that gave her away. Jennings stared at them as they darted about the carriage, never once resting on him, but knowing full well that they were being studied. He could see that tell-tale glint in the corner of each one, a clear indication that she was fighting back the urge to burst into tears. Here was an intelligent and very wealthy woman. Jennings guessed her age at thirty-five, but still extremely attractive, for a married lady. Her black hair had been meticulously coiffured in a way that Jennings found rather strange, but which he guessed to be the height of current French fashion. Every delicately curled ringlet was in place and the whole style was enhanced by the most exquisite pearl earrings. Her gown was of pale pink satin, embellished by red floral embroidery, and was cut quite high at the neck where it was surmounted by a pearl choker. Her figure was largely hidden beneath the large quantity of material, but Jennings was convinced that a lady of such class would be perfectly proportioned. Her husband would have been able to select a wife from the most attractive of French society women.

"We shall be in this coach for rather a long time, Madame. I suggest we get to know each other. My name is Monsieur Jennings, what is yours?" The lady kept silent.

"Oh, come now, there is no harm in telling me your name," coaxed Jennings in his most friendly tone of voice. It seemed to have some effect: she appeared to relax

202

the tension in her muscles a little, though her face remained as impassive as she could make it.

"Why should I?" she questioned.

"Because I can probably find out, by one means or another. Why not be friends with me? I've no wish to hurt you. I just want to get to Calais. When I am there you can continue with your journey unharmed…"

"… And without my husband," she cut in.

"You really must not be so concerned about him. He, like you, is unharmed. He looks like a resourceful fellow; he will catch you up at your destination." Jennings was turning on the charm. The lady was not fooled, however. She did not trust him in the slightest. The man obviously fancied her and would be as nice as possible for a time, no doubt with the intention of persuading her to sleep with him. If she refused he would rape her anyway. Men were like that. She would have to be very careful. She knew that her only hope of escape would be by using her intelligence and her female guile. This man was but a primitive animal wearing clothes. No civilised, intelligent human being could behave in such a manner. Surely she could outwit this serpent? She would tell him her name. He was right: he would probably find out anyway.

"My name is Marie."

"A beautiful name for a beautiful lady," replied Jennings. Marie was not impressed. She did not need compliments from a criminal.

Then Jennings realised that he had other problems. In contrast to the man whom he had left standing forlornly in the road, Jennings was still wearing his prison clothes. He looked around the small compartment. In every available space there was luggage.

"You carry an awful lot of kit with you, don't you? Where are you going, for heaven's sake?" As he said so he picked up a canvas bag. An engraved nametag was affixed to the outside of it just below the handle. It said "Mme. la Marquise d'Arranda de Darrax." He read it and whistled quietly.

"Well, well, a real, genuine member of the aristocracy? I am honoured, Madame." He reached across the carriage, took her hand and kissed it whilst bowing his head in mock reverence to her station. Then he sat back once more, picked up the bag and began to ransack it. Inside were items of female underwear.

"Keep out of there," snapped Marie, "that's none of your business." She snatched the bag from his grasp and he made no attempt to stop her. "If you're looking for money, there isn't any," she added, unwisely.

"No money? Well, well, times is hard, Marie. You, a titled lady, travelling all this way, with all this luggage… and no money? Very sad." The sarcasm was bitter. "I'm not looking for money anyway…" The lady looked relieved…"Yet! What I need is new clothes. I can't travel with a noble lady such as yourself with me in these rags, can I?" Marie bit her lip. She knew he would find her husband's clothes sooner or later. It might as well be sooner lest he ransack every other item of baggage. She decided to humour this evil criminal as a way of overcoming him.

"There are plenty of clothes on board, but they are outside on the roof," she said. Jennings looked her straight in the eyes.

"If you are devising some sort of trick to play when I stop the coach I should forget all about it." The woman was in no doubt about the severity of her position. This man was very dangerous.

"No, honestly, it is no trick. My husband's cases are on the roof of the coach behind the driver. The one you want is a large brown leather bag with two black straps across it.

You'll find all you need inside."

Jennings glanced out of the window and saw that the coach was passing through another wooded area. The woman's husband had been left miles behind. He opened the window and shouted.

"Driver, stop the coach." The driver complied. "You stay inside and be warned, no tricks." said Jennings menacingly. He picked up the pistol, opened the door and jumped out. "Throw down that large brown leather bag with the black straps." The driver unfastened a lashing which had been securing the case to the coach and carefully handed down the bag. He was not prepared to throw about any of his master's belongings. With one eye on the driver Jennings opened the case and rummaged about for some suitable clothing. As he did so he selected several items and tossed them up to Pierre, who was also in need of some different clothes. Eventually, dressed in a very expensive looking costume that did not suit his rugged, bearded face, he remembered a further instruction to the driver.

"Listen carefully. We are going to Calais and I know how far away it is. It will mean spending the night at an hotel, as well as changing the horses. I shall be riding with Madame inside. If we are stopped by anyone you will tell them that Monsieur le Marquis and Madame la Marquise are inside. If there are any problems at all, Madame will receive a blast from this pistol, which will prove fatal. Is that quite clear?" The driver nodded solemnly as Jennings waved the gun in the air to demonstrate that he meant business. Madame was a hostage and the driver had no choice but to do as he was told if his mistress was to live. "Pierre, you stay up there with him and keep your mouth shut. Make sure he behaves himself. Now drive on."

Jennings returned to his seat and relaxed as the carriage burst into motion once more. He looked about him and noticed that several items of luggage had been moved, though only slightly, from their original positions. Suspicious of the lady's actions while he was outside the coach, he looked carefully around the inside of the compartment but tried hard not to let her know that he was doing so. For her part, she sat quite still, gazing in apparent contentment out of the window at the passing countryside. Then Jennings analytical gaze fell upon a small lump beside her on the seat and underneath the material of her dress. While he had been changing his clothes she had not been idle. Quick as a flash his hand flew across the carriage to uncover a pistol. Marie recoiled in sheer surprise at the sudden movement. Then, when she knew that her plan had been foiled, a look of dire misfortune filled her eyes. It was obviously the only pistol she had and now that it had been discovered she would have to think of something else. Jennings turned the small weapon over carefully in his hands to acquaint himself of its mechanism, for he had not seen one like it before. As he did so, he cocked it and held it an inch away from the very frightened lady's nose. She shrank back as far as the seat would allow, to no avail.

"That was very stupid of you, Marie. You will make me very angry if you try anything else like that. Promise me you'll behave yourself." She hesitated. He drew even closer until his face and hers were but inches apart, the muzzle of the gun between the two. Marie smelled the foul breath of her captor for the first time. This man was truly horrible; she was afraid. "Go on... promise!"

"I promise... Oh, why don't you leave me alone? I promise..."

Having got so close to Marie's peach smooth complexion and quivering red lips, Jennings could not restrain himself. He pushed his unshaven face into contact with hers and treated himself to a long exploratory kiss. It tasted good. Marie in terror did not resist.

Releasing first his lips and then the hammer of the gun, Jennings retreated to his seat and tucked the small weapon into his breeches.

"Now, Madame. Tell me why you, a titled lady, a member of the French aristocracy, are making a considerable journey with your husband and all this luggage, but no money." Marie had had time to think of an answer. She replied quickly and convincingly.

"Monsieur Jennings, is it not obvious? It is for precisely an occasion such as this. Do you think that we would carry great wealth around with us and wait for any passing criminal to rob us? Of course not. Yes, I have enough money for the journey and that is all."

Jennings said nothing but simply held his hand out palm upwards and looked expectant. Marie turned to her hand luggage and handed him a purse containing a considerable number of coins.

"Thank you, Madame. Are you sure this is all there is?"

"My husband had more... but you left him behind." She said it with a smile of satisfaction; at last she had won a round in the battle with this monster.

The coach travelled several more miles before, without warning, it began to slow down to a walking pace. Jennings, who had just begun to relax and enjoy the journey, was immediately on his guard. He disturbed the lace curtains as little as possible whilst taking a surreptitious look out of the window. He saw uniforms that looked very similar to the ones he had seen in Rennes prison. He had known all along that they would meet a roadblock. He tried to relax and appear normal. For a few minutes he was going to be a French Marquis travelling with his wife.

"Why are we stopping?" asked Marie.

"Nothing much." He was not going to tell her anything just yet. "Sit where you are, relax and everything will be all right. If you try anything silly - anything at all - I will kill you. Do you understand?" He looked her straight in the eye. She believed his threat and nodded. Both sat erect in their seats facing each other in the privacy of their luxurious travelling apartment. Jennings could hear words being exchanged outside. Though he could not make out every word of the conversation, he was able to follow the gist of it. The driver had done as he was told. The coach began to move once more and as it did so a line of soldiers passed the window. Each man was at attention and the last of the line, which Jennings assumed to be the officer, was saluting.

"The army!" said Marie in surprise. "I wonder what they wanted." Jennings was silent, but his unrestrained smile gave the game away. Marie was able to work out the answer to her own question. "They want you, don't they?" Jennings laughed aloud and then, jumping across the carriage, threw another kiss at her. His plaything was unresponsive but unresisting. His tongue explored her teeth and gums; her saliva was like nectar. Then he withdrew and replied, "Yes, my dear, but with you by my side I can go anywhere... anywhere at all.

Apart from a brief stop to refresh the horses and relieve troublesome bladders it was not until evening that the carriage clattered across the cobblestones of a courtyard in the centre of Rouen. The driver, being the only person in the party with any knowledge of the area, had selected a suitable place to spend the night. Marie was quite exhausted, despite having slept for several hours in the afternoon, for the vibration of the carriage on the inadequate French roads had been tiresome. Furthermore she'd had nothing to eat; Jennings had not cared to stop and delay his progress.

As the coach drew to a halt outside the door of the chosen hotel, Marie was just stirring from yet another catnap. The driver, who had already been briefed by Jennings at the earlier stop, disappeared into the hotel to book a room for his 'master and mistress.' Within seconds he reappeared and approached the carriage. He opened the door and held it open for the occupants to alight.

"Your room is ready, Monsieur, Madame." Marie hesitated. The moment she had been dreading had arrived. It was an inescapable fact that she was going to have to share a room for the night with this monster who was pretending to be her husband, and there was no doubt in her mind that he had every intention of using her husband's privileges. Her driver was in an impossible situation and dared not help for fear of causing his mistresses death. Jennings would remain inches away from his hostage to ensure that his plans were not foiled.

"Come on, out you get," ordered Jennings tersely. He was impatient again as the thoughts of bodily pleasures raced through his mind. Marie did as she was told. "Take care of the baggage, Pierre... Albert, take the team." Jennings liked giving orders, especially when he obtained the sort of instant reaction that those in fear of their lives are bound to give. He closely followed his 'wife' into the hotel where they received a courteous bow from the manager and were shown to the best room in the hotel. The room turned out to be a suite and was on the first floor at the far end of a passageway. The manager assured his important guests that there were no other guests in the vicinity and that they would not be disturbed. Meanwhile, if there was anything he could do? There was - dinner for two, to be brought to the room.

206

Whilst poor old Pierre huffed and puffed his way several times to the private suite with armfuls of luggage and other items, Marie carefully considered her position. She was quite certain that this man Jennings meant everything he said: he would kill her if she tried to escape. Likewise, he was going to have his way with her before very long, whether she liked it or not. There was no alternative but to accept the fact that to resist him would be suicidal. Marie did not want to die, neither did she want to give in to this brute. Her husband had been the only man ever to lie with her and she wanted to keep it that way. On the other hand, if she was to escape at all then her best chance would be created by a little softening-up. Marie was an educated lady. She knew that all men were the same when it came to sex. A little bit of feminine attention could go a long way. A man treated properly could be made to do anything. She approached Jennings who had collapsed on the bed temporarily, but who was still keeping a careful eye on his insurance. Marie put on her most enticing air.

"I'm going to have a bath. It will freshen me up and then perhaps we can get to know each other better." She stroked his chest. Jennings' eyes widened and glistened. He could hardly believe his ears. Slowly he sat upright. Marie put her hands around the back of his head and pulled his dirty face towards hers. Then she pushed her tongue right inside his mouth and kissed him as he never was kissed before. He threw his arms around her and hugged her, but she broke away and smiled cheekily. "Wait until I've had a bath," she said. For a moment Jennings watched as she walked into the adjoining room where they had previously been shown the very latest in bathtubs. Then, suddenly suspicious, he leapt up and ran into the bathroom where he checked that there was no means of escape. There was not. He called the maid and soon the bath was filled with hot, soapy water, whilst a huge pile of the freshest, fluffiest towels in the establishment towered over the bath from an adjacent chair. Then the door was closed for a whole hour as Madame la Marquise soaked away the stresses of the day. She was relaxing for her man.

Meanwhile, Jennings was not idle. Systematically he searched the luggage that had been brought in considerable quantity into the bedroom. As he searched he could hear the splashing of water and imagined the soft, white, voluptuous flesh of the lady who was about to submit to his desires. At the same time, the chink of china and metal indicated that the waiter was laying the table for dinner in the last of the three rooms that made up the regal suite. Jennings, however, had another thing on his mind.

Madame and her husband were surely moving house? Surely they would be carrying more than just a purse full of coins? One particularly large, heavy case attracted his attention. It seemed a good deal bulkier than its internal size indicated, and although filled with Madame's dresses, furs and other female accoutrements it seemed especially heavy. Jennings emptied everything onto the bed and examined the case. Made of black leather, it opened outwards into two halves from the top and had heavy leather fastenings with bright buckles. On the inside, the bottom was in obscurity, a solid base enveloped by darkness within the container. He felt around the inside very carefully and then looked at the outside. Suddenly, he found what he was looking for. He Released four, small, concealed catches and removed a false bottom from the case. His eyes gaped in disbelief, for there in the darkness he caught sight of real wealth.

Since earliest history, jewels have been greatly prized and universally acceptable in purchasing power. In any corner of the world a well-cut and polished jewel will buy almost anything. John Jennings, being the son of a poor working family, had never seen a real jewel before, but was still able to recognise priceless gems. His mother had possessed several items of jewellery, which, as a child, he had thought were diamonds, but as he grew older he realised that they were merely coloured glass. Only rich people possessed diamonds, for these glass-like stones have a value far greater than their size would suggest. This is because of a unique property. In almost total darkness a diamond collects every last ray of light that falls upon it and absorbs them deep within its crystalline interior. There the light is gathered together and reprocessed, whereupon it is re-emitted into the darkness in a blaze of radiant energy, sparkling, dazzling the beholder in a myriad of spectral splendour.

Jennings' eyes had fallen upon Marie's jewels. Marie was indeed a wealthy woman. She was married to a Marquis, and she adored diamonds. There were bracelets, rings, earrings and all kinds of brooches, some of rubies and emeralds, others of pearls, but most of diamonds. Carefully, Jennings removed the jewellery from the case and laid it on the table beside the bed. Here was what he had suffered so much for. All that had happened over the past year had been the spawn of destiny, a series of small decisions and events which when pieced together had led him to this hotel bedroom in Rouen. How could he ever have known that he would be so lucky? His life during the previous twelve months had been unbearable at times. Here was a reward for his trouble.

The case seemed to be empty but then he noticed a black box within the hidden compartment. He pulled it out and studied it before opening it. It was covered in black velvet and had a single brass catch. As he flipped the catch across and threw back the lid he gasped in amazement. This was surely Marie's prize possession, the most beautiful diamond necklace he could ever have imagined. In the dim light of the bedroom it almost dazzled him with its brilliance. He took it nearer to the lamp where the stones absorbed more rays of light, magnified them and cast them dancing into the glazed, greedy eyes of the Kentish man. The necklace was an exquisite setting of thirteen diamonds, which grew in size towards the centre where the queen of them all rested in its gold mounting. This diamond alone Jennings estimated to be worth a fortune, for its size and brilliance were beyond belief.

Sounds of activity at the dining table brought Jennings back to reality. Quickly he shut the box and looked around the room. He saw the small canvas bag that he had ransacked on the coach. The bag was just the right size. He picked it up and emptied its contents into the large black case. Then he carefully placed all the jewels in the innocuous looking bag and closed the fastening. Next he re-packed the false bottom of the case and replaced all the clothing he had removed from it. Unable to refrain from smiling, he clutched the container of his life's fortune and considered where best to keep it safe. He placed it under the bed where he would be able to reach down and touch it during the night.

"Dinner is prepared, monsieur." The polite tones of the waiter came from just outside the bedroom door.

"Very good. You may go."

"Thank you, monsieur."

The footsteps receded and there was barely a sound as the servant closed the door into the passage behind him. Jennings re-entered the room where the dining table had been set with all manner of china and cutlery, the like of which he had not seen before.

"Are you ready to eat now, ma cherie?" asked Jennings in the best of moods.

"Coming," was the reply.

As he waited for his 'wife' to emerge refreshed and ready to submit herself to him, an idea occurred to him that he should have thought of before. He crossed the room and, reaching the door through which the waiter had just left, Jennings turned the key in the lock and pocketed it. Then he made quite sure that all the windows were secure. He did not want his companion to escape at this stage in the game. Everything was going his way and he was determined to remain cautious whatever happened. Then the door to the bathroom opened and in its frame stood Marie, fresh, relaxed and wrapped in a pink bathrobe. Her hair remained immaculately groomed and her complexion looked smoother than the silk of her gown. She posed for a moment to allow Jennings to take it all in. Then, with the gait that only a lady possesses, she crossed the room to where Jennings stood aghast at her beauty. She reached for his hand and led him towards the bed, which was still covered in bags and other trappings. Jennings felt foolish and removed them at top speed, his heart beginning to race as he began to appreciate the extent of his desire for this woman.

When the bed was clear, Marie approached once more and stood close in front of Jennings. She sat on the bed as he allowed her to loosen his breeches. Jennings eyes closed in delight as a soft female hand grasped his vital parts. Gently, so gently, he was caressed. The grip was tightening, but still ecstatic. Marie seemed to be getting carried away. Then in an instant the grip became a clamp. With all the strength she could manage, Marie squeezed until she could manage no more. She, a mere weakling in comparison to this vicious killer, could use her soft, delicate hands to inflict overwhelming pain on her adversary. Jennings cried out in agony and collapsed onto the floor, doubled up and writhing with a pain that was not a pain, an ache that was not an ache, a sickening, incapacitating feeling that was far worse than any other injury for it stemmed from the most vital area of all.

Marie had waited so long for this moment. She had planned her escape, acted her part and suffered the hideous man's body in order to free herself from his malevolence. Now that the time had finally arrived and she watched him squirm totally helpless on the floor she almost felt like waiting a moment longer to gloat over man's ultimate weakness. She had won. Her superior intelligence her class, her upbringing and her education had finally triumphed over this pathetic male creature.

All that strength, all that brutality had been overcome so easily by a woman's grip in just the right place. What a weakness!

But Marie did not wait, nor did she gloat. She dashed across the room to the door. Moments more and she would be outside and free. She gripped the handle and turned, but it would not open the door. She tried harder, to no avail. Her heart pounded within her and her eyes filled with tears of incredulity. She had forgotten a very important part of her escape. The bastard had locked the door. Panic-stricken, she looked around the room. Surely there was another way out? As she did so, a poor, pathetic form came crawling along the floor from out of the bedroom. This deadly snake that she so much feared had managed, despite continued excruciating pain, to slither from his prone position in the bedroom to a place where he could see the terrified marchioness with her back to the door. Then, with the cold, deliberate and unquestionable intent of an injured serpent, deadly metal venom spat from the fangs of Jennings' weapon, straight through the heart of the lady.

All the horror, the disbelief and the pain of a single moment became engraved upon the freshly bathed countenance as Marie slid down the door into a sitting position. The duel, which had begun from the moment that the Christian, caring lady had instructed her driver to stop and help a sick man, had finally ended. It had been fought largely in the mind, a duel of two intelligences, hers, a lively, imaginative and ambitious wit, his, a single-tracked malevolence. Both were equally devious and determined to succeed, but she, Madame Marie la Marquise d'Arranda de Darrax had lost. Her frightened, pathetic and still so beautiful eyes would dart no more. Their gaze rested on Jennings still, but saw naught.

24 PIERRE GALLOND

Guy Rodier was a honourable man who always kept his word. William Knott junior found every day in St. Nazaire jail a trial of all his physical and emotional strength combined, but he could never have known how much worse it might have been if the Lieutenant had sent him to Rennes instead. Even at St. Nazaire his life was considerably more comfortable than it might have been because the army officer had instructed the jailer that Will was to be well treated in return for his co-operation with the army. As a consequence he was allowed several privileges that were forbidden to the other prisoners, and the most important of these was to be visited by his dear Isabelle.

The town of St Nazaire was a small one with a population of around two thousand. Its location at the mouth of the Loire had sustained its steady growth as a fishing port. Furthermore, in the latter part of the seventeenth century the military had made use of the town's geographical advantages and set up a small garrison.

The journey from Le Croisic to St. Nazaire was quite long on the poor roads and occupied a whole day in each direction. Isabelle was therefore not able to visit Will as often as she would have liked. Her father drove her there in their cart whenever he could spare the time, and indeed, sometimes when he could not. Then, despite their limited means, they found accommodation in the town and Regis made use of the opportunity to do business while Isabelle visited the prison.

Although Will's confinement was comparatively luxurious, he found it almost unbearable, and on numerous occasions had seriously considered suicide. Isabelle's visits were the only incentive for him to stay alive. During the painfully long weeks and months, he thought about his future constantly, and soon concluded that he could not face a life of any kind without Isabelle. During each of the visits that Isabelle made to the prisoner, they promised each other that they would marry as soon as Will was released, and Isabelle had said that she would go home to England with him.

Unbeknown to the two lovers it transpired that they had a much better friend in Guy Rodier than they could have guessed. The officer had been very pleased with the information that Will had given him. A mysterious crime had been solved and a dangerous criminal uncovered and brought to justice. Furthermore he had taken the couple to heart. Isabelle was a kind girl whom he had known for years. The Englishman too had impressed Guy as a sincere and honest seaman with no grudge against the French people. He had even had the resource and initiative to become fluent in the French language in a short time. Guy was convinced that the two youngsters would form a strong marital bond and wanted to help them. As soon as he had delivered Will to the jail, he sent a very favourable report to his superiors in Paris in which he requested permission to have Will released. In it he stated that the prisoner was hardly an enemy of the nation and would almost certainly marry and settle in France. The Lieutenant's request was, of course, contrary to all the regulations so it was not really surprising that Guy's supplication was denied. No reasons were given for the decision and Guy was saddened by the apparent total lack of compassion on the part of his commanding officer. There was no question of Guy disobeying such a decision, which he thus accepted with a heavy heart. It seemed that Will was destined to remain at St. Nazaire, at least until the cessation of hostilities, whenever that might be. Guy's only consolation was in the privileges he had ordered for the lad in order to try to ease the anguish. The area commander, however, must have been impressed by Guy Rodier's highlighted abilities when, in the spring of 1760 the officer who had done so much for Will and Isabelle was transferred to a new post in Paris in which Guy would almost certainly be able to earn his promotion. Such was the speed of the transfer when it came that Guy was given enough time only to pack his suitcase and be on his way. Neither Will nor Isabelle ever saw him again.

The number of internees at St. Nazaire gaol grew slowly as the war progressed, although but a fraction of them were English. Eighty Frenchmen who had transgressed their own laws filled the majority of the cells and included several who were to face the death penalty. The remaining fifty or so English soldiers and sailors had arrived in captivity at St. Nazaire by various means and were all eagerly awaiting the end of the war when, it had been promised, their freedom would be given back to them. Although Will was allowed to socialise with the other Englishmen during recreational periods, he was kept in a cell of his own so that he could receive the special treatment that had been ordered for him.

The time between each of Isabelle's visits seemed to become progressively longer, and, during the single hour that they were allowed to spend, looking at each other across a table, they rarely spoke. Conversation flowed between their twinkling, tear-filled gazes as silently as the seawater currents not a hundred yards from the gaol. The only physical contact allowed was that between eager fingers, and the touch of each other's warm flesh was enough to accelerate their heartbeats even faster. Then, far too quickly, the hour was past and Gallond the jailer was ushering Will back to the cell where he was to remain for the next three years.

It was almost three years exactly after the day when Will was first enclosed behind those St. Nazaire bars that the first talk of peace was in the air. Gallond, a rather miserable old soldier who had seen better days, had very little to do during the long winter evenings. To relieve his boredom he would often chat to Will, whose French was becoming as good as the natives. The topics of conversation were rather limited and usually relived the wars in which Gallond had served. Will enjoyed talking to the old man for it hauled his mind out of the numbing tedium of imprisonment and exercised his oral powers. Then one day the jailer began to speak about the ongoing war in a way which seemed to intimate that it would all be over soon. Will could hardly restrain his excitement, and did his best to extract every scrap of information, whether fact or total hearsay, from his informant. Within a month, the rumours were transformed into cold historical fact by a peace declaration between England and France. Seven years of wasted lifetimes had ended with little real gain by either side. No sooner had the news reached Isabelle than she was on her way to St. Nazaire once more. By this time she had developed a standing arrangement with one of the merchants who regularly travelled the roads. She could ride on the trader's waggon and stay at the house of a friend she had acquired during the course of her three-year pilgrimage. Regis was no longer required to ferry her about.

The day for which Isabelle had waited so long was close at hand, How long would it be before Will was released into her arms for ever? It took more than two weeks after the end of the war for orders to filter down from the High Command in Paris. No time was wasted in the execution of the orders, once received. It was early in the morning just as Isabelle was about to set off from Le Croisic to visit Will that the order releasing all the English prisoners-of-war was delivered to the gaol by a tired horseman. Will was anxiously pacing his cell in anticipation of Isabelle's arrival when the jailer entered holding a document in his right hand.

"Good news, boy. The order has arrived; you're to be set free." he said with not a trace of emotion on his face. Will leapt into the air with a shout and almost knocked himself unconscious on the low ceiling.

"Let me see it, let me see it," he said impatiently, snatching the document from the hands of the old man who had jumped back in surprise at Will's sudden outburst as if it had been unexpected. Will eagerly read the wording of the document. Each sentence had to be carefully translated in his mind before moving on to the next,

212

but he was able to understand it all. Slowly his excitement abated and he became worried. "It says here that all English prisoners are to be sent back to England forthwith," he queried, in the hope that his new linguistic powers were not so good after all and that he had misunderstood. Gallond confirmed his fears.

"That's right. A ship has been chartered by the government to take you home."

"But I don't want to go back to England - well not yet, anyway," said Will anxiously. "I'm getting married first. I hadn't planned to return to England for some time."

"Well, I'm afraid it says here 'all fifty-three English prisoners' and that includes you."

"When are we due to leave?" asked Will in dread of the reply.

"Tomorrow," said the jailer clinically.

"Tomorrow! But that can't be true. I can't leave without my fiancée." Will was in despair. He hardly knew what to do. He flung himself on his bed and buried his head in his hands in disbelief.

"Sorry, boy, but that's the orders. You know I can't go against the orders. The ship's coming in this afternoon, and she sails at ten tomorrow. Cheer up, boy, you're going home to your folks. You should be pleased." Gallond looked at Will and upon gaining no response he shrugged his shoulders and left the cell grumbling, "Some people are never satisfied."

The twenty-four hours that followed the delivery of the release order were a terrible time for Will. During the three years of imprisonment he had probably spent only a dozen hours in the company of his beloved. He yearned for nothing less than to be with her constantly. Now he was to be deported back to England without even being allowed to say goodbye. What would Isabelle think? He could not dismiss fears that crept into his heart, no matter how hard he tried. Perhaps she might doubt his love if he left without confirming their betrothal one last time. She had been expecting his open release so that they could marry and live in France for a time before eventually returning to Will's home. Isabelle would naturally expect a strong bond to reform between Will and his family if he returned to England without her. She could be forgiven for thinking that he would choose his home in England rather than life with her. Perhaps she would resign herself to never seeing Will again. Women in such a position often marry the first eligible male they meet for fear of being left on the shelf. Will worried intensely that Isabelle's commitment to him would lapse, and by the time he were able to return to France once more to claim her for his bride, she would no longer be his.

Throughout the day Will had alternating periods of confidence and despair. When his senses were alert he was certain that, after all they had said and done together, Isabelle would be his woman forever. She had waited for him all this time. She had surely suffered as much as he. Isabelle would never desert him now, whatever happened. They would both surmount all obstacles that stood in the way of their marriage. Perhaps Isabelle would even follow him to England alone?

213

As he tired, Will began to doubt her resolve and the all too familiar feeling of inevitable failure seemed irresistible. In the pit of the Slough of Despond he even began to curse God for failing him. Why had He saved Will from certain death in the seas adjacent to *Resolution*? Why had He allowed Will and Isabelle to form such a beautiful relationship together, only to destroy all their hopes and happiness at a stroke? He had always tried to be a good, honest man of honour and principle. He had been brought up by his parents to believe in God and His ever-caring Son. Why had he been deserted in this way? What had he done wrong? In his agonies Will uttered many things for which he was later sorry.

Hardly for a moment could Will sleep that night. No matter how logically he reasoned with himself he could not dispel the doubts. Every argument and counter-argument reverberated in his mind's eye over and over again. He wriggled around in his bed so much that his muscles ached and the bedding became dishevelled to leave him cold and more tense than ever. On numerous occasions he cried into his pillow until it eventually became so wet and cold that he tried discarding it completely. Still he did not sleep. Sometime after midnight he got out of bed and paced the cell. It solved nothing.

It was a mere two hours before dawn that he became so mentally tired that his brain succumbed to the physical needs of his body, but still the dreadful reality of losing Isabelle lingered in his dreams. Magnified into dreadful proportions, the dreams turned into nightmares that were not dissipated at daybreak. The nightmares were real. Soon he would be on board ship with their love in tatters, shredded by a score of intangible doubts. So tired was he that, even awake, he seemed dazed. The moment for which he had waited three years would never come.

The routine chores of the prison had still to be done, if only for the last time. Breakfast was served at the immutable time, although on this occasion a piece of cheese had been added as if in celebration. Then the cell had to be swept and tidied, the bed made up immaculately with no creases in the blankets. Then, after prisoner inspection at eight, Will collected the few belongings he had acquired during his three years confinement and was taken from his cell for the last time. An armed soldier whom he had not seen before ushered him to the prison yard where he was mustered with the other fifty-two prisoners-of-war. They were counted three times. That alone seemed to take a very long time. The guards were not used to handling such a large number of men at one time and were being careful to do it correctly. The officer in charge was the same one that had delivered the order to the jail. He marched up and down with a severe look on his face, as if the exercise was really too much trouble. Gallond too was in attendance, supervising the muster.

Then to Will's great joy, he saw Isabelle walking towards the group inside the gates of the prison. His heart began to beat vigorously and his chest tightened. His eyes filled with tears as he saw the vision of his dreams. Anxiously he called old Gallond, for he feared breaking ranks at so delicate a point in the proceedings. The guards glared at him uneasily, but Gallond stepped quickly to where Will was standing. Will did not have to say much to the jailer. A few words of French and a pointed finger in the direction of Isabelle were enough to explain the problem. His friend Gallond nodded and told him to remain where he was. Then he walked briskly to Isabelle and whisked her into his office only yards from the point where they all waited. Will's excitement was mixed with extreme anxiety about his chances of speaking to Isabelle before the party left for the transport. His association with the grumbling Gallond over the past three years and his readiness to listen to the interminable tales of woe had finally paid a dividend. The old soldier reappeared from his office without the young lady and proceeded directly to the officer-in-charge. There he explained the situation on Will's behalf as politely as he knew how.

"This prisoner Knott, sir - he's been allowed the privilege of seeing his fiancée...Lieutenant Rodier's orders, sir. With your permission, sir, he'd like to speak to her for a few minutes before being deported."

"This is most irregular, sergeant. These men are about to leave. I am taking fifty-three men to the ship, not fifty-two. There isn't time." Fortunately for the couple, Gallond did not give up.

"I guarantee to deliver him to the ship before she sails, sir. Knott is a good prisoner. He probably won't see the girl again, sir."

"Oh, very well. He's your responsibility. The ship sails with the tide at midday and he'd better be on it. Corporal! Fall out that prisoner - the rest, move out."

Will dropped out of the squad, and ran to the door where he had seen the jailer take Isabelle. He threw the door open to be greeted by his beloved who hugged him tightly around the neck. She kissed him hard on the lips until he had to pull away for breath.

"What's going on, darling? Are they taking you away?" Isabelle was baffled by the events outside and quite ignorant of the state of affairs. The guard at the gate had recognised her face and let her in without a word.

"My love, I thought I would never see you again. I'm to be deported to England on the next ship. It sails at noon and they say I must be on it. They won't let me stay and they won't let me take you with me. It's terrible. I..." The door opened slightly and the unsmiling Gallond put his head through the crack.

"Excuse me. I can give you half an hour - no more." Then, uncharacteristically, he smiled. Will had never seen him smile before and suddenly he seemed to be their friend. "Make yourselves at home. You won't be disturbed - I'll see to it." He closed the door and a key was turned in the lock from the outside.

"How kind of him," Isabelle said sweetly. She looked around and in the corner of the room noticed a comfortable-looking couch. She took Will's hand and led him to the seat. Then she hugged Will as tightly as she could manage, snuggling her face into his neck and shoulder. Will caressed her hair and noticed how beautifully curled and fresh it looked. She had obviously spent a long time preparing for her visit. He clutched her tightly to his chest and felt her bosom heaving ever so slightly. Then he detected the muscular contraction, which always signifies tears. These were silent tears, restrained tears, which burst through involuntarily. He pulled her face away from him and cradled her cheeks in his hands. Will kissed the tears away and then began a long, intense kiss in which he explored her lips and mouth with his tongue. Isabelle responded warmly and clutched him even tighter as their passion grew.

"Dear Isabelle, you know that I love you. Will you wait until I come back to France again? I shall return by whatever means I can manage - even if I have to swim back. Please wait till then."

"Oh, Will, of course I'll wait, my love. You know I always said I'd marry you and I mean it."

"You won't marry some other eligible young man while I'm gone, will you?"

Isabelle looked into his eyes with an expression that seemed to say, "You don't trust me, do you?" She said nothing. After thinking for a moment she wiped away the last trace of tears from her face and looked up. She noticed that the curtains to the small windows opposite were still open. In silence she rose from the couch, crossed the room and drew the curtains. The light level dropped considerably, but there was still sufficient light in the small room. She turned, and looking Will straight in the eye, began to unbutton her blouse and bodice. Will's eyes widened. In an instant he knew what she was going to do. His heart began to race furiously and his breath suddenly felt short. He uttered but one word in surprise.

"Darling!"

Will was awe-struck as the beautiful little French girl of whom he had dreamed so much, slowly and tantalisingly slipped out of every piece of clothing she was wearing. Will had never seen a naked woman before and realised that his cheeks were on fire. He felt deeply embarrassed as he remembered how they had both promised Regis that they would be good, but suddenly promises made so long ago seemed unimportant. It had been a promise made to avoid compromising Regis in his own house. Things had changed a lot since then. Naturally, Will had dreamed about having sex with Isabelle one day, but the idea of making love to her that morning had been the last consideration in his mind. Stupidly, he looked away out of politeness, but seconds later his eyes returned to the delightful female form that was all his own. He found her body unbelievably attractive and almost unreal as she posed naked for him. To have known her for so long and never to have realised the true beauty of his beloved was astounding. How could such a lovely body be concealed so effectively and for so long beneath half a dozen garments? Her beauty had until now always lain in her face and in her eyes, enhanced by the subtle choice of dress, a trace of perfume or a change of hairstyle. Here was a new Isabelle, totally different from the one engraved upon his mind's eye. The Isabelle he had known until now had been clean living and virtuous. Suddenly she had become naughty. He had been seduced in the nicest way he could possibly have imagined by someone he loved intensely. Was it really naughty? This woman was his own woman, not one who acted thus with everyone she met. Isabelle had matured from being a Frenchman's innocent daughter into a wholesome wife. Suddenly there was so much more of her to enjoy. He stared at her small, firm breasts until his vision blurred and he blinked quickly. Then his gaze lowered to Isabelle's ample, well-shaped hips and a strange dark shape in the centre that he had never imagined before. In his fantasies he had been able to imagine

216

breasts; fantasies coined from the views of women wearing revealing party dresses. Here, however, was a new feminine attribute. He felt ashamed of himself for looking at her in such a manner. His entire upbringing had taught him to respect a woman's body as private, yet here he was being invited to inspect one for himself at close quarters. He could not quickly overcome the instinctive feeling that he was looking at forbidden territory.

He realised that she too was blushing and beginning to feel embarrassed. He knew it had taken a lot of courage on her part to strip for the first time so openly and with such warmth. He admired her more than ever and tried to lessen her discomfort.

"My God, you're beautiful," he said, shaking his head in sheer disbelief. He got up from the couch. His clothing felt uncomfortably tight and awkwardly he shuffled towards her. Slowly she walked towards him and when they met she held him tightly around the waist. Even through his own clothes Will could feel a pulsating feminine body summoning him. It was an animal instinct, so irresistible, so indefinable, and so pleasurable. His hands caressed her warm back and found their way down to her buttocks. So soft and smooth... such silky flesh... He pulled her tightly to him. Momentarily she pulled away and began to undo his clothing. Will could hardly contain his embarrassment. He almost asked her to stop when she came to his underwear, but realised how stupid he was being. Her warm hands explored his body and Will's intense pleasure almost made him faint. He gasped a deep breath.

"We promised your father," he said, half-heartedly.

"Papa would entirely approve in the circumstances," she replied reassuringly. Isabelle led him to the couch and spread herself invitingly upon it. "Do you still think that I'm going to marry someone else?" she said. Will was dumbstruck again. He felt so naked and tried to cover his embarrassment. "Don't just stand there," said Isabelle. "Are you going to kiss me, or not?"

Will was very ashamed of his naivety and tried hard to overcome it. He sidled quickly up to the couch, still glaring at the pink, warm body lying so seductively before him. He bent down to kiss her lips. "Not there, silly," said Isabelle. She sat up and thrust her breasts right into Will's face. It was the final action necessary for him to discard his shyness. Isabelle was to be his wife. All their inhibitions must be forgotten. He must not let her down now. Isabelle had given him a demonstration of her ultimate trust and he must do likewise. It would be a long time before they saw each other again. He must seal their love once and for all.

"Be gentle with me," whispered Isabelle as his mouth explored her neck. "I love you."

25 JEAN-PAUL CARTIER

Isabelle was feeling delighted with herself at having finally consummated her love for Will, even though she was rather tender from the experience. Somehow the reality of imminent parting had not materialised and the exquisite sensations of their union still pervaded her whole being. The young couple's lovemaking, though slow to initiate, had been rapidly completed once Will had overcome his shyness and, as they lay basking in the afterglow, the world at large seemed so unreal in comparison to the zenith of human experience they had both enjoyed. Soon, as the minutes of their half-hour meeting ebbed away, the lovers dressed quickly and just had time to tidy up old Gallond's room when the sergeant's purposely-noisy footsteps signalled his return. Isabelle hastily rummaged in her handbag and pulled out a small crucifix that she gave to Will.

"Take this, my lovely," she said softly, "I carry it with me whenever I am travelling. It will look after you and keep you safe until we are together again." Will was overwhelmed by the gift, besides being greatly troubled because he had nothing to give to Isabelle in return. "Don't worry," said Isabelle reassuringly, "You have much farther to travel than I: you will have need of it. In the meantime, I have your love - that is all I need to keep me strong." Will took out his handkerchief and wrapped the crucifix carefully within. Then he tucked it well inside his shirt for safety and kissed Isabelle in gratitude. Then it was time to leave.

Even as Gallond ushered the lovers from his quarters and out of the prison towards the docks, the wonderful feeling that would live in both their hearts for many a year continued to bubble up inside them. Out of consideration for old Gallond who'd done so much to cement their relationship, Will did not try to delay his departure any longer. He knew he must leave and that the old chap would be in trouble if he were late. As they stepped out briskly along the cobbled road to the docks Isabelle tripped lightly along at Will's side, never once letting slip her grasp of his hand, but that journey was like a dream and Will never remembered a single step of it in later years. His only recollection was the final heart-rending embrace on the quayside as he bade a last farewell to his love. He did not subsequently remember the first view of the *Mistral*, a medium sized merchant vessel that had been specially chartered to take him and the other English prisoners-of-war back to England. Neither did he recall the anxious looks of the French mate who hurriedly pushed him aboard lest they miss the tide. He forgot even his last farewell to his friend Gallond who had been so good to him.

At ten o' clock the freighter slipped her moorings and proceeded quietly away from the quayside and out into midstream. Will watched helplessly as his dearest love waved frantically from ashore. Would they ever see each other again? Will had promised himself that he would not rest until he was able to return to claim Isabelle for his wife, but try as he might he could not dissipate the thought that he might never see her again. The feeling seemed to diffuse into the deepest recesses of his soul like an evil spirit from the past that was haunting him and trying to prevent their goal being achieved. Had God Himself ordained this? Was God displeased at their act of immorality back at the prison? Will could not understand how something so beautiful could be a sin. He remembered the little package tucked inside his shirt and having clutched it to ascertain its safety, was instantly reassured by its presence.

Will stood on the upper deck until he could see Isabelle no longer, and as the early March wind picked up across the open river he felt cold. As he stood dazed and motionless he was pushed out of the way several times by busy seamen going about their duties, but they ignored Will's presence and he continued to gaze entranced in the direction of his woman. Then, as the merchantman finally drew away from the shore and into the open sea he thought he ought to begin to look around the vessel. No thought had entered his head of the other English prisoners or of where he was to spend the night. Only one thing had occupied his mind: his love for Isabelle. Now that she was gone from him, he was forced to re-enter the real world once more.

It seemed strange to be on a ship at sea once again. This time it was as a passenger, for that is what he imagined he must be. He was no longer a prisoner, for the war was over and he had been released. The French sailors had no cause to imprison him within the ship. Equally, there seemed no reason why they should be made to work their passage, as they would have done on board *Resolution*, for the ship had a full complement. The Frenchmen would have to sail the ship whether the English were there or not. Indeed, the English would probably get in the way. It appeared, then, as if he really were a passenger. He felt sure that he would have quarters assigned to him somewhere on board the *Mistral*, but no-one seemed to be interested in him. Experience told him that he should be for'ard rather than aft, so he decided to begin his tour of the ship by looking for his countrymen in the area of the bow.

The first place he chose to look was beneath a canvas hatch cover that was in the deck nearby. The hold was very dark so he threw back the cover to let in as much light as possible and began to descend the ladder into the darkness. As his head entered the space below deck and his eyes became accustomed to the blackness, he was able to make out a large stock of barrels as well as dozens of cases of dusty dark glass bottles. Just as he was about to have a closer look, a French voice barked at him in distinctly unpleasant tones. By the authoritative way in which the newcomer had accosted him, Will took the man to be the mate and apologised profusely, saying that he was looking for his quarters. The mate replied rather rudely that Will had no business to be in this hold and that his quarters were in the for'ard cargo hold, along with the other English pigs. Will thanked him politely, despite a strong inclination to give him a lesson in manners. He knew that he must take care not to cause any trouble as a passenger or his voyage would become much more like his past experiences in *Resolution*. He could not have known of the troubles to come.

Will climbed out of the forbidden hold, whereupon the mate began to secure it lest the event be repeated. Will looked about him for the hatch which would lead to his designated sleeping area and where, presumably, his compatriots would be found. He did not have to look hard.

"Hey, you, come over 'ere."

He looked towards the sound and discovered that the gruff voice belonged to an even coarser man who'd half emerged from a hole in the deck near the bow. Will thought for a second and consciously told himself that the command had been spoken in English. At last he had discovered the location of the English contingent. He complied with the instruction and climbed down the ladder into the hold where the remaining fifty-two ex-prisoners had nearly finished lashing their hammocks to every available support beam. At once memories came flooding back of his time in the *Medway Lady*. The smell, the darkness, the motion, all instinctively repulsive to him, even after so long away from it.

"You're the special prisoner, ain't ye?" The voice came from behind and he turned to face the speaker. He found himself facing a group of half a dozen men, none of whom looked particularly friendly towards him. He did not like the sound of the welcome that had been given him and began to feel afraid.

"What do you mean?" he asked.

"You knows what I mean. You 'ad privlidges - we didn't 'ave none."

Will began to defend his position without thinking. "I did not have any privileges…" He started, but realised he was lying and that they all knew it.

"Oh, no? A cell of yer own, nice food, a woman to come and visit you every month…"

"It wasn't every month…" Will protested, but it was no good. He knew that the other English prisoners were not going to let him get away with special treatment. They'd all had to suffer the poor French prison conditions, whilst, in their eyes, he seemed to be living in luxury. Will had never considered his imprisonment in that light, but it hardly mattered now. These men were going to make him pay for his privilege.

"We don't like it when some gets special treatment. It makes us think that you've been helping the Frogs - perhaps even giving special information about us. We don't like pigs who pretend to be English but speak their lingo. We think you're a spy…"

"That's not true," shouted Will in his own defence. Mistakenly, he tried to reason with them. "I am an English sailor off the *Resolution*. I come from Dover in Kent. I helped the French to solve some murders, yes. I got to know Lieutenant Rodier well because he was interested in them. I knew how to speak French and it helped a lot. He said he'd help me…" Will was gabbling out his story in the desperate hope that he could make them see sense. Unfortunately, rational thought was not attributable to these men.

"Only spies speak French and English too," came the menacing reply. At once, Will knew that all his efforts to protest his innocence would be wasted. They had been locked up in the same prison as he, many of them for much longer periods. No amount of argument would appease their sense of injustice. In the relatively short time that Will had been away from his home in the sleepy Kentish village, Will had met many men of this type. John Jennings was a good example, a man with a mind that was evil, through and through. There could never be any cold reasoning with such a burning insanity. Every moment that Will spent in that hold would decrease his chances of surviving to see Isabelle again. Instantly he made the decision to run for it. As he faced the men in a half circle, the ladder was slightly to the left and between him and them. As quickly as he could he gripped the sides of the ladder and almost jumped up it, six rungs at a time. His judgement was perfect for he was out of the hold before the aggrieved prisoners had time to grab at him. But having escaped from the hold, his problems had only just begun. Where was he to go next? The merchantman was not a large ship; he would not be able to hide away for the whole journey.

Will had not had time to think logically. In sheer panic he ran aft, pushing aside several French seamen as they made their way amid the deck rigging. He hoped to reach cover before the others were able to escape from the hold and spot him. He came to the aftercastle where he noticed an open door and leapt inside. To his dismay there was a ladder immediately inside and he fell heavily to the bottom with a loud crash and release of expletives. His shoulder and thigh were badly grazed and he sat in a pained heap for a moment while he massaged his injuries and wondered what to do next. A gruff French voice bellowed out a complaint, and its owner was in close pursuit. Will was at once on the alert; it did not seem to be a good day for making friends.

Though he did not appreciate it at first, Will had come face to face with the Captain, who was rather upset at the intrusion into the privacy of his private apartments. Once again, Will's ability in the French tongue proved to be his salvation.

"What is the meaning of this? Who are you?" asked the Captain.

"I beg your pardon, sir, but I am trying to escape from the English prisoners. I think they are going to kill me," said Will, still rubbing his shoulder.

"Why should they want to harm you? Are they not your own countrymen?" The Captain was less annoyed than confused. Will quickly explained the situation whilst the Captain listened intently. When Will had finished, he said simply, "I see." Then he gently pushed Will aside and climbed the ladder to the upper deck. There he saw eight scruffy English passengers looking for Will. He barked an order to the mate. "Get those men below in their quarters and make sure they stay there. They are not to leave that hold under any circumstances, is that clear?"

"Aye, aye, sir," came the reply. The mate quickly mustered several of his men and, one by one, the English were rounded up and thrust below. Then, just as the last was being sent below to his swaying hammock, another English sailor emerged from the same hold that Will had first explored. The Captain saw him and went wild with anger.

"Get that man out of there. I thought I told you to secure that hatch so that no-one... no-one I said... can go near it. The mate was obviously very embarrassed by his gaff.

"But I did, sir," was his feeble response. The Captain's scathing comment was only to be expected.

"Then you did it badly. Seal that hatch once and for all, and if one more man sets foot inside I'll have his guts for a painter with your neck for a mooring post. Is that understood?"

"Aye, aye, sir." The mate dared not make any more excuses, and Will, who had heard all the exchanges, decided that he had better not say anything about his short foray into the forbidden hold. The final Englishman was dispatched into the for'ard hold and the hatch secured. However, the damage had been done.

As the Captain returned to the ladder which led into his quarters, he found Will peeping timorously over the top. He signalled to Will that he go back down and then followed the lad below. Once in the comfort of his cabin, the Captain regained his composure and invited Will to join him for a drink. By now Will had guessed who his host was. The hospitality was warm; he was offered the choice of rum, whiskey or finest cognac. Not being one for strong drink, Will tried to refuse politely but the Captain would have none of it. Soon Will was lounging in a comfortable chair with a glass of the Captain's best cognac between his fingers.

Captain Cartier was an experienced merchant Captain who had been sailing the seas ever since he had run away from home at the age of nine. Although the recent war with the English had caused some restrictions on the movements of his ship, he had never been directly involved with the fighting and had continued with his trading, mostly between St. Nazaire and Amsterdam. He knew the English Channel routes as well as anyone and always felt most at home there. With no personal animosity towards the English, he had no reason at all to dislike his passengers, other than that they seemed such an ill-disciplined bunch of ruffians. To him, they were simply passengers to whom he owed as much responsibility as to the rest of his cargo.

Will found every second of conversation with Cartier a fascinating experience, although it always seemed to be Will who was doing the talking. The Captain was an extremely good listener and, by means of a subtle question interposed at just the right point in the conversation, was able to extract the maximum amount of information from the person to whom he was talking. Will fancied that he would have made an excellent interrogator. Soon, Will had told the Captain the whole of his life story. Indeed, for the first time he realised exactly how much had happened to him since he had run away from his lighthouse so long ago. When the conversation at long last began to dry up, the Captain rose from his seat and summoned his steward. He ordered supper for two, and as the servant left the cabin Cartier took a particularly large sip of cognac.

Will used the opportunity to ask questions of his own.

"Where are you taking us, Captain?"

"That's no secret, my lad. Why, to Chatham, for I have other business there. The passengers are not my only reason for going to England," he replied enigmatically. Will waited for a second to see if the Captain would volunteer any other information, but he did not. Suddenly Will remembered the bottles and barrels in that forbidden hold. Somehow, the words slipped out before he could prevent himself from saying them.

"I don't suppose it could have anything to do with all the liquor you have on board, would it?" he asked cheekily. As soon as he had uttered the words he knew that he had committed an indiscretion for the Captain's face froze into an icy expression that seemed to penetrate to Will's very soul.

"How do you know about that?" he asked sternly. Will told him how he had accidentally climbed into the hold while he was looking around for his quarters. His simple answer, given freely and without a hint of deceit, induced a thaw in the

222

Captain's manner. He looked away towards a scuttle and drained his cognac. "You are quite correct, young man. I have a large consignment of the finest cognac on board. It is a gift from my government to yours - a simple gesture that there is no lingering animosity between our two countries as a result of the war. The shipment was authorised at the highest level, probably by our King himself, and I am to deliver it in Chatham to one of your King's ministers who will take it directly to the royal cellars. The idea of taking you all along as passengers was an afterthought, arranged at the last minute by our Minister-of-War. He wanted to get you all off his hands and this was the only ship going to England. Of course, he will gain politically, for your King will undoubtedly better receive the gift if it comes with a band of released prisoners. However, as far as I am concerned, the mixture is not a good one. I know that I can trust my own men in the presence of so much liquor, but fifty-three English prisoners-of-war?" He broke off, shrugging his shoulders as if in despair at the thought of his passengers on a drunken orgy with France's finest ambassadorial cognac.

"There are only fifty-two untrustworthy English sailors, Captain. This particular one is completely honourable." The Captain rose and slapped Will on the back good-naturedly.

"Well said, my lad. After all, why should you need to steal it when you can sit here in my cabin and drink as much as you like, eh?" He laughed. Will felt embarrassed, after all, it did look rather like cupboard love. He blushed and tried to protest his honour, but the Frenchman merely laughed louder still, took Will's glass and refilled it to the brim. "Come, Will, let's have no more of that. I want to hear about your plans when you get home."

"Well, I haven't any really - except that I want to get back to France again as quickly as I can."

"Oh, surely not!" exclaimed the Captain, settling himself down into his favourite chair once more. "All for the love of... what's her name? Isabelle? She's never worth it, you know." Will was downhearted that Cartier should think so little of his love for Isabelle. This grey-haired and weathered old salt had long since forgotten how the mind of a young bachelor really works, for within those wrinkled temples rested the mind of one who had spent his entire life in the service of seafaring, the mind of one whose first love is always the ship in which he currently sails. Captain Cartier had never known true love for a woman. He could never appreciate the force that, even as he spoke to the young Englishman, was drawing the two young people together.

"Don't you want to see your parents again? How long is it you've been away?" asked the Captain.

"Yes, of course I do, dearly. I've had a lot of time to think about this. Eventually I have to leave home and start a new life with another person. Much as I love my parents, I believe that day has arrived now that I have met Isabelle. After I've seen my folks once more I shall be straight back to her. We're promised to each other now, you see." Will stopped talking and for a few moments there was silence. He sipped the cognac and it burned his throat again. He did not like the stuff and wondered why he was, drinking it. Suddenly, they had become very serious and Will was wishing himself in the arms of his beloved once more. The Captain winked at him.

"Well, I admire your sincerity, lad, and I wish you well, but don't forget your folks, will you? They've worked all their lives to raise you. You must not desert them too readily. You owe them a thought too, you know." Will knew that the Captain was right. Why was his life always beset with problems? Then another thought occurred to him.

"May I ask you why you are looking after me so well? You did not know me at all until a few hours ago. Why didn't you just feed me to those English wolves up for'ard?" The Captain smiled through his grey beard and Will could see that he had a number of brown, tobacco-stained teeth, yet he had not seen the Captain smoke whilst they had been talking.

"Well, my boy, to tell the truth, I thought I might have some trouble with that bunch from the moment I saw them. When I discovered how well you speak both languages I thought you might come in useful as an interpreter."

"I see," said Will thoughtfully.

"After all," continued Cartier," it's not often that you meet someone who is as proficient in two languages as you are. Honestly, I admire you. I've always felt so useless when I've been in other countries and unable to speak to the natives. I think you've done very well to learn French so quickly."

"Well, I had a good incentive," said Will, cheered by the compliments paid to him. "You'd have done it too if you'd been living with such a pretty girl and you couldn't speak to her." The two men laughed aloud as the servant returned to commence laying the table for supper. The Captain stood up, as if he had suddenly remembered his responsibilities on deck.

"Look, through there is a cabin which I keep for my special guests." Cartier indicated a door in the corner of his spacious apartment. "Make yourself at home, have a quick wash and brush-up. When you're ready we'll have dinner. I like you. We'll make good conversation tonight, you and I. While my man prepares the table I must see how we go." So saying, he was gone up the ladder and Will was left to explore his new cabin alone. It was well appointed with a comfortable-looking bunk along the length of one bulkhead and a few other small items of furniture. He found a small bowl of water, some soap and a towel, and proceeded to freshen himself up, though he had no clean clothes in which to dress for dinner.

Just as Will was finishing a delightful experience with soap and water, he heard the noisy footsteps of the Captain returning for his meal. Will re-entered the Captain's cabin to find the small table attractively laid for two persons and his host eagerly awaiting the arrival of the first course.

"I feel better for that," said Will as he seated himself opposite Captain Cartier.

"Are you hungry," asked the Frenchman.

"Ravenous," replied Will, as he remembered that he'd had nothing since breakfast. "How goes the voyage?" he asked courteously.

Cartier looked pleased. "Ah, we'll be there in no time. A following stiff southwesterly wind and we're positively flying along. This lady is one of the fastest afloat when she gets moving," said the Captain with a twinkle in his eye.

"Yes," thought Will, "This is the love of Cartier's life; no woman for him, other than the sleek lines of the *Mistral*." Then aloud: "Tell me about her - the ship, I mean," Will clarified himself. "When did you become Master of her?"

The question was never answered, for, as the words left his lips, there was a terrific crash from the ladder. The Captain's steward fell heavily to the bottom where he remained firmly unconscious amid broken plates and greasy food. The Captain was on his feet in a trice, but within seconds four heavily built and very threatening thugs appeared as if from nowhere. Then, as these men approached menacingly, more were descending into what were supposed to be private apartments. The Captain lost his temper and began to scream at the men to return to their quarters, but they did not appear to understand for they showed not the slightest sign of compliance. At first, Will wondered what the men could possibly want, but very soon he became aware of a very thick smell pervading the atmosphere. It took only seconds to identify the stench of alcohol-laden breath, and then he knew what the problem really was. Even as his powers of observation were working to unravel the situation, the fifth man had reached the bottom of the ladder and as he turned to face Will it was apparent that he had a number of bottles of cognac on his person. Captain Cartier saw the cognac at the same time as Will. He marched forward without a hint of hesitation, cursing the men in French all the while, and laid hands on the fifth man in an attempt to recover the stolen alcohol. As a group, the men closed ranks on the Captain and, ignoring Will, began to bustle the Frenchman into a corner. Without thinking Will did something, which he was later ashamed of, but which, in retrospect, saved his life. He bolted up the ladder almost as quickly as he had done from the for'ard hatch, although this time his stiff limbs retarded him a little. On this occasion his speed mattered less than his desire to stay and fight, for the invaders were uncoordinated through drink and would have been no match for Will in a race.

As Will vanished from the scene, Cartier fared not so well, for against the combined strength of five seasoned English salts, he stood little chance. Within moments, one of his precious bottles was smashed to pieces on the crown of his head, its contents drenching all who were involved in the struggle. Then, as the poor Captain slumped unconscious to the deck and the men's immediate problem had been dealt with, the ringleader realised that Will had gone.

"Get after that one, Tom. I want him brung 'ere, now."

Poor Tom, the fifth man, even without the handicap of his bottle burden, found the ascent of the ladder much more of a problem than the descent. By the time he had reached the top, Will had completely disappeared, and it was necessary to mount a more considered and methodical search for him than Tom was really capable of. Tom spotted a couple of colleagues emerging from the liquor hold and called on them to help him find the French spy.

Meanwhile, Will was at his wits end. He had deserted the Captain, half hoping to get help from the French crew, but, now that he had arrived on the open deck, there seemed to be no sign of a crewman. He found temporary cover beside a bulkhead just for'ard of the quarterdeck and knelt in despair. There seemed to be no escape from these drunken English matelots. Where on earth had all the Frenchmen gone? Why was there no resistance to this mutiny? He remembered his crucifix and, pulling it from its place of safety, unwrapped it gently. "I need your help," he said, kissing it lovingly. With a tear in his eye he looked into the calm face carved in miniature before him. Then, just as he was about to return his treasure to its hiding place, a ruffian, unseen from the shadows, snatched it from his grasp. In his misery he had momentarily excluded the world from his sphere of awareness and failed to notice two of his countrymen approaching stealthily.

"Give me that," snapped Will, "It's mine - you've no right..." He lunged at the cross in a vain attempt to retrieve it from the hands of the enemy. Simultaneously, a smooth, muscular motion of the thief's hand sent Isabelle's gift whirling away up over the quarterdeck into the darkness on the port side of the ship. From the angle of its trajectory Will had no doubt that his most precious possession, the crucifix, had gone overboard. In the available moonlight he could see the smug expression on the face of the perpetrator.

"Oh dear, my hand slipped." The evil face sneered unforgivably.

"You bastard," exploded Will, "you'll pay for that." As the words left his lips he unleashed a blow, which, in his anger, contained more energy than any other blow he had struck in his life. The tightly clenched fist of his right hand landed with maximum effect on the left hand side of the sailor's jaw, fracturing it in several places. The wretched man's teeth, which had been slightly separated in the position necessary for a smug smile, were brought together with great force, severing the tip of the man's tongue. As the blood began to issue from the corners of his forcibly closed mouth, the momentum of the punch had been translated into a backward motion of his body. The combination of instant pain, shock and an alcohol-laden bloodstream, divorced the Englishman from all consciousness and his unfeeling body crashed to the deck where it lay motionless amid a considerable coil of cordage.

The second of Will's two opponents merely watched in amazement as his friend was subjected to the enormous effect of Will's wrath. He took one look at the crumpled form with its bloody grin frozen in anger and, fearing similar treatment at the hands of such a deceptively able pugilist, fled in search of assistance.

Despite the devastating effect of the single blow, which had amazed even Will with its ferocity, he had now reached the depths of despair. What more could he do? He just wanted to give up now that his final morale-raiser had been so cruelly taken from him. Will's agony was worsened by the fact that, so soon after asking the Lord for help, his dearest possession had been plucked from his grasp and thrown overboard. There could be no other interpretation than of being spurned. Will was angry. Why should God desert him like that, just when Will needed Him? Perhaps it was punishment for his immoral behaviour with Isabelle. He remembered the Captain. Perhaps it was retribution for having deserted the Captain at his moment of need. But, surely, not? God was not vengeance seeking... was He? Will was confused, desperate and terribly alone. With no plan of escape in mind he climbed the ladder to the quarterdeck and walked aft as far as he could go until he stood at the very stern of the vessel. The moon was behind the ship as she sped her way onward, presumably toward England. Her wake seemed strangely luminous in the night. For a tantalising moment all was tranquil. Then he was spotted by the quartermaster, whose post was now filled by a liquor-supping matelot with more of an eye for the level in the bottle than the course of the ship. The English-spoken alarm captured the attention of Will's pursuers on the deck below. At once his problems were upon him again...

From where he stood there was only one way to evade capture. In an act of utter and complete desolation Will gate-vaulted over the stern of the ship, fully expecting to plummet into the icy March waters of the English Channel. Was it really the end of his adventures at last? Had he come through so many dangers only to perish in this way? No! His feet fell firmly onto a solid wooden balustrade that bordered the stern above the windows of the Captain's apartments. This ledge led around both port and starboard quarters of the *Mistral*, mostly for decorative purposes. Its designers had never intended it to be used in such a manner by a broken man at the end of his tether. Will kept low, keeping a firm hold on whatever convenient timbers were at hand, and then crept around to the port quarter. Within moments of his rounding the corner his adversaries arrived at his point of departure from the quarterdeck.

" 'e's jumped! The bastard's gone overboard!" was the decision. Will guessed that from the angle at which the stern fell away from the top of the deck, his escape route was not easily visible. Certainly, he had not seen it himself whilst studying the turbulence of the troubled wake astern.

"Well that's 'im out of the way," observed a second voice. Its speech was slurred enough for Will to picture the state of inebriation of the speaker. "Let's get another drink," it added predictably. Will clung onto the ship's side for several more minutes after he imagined the men had departed. He could hardly believe his luck. His fortunes seemed to change so quickly from good to ill and back again, that he dared not speculate about the future. He was safe for the moment now that they thought he was drowned, but he was still aboard an unfriendly vessel and in an alien environment. In the immediate future he needed somewhere more permanent to hide, for he could scarcely travel all the way back to England whilst clutching forlornly the seaward side of the decks. Anxiously he looked all about him and saw a longboat hanging from its davits about twenty feet for'ard of his position. The biggest problem was that the ledge fell short of the longboat by about ten feet. In order to reach his goal he would have to dangle from the guardrail at quarterdeck level and inch his way forward without attracting the attention of the quartermaster. A vision of the drunken dutyman flashed through Will's mind and Will gambled that he had nothing to fear. Besides, it was his only hope. Carefully, he edged his way forward to where the longboat hung invitingly against the ship's side. With a burst of energy and a quick prayer that he would not be spotted, he swung on the guardrail and hoisted himself over the side of the longboat. There he collapsed in exhaustion on the hard but deliciously comfortable carvel planking. At last he was safe. These men had no need of a longboat and he had convinced them that he had jumped overboard. The odds were now firmly in his favour and he gave thanks for his deliverance.

For a time, he lay in luxury, cooled by the chill of air, but sheltered from the fresh wind which had now swung around to the south-east and, unbeknown to the uncaring ragamuffins in control of the ship, was taking them along a rather different course than Captain Cartier would have liked. Had the alcohol-ridden crew possessed even a fraction of the knowledge of the Captain, who at that moment lay with a fractured skull in his own cabin, they would have been making preparations for a change of canvas. Not that there was the slightest chance of any one of them actually having the balance necessary to climb the rigging and reduce the area of sail. None but Captain Cartier would have predicted the rainstorm that, in these parts, usually followed close behind a southeasterly.

The first spots of rain that fell on Will's face as he lay recuperating in the longboat were not sufficient to waken him. He'd had an exhausting day and the sudden relief of nervous tension had enabled him to fall asleep even on the comparatively hard wooden floor of the boat. Even the conversation that sprang up at the wheel did not wake him immediately.

"Where's all they Frogs then?" The man who was standing-in for the rightful quartermaster still possessed enough savvy to attempt a reasoned conversation with the colleague who had arrived on the quarterdeck to replenish the first man's stock of liquor.

" 'Ere's yer bottle. Ah, don't worry yerself about they. Us got all they locked up in their little 'ouse this afternoon. Didn' take much to get 'em in there. Bloody soft bunch they were. Even that Mate - all mouth 'e is." The second man extracted a cork with ease from a bottle he was carrying and swigged the contents, carelessly spilling much of it down the front of his clothes.

"So 'ow long am I s'posed to steer this bloody thing then? I bin 'ere 'ours."

"You just sit there, my 'ansom, and trust yer old mate George. I've got it all in 'and. Now let's see now," he raised his eyes to the heavens and looked about. He located a few stars in the direction from which the moon still radiated energy before being covered by the rain clouds. Unfortunately, the new position of his unbalanced head, coupled with a roll of the vessel, caused him to stagger almost the whole length of the quarterdeck before saving himself on a convenient piece of rigging. Recovering his stance and returning to the helpless wheelman, he tried once more to instil confidence in the troubled mind of his companion.

"Well, that there is Sirius… see it over there, look!" He pointed unsteadily. "Now at this time of year, let me see…

He scratched his chin as he struggled to recall the little knowledge of navigation he thought he possessed. Then something caught his eye. It was in the distance and on the port bow, a faintly twinkling light, low down, too low for a star. George jumped in the air with glee. "That's it... there... look!" he pointed excitedly. "It's the Eddystone lighthouse, it's got to be. There ain't no other lights around here like that. It's not the Lizard, the Lizard's a big fire, I've seen it before. That's not the Lizard - it's the Eddystone, I tell you." He clasped his friend by both shoulders as if to instil the supreme level of confidence in a worried relative. Looking him straight in the eye, he said, "I told you to trust old George, didn' I?" Unfortunately, his enthusiasm was wasted on the dumb wheelman, who had no conception of where the Eddystone lighthouse was anyway. Still, if it made George happy, perhaps he should feel happy too? George released his grip and stumbled to the port side, knocking back yet more liquor as he did so. "Ah, we 'm all right now, boy. I knows exactly where we are now."

"So where are we going ashore then, George?" George realised that he had not really thought about that yet, but tried to cover up his inadequacy.

"Well, I thought we could go into... er... what about Torbay? That's a good place...or Weymouth... even better. We won't go into Plymouth - there's too many naval ships in there. No. Let's keep clear of there, away from the navy. Weymouth, that's the place."

"How do we get there then, George?"

"Don't you ever stop askin' questions?" George began to get a little impatient. He pointed, "You just keep us goin' that way, there, understand? Keep well south of the Eddystone, there's some pretty nasty rocks there - that's why the lighthouse got put there. South... stay south. We'll be all right on this course for now."

The rain had begun to patter down onto the deck as well as stream down the flushed, insensible faces of the drunken crewman. Will, too, had been disturbed by the rapidly falling raindrops, but had listened in some amusement at the bantering brogue of sozzled George. Cautiously, Will peered over the side of the longboat, whilst taking care not to let anyone see him. He was able to discern the faint but clear signal cast across the sea from the Eddystone lighthouse, assuming that George was at least correct in this. It seemed a reasonable decision to make in view of their presumed position. Will remembered the occasion when, years before, he had sailed past it in the *Resolution*. He had studied it with an educated eye and had admired the streamlined shape of the grey, granite tower as it pierced the monotony of the seascape. Now, he was overwhelmed to see its heart-warming beams telling all seamen their position, for although it was warning of terrible danger only when a ship came too close, the lighthouse served as a navigational aid for those at a safe enough distance to have no cause for concern about the reefs it guarded.

Slowly, *Le Mistral* passed by the lighthouse. George and his friend, aided and abetted by their newfound confidence in navigation, had entered upon a new bout of alcoholic celebrations and were in no mood to bother about anything else. Even the rain, which still beat down steadily, did not concern them. The stiff wind was not so strong as to cause problems, but the light from the moon had long since been obliterated by the racing clouds high above. Brighter than ever, the warm, penetrating beams from the lighthouse sparkled at the ghost ship, the ship with a drunkard at the helm and an incarcerated crew of hungry, frightened Frenchmen, the ship with a dead man, fugitive from his own countrymen and hidden in the longboat.

Steadily, surely, *Le Mistral* sailed on to the point four miles southeast of the Eddystone reef where a lesser-known relative lies just a few feet beneath the barely troubled surface.

George's senses were being assailed by the huge doses of alcohol that infused his cerebral substances. His friend had been reduced to a state of tacit concurrence with all that George said and did.

"Ah tol' ye to chus me din ah?"

George's confidence reached an all time high just as the hull of *Le Mistral* sliced into the jagged, immovable mass which was known to the local seamen as the 'Hand's Deep'. An enormous hole was torn in the port bow of the merchantman as the sudden change of momentum sent everything smashing down into chaos. Will knew at once what had happened. A sickening feeling swept over him as he remembered vividly the night that the *Resolution* had struck *Le Four* shoal. It was true that the ship did not sink on that occasion, but it had been enough to cause utter pandemonium on board. *Le Mistral* quickly began to list to port and Will found his longboat dangling at a sharp angle away from the ship. As the list grew larger, the two incapables on the quarterdeck found it increasingly more difficult even to remain on the deck. Both were thrown down towards the port guardrail, below which Will still sat in his longboat. Inevitably, they all came face to face.

"Come on," shouted Will, "help me to get this boat released. We've got to get out of here."

"Oo're you? 'Ere, you 'm that spy int ye?" George's brain was not yet totally useless.

"Never mind about that, let's get this boat away or we'll all die right here." Will issued orders to the men. "You, get in: you aren't going to help much in your state." That was to the wheelman. Then he ordered George. "Unfasten that bend and pull that pin - no, not that one - the one under your left hand... yes. Quickly now, come on!"

Fortunately for Will, George was able to carry out his orders, albeit rather slowly. Between the two of them, they managed to lower the longboat into the water, by which time it was obvious that *Le Mistral* was going to sink quite quickly. She seemed to be well down in the water at the for'ard end although the combination of rain and darkness made it rather difficult to see clearly. It was more easy to predict the imminent sinking by simply looking at the attitude of the ship in the water which was now dramatically inclined towards Davy Jones' locker. A number of men managed to escape from the entrance to the Captain's quarters, but with very little control over their alcohol-filled nervous systems they found themselves sliding down the wet deck and catapulted into the water. Will was not able to see them in the darkness, but he could hear their screams and shouts and decided to try to rescue them. George and his companion were flat on their backs in the boat and making no effort at all to help themselves.

"Come on you drunken bums - get your skins on these seats and let's pull across there and save those men."

As Will looked in the bottom of the boat for the oars a tiny glint of reflected light caught his eye. There was something lying in the front of the longboat, partly hidden by the seat. He put his hand down to discover what it was and there, to his great delight, he found his lost crucifix. It had obviously flown through the air and dropped into the boat rather than going into the sea, as it had looked from where Will had been standing. Will suddenly felt as if all his troubles had been whisked away. He kissed the cross and said simply, "Thank you, Lord." Making quite sure to tuck it very safely away, he picked up the oars and handed them to the other two.

"Now come on, you two. We're going to pull this boat over there. Make an effort. Those chaps lives are depending on you."

The three men began to row the longboat; there was never much hope of unity of effort, but at least they managed to make the craft move slowly through the waves in approximately the right direction. Soon, Will could barely see several men splashing about in the water. The act of recovering men from the sea into a longboat is never easy when they are reasonably fresh, but the act of hauling cold and exhausted drunken men over the gunwales was almost superhuman. It took numerous efforts to hoist three men on board. Will noticed a fourth man floating face down in the water. He reached over the side, and, grabbing the man's shoulders, tried to turn him face up. As the seaman rolled over in the water Will came to see the purple face and staring eyes of a drowned man. Will had never seen such a sight before and found the experience both sickening and frightening. After the initial inhalation of seawater, the lungs go into immediate spasm as they try fruitlessly to obtain oxygen, which, though present in seawater, is quite useless for breathing purposes. Quickly the oxygen supply in the bloodstream is exhausted, the healthy, pink skin coloration becomes purple with deoxygenated blood and the brain dies in minutes, starved of oxygen. The man's eyes reflected the last moments of his thoughts as his brain, his heart and lungs ceased to function. Will closed his eyes as he released the body and prayed that it would never happen to him.

Le Mistral was almost submerged, though in the darkness it was difficult to assess just how much longer she would last. Will overcame his revulsion at the sight of death and with no further hesitation took charge of the pathetic rabble he alone had saved from death.

"Right, you lot. Since I'm the only one amongst us who's sober, I am taking charge here. Every man is to take hold of an oar. I don't care how much you've had to drink; you'll sit up on the seat and bloody well row. We're going to pull to the Eddystone lighthouse. It's not far away - over there." He indicated the direction in which the glow of the lighthouse could still be seen clearly. "Now come on, try to sober up. Concentrate on your rowing. Let the rain wash down your face. The wind is

with us, the tide is not too bad. Now, are you all ready? Then let's heave - two, six…
heave! Two, six… heave!"

26 JOHN HATHERLEY - 2

Dear Sir.

A letter should always begin with that, thought John Hatherley. Perhaps it should be 'Dear Mister Smeaton.' No, that would be presumptive. He knew John Smeaton quite well, but Smeaton was a gentleman and he, Hatherley, a mere lighthouse keeper. He wrote the words 'Dear Sir.' That was a start.

Hatherley did not feel comfortable with a pen in his hand. By the standard of many folk he was well educated, for he could write with a modest amount of confidence. His handwriting was a little untidy and his spelling unreliable, but at least he could express himself on paper. The trouble was that he did not practise enough. He had no need to write many letters for the few of his relatives who were still alive could not read. The quill was therefore a rather clumsy tool for Hatherley. This particular one was rough and scratched the paper because he had not used it before. The ink was rather thin and he felt sure he would not get far into the letter before he made a blot. He could only do his best, however. The contents of his letter were more important than the form of their delivery and he felt sure that Smeaton would understand.

After his experiences in several bad storms his resolve to report the events to Smeaton had been growing daily and he'd finally found the courage to make his report. But it was difficult. Hatherley stared vacantly at the two words that stood alone on the paper. He tried to string his thoughts together sufficiently well to enable him to continue. Then he realised that he had not written the date. He did not know what it was and he had no calendar or diary, so he guessed it. He knew that it was March and that would surely be good enough. Carefully he dipped his quill into the inkpot, allowed the excess ink to run off the nib onto the inside of the inkpot, and wrote the date above his earlier greeting. "March 1763." He thought that it was Thursday, but he did not write that. Now what? He rested his quill and pondered how best to start his report.

The small table at which he sat in the living room of the Eddystone lighthouse was shaped so as to fit against the circular wall. Directly above it a small bookcase was mounted on the wall. Hatherley had made the bookcase himself to store neatly his few personal volumes. The wood had been rescued from the reef below as flotsam from a long-gone shipwreck, left in store for six months to dry out, and fashioned with all the skill of someone who has all the time in the world at his disposal. Hatherley was much more at home with a chisel and a saw than with a pen. Alongside the bookcase was a small painting of a man-of-war that Henry Carter had crudely painted. Henry painted as often as he could, but this was the only painting his colleagues would allow him to hang in the tower. To the left of Hatherley was a small window, one of three equidistantly spaced around the circumference of the room. As he glanced at it he could see that the panes of glass were still being regularly drenched with seawater. It was raining quite heavily, but the steady impact of the raindrops was punctuated by an intermittent deluge of seawater that clattered on the glass of the room in which he sat, some forty feet above sea level. He could see not an inch farther than the thick glass of the windows, for it was night and he had just started the middle watch.

Apart from seamen, only the lighthouse keeper knows the feeling produced in the pit of the stomach by the words 'middle watch'. Positioned in the middle of the night it induces a strangely satisfying feeling of responsibility and awe: the responsibility of alone guarding the lives of one's friends and work-mates while they sleep peacefully, the awe of the darkness, solitude and solemnity which duties always assume at night. When darkness was coupled with bad weather, the lighthouse keeper found the solemnity to be magnified fourfold.

For four days the lighthouse had suffered gale force southwesterly winds combined with two days of heavy rain. The hours of daylight were still short and the days seemed to be greatly overwhelmed by the nights. The wind was now southeasterly, and the seas, though moderating, were still greatly troubled in the vicinity of the reef. John knew from long experience that it would take several days for the heavy seas around the rocks to quieten down again, even if the weather abated quickly. The worst of the winter must surely be over: it was nearly springtime, but as Hatherley tried to put his thoughts down on the paper in front of him he cast his mind back over his time in the tower. He and his colleagues, Henry Carter and Henry Edwards, had successfully kept the light going through three winters since Smeaton's tower had been completed. It had been fully tested by some of the most violent weather and there had been very few problems. One of them, however, was serious.

The first spell of bad weather had occurred very soon after Smeaton's last visit to the tower. Hatherley vividly remembered the occasion back in December 1759. During this particular storm, they suddenly felt the tower lurch violently when it was hit by a powerful wave. Henry Carter, who had been on duty at the time, had lost his nerve completely for several hours.

Carter had come down the ladder in such a panic that he had fallen the final four feet and landed in a heap on the floor. Edwards and Hatherley had themselves been surprised by the severity of the tremor that had caused several items to fall from their appointed places onto the floor. Both men were worried by it, but fortunately they had great confidence in the strength of the tower and were not afraid. Carter, on the other hand, had really taken fright. The second lurch, which followed about ten minutes after the first, reduced him to a blubbering, panic-stricken coward. It had taken all Hatherley's efforts, together with a good dose of Plymouth gin to calm him. Eventually he began to overcome his fear, but was still concerned about his safety and would have deserted the tower readily.

Hatherley, too, was most concerned, though he did his best not to show it for Carter's sake. His experience on the old wooden tower had given him much confidence, for he had already seen the worst that the ocean could do. Rudyerd's tower had been unnerving on occasions, and it too had trembled quite dramatically, but not as badly as they had experienced in Smeaton's tower. Hatherley was not a man to be frightened easily. He had almost lost his life on two previous occasions, besides spending the bulk of his years employed in dangerous situations. He had formed the conclusion that when his time was finally up he would have very little say in the matter, and there was thus no sense in being afraid in such situations. At the end of a third winter during which the tremors had been particularly bad, he was convinced that the problem was worsening. He had decided to tell the designer and engineer in the calmest way possible that all was not well. It had, however, been a difficult decision to make. How could he, a mere lighthouse keeper, deign to tell the world's greatest engineer that there was something wrong with his tower? Furthermore, he was not all that good at letter writing and it was proving to be a struggle to say what he really meant. After delaying the task for so long, he had finally overcome his reluctance to write. He must tell the truth - it was his duty. The letter need not be rude or insulting if he kept only to the facts of the matter. Surely the great engineer would be able to provide a simple solution to the problem Even to Hatherley's simple mind, it was obvious that, left unchecked, such a tremor must ultimately weaken the structure which had been built to last for ever. Hatherley was quite sure that there must be a fault in the tower. Equally, he was convinced that if Smeaton could allay his fears he would, in due course, get used to the vibrations. Other keepers might be greatly frightened by it in the same way that Carter had been. This was most undesirable for a number of reasons. Carter had been so incapacitated that Edwards had had to take over his duties for some time. Carter eventually overcame his worst fears, but remained jittery whenever the weather was bad. A great strain had been placed on the three of them. Indeed, it was a good thing that there were three of them on the lighthouse, for, with one man incapable of work, the other two were still able to cope. If there were only two keepers and one of them were ill it would be impossible to manage the lighthouse effectively. This had now been recognised by the lighthouse owners ever since poor Henry Hall's dreadful experience, and three keepers were now always assigned to a rock lighthouse. On numerous occasions Henry Hall had told Hatherley the appalling tale of the time he had been forced to live in Winstanley's tower with a corpse tied to the balcony lest he be accused of murder. The story was imprinted on Hatherley's mind. For John, however, nothing could surpass his own escape from the inferno that Rudyerd's tower had become on that December night seven years ago. He had been very lucky to survive. Poor Tom had been mentally destroyed and was now permanently committed to an institution. And as for poor old Henry Hall, he had died a grizzly death with a large piece of lead filling his stomach, so they said. Hatherley felt sorry for Henry. They had known each other well. Henry had been a keeper for a long time: the most stalwart of the new breed of watch-keepers. He had amazing stamina for a man of his age Hatherley reckoned that but for the fire Henry would have lived to be well over a hundred. What a ridiculous way to die!

'It is my humble duty to inform you of the effects of the sea upon the structure of your new lighthouse during winter storms.'

That was a good start to the letter. Hatherley was pleased with the grammar. What next? It had taken him almost half an hour to get this far. He needed a drink and stood up to put a kettle onto the range. Even the thought of refreshment must have provided him with inspiration, for having sat down again he found the next sentences easier. Perhaps it was the confidence acquired by his sound opening sentence, but it mattered little, for, by the time the kettle had begun to produce its cloud of scalding vapours, John had finished his letter and was searching for a stick of red wax with which to seal the message. It occurred to him that his pathetic letter, the scruffy, ink-smudged missive of which he was so pleased, might prove to be the saving grace of the lighthouse. If it were not sent, the problem might never be reported and the tower might collapse into the sea without warning. He felt proud. He had done his duty and the great pressure he had suffered in anticipation of the task had been removed.

John set aside his letter, took the kettle off the heat and, before pouring his hot refreshment, climbed the ladder into the lantern room to inspect the candles. All was well. They had been changed an hour before and were barely a quarter burned away. The twenty-four thin cream-coloured fire-sticks seemed so pathetic and futile in comparison to the efforts that had been expended to put them there. And when compared to the forces of energy that prevailed outside the lantern at that moment, the light energy they produced was immeasurably small. The night seemed even darker than before and through the roars of the wind John thought he could hear the shout of a man in distress. He was all too familiar with the various manifestations of human emotion during the middle watch. He made a strict habit never to drink either before or during a duty, but even so he frequently thought he could hear the shouts and screams of men going to their deaths, and the creaking of ships timbers under the force of the storms. Past experience told him that the noise he had heard was simply Mother Nature imposing her Reginal authority over her subjects. Man should always be aware of his position in the scheme of things. He was a fragile life form, which, like the candle flame burning feebly above his head, could be extinguished at the slightest whim of his Creator. Let him forever be in awe.

John had lived too close to the fulcrum of life and death to lose his respect for the elements. That had partly contributed to his motivation for the letter to Smeaton. Even the world's greatest engineer might have made an error in his estimation of the power of the universe. Hatherley marvelled at the similarity of the whining wind with the sound of the human voice. He had actually placed his foot on the rung of the ladder down to the kitchen when something inside his head made him think that just for once the sound was a little too realistic. He dismissed the idea as absurd and, after a brief hesitation, returned to the kitchen. Once the idea had entered his head that there might actually be someone outside the tower, he could not resist the urge to look outside and see. That was another peculiarity of the middle watch - a mixture of assumed bravado and disguised fear, which causes the watch-keeper to investigate even the slightest unaccountable noise. During the day he might not even have noticed it, and if he had, he would probably have dismissed it as trivial. But during the middle watch, every sound had to be analysed and, if unexplained, investigated. Thus, from the moment when John had first heard the wind make a noise like a voice shouting from the void, there was never any doubt that he would investigate to see if it were real. Common sense dictated that his imagination had played tricks with his consciousness. How could there be anyone outside? John could not rest. He had to find out if the noises were real or not, but he was afraid as he climbed the ladder to the lantern room once again. In such a God-forsaken place as the Eddystone reef during the middle watch fantasy outstripped reality. Could it be that the ghost of one of the countless drowned seaman had returned to punish the keepers by haunting them until eternity?

John's fear of the unknown was transformed into terror as he opened the door of the balcony. What was he going to find outside? The sudden draught caused four of the candles to blow out and the rest to burn furiously with streams of hot liquid wax running down into the holders. In a few seconds the door was closed behind him. The weather atop the eighty-foot high tower was severe. He gripped the steel handrails with all his strength and stared into the darkness and driving rain. He moved his grip, hand over hand, around the safety rail and inched his way carefully around the exterior of the lantern on the three-foot wide gallery that Smeaton had provided for cleaning the vital glass windows. He heard it again. He was certain that it was a shout from below. He could see nothing but the sound seemed to be coming from the vicinity of the exposed group of rocks that made up the centre of the three arms of the reef. The lighthouse had been built on the westerly group of rocks, and between the two groups was about twenty feet of angry sea that had been christened the 'Gut'. It was about two o' clock and the tide was at its lowest.

"Ahoy, there! Is there anybody below?" John bellowed at the top of his voice. The response was immediate, though indecipherable. There were men on the reef! "Hold on, I'm coming." Again, an incoherent reply was received, but in a tone which suggested great excitement. John cautiously, but quickly, returned to the gallery door and re-entered the lantern room. More candles blew out but he had no time to re-light them just yet. He almost fell down the ladders to the bedroom in his excitement to awaken his colleagues. Henry Carter was already awake, having heard John shouting from above.

" 'Ave you gawn out o' yer brains 'Atherley?" he grumbled. "Folks is tryin' to sleep down yer."

"Nay, George, folks is queuing up on the rocks to visit thee an' me... come on, quickly... get up and bring a lantern." John began to shake Henry Edwards who stalwartly resisted all efforts to waken him muttering, "Sod off, Carter, ye bugger, I paid fer 'er... she's mine... sod off I say..." It took several minutes to convey the urgency of the situation to the other keepers. Carter flatly refused to believe that there could be anybody on the rocks in such weather, whilst Edwards was in a foul mood with John for waking him up at a particularly bracing moment of his dream. Eventually, John's own mood suggested that they ought at least to see what was going on, by which time John had found himself a lantern and had begun the descent to the entrance door.

236

Unfortunately, the door was on the wrong side of the tower for him to simply look out and see the refugees. He would have to climb down onto the reef and circle the base of the tower to a point adjacent to the place where he guessed the shouts were coming from. He had the presence of mind not to leave the lighthouse until Carter arrived with a long length of rope. Even though it were low tide, only one devilish wave would be needed to sweep him into the cloven claws of death. One end of the rope was fastened around his chest with a bowline and the other to a solid fixture inside the tower.

With great care Hatherley climbed down onto the slimy rocks with a lantern in one hand and a second length of rope in the other. Despite the light from the lantern, his path was extremely treacherous for the rocks were very uneven and highly slippery. There was no shelter of any kind from the weather; the rain swept in from the southeast and made vision of any kind almost impossible, even with the lantern. Fortunately, it was not as cold as it might have been in early March and John had known the weather to be far worse than this. He heard more shouts and was barely able to make out a small group of men gathered on the very top of the centre reef. How on earth they came to be there was of great interest to John, but he had sense enough to know that information of that kind could be obtained in the comfort of the tower once the men had been brought to safety. In the meantime, the men had no access to the reef on which the lighthouse stood. Somehow, a means must be found to transport them across the twenty feet of raging sea that with monotonous rhythm beat its way into the 'Gut'.

"Stay where 'e be. Any folk hurt over yon?" shouted John. The men were mostly sprawled across the jagged rocks, all except for one young man who seemed much fitter than the rest and who did all the talking.

"No-one is injured, but there are four men here who are very tired and quite drunk," shouted the voice.

"Drunk! What the hell 're 'e doin' out there gettin' drunk!" John could hardly believe his ears. For a moment his head fell loose on his shoulders and nodded limply in disbelief. "What a bleddy silly place for a party!" he muttered.

"How can we get across this gap?" shouted the young man. "We had a boat, but it got smashed up on the rocks down there." He pointed away to a place which was consumed in the darkness, but which John knew to be the southern end of the reef on which they were marooned.

"Don't 'e go movin' now while I works out what to do." It was a stupid comment.

"Don't worry, mister, we're not going anywhere at present."

John remembered a stanchion that had been set into the centre reef by the builders. This formed part of the heavy lifting gear that had been necessary to get the huge stones out of the boat and onto the building site. "I knows. Move to your right, about thirty feet. 'E'll find a big metal post set into the rock. There's a ring in the top of 'un and if I 'eaves this line to 'e then 'e can come over on it."

237

John watched as the young man got down onto all fours so as not to stumble on the slippery rocks and made his way very gingerly towards the life-saving metal post. Though neither man could see their goal in the darkness, John had a very good idea of the geography of the reef, and by giving more directions was able to talk the survivor into finding it. Edwards arrived on the scene and the second lantern that he had brought shed a little more feeble orange light on the immediate vicinity. To their left was a man anxiously clutching the lightly rusted wrought-iron stanchion and awaiting fresh instructions. To their right was a small group of apparently exhausted men spread-eagled across the rocks like human flotsam. Behind them loomed the huge black shadow of the lighthouse that was their refuge, whilst all around waves crashed incessantly into the unyielding reef. Fortunately for all concerned they were not breaking over the top of the rocks, as they would have done at high tide. The whole scene was, however, being drenched with rain and sea spray and all those present were soaked to the skin.

John carefully made his way to the point nearest to where the youth was clutching his post. He heaved the line across whereupon it was made fast and Hatherley tied his own end to one of the iron rungs which led to the entrance door of the lighthouse. The rope was made as tight as possible.

"Right, now ye can cross, 'and over 'and," shouted John. Edwards was looking anxiously over John's shoulder.

"No, they'll never make it. I can do it, but they're too drunk - they'll fall off if they try," replied the youth.

"Drunk? What do 'e mean, drunk?" Edwards too was incredulous, and the tone of his voice achieved a pitch even John had not heard before. "They 'm gettin' pissed over there and we 'm over yer. Gimme that rope. I'm goin' over for a tot. Don't see as 'ow us cant get no invite."

John grasped Edwards by the arm and restrained him. He tried to bring the excitable keeper to his senses. "Don't be so bleddy silly 'Enry. Go into the tower and get more rope and a knife. We 'm goin' to 'ave to fix up a chair for 'em." John wiped the rain from his eyes and combed his hair back with his fingers. Edwards was not pleased but complied with John's orders.

"Bleddy 'ell, what next?" he muttered as he disappeared into the night.

"Get the rest of 'em to move over to where 'e be now," shouted Hatherley. "We'll get a chair fixed up for 'e."

While this was accomplished, John waited impatiently for Edwards to return. He was beginning to get very cold from being so wet and he shivered freely as he wondered where Edwards had got to. The men on the other reef must be in a bad way by now if he himself were suffering. Where the devil was Edwards? John was on the point of returning to the tower in search of Edwards when his colleague returned carrying an armful of gear.

" 'Ere's what 'e wanted," he said. "Carter fixed it all up for 'e when I told 'im."

"Good on yer, Carter," shouted John, pleased that a difficult part of the task had at last been done for him. The 'chair' that Carter had made took the form of a loop

238

of rope, designed to fit around a man's chest and under his arms. This loop was to be secured to a snap hook that, in turn, slid along the fixed line that they had already set up. All that was necessary now was to fix two more lines to the loop, one each to pull the chair in either direction above the snarling foam within the 'Gut'. Hatherley attached the chair to the line using the snap hook and then heaved another line to the survivor on the adjacent rocks.

It was not an easy task to get the chair properly fitted around a man who was almost unable to help himself, but the young man accomplished it and then lifted the first drunken sailor onto the line. Hatherley and Edwards took the strain on the pulling line. Though at first the man slid easily along the rope in his simple but cleverly constructed truss, there came a point in the middle of the sagging rope where the man was at his lowest height above the sea. From there on it was an uphill pull to bring him to the side of safety. Edwards and Hatherley needed all their strength to bring home the limp, semi-conscious body.

As each of the remaining three drunken men were fitted awkwardly into the chair, the two keepers, with much heaving and cursing, pulled them to safety across the 'Gut'. Finally, the young man himself was brought across the void in the magnificent fashion devised by Hatherley and Carter. Next, the fit men assisted those who could barely walk, by almost pushing them up the rungs of the ladder and into the safety of the tower. This, too, was accomplished by no small effort, but when at last all the survivors were inside the tower with the mighty gunmetal door closed firmly behind them, they were slowly ushered up the ladders into the warmth of the living accommodation. Nothing much could be done for the drunkards until they sobered up, so they were stripped of their wet clothing and tucked up in the keepers' own beds to sleep off their stupor.

The youth, on the other hand, was full of enthusiasm at having so miraculously reached a haven of peace and friendship. He sat close by the kitchen range where the radiant heat would soon restore his numbed limbs. Then, while Hatherley found him some dry clothes, Edwards made him a hot drink. The latter, having recovered from the urgency of the rescue, lapsed into his usual lackadaisical, spiritless drone.

"Now, you just tell I 'ow five bleddy idiots appear, as if from nowhere, miles out at sea and pissed as farts. I jus' got ta yer answer."

Hatherley re-appeared and handed over a towel and some fresh, dry clothing. Then, as the young man towelled himself dry, slipped his head and arms into a sea jersey of Hatherley's, and reminded Edwards that he was quite sober, he began to recount the incredible story to the three lighthouse keepers. They, in almost a hundred and twenty years between them, had heard almost every possible sea story that could be told. Not one had heard of drunken, shipwrecked sailors before, neither could they even begin to imagine how they came to be on the reef. Needless to say, the keepers were keen to find out. The youth told of his entry into the navy at the hands of the press gang and his travels in HMS *Resolution*. Edwards was impressed as he told of the events which caused him to fall into the sea and drift ashore into enemy territory.

Then, when it was told how he had been rescued and cared for by a beautiful French damsel and hidden away for months, gasps of envy slipped from the lips of the sexually deprived keepers. The subsequent imprisonment and the three years of hardships caused three glum faces of those sympathetic to the enforced separation from the luscious brunette. These expressions relaxed into smiles as the release from jail was related. The tale of putting to sea with a cargo of French brandy and liquor-starved English sailors made the listeners burst out laughing from the sheer folly of such a venture. Carter, who had a mouthful of hot tea at a crucial point in the story, nearly choked on his laughter. All proclaimed vociferously that they were not at all surprised the men took the ship over. The young man's adventures whilst trying to escape the wrath of the mutineers made them bite their lips, and the final shipwreck on the Hand's Deep concluded the whole tale on a note that the keepers found all too familiar. They could not help but be filled with admiration for a young man who had come through so much peril to be saved in such dramatic circumstances.

The story was fragmented, but compulsive listening. It was funny; it was serious. It was incredible, and tragically sad. The young man had been forced to leave his sweetheart behind, and Hatherley felt his spine chill in sympathy for the lad who must be just half his own age. The story of the shipwreck was very much like his own life, thirty-three years earlier.

When the young man had finished and sat quietly sipping his mug of tea, the keepers were still for several minutes whilst they assimilated the details of what was a remarkable tale. Suddenly Edwards piped up.

"What be called, bye?"

"William Knott; just call me Will."

Hatherley froze rigid. The name, even after thirty-three years, was as fresh in his mind as it had been then. Surely this must be a coincidence? Then he recalled the early part of the lad's story. Almost afraid to ask, he said, "Did 'e say 'e was from Dover?"

"Yes, I did."

"Where 'bouts exactly?"

"My home is in the South Foreland lighthouse. It's a…"

Before he could finish, Hatherley had leapt from his chair with a mighty shout and thrown his arms around the bemused boy.

"Welcome, Will, welcome. Thy father be called William too. He saved me life a long time since…"

Carter and Edwards gaped.

27 SAMUEL GRAVES - 2

As the heavy, oak, front door of Thanckes House was opened by a servant, a sudden gust of early morning cold March air lifted Captain Samuel Graves' cap, which he'd only lightly placed upon his head. He reacted quickly to prevent it blowing off, and then turned to bid farewell to his great-niece Matilda.

"Stay inside in the warm, my dear, you might easily catch a chill," he advised the attractively dressed teenage maiden. "Thank your father for his kind hospitality. It has been a delightful stay." He quickly reached for Matilda's hand and kissed the back of it courteously. A matter of feet away from the entrance porch, a carriage and driver awaited their passenger. A second servant carried three pieces of hand luggage past the elderly sea captain and his the bags on a special rack at the rear of the carriage. "Goodbye, my dear. It has been so nice to see you again."

"Goodbye, Uncle Samuel. Do come and see us again soon. Have a safe journey."

The Captain wasted no time in climbing into the carriage and the mansion door closed with a firm thud as he settled into his seat. He looked to his left and briefly admired the panoramic view before him. The land in front of the house fell gently away to the banks of the river Hamoaze, a composite estuary into which the rivers Tamar, Tavy and Lynher all flowed. It was the Hamoaze that had so impressed William of Orange that he'd commanded the setting up of a naval dockyard for his warships. Graves' view of the scene a hundred and fifty years later bore witness to the wisdom of the decision. There, on the other bank and to the south of where Graves was sitting, a busy port had sprung up and extended along a full mile of riverbank. Its wharves, docks and moorings were all occupied with the assembled forces of seven years of naval warfare. The crewmen of the scores of ships were, even at this early hour of the morning, busying about their individually trivial and collectively urgent tasks with an efficiency found only in a disciplined service.

The carriage driver issued a short, sharp command to the obedient mare that instantly, but smoothly, pulled away from the front of Thanckes House. Then, instead of turning to the right, which path would have led towards the village of Torpoint, the driver deliberately steered his vehicle to the left along a gently downward sloping, well-tended gravel drive towards the river. For almost three hundred yards the carriage squeaked and jolted its way through the woodland of Thanckes Park, as it transported its passenger to rendezvous with a waiting longboat at Yonderberry Point.

Thanckes House was a large stone-built castellated dwelling of about sixty rooms. From a commanding position atop a wooded promontory, which had become known as Thanckes Park, it was master of superb views in all directions. In the northeast lay the perennially dark uplands of Dartmoor, whilst Bodmin moor was to the northwest and the Rame peninsula to the south. The immediate vicinity, however, was dominated by the expanse of grey, motionless river.

The crossing of the Hamoaze estuary had always been a problem for travellers in southern Devon and Cornwall, who had been diverted as far north as Tavistock to achieve their aim. A boat crossing had been available for use by foot passengers between Devonport and the Cornish bank, but it was during the middle part of the eighteenth century that popular demand was finally satisfied and a floating bridge established between the two counties. This allowed passage of the vehicular through-traffic that was becoming increasingly prolific. The Devon side of the Hamoaze was taken up with the towns of Plymouth, Devonport and Stonehouse.

Plymouth was a fishing town and fortress; Stonehouse was a busy garrison town. Devonport was centred almost exclusively on the Royal Dockyard. Each had a population of several thousands. On the Cornish side, Torpoint was but a tiny hamlet home for two hundred people. The floating bridge at once became Torpoint's greatest asset and created not only instant growth, but an ever increasing dependence on the Devon bank for its livelihood.

Thanckes House had come into the possession of the Graves family when Samuel Graves' brother, whilst in command of HMS *Dulwich*, visited Devonport in 1716. He fell in love with Mary Warne, a rather ugly but well-endowed daughter of a local landowner who was also Superintendent of the King's brew house at Insworke near Millbrook. Even so, it was a love of the heart rather than the wealth of which each partner had plenty. Mr Warne was so pleased when the young Graves announced his intention to marry Mary, that he promised that they should have Thanckes as a wedding present. It was duly presented to the newlyweds, Mary and Thomas Graves, on their wedding day in that year. The arrangement was ideal, both for Mary, the local girl with family and friends nearby, and for Thomas, the seafarer with ships regularly in Devonport. Unfortunately, their union was tragically ended after just two years by Mary's death at the age of twenty-four. Thanckes, however, was Thomas's and it was by Elizabeth Budgel, his second wife, that his children were born members of the Cornish gentlefolk.

During the years that passed, Samuel became a habitual visitor to Thanckes, and, even when his brother died in 1756 and left the estate to his eldest son, also Thomas, Samuel continued to pay regular calls on his relatives. This was partly for mercenary reasons, one of which was his great-niece Matilda, in whom Samuel delighted. The other more practical reason was the convenient location of the house adjacent to the usual moorings midstream in the Hamoaze. There could be no better accommodation ashore for a naval Captain than Thanckes. So busy was the dockyard by 1740, that it was usual for there to be no berths available alongside the wharves. Thus a number of heavy mooring buoys had been laid in the river. This in itself resulted in a frenetic stream of small Devon craft between the moored warships and their supply depots in the dockyard. One of these small craft was the Captain's longboat, which had uniquely steered a course towards the landing stage on the Cornish side of the river at Yonderberry Point.

The Captain's carriage drew to a halt at the landing platform and the crew of the longboat sat smartly to attention. The Bosun greeted his Captain with a salute.

"Good morning, Mister Spicer... a fresh wind today... that will speed us along our way to Chatham."

"Indeed, sir. All supplies are on board. The ship awaits your sailing orders."

"Good," said Graves, stepping into the boat and taking his seat at the after end. "Then let us be on our way."

The longboat was cast off and to the precise orders of the Bosun the crew dipped and pulled their oars in a rigorously rehearsed fashion that left no room for error on the part of a single man. The south-easterly wind caused them to work hard, for they were heading precisely against it, but the short distance to the *Duke*, which lay majestically in the river about a quarter of a mile downstream, was covered comfortably by the professional oarsmen.

The *Duke* was on her way back to Chatham to pay off at the end of a long, hard campaign against the French and the rebels in the New Continent. Hostilities had ceased only a matter of weeks earlier, but their Lordships had deemed that the services of the *Duke* were no longer required. It seemed almost an insult to a ship which had seen so much of the action over the seven years of war, but that was the way of the Navy. It was too costly for the King's purse to retain heavily manned warships when there was no war. A number of ships would always be kept to form the nucleus of the nation's defences in peacetime, but wartime strength could never be justified in the absence of an enemy.

Samuel Graves and his crew had come to the end of a long winter deployed along the eastern seaboard of the New World in America. Their landfall in old England had not come too soon and Captain Graves had permitted himself the luxury of a courtesy call on the Port Admiral at Devonport, as well as the opportunity to re-store for the last leg of the journey to Chatham. The fact that he'd also been able to spend two nights at Thanckes was an added luxury allowed only to himself, for his men had, of necessity, remained on board the ship where they had impatiently but obediently awaited their chance to step ashore after so long at sea.

Graves pulled his cap even tighter onto his head and braced himself against the chilling southeasterly that swept straight into his face. He glanced up at the sky; it looked as if it would rain soon. The weather had been vigorous for most of the night. From the comfort of his bed he'd lain awake and listened to the clatter of the driving rain of the windowpanes. He'd always slept in a room at the front of Thanckes House from where he could look out at the river. Usually this was the sheltered side, for the prevailing winds in these parts almost always were from the southwest. Last night, however, had been different and the noise had kept him awake for some time. He thought how strange it was that the windy, wet weather should keep him from his slumbers - he who had known so many storms at sea and never once been bothered by any of them. He'd always had the utmost confidence in his ships and his men: why should he be afraid? Last night, however, the rain had kept him awake because he was in a new situation. The noise of the wind, though far less than the gales he'd been used to at sea, had quite a different texture as it percolated through a thousand leafless trees to rattle the windows and loosen the roof slates. As he lay, warm in bed beneath the crushing weight of sheet, four blankets, eiderdown and counterpane, the warship captain had felt that the weather outside was trying to enter the house like some malevolent burglar, testing every window catch, rattling every door latch, searching diligently for the one weak link in the house's defences which, when broken, would allow in the intruder in all his fury. Strangely, Graves had not for a moment thought about those at sea in such weather. He did briefly consider the security of his ship's moorings, but in an instant had dismissed any misgivings he might have had. This was no storm - just a bit of rough weather. It had, however, been sufficient to prevent him from sleeping and he was not pleased.

Graves could not restrain a yawn as he pondered his loss of sleep and watched the *Duke* draw ever closer. The longboat came alongside just as the rain commenced. Samuel Graves took no notice of the damping droplets as he was piped aboard his ship at precisely thirty minutes after eight o'clock.

The tide was running higher than usual as the three-masted ship-of-the-line cast off her moorings and set sail for the journey through Plymouth Sound to the English Channel. The red and white paying off pennant was broken just as the mooring cable was slipped and the flag unfurled from the masthead like a paper streamer. It was the last time that Devonport's dockyard would see the bold lines of the *Duke* in the predictable future. The current public opinion was that there would be a lasting peace; ships such as the *Duke* would be required no more. Having served her nation well, she would soon be consigned to a life of slow decay, a ghost ship haunting the upper reaches of the Medway with her glorious memories of battles past. Abandoned and forgotten by her crew, her employers and the nation, the stout wooden lady headed home to retirement and a lingering death.

As she slid silently past Admiralty House at Mount Wise, her immaculately polished cannon fired thirteen guns in salute to the flag. Nine were returned for Captain Graves. Slowly, she glided past the landmarks of Devonport for the last time; the luscious wooded slopes of the Edgcumb estate and Rame on the right, the vast victualling storehouse with its grey, prison-like frontage on the left. Behind lay the Stonehouse garrison and its associated housing. Next came the basin and workyard at Millbay, which Smeaton had used for preparation and dispatch of the stone for his marvellous lighthouse. From the foreshore and promenade of the Hoe small groups of people gathered to wave at the beautiful dancer as she gambolled her intricate routine between the mainland and the tiny wooded St. Nicholas Island. After a workmanlike turn to starboard across the wind, the well-disciplined sailors trimmed her sails for the passage along the narrow channel that, invisibly, led the way out to sea.

To the Captain, the excitement was now over. Once amid the vast expanse of water the ship required little handling and there was a concomitant reduction in the orders emanating from the quarterdeck. Under normal circumstances Samuel Graves would have been able to retire to his cabin, but on this occasion an unexpected turn of events was to unfold. As the *Duke* began to bear off to the east for her passage to Chatham a vigilant lookout espied something unusual.

"Sir, the Eddystone lighthouse is flying a distress signal," he shouted to his Captain. The latter promptly focused his telescope upon the tower where, partly obscured by the veil of misty rain that continued to fall, Graves was able to make out the inverted Union Flag.

"Helmsman, steer two one zero."

The course would take *Duke* to the Eddystone Rocks. Graves glanced at his First Lieutenant who was also studying the flag.

"Let us hope that it is not an error of ignorance on their part," he commented. He would be very annoyed if the deviation to his schedule proved to be a false alarm.

"Aye, sir, but if I may say so, I think that it is a genuine distress call. The keepers are all seamen and know the significance of what they have done," he observed.

As the new course took them closer to the dangerous rocks, which had been the scene of so many disasters in the past, the sizeable waves were almost on the beam and *Duke* rolled heavily in their wake. To professional seamen, however, it was not sufficient to cause concern, although Captain Graves wondered about the nature of the distress. Whatever the problem it would be necessary to send the longboat to the lighthouse and he decided that one of his officers, Lieutenant Rowles, should be sent to investigate. He considered with care how he would manoeuvre the ship when once he'd drawn within the range necessary for the ship's boat to approach the rocks. Both swell and waves were large enough to make the boat's journey hazardous, and by careful positioning of the *Duke*, Graves could greatly assist the boat's crew. Graves was not of the South Devon coast, however. He could navigate the waters as well as any other seaman, but to approach such a dangerous reef as the Eddystone he would need specialist knowledge. Graves was not too proud to ask for expert advice when he needed it, and this was such an occasion. He shouted for the bosun; the response was instant.

"Bosun, I intend to send the longboat to land on the Eddystone. You are a local man. What is the best approach?"

"From the south-west, sir. There is a narrow channel between the main branches of the rocks. It will be sheltered enough in this sea for the men to land."

"Are there any other hazards in the vicinity of the reef, let us say, to within a cable on that side?"

"For the *Duke*, sir?" queried the trusted seaman.

"Aye."

"None, sir."

"Excellent. Thank you for your advice, Bosun." Satisfied with his information, Graves had confirmed his plan. As *Duke* approached from the north-west, he amended the heading slightly, in order to take her around the rocks on the eastern side so that he could turn in close to where the Bosun had suggested. Then he summoned the officer who was to take charge of the landing party.

"Lieutenant Rowles."

"Sir."

"Take the longboat and six good men. Find out what the problem is in the lighthouse. I will lay off on the southwestern side at about a cable. Take the Bosun with you - he knows the reef well and will show you the best direction of approach."

"Aye, aye, sir."

"And you had better arm the men, just in case. We do not know what is wrong inside so it is wise to exercise caution."

245

"Aye, aye, sir." Rowles was a young officer for whom Graves had high hopes. Graves had served with Rowles' father many years earlier and, although their ways had parted soon afterwards, Graves had developed a great bond of friendship with Rowles senior. When the young Lieutenant had been appointed to the *Duke* Graves had been delighted to find the son a keener, fitter and more able officer even than his father had been. Graves judged that the young man would, without doubt, rise to high rank in due course. In the meantime he would need plenty of experience in as many different situations as possible and this was just such an opportunity.

As the *Duke* made headway into position the longboat was made ready and its crew prepared themselves for the short but demanding journey to the rocks. Meanwhile, the presence of the *Duke* in the Channel had long ago been noticed from within the lofty observation gallery of Smeaton's tower. The occupants of the lighthouse had streamed out onto the balcony and waved furiously to attract the attention of the seamen in case their distress signal had failed to do so. However, when it had become apparent that the unidentified Royal Navy vessel had altered course and was bearing down upon the reef, they contented themselves with merely observing the arrival of the ship which would, with luck, release them from the confines of their overcrowded lighthouse. The drunkards had sobered up and, with sore heads and loose bowels, they chose to loll about inside the tower to nurse their finely balanced constitutions. In the cold light of day they'd discussed their predicament at length among themselves and all bitterly regretted their behaviour aboard the *Mistral*. They'd resigned themselves to being brought to justice for their crimes and were thoroughly miserable human beings at the thought of further lengthy prison sentences, which, they felt sure, would ensue their impending arrest by the Navy.

Will Knott and John Hatherley watched from the balcony as the *Duke* hove to, about two hundred yards from the reef. Then, as they watched the dispatch of the longboat and the smooth, professional approach of the small boat to the hideously dangerous rocks on which they stood, Will realised that he and John had become firm friends in the duration of just a few hours. The remarkable coincidence that had brought them together seemed to have cemented an invisible bond between them. To Will, it was as if he'd met a long-lost uncle. They seemed to have so much in common - so much to talk about. Will had heard so many of his father's stories about John that he felt as if he'd known John for a very long time. Since that first hearing of the wreck of the *Prosperity* Will had formed a mental image in his impressionable juvenile imagination which had remained with him throughout each subsequent retelling of the narrative. In Will's experience, he found that when this happened, the real person always looked very different from his imaginary counterpart. In this case, Will was amazed to find that John was an accurate representation of the character he'd nurtured in his sub-conscious mind for so many years, older perhaps, but, in the main, uncannily similar.

John, felt the same way. It was as if William senior had been preserved in the passage of time by some magical fountain of youth and, without warning, transported to the Eddystone. The son was an image of his father as John remembered him thirty-three years before. All this had contributed to the mutual feelings of trust and camaraderie that seemed to exist between them from the moment they realised each other's identity. Their conversations had continued until the first strains of morning became hard daylight. Neither of them had slept that night. Will, in any case, would have found it hard to sleep. His mind had been so active after the events of the past few days that he'd been only too pleased to sit up and chat to his new 'uncle' whilst the other survivors slept off their drunkenness. Furthermore, with so many bodies aboard the lighthouse all the beds had been filled. Will could not have slept, except in a most uncomfortable posture on the cold limestone floors of the tower. He'd been quite content to spend the hours in conversation with John. Will's father had been so impressed with John's stories about lighthouses and keepers and his desire to be a keeper that William had taken up the career for himself. John's influence on William had been responsible, in part, for Will's happy and contented upbringing at the South Foreland lighthouse. Will had a lot to thank John for. Both William and John now spent their working lives in charge of the lights at their respective lighthouses. Will loved the life also and during the many months he'd spent away from home he'd yearned more and more to follow his father's lead. Given the opportunity, Will would gladly be a keeper too, but first he must return home…

Will watched the entry of the *Duke's* longboat into the Gut and prayed that this would be the start of the last leg of his journey home. Then, he and John left the balcony and hastily descended the levels of the lighthouse until they reached the entrance door. There they met Carter and Edwards who had just opened the gunmetal door and were exiting the tower to greet the visitors. The four men followed each other out onto the wet, slippery granite and passed around the base of the tower until they could see the boat. Already, under the safe and expert guidance of the ship's bosun, it had guided into the foaming waters of the Gut and come alongside the rocks. The officer was just jumping onto the infamous reef as Hatherley approached him. John found himself being covered by half a dozen pistol barrels. He should not have been surprised, for the Navy were not to know the circumstances of the distress and were simply exercising due caution. John, however, anxiously requested the officer to instruct the men that they had no need for their weapons. Lieutenant Rowles was not prepared to accept the word of someone whom he did not know and therefore could not trust. With his own weapon levelled at the keepers, he advanced.

"What is the problem here?" he demanded. Will decided to take upon himself the task of spokesman. After all, it was because of him that all this was necessary.

"There is no problem, sir. I and four other Englishmen were shipwrecked last night on the rock they call Hand's Deep. We are prisoners-of-war from France and we were being brought back to England on board a French merchantman when she struck the rocks in the rough weather last night. We are the only survivors. We were lucky enough to escape in the ship's boat and make it here to the lighthouse where the keepers have been very kind to us. They have looked after us for the night and now we would like to be allowed to return to our families."

"What is your name?" asked the officer, still not entirely at ease with the situation.

"William Knott, sir. These gentlemen are the keepers and my four companions are inside the tower where they are resting after their ordeal." Lieutenant Rowles thought to himself for a minute and then dropped his weapon to his side.

"Very well," he said in a more relaxed tone, "go and summon your friends. You may return with me to HMS *Duke* where we will investigate this more fully. I am sure that my Captain will be happy to take you to Chatham which is our next port of call." Will could hardly restrain a beaming smile as he heard the Lieutenant mention Chatham.

"Aye, aye, sir," he replied and quickly turned on his heel to fetch the others. Hatherley followed Will into the tower, leaving his colleagues to spectate from their chosen position on the rocks. As Hatherley caught up with Will in the storeroom he questioned his friend.

"So thee's not going to run 'em in then?" Will knew who John was referring to. They had been on his mind for hours, though he'd said nothing.

"No, I can't. There's only one of me and four of them. It's easier all round if we are simply shipwrecked sailors. There are no witnesses to the events on *Mistral*. Let's leave things uncomplicated. I've no grudge against them. We all want to go home to our families. I think this is the best way of doing that."

"Thee 's right," said John, nodding his head in agreement. "Take care and say 'Hello' to thy father for me. I always wanted to visit South Foreland again, but... well, there's no excuses really, I just never was there."

"I know," concurred Will. "Don't worry, he'll be so pleased when I tell him what has happened. I wouldn't be here today if it weren't for your rescue last night."

" 't was my repayment of a long outstanding debt, Will, the most rewarding I ever done in my life. Goodbye, Will." He embraced Will like a son.

"Au revoir," said Will instinctively.

"Eh?" John did not understand. "Sorry, Will, what did thee say?" Will flicked his eyes up and laughed as he realised what he'd said.

"Sorry, I didn't think. The French don't say goodbye. It means, until we meet again," explained Will.

"What a bloody good idea," exclaimed John. "That's the only sensible thing I've ever heard about the Frogs."

28 FINALE

The voyage from Plymouth the Chatham on board HMS *Duke* was, for Will, a marked contrast to the one that he had made in the opposite direction four years earlier. Then, he had been an inexperienced youth who had rashly signed away his civilian freedom in the mistaken belief that he was asserting some form of independence to his family. His naval career had started very badly however, and as he sailed west he had been desperately unhappy. Now, he was a mature seaman who had fought for his country, languished in prison and come through a score of adventures. But most important of all, he had formed a relationship with a woman. When he had left Chatham on that miserable day in 1759, Will had not known what it was like to be in love, and had very little idea about sex. Isabelle had changed everything. She had brought about a complete reconstruction of his emotions and his ambitions, and although his desire to return home to his family was great, the desire to be with Isabelle far outweighed any other. It was an intense ache that seemed to emanate from deep within his chest, and whenever he remembered that precious time in the jailer's apartment when he had first experienced intimate contact with the soft white flesh of his beloved, the heartache within him became so unbearable that it induced a feeling of nausea. His whole body was pining for the company of the only human being in the world who could satisfy his desires. Yet his love for his family was in some way different. They would always be his family and that love that existed between Will, his parents and his brothers and sisters, was as sure and as constant as the tides. But the love of Isabelle was much more intense and worryingly fragile. He had no doubt whatever that he would love her until he died, but how could he be sure that Isabelle would do the same? At any time she might meet a young French beau, perhaps a wealthy son of a gentleman who would sweep her off her feet and marry her before Will had the chance to claim her for his own. Then she would be lost to him forever; the rest of his life would be spent in spiritual ruins. He would never be able to rest until she was his wife, and at present he was not able to even guess when he might be able to return to France for her. Perhaps his family would even refuse to allow him to go?

The uncertainties of his future detracted from what should have been a joyous homecoming for Will, but he still enjoyed himself and eagerly awaited the moment when he could set eyes on his lighthouse home once more. Will and his four companions were not idle passengers. They were made to work their passage, and, in addition, Captain Graves was not prepared to let the matter of their shipwreck go without investigation. He instructed Lieutenant Rowles to delve fully into all aspects of the case before the ship arrived in Chatham. Even then, when the ship had berthed in a dockyard which was crammed full of redundant warships, Will was not allowed to leave the ship until an official report had been rendered to the authorities. Furthermore, Graves ordered that a complete check be made to ascertain whether any of his unexpected passengers were wanted men. Fortunately for Will, it transpired that he was not being sought by the Navy for past, unprosecuted crimes. Even though he knew that he had not committed any, it had occurred to him on more than one occasion that he might be listed as a deserter from the *Resolution*. His shipmates had obviously conveyed the true facts of the incident and the Navy therefore believed him to be innocent. It did not enter his mind, however, that the Service might believe that he had been drowned. This, indeed, was the real reason why there was no mention of Will on any of the official wanted lists which Graves consulted before finally releasing him a week after the return to Chatham.

249

It was a two-day journey to St. Margaret's. Will walked the majority of the distance, but on several occasions he was able to gain welcome relief for his feet by riding on a cart for a mile or two. In one case a particularly patriotic farmer, who was delighted to offer food and shelter for the night for a returning war hero, befriended him. So it was not until late in the afternoon of the second day that Will finally directed his feet along the main street of the village that was his home. There was very little activity. He saw only two faces that he recognised, and then only from a distance, so that no-one was aware of the return of the long-lost Knott. As he turned the corner of the churchyard to take the track to the lighthouse he found himself running as fast as his sore feet would allow, but he was unfit after the years in prison and soon he panted vigorously. He slowed to a fast walking pace, his heart beating out a noisy rhythm that reverberated in his eardrums. He told himself that there was little point in arriving home so out of breath that he could not speak. He had waited years for this moment; a little longer did not matter. The lighthouse grew larger as he approached. It had not changed at all and was exactly as he remembered it. There was no sign of his brothers and sisters, but they would be much older now and no longer playing games within earshot of their mother.

Elizabeth had her back to Will as he opened the door of the cottage and took a step into the relative gloom of the living room. Disturbed by the noise of the latch, she turned, half expecting to see one of the children returning from a fishing trip. The sight of Will was a great shock to her. She cried out and clutched her breast.

"Oh, Lord save us, it can't be true?"

"Hello, mother," said Will, crossing the room with his arms outstretched. Elizabeth needed no invitation to greet her son. She burst into tears of joy and incredulity as she flung herself into his embrace. Together they hugged and danced around the room as Will too succumbed to the emotion of the moment and cried like a baby.

"We thought you were dead, Will! Our prayers have been answered. Oh, Lord, what a surprise!" She could hardly get the words out between the sobs.

"I'm fine, mother, just fine. I've missed you all so much," said Will, pulling himself together. "Where's father?"

"Need you ask?" replied Elizabeth. She raised her eyes to indicate silently that William was in the lighthouse. Will kissed her cheek with an intensity he had never used before, except on Isabelle. Then he ran up the steps of the tower to where his father was preparing the fire for the approaching evening. There, a demonstration of love and amazement similar to that with Elizabeth was performed.

"Son, I didn't want you to go like that," said William, brushing away the tears from his cheeks. "I blamed myself for all that happened, and when they said you were dead I wanted to kill myself. It was only the thought of your mother and the kids struggling to survive that stopped me doing it. I'm sorry for it all, Will. It was all my fault."

"I'm sorry too, dad. I should have had more courage to come back and face you. I shouldn't have run off like I did. And Lizzie? How is she?"

250

William smiled contentedly and rubbed his eyes. "She's fine, she really is married now with a little son. They come over here quite regularly."

Will realised how foolish he had been. Family arguments never last long, no matter how serious they appear at the time. As a result of his impulsive act he had caused his family four years of anguish. "Who told you that I was dead?" he asked his mother, who was just climbing the last of the stairs to join them in the lantern room.

"It was the vicar. He had received a letter from a friend of yours, Jacob Evans." She put her arm around her son's waist in her delight to have him home again. "The letter said that you had got into a fight with John Jennings and that you fell over the side of the ship and were drowned. I refused to believe it, but we never heard any more from you, and I suppose that deep down in my heart I thought that it must be true." She clutched him tightly to prove that he really was flesh and bone rather than a figment of her imagination. William reached out for his son's hand and held it tightly.

"It's wonderful to have you back, son. We can't believe it's really you, but we thank God for your safety. Now let's go downstairs and sit in comfort. We've so much to ask you. It'll take months to find out the answers."

William was not far wrong in his estimation. It was in fact weeks before all of his son's adventures had been described in full to his excited family. The younger members wanted to hear every detail, often more than once. To have a real war hero in their midst was the most exciting thing to happen to them since George Goldsack's horse had bolted and killed the youngest of the Pilcher children outside the *Green Man*. Lizzie, too, was spellbound to hear of Will's exploits, but she was far more interested in Isabelle and how Will was going to get back to France to see her again. Lizzie was anxious to help Will in any way that she could but she was concerned that if Will left again so soon after returning 'from the grave' their parents would take it very badly. She spoke frankly to Will about the matter and expressed her doubts about the method by which Will was going to travel such a distance, but she succeeded only in depressing her brother to a considerable degree. Will, despite being desperately in love, was able to appreciate the logic of his sister's arguments. When once the novelty of being at home had worn off, he spent several weeks pacing the cliff-tops, deeply depressed and convinced that he was never going to see Isabelle again. His parents, unable to offer any advice or assistance, soon noticed his problems. They were not well off and there was no question of money being available for such a journey. Furthermore, they were not in the slightest bit happy with the idea of their son leaving home forever to live in France. Will told them that he would marry Isabelle and bring her back to Kent to live, but he knew that he would have enough difficulty getting to France and that there was no hope of completing a return journey as well. William and Elizabeth tried to discourage his ambitions in the hope that perhaps time would heal the wounds of separation: either his passions would cool off or he would fall in love with a more available local girl. On several occasions they attempted to cheer their son up by arranging for him to be in the company of an attractive young lady, but Will was not to be swayed from his devotion to his lady from France.

It was about seven weeks after the homecoming that matters finally came to a head. Will had been particularly depressed and had taken off to his sister's house at East Langdon to seek comfort from her caring, feminine attentions. It was dusk when he arrived home and without bothering to go into the cottage he climbed the tower to speak to his father. He knew that William would be engaged in lighting the fire at this time, but he had made up his mind that he was going to attempt the journey to France and he had to tell his father while his determination was at its greatest. It would be a difficult thing to say, but he was old enough to make his own decisions and he felt sure that his father would respect him for it. He did not want to leave his family so soon after returning home, but he could not wait any longer. His love was burning all other thoughts from his mind. He could think of nothing other than to be with Isabelle. Surely his father could appreciate that?

When Will arrived in the lantern room, William was setting light to the fire and applying the bellows to assist the combustion process. Will did not wish to broach the subject just at that moment for his father was busy and would not want to discuss such important topics. Instead, he engaged his father in small talk, awaiting his chance. It was, however, William who initiated the subject that Will was so anxious to discuss. As the fire caught up and a bright light was cast in their faces, William rose to his full height and took a deep breath. He mopped several beads of sweat from his brow.

"Son, I want to have a talk to you about Isabelle." Will became agitated. He wanted so much to blurt out what had been spinning around in his mind for hours but his father had begun; Will must at least hear what he had to say. Perhaps he'd had an idea that would help Will get back to Isabelle. "Your mother and I have talked for a long time about you, son. We don't like to see you so miserable. Now, we've thought of every possible way in which we might be able to help you and we can really only come up with one answer," Will was excited, his heart beating quickly. He looked nervously around the lantern room. "We really don't think that this idea of yours is a good one, Will. It is so impractical. It's not just the travel, though heaven alone knows how you'd manage that. No, what happens when you get there? Will you bring her home again? I don't think so - it will be difficult enough for you to get there without a return journey for both of you. You would have to remain in France and we would never see you again. And what about work? What will you do? How will you support her? Where will you live? There are so many questions that cannot be answered."

Will was speechless. He stared into the flickering flames and hardly believed the messages of his ears.

"Then, of course, there is one other unanswerable question - will she still be free to marry you?"

"Of course she will!" The young man was indignant.

"But you don't know that, do you? Look at Lizzie, your own sister. She thought she was in love with Edward Gibbon and when she found that she couldn't marry him she fell in love again and married just weeks afterwards. How do you know that Isabelle will not do the same?"

252

"Father, I know that she will wait until I return, she promised me." Will was nearly in tears. "She waited for me while I was in prison for three years." he reasoned.

"Yes, but you were a lot closer to her then. You might never be able to get back to France. She must realise that."

Will was silent and wiped a tear from the corner of his eye. Suddenly his resolve which had been built up during the day spent at Lizzie's had melted away in five minutes discussion with his father. William was consoling.

"Look, son, as I said, your mother and I have had a very long talk about you. We both know that you will be just as happy if you marry a local girl. We want you to give our idea a try - for our sake. Now we've invited a pretty young girl to tea this evening in the hope that you might talk to her and perhaps take her walking afterwards. We know you'll like her if you will only give it a chance."

Will was confused. He knew that his parents were acting with the best of intentions. They wanted him to be happily married like his sister. He understood all the arguments his father had put forward, and could not disagree with any of them, but all he could think about was Isabelle.

"She's here now, Will. Come down and talk to her, please. You'll like her... I know you will. I know that she approves of you too by her reaction when I invited her to tea. What do you say, then?"

His father was very persuasive. Will could not be angry or uncooperative. Almost automatically, Will found his feet carrying him down the stairs to the foot of the tower. His father was behind him, encouraging him lest he change his mind. As Will approached the cottage door he began to have second thoughts. What about Isabelle? How would she feel if she knew he were entertaining ladies to tea? William almost pushed him through the door of the cottage. Will wondered if she would be as pretty as his father had said. He stood in the doorway and for a few seconds his eyes were insensitive to the low level of light within and he could not recognise the occupants of the living room. Before he had time to cross the threshold a feminine form flung herself across the room and clutched his neck tightly. Will was stunned as the lady showered him with kisses - his face, his neck, his eyes - all moistened by the soft lips of a lady. Something was familiar. The perfume, the passion, the dark hair?

It was Isabelle.

So surprised was he that she ceased her assault to ask why he was not embracing her also. The sight of her dark face sent his spine tingling with delight. Then it was his turn to smother his affections on his loved one. He held her so tightly she could scarcely breathe, but she did not attempt to break his grip. He swept her off her feet and whirled her around the room, kissing her vigorously as he did so. Isabelle's response dispelled any doubts he might ever have had about the depth of her love for him. Will was spellbound. The warmth of her body through her clothing, her pulsing breast, the touch of her skin were unlike any other experience - except for that wonderful hour in the jailer's room. Will felt that he should be dreaming: minutes before he had been in the depths of despair and now he was happier than he had ever been before. How was it possible? He realised that someone was clapping.

"Bravo! Vive l'amour." A voice, which Will did not recognise, came from the corner of the room. This person, whoever he was, was applauding the love-scene. Will had forgotten that people were watching and became suddenly embarrassed at his public display.

"Perhaps we should leave the room, Elizabeth?" That was Will's father. Will released his grip on Isabelle to find that he had been performing his amorous antics in front of his whole family. His mother and father, even his brothers and sister, all looked on smiling. But there was a stranger present. He was extremely well dressed and Will had no idea who he might be. For a moment he was not really interested anyway, for all that mattered was that he was reunited with his dearest. His blushing was matched only by the nervousness in his voice.

"I'm sorry everybody... I just got carried away... I can't believe it." Still incredulous, he found a smile rather difficult and preferred to hide his embarrassment by gazing into Isabelle's eyes in disbelief. Suddenly he remembered his discussion in the lantern room of the lighthouse only minutes ago.

"Dad! That was rotten trick you played on me," he said severely, to which everyone burst out laughing. Will's frown finally melted into a beaming smile once more - something that had not been seen on his face for a considerable time. "What's going on? Everyone seems to know except me," he complained jocularly, whilst hugging Isabelle yet again.

"The joke was my idea, son," explained William.

"I'm sorry, but it was all in good fun. I knew you wouldn't mind when you discovered the truth. Isabelle, my dear, you'd better tell him your story before he bursts!"

"Mon cher, before I begin, let me introduce you to Monsieur d'Arranda." She courteously introduced Will to the stranger who rose to shake Will warmly by the hand. "Monsieur d'Arranda is from Paris. He is the kind gentleman who you must thank for my presence here today. It is a long story, shall we sit down?" The younger children found stools for themselves and gave up seats for the couple to sit close together.

"After you had gone - I think it was about two weeks - I was visited by this kind gentleman who asked about you. In fact, he asked me a very large number of questions, but he was most interested in your friend Jennings…"

"He's no friend of mine, love," interrupted Will.

"I'm sorry, I didn't mean it like that, mon cher. Oh my English is not so good…" Isabelle shook her head.

"Nonsense, your English is excellent," asserted William. "Carry on, please. Will, be quiet."

"Well, Monsieur d'Arranda was most anxious to trace this man Jennings. You see, the evil man had murdered Monsieur d'Arranda's wife three years ago." Suddenly the people gathered in the tiny room became still and all sign of the smiles disappeared.

"I'm so sorry, Monsieur… mais j'ai oublie. Parlez-vous Anglais Monsieur?" asked Will politely. He received a courteous nod from the foreign guest.

"Yes, Will, I learned English when I was a boy. I understand you perfectly. Thank you for your concern about my wife."

Isabelle went on. "He searched the country to find the killer and managed to locate an old man that Jennings had taken with him in his efforts to flee the country. The old man confirmed Jennings' identity as an English seaman and that they had come from Rennes where they had both been imprisoned. He was unable to be of any further help and it seemed that Jennings had vanished completely. Although Monsieur d'Arranda visited Rennes prison he was unable to find any further clue about Jennings' whereabouts. All his enquiries had come to nothing. He was on the point of giving up and had returned to his home in Paris when, by chance, he met our friend Lieutenant Rodier who, you remember, had been posted to Paris. The Lieutenant remembered Jennings well and the crimes he had committed at Le Croisic. He was able to tell Monsieur d'Arranda about Jennings and his association with you. Naturally, it was the obvious thing to come and see me, since I knew you so well. That is just what he did! Unfortunately, he had missed you, but I was able to tell him that Jennings came from the same village in England as my beloved. Of course, I told him about our relationship and at once he offered to bring me to England if I would be his guide and bring him here to St. Margaret's. So here we are!"

Will was amazed. "What a story. It's unbelievable. Monsieur, how sorry I am about your wife. You say Jennings did it?"

"Oui, monsieur," replied the gentleman. "There is no doubt. He shot her dead and took almost all the jewellery she possessed. My only problem is to find him and make him pay for his crime. Unfortunately, we have already enquired in the village he is not here."

"No, he isn't," confirmed Will. "That was one of the first things that I wanted to know when I got home. He hasn't been seen in the village since the day we were both pressed into the navy. That's a good thing too, if you ask me, though I do hope that you find him and bring him to justice. He is the most evil man I know and this village is better off without him."

"Never mind, monsieur, it has brought me great pleasure to see you two young people brought together once more. It is obvious that you love each other and I wish you the best luck in the world. I shall continue my search for this man alone, and I shall not rest until I find him," The Frenchman rose as if to leave but Elizabeth would not allow it. She insisted that tea was served for all and produced a marvellous spread in celebration of what everyone assumed was the engagement of Will and Isabelle. The small cottage was too cramped to allow Isabelle and Olivier d'Arranda to spend the night, but William thought that he would be able to arrange accommodation at the vicarage. Besides, it was a good opportunity to talk to Reverend Marsh and decide upon the earliest possible date for the marriage ceremony. While William was away making the arrangements, Will was deputised to look after the light, which was now casting its glow over the surrounding grassy slopes and out into the depths of the night. Will did not mind at all: he was glad of the chance to be alone with Isabelle. As they stood in the lantern room side-by-side, Will felt a warm glow of satisfaction within that was far greater than from any fire. They embraced eagerly, thankful for the privacy that the lantern room afforded them. Then Will gazed into the night and contemplated the future.

"Well, my darling, we can marry as soon as possible, but I must find a job if I am to support you. We cannot expect my parents help any more."

"I think, mon cher, that your father has another surprise, how do you say, in his sleeve?" Will looked at Isabelle in surprise.

"Really? You have been playing games behind my back today, haven't you?" he said in fun. "Well, tell me then, I must know."

"I don't think he will mind if I tell you," continued Isabelle. "While you were away at your sister's house today we had a long discussion about the future. Your father told me that the keeper of the other lighthouse... what is his name again?"

"Saul Goldsack."

"Yes, well he wants to leave his job and is looking for someone else to be the keeper. Your father wants you to do it."

Will was amazed. How many more surprises were in store for him today?

"But do you want to live here in the lighthouse, my darling? Will you be happy?" Will asked considerately.

"Of course, mon cher. If it is what you want then I want it also." She clutched him and they kissed passionately. The flickering flames of the fire reflected the intensity of the emotions that welled up inside them. And as the seamen who were passing the two South Foreland lighthouses at that moment looked up at the brilliant glow from the cliff-top, they could never have guessed the story of the keepers' newest recruit.

THE END